EVER PRESENT DANGER

Enjoy the read!

C. S. Peters.

C S Peters.

authorHOUSE®

AuthorHouse™
1663 Liberty Drive
Bloomington, IN 47403
www.authorhouse.com
Phone: 1-800-839-8640

First published by AuthorHouse 11/16/2011

ISBN: 978-1-4670-0850-1 (sc)
ISBN: 978-1-4670-0851-8 (e)

Printed in the United States of America

*Any people depicted in stock imagery provided by Thinkstock are models,
and such images are being used for illustrative purposes only.
Certain stock imagery © Thinkstock.*

This book is printed on acid-free paper.

1

March 1942 began very cold and miserable. Up in Lincolnshire, for the first two days of it especially, there had been flurries of snow. Now into the second week of the month there was lovely bright sunshine and, although still cold, it was the sort of weather for putting on a warm overcoat and scarf and going for a long walk in the country.

As the train approached Liverpool Street Station just after eleven, the extensive bomb damage in the streets either side of the railway was starkly apparent. It was the first time James had been to London since mid-August 1940 - before the Blitz started. Then it had been at night with John, Paul and Malcolm when, because of a spell of bad weather, the Squadron had been stood down for 48 hours and they had travelled up to see a show. He remembered the times during the blitz when he and his Squadron pals gathered around any available wireless set in the Mess, Dispersals hut or pub or read the heavily censored newspapers, to learn of what was happening to London. And then later in the year, when he was recovering in hospital, as the news concerning the blitz worsened, how he and the other patients had listened horrified. The damage and devastation he was seeing now from the railway carriage was far worse than he imagined. He wondered when he got out of the station shortly, whether the damage would be as bad or even worse than he had seen during the last few minutes.

A pleasant-looking woman and her young son had shared the compartment with him and during the journey they had struck up a conversation. The woman's husband was away in the army fighting - all she knew was he was somewhere in North Africa. She was understandably worried for her husband's safety and James felt desperately sorry for her, as news from that particular theatre of war had been going from bad to worse from the allies point-of-view. The little boy was shy at first, and spent the first part of the journey - in the way children do - staring at the large still-livid scar above James's eye, in spite of his mother's quiet discouragement and apologies. The boy also played with two model aeroplanes - the ones highly popular with children in the forties and made be Messrs Lines. Similar models had also been used as a tool for training in aircraft recognition for James and all other airmen. They were models of a Dornier 215 and a Hurricane. James well and truly broke the ice with the little boy when he revealed he had flown a Hurricane two years before. For the rest of the journey they became friends. At the platform, as the engine hissed its relief at the end of its work, James opened the carriage door for them and helped the woman with her small suitcases. For a moment the little boy hung back. James could tell there was something he wanted to say as he fumbled in his pocket for a scruffy piece of paper.

'Please sir? I've never seen a pilot before.' He thrust the scrap of paper into James's hand. 'Could I have your autograph please?'

Embarrassed, the little boy looked down and concentrated on the ground. James laughed and playfully tousled the boy's hair.

'Barry! That's naughty. You mustn't be rude ...'.

James smiled at the boy's mother. '…It's all right - I'm rather flattered - I would be pleased to oblige.' He reached inside his coat for the silver pen June had given him for their first Christmas together and signed his name along with a little message. The woman and her son thanked him. He shook the boy's hand. 'Now Barry you look after your mummy. Remember, while your daddy's away you're the man of the house.' The boy nodded, his mother smiled warmly. 'I hope you get some good news from your husband soon.'

'Thank you. So do I - I really hope so.'

They said their farewells and James watched the pair disappear into the crowd ahead. He looked fondly at the pen still between his fingers - it wouldn't be long now before he saw June again. He replaced the pen in his pocket, picked up his luggage and hastened his steps toward the ticket barrier. This was manned not only by the ticket collector but also by police and members of the military, obviously on the lookout for anyone suspected as a spy or absconding from the Services.

June, by wangling and exchanging some duties and leave, had managed two days off to be with James whilst he was in London for his mysterious interview. He had booked a room in a small but pleasant hotel in Kensington near the Albert Hall. His father had frequently used this hotel when meeting or entertaining visitors in the course of his work. James's interview was to be on the morning of the following day, and it was a marvellous and rare opportunity for them to have some time together whilst exploring some of the sights of London. He was due to meet June at Victoria Station in about two hour's time - time enough to look around part of the City before catching a connecting underground train.

James passed through the barrier where the ticket collector closely examined his ticket and, a policeman and an officious serviceman scrutinised him and his documents suspiciously for what seemed like an inordinate amount of time. Now outside in the bright sunshine, a gentle rustling above him attracted James's attention. A large barrage balloon, on its anchor wires, quivered in the breeze and cast a shadow over the roadway in front of him. Other balloons positioned further away dotted the skyline like a school of stranded whales.

James started to walk down Old Broad Street, in the direction of the Stock Exchange and Threadneedle Street and the Bank of England building. Life seemed to be continuing, much as he supposed it had before the war started. Men and women in their business clothes scurried about to-and-fro in business-like fashion. However, there was something surreal about the images and sights he was witnessing. The majority of men and women he saw were in the older age group - those in the younger age groups, he presumed, were away in the armed services or now engaged in one of the multitude of "war effort back-up services" which had proliferated since 1939. About half-way along Old Broad Street, scores of office workers milled around, were grouped on the pavements and roadway as if waiting for something. It looked as if a good many of them had been locked out of their offices. Some of those waiting partook of the refreshments made available by the Salvation Army's refreshment station nearby. Edging his way through the crowds, James found further progress was prevented by a barrier. In front of this stood a police officer and a warden. A notice bearing the words: "Beware UXB", was propped against the barrier.

Seeing James's uniform the warden called: 'Hello sir. My sons in the RAF. Air-gunner on Halifaxes he is.'

'A vital member of the crew. The Halifax is a wonderful

aircraft too.' James nodded towards the barrier. 'How long has this been here?'

'The bomb's a biggun' replied the warden. 'A "tip-and-run" raid. A Hun bomber came over just after midnight and dropped it.'

'Where are you wanting to get to sir?' Asked the police officer.

'I just wanted to have a look at St. Paul's whilst I was in London.'

'It's all a hell of a mess around there' said the warden.

'Yes' added the policeman. 'They're clearing away and demolishing a lot of the buildings destroyed in the blitz you see. They've blocked off many of the roads whilst they're doing it.'

The warden pointed to his right. 'Your best bet would be to go down Throgmorten and Lothbury, then cut through Old Jewry to Cheapside.'

James was confused. His knowledge of London wasn't that good. He smiled politely. 'Thank you both. I'll see how I get on.'

Turning into Throgmorten as directed, James continued on his way. Now and again he spotted men dressed in the uniform of the Home Guard - no doubt fitting in their service in that organisation with their normal, daily, City duties in financial, banking and insurance institutions. Everywhere, mounds of sandbags protected doorways of the buildings still standing. Every now and again James saw large signs proclaiming the position of a public air-raid shelter. Dotted here and there, more refreshment stations - manned in time of need by the Salvation Army or WRVS - stood on the pavement. Along the sides of Old Jewry and Poultry and, in the many lanes courtyards and passages that lay off them, were ugly gaps where once stood buildings - now already being colonised by weeds and shrubs. In other places, partial and safety repairs had been made or started to damaged buildings. In yet other places the fire-blackened walls, pillars, columns and window frames of disembowelled offices and buildings stood like blackened ribs and skeletons of large creatures. Before turning into Old Jewry, James stopped to look at the road almost opposite. The road name board bore scorch marks and he could just make out the words "Coleman Street". The wall bearing the blackened name board was the only wall remaining of a building once standing on the site. As he looked up Coleman Street, as far as he could see, there appeared to be no building whatsoever now, not even a mere empty shell. Looking to the left of Coleman Street and beyond nothing remained but acres of complete and utter destruction - marked every so often by huge mounds of rubble and debris.

The sight of two Wren Churches destroyed - St. Mary-le-Bow in Cheapside and St. Mildred's in Bread Street - provoked a remarkable sadness within him. Of both Churches, only their towers and steeples had survived extensive damage. As James stood looking at the forlorn tower of St. Mary-le-Bow, he overheard a woman talking to her son as she clutched his hand protectively.

'This was a famous old Church David. Do you remember your Grandad and Granny telling you about Bow Bells?'

'You mean when they said they were cockneys?'

'That's right. Because they were born within the sound of Bow Bells.'

'Cor! Really?'

As he moved away James remembered Louise - one of the Nannies who looked after him and Colin many years before - singing them a Rhyme mentioning "Bow Bells" as they got ready for bed.

For a while he stood on the corner of Cheapside taking in the huge magnificence of St. Paul's. Like many others he wondered what divine miracle had spared the Cathedral when all around it lay in such devastation. Yet there it stood like a phoenix, standing defiant amidst acres of rubble, ashes and death. James had learnt from a fellow patient, when he had been in hospital, that incendiaries had indeed set the roof aflame during the terrible raids on London in late December 1940. Then, hearing later, because of the dedication, single-mindedness of the Fire Service and Cathedral staff, how the fire had been contained and extinguished. It had been widely believed that Churchill, aware of the psychological affect the destruction of St. Paul's would have on the British peoples, had personally insisted maximum effort be put in to saving the building by diverting Fire Brigade resources away from other areas. Whatever, from where James stood now, he could see no real evidence of the fire in the dome. All around Paternoster Square the area had largely been cleared of bombed buildings, leaving a large square void amidst a boundary of other blackened ruins. On the furthest corner of this cleared area, static water tanks had been placed. He remembered his father, in a recent letter, telling him these had been erected last year to ensure The Fire Brigade had a ready source of water to quell fires in the event of future Luftwaffe attacks.

An old man, whom James presumed had been displaced from his home, was laying on some nearby steps clutching a box of pitiful belongings. James took a few steps towards him and placed a few coins into the old man's dirty hand.

'Cor! Thank yer guv and Gawd bless yer sir. I fought at Ypres in the last lot and lost an arm. This time I've lost everything in the bombing - me wife, me 'ome, even me little dog.'

James smiled at the old man and exchanged a few friendly words. He looked at his watch. Hampered by his injured leg, the walk had taken longer than anticipated. He realised it had probably been his longest walk on a hard surface since the injury and his leg now ached like hell. He saw the sign marking St. Paul's station and made his way to its entrance.

The train was not crowded and he eagerly took a vacant seat, knowing he would have to endure stairs or escalators and changes of trains before arriving at Victoria to meet June. At St. Paul's station and, at others on the way, James had noted the array of bunk-style beds on the platforms, installed *albeit* reluctantly by the authorities, as the blitz had progressed. Although the bombing had lessened, underground stations were still being used as shelters. At the stations, all pervading, was the smell of human night-time habitation - urine and sweat. He had heard, when the poor souls sought sanctuary from air-raid warnings, people were not always able to obtain an "official" bed and, as a whole family they would go down onto the platforms armed with their own mattresses and bedding. Again tonight, no doubt, people in large volume and their treasured possessions would cover the entire platform surfaces in a crush of nervous humanity.

He and June had agreed to meet at the buffet bar where they first met, before their train journey to Sussex, almost two years ago. James got there with a few minutes to spare. The buffet bar itself had been largely rebuilt and redecorated in the intervening time and, as he waited, he observed the goings on around him. With the exceptions of the inevitable increased presence of police and the military and, the utilitarian clothes of the majority of men and women and children criss-crossing the concourse and, of course, the obligatory gas mask boxes they carried, one would not think anything was really different from normal. Suddenly James saw June passing through the barrier and looking around to get her bearings. He waved wildly to attract her attention.

On seeing him she ran like a delighted schoolgirl towards him. She wore her ATS uniform and carried a small, brown suitcase. He lifted her off her feet as they embraced and kissed. The lovely moisture of her lips, the feel of her soft skin, the familiarity of the gentle light scent of her perfume and hair were heavenly.

'The train journey seemed to take for ever darling. I thought I'd never get here.'

They continued to hold each other.

'Surprisingly, your train got in on the crack of time.' Then, jokingly 'It was your desperation to see your husband which made the journey drag I expect.'

She stroked his face. 'Um! That scar is still looking angry. How is your leg - how are you?'

'Oh so many questions Nurse Graham! I'm fine thank you. Well, except my leg, it aches a bit that's all. I had a couple of hours to spare after I got to Liverpool Street, so I walked around and to St. Paul's. Overdid it a bit I suppose. How are you sweetheart?'

'Oh James!' She exclaimed with disapproval, ignoring his question.

'How are you June?' He asked again.

'I'm fine thank you. Perhaps a little tired but apart from that. I'm better for seeing you.'

James jerked his head toward the buffet.

'Fancy having a bite to eat in here? Where we first met?'

She laughed and kissed him again.

'That would be very romantic. However, shall we save that for tomorrow before we travel back? It's such a lovely, bright day - too good to be stuck inside in a smoky station. I stayed at mother's last night and dear Ruth has concocted some of her delicious sandwiches. I thought perhaps we could find one of London's famous parks in which to eat them.' She paused. 'But if you're hungry ...?'

' ... I can wait a while. Before I left I managed to have a good Mess breakfast. The thought of one of Mrs Fuller's sandwiches makes it worth delaying our lunch.'

With their arms around each other's waists, they walked out of the station. It was no problem to take their small items of luggage with them and check into the hotel in Kensington later in the afternoon, so James hailed a taxi asking the driver to take them to St. James's Park and drop them off in Birdcage Walk.

Beside the lake they found one of the few benches remaining and sat down. Although the park still looked lovely in the bright March sunshine it had the appearance of neglect. Shrubs remained un-pruned and straggly, flower borders were left unattended. In places though the Government's "Dig for Victory" campaign had been heeded in part and some areas had been put to vegetable growing. The part of the park bordering The Mall was scarred with anti-glider trenches and other anti-invasion devices. By now they were both feeling hungry and began to eat their sandwiches. June scattered some crumbs from her lap to the fearless Sparrows playing around their feet.

'What is the interview for James? I always thought moves within the RAF were by postings and one didn't have much say in the matter.'

'Well, that's the funny thing about it all. I don't really know much about it myself. I wish I did know more - it's all rather strange.'

'And your superior officer just said he's sending you for an interview?' She asked incredulously. Looking rather concerned she offered James another sandwich. 'It's not about some dangerous mission is it James?'

James laughed lightly.

'Umm! These sandwiches are delicious.' He put his other arm around her shoulders reassuringly. 'Oh I shouldn't think so! Anyway, who would send someone on a "dangerous mission" - as you put it - with a dodgy leg and an eye like Admiral Nelson? I'm sure it's nothing like that. Now don't you go worrying your pretty little head about it.'

She slapped him playfully. 'Oh James! Honestly! I do worry, you know that. It was bad enough when you were flying Hurricanes. I thought you were now in a relatively safe job. And, Mr Graham, your leg is not "dodgy" - not too dodgy anyway - and your eye is not like Nelson's.'

She seemed somewhat reassured. They watched as three swans landed noisily on the lake in front of them.

'How's your mother? You said she was rather depressed. Understandable of course.'

'She doesn't seem too bad at the moment considering. I think, what with it being the first Christmas since daddy died, it was a very bad time for her. Also, Richard and Stephen being away as well for the Christmas didn't help. When she's not at the hospital - and I'm off duty - of course whenever I can I go and see her. Some times I stay with her at *Oakfield*.'

'Yes. Times like Christmas and other occasions, like birthdays or anniversaries, must be worse for someone bereaved.'

'Personally, I don't think mummy allowed herself enough time to grieve - being so busy at the hospital and, at Penley Manor. She threw herself into her work. She seemed, at the time, so in control of herself.'

'Yes. My Grandmother was a bit like that. Insisted all the time in putting on a brave face.'

'I think also what made it worse - well, with daddies' injuries - things were very difficult for him and mummy. In so many ways - after he came home - at various times - he wasn't the same man I knew as my father, not the same man she knew as her husband. I think she also feels some guilt that, despite doing as much as she possibly could for him, she was unable to do more. She also keeps asking herself why it happened to him. I suppose, a question, everyone asks themselves at such times.'

'All you can do June is just support her as much as you can - we both will.' He paused. 'I suppose it's not possible for you both to take some time off - the pair of you take yourselves off for a little holiday somewhere?'

She shrugged. 'At the moment there's not much chance of that, what with my duties and everything. And mummy's so busy at the hospital at the moment.'

'I just thought perhaps things may have got a bit quieter at the hospital?'

'She says there's now such a shortage of doctors - shortage of everything. And they're dealing now much more with other things: the result of the previous air-raids and the war in general - diseases like Diphtheria and TB; diseases caused by the damage to drains, water supply, sewers and housing; general inadequacies now in the diet.'

'Of course. I suppose those of us being in the services and away from normal everyday life as it were, tend to forget the struggles and problems of those back home.' He held her close to him. 'Reading your letters June, what you've achieved - what with your promotion and everything - I'm so proud of you.'

She kissed him.

'James you say such lovely things.' She paused. 'By the way. Before I forget. I've received an estimate for repairing the chimney and replacing that part of the roof.' She reached in her handbag and handed him a sheet of paper. 'Seems rather expensive to me. Still, he's the only one able to do the job within the next few weeks. The estimate arrived yesterday.'

James studied the estimate.

'It doesn't seem too bad to me. And Keating was recommended to us by your mother's neighbour and, lord knows, that old so-and-so is so critical. If he was satisfied by Keating's work, that's recommendation enough. Yes June. Give him the go-ahead when you get back please?'

'Well if you're sure.'

'We need to get the job done as soon as we can. After all, it's only early March. Still time for more severe weather.' He kissed her. 'I can't wait to see our little home again. Since we bought it, I hardly seem to have been there.'

June told him about the difficulties she was having obtaining suitable curtaining and soft-furnishing fabrics. Also of the other jobs she had managed to do to the inside and outside of the cottage. Billy, who still did the odd jobs around *Oakfield,* had helped June with some of the heavier manual jobs.

'It sounds as if you've been working very hard darling. I can't wait till I get some leave and can spend time at home. It's wonderful Billy has been so much help to you. We must think of a way of giving him some special treat of some sort.'

'He would love that. Poor Billy. He used to love doing the garden and making it look pretty. He was quite devastated when my parents decided to be like everyone else and dig up most of the shrubs and flowers. Oh I know the growing of vegetables is important now and takes a lot of work but, he seems to miss seeing all the colours in the borders.' She gave a little laugh. 'Still, he enjoys looking after all the chickens and ducks mother has now. You ought to see him James collecting the eggs and trying to guide them back into the hen house in the evenings. That big cockerel mother got the other week chased Billy all round the chicken run the other day. I shouldn't have laughed but, James, it was so funny I couldn't help it.'

'How about having a little walk before we go to the hotel?'

'That would be nice. But what about your leg? You've already walked a lot today.'

'It feels better now for having rested it a bit.'

They got up and walked alongside the lake for a while. Near Buckingham Gate they passed the headquarters of the local Home Guard platoon. In the compound around it was a motley collection of vehicles - some of them, James was certain, requisitioned to assist the platoon in its endeavours in repelling fifth columnists or the German army itself. After watching the group - mainly senior gentlemen - practice their parade drill they left the park to catch a bus to the hotel.

The Bus Conductor was a cheerful man, causing June and James much amusement as he noisily regaled passengers with the latest news of the war; about the constant diversions to the bus route caused by recent bomb damage or by the various unexploded bombs being discovered at miscellaneous points along the route. What he would personally do to Hitler if he was ever able to get hold of him was a sound to savour.

2

They stood at the farm gate waving farewell until the coach disappeared from view. Lucy, Sandra and Carol were still crying when they re-entered the farmhouse. It was 1942 and now into the second year of the youngsters' evacuation from London. Strong bonds of friendship had grown between all of them and Lucy and parting had been painful. In the time he had been living in Somerset, John had changed considerably from an unpleasant, bitter delinquent into a very pleasant and helpful young man. Although not tearful like the others, he too had found the farewell to some of his fellow evacuees upsetting. So had Sandra's brother Robert whom, although not one of the original evacuees, had been an almost daily visitor to the farm since he, Sandra and their aunt had moved into Mr Simpson's cottage.

Peter and Sylvia's departure was as a result of the trend - starting as a trickle at the beginning of the year - and which, within a few weeks, had developed into a flood of evacuees back to London. This return to London was alarming the Government as, although the number of air-raids had abated, there were still sporadic attacks. However, many of London's population considered the threat of invasion had diminished, and there were now strong feelings amongst them that they wanted to be re-united with their families and children. Carol's parents, on the other hand, thought it best - at least for the time being - that she remained with Lucy. Also, John's mother was now safe at last from the brute of a man she had been involved with and, John and she now managed to see each other fairly frequently down in Somerset. Seeing how her son was now maturing from the type of individual he had been and, becoming aware of his apparent natural practical ability with his hands, she had come to realise he would benefit from remaining in Somerset.

This realisation had coincided with Lucy's concern over Walter's increasing age and failing physical ability. She hadn't, for a minute, considered saying anything about this to Walter but, having someone younger and fitter to help with what was increasingly heavy and demanding work was ideal. The girls of the Land Army were excellent and she would not have been able to cope without them but it was good to have another male about the farm and Lucy had offered John the chance of working for her as an employee. He had readily accepted and was fully re-paying Lucy's faith in him.

'I'm glad Tommy and his mum were able to come and say goodbye to Sylvia and Peter yesterday' said Sandra as she put the kettle on to boil.

'Yes I am too. They seem very settled and happy staying with Mrs Hawkes. Tommy's mother was saying she's started working voluntarily at the school.'

Robert, playing with one of the kittens under the kitchen table, piped up. 'I'm going to miss playing with Peter. Tommy won't be going as well will he? I don't want him to go as well.'

Sandra smiled and tousled her brother's hair affectionately.

'No. Not for a while anyway.'

Watching Sandra with her brother, Lucy realised what a

pretty young woman she was growing into. It had been long since she had regarded Sandra as an "Evacuee". She looked upon her as more of an adopted daughter or niece - a friend. Last August, Sandra celebrated her seventeenth birthday. For the occasion Enid, Robert and Lucy had arranged a party for her. The evacuees in Lucy's care and some other friends Sandra had made, had all been there. Also Walter and even Mrs Appleford.

'Well Mrs Hughes' said John putting on the cap he had recently taken to wearing. 'I'd better get back to help Walter finish off that muck-spreading. There's still quite a bit to do. Then Sally can go and help the other girls working in the barn.'

'What about your mug of tea?'

'It's all right Sandra. I'll have one later on. Best get finished first. It won't be long now before it gets dark.'

'Make sure you're warm enough John' said Lucy. 'It's turned very cold today. The field up there is exposed, the wind really rips across the valley.'

'I'm fine Mrs Hughes. See you all later.'

After the door closed, Sandra gave a little chuckle.

'If you ask me, John has taken rather a shine to Sally.' Sally was the youngest of the Land Army girls. Had worked at the farm since the Autumn of last year. Sandra continued 'Wherever she is, John seems to find some excuse or other to see her or have a chat.'

Lucy also chuckled.

'Really? But she must be a good two years older than him.'

'I know. Walter pulls John's leg about it. You should hear the pair if them when Walter starts teasing him about it. It's really funny.'

Sandra poured the tea and handed a mug to Lucy.

'I can't get over how John has changed in the two years

he's been here. When you think how disagreeable he was when he first arrived.'

'I know. It's amazing. I really detested him. So did the others.'

'At one stage I nearly insisted Mrs Appleford tried placing him elsewhere. Although, I must admit, I felt so sorry for him in a way - what with his background and everything. I'm so glad he's turning out the way he is. Now, now that I'm employing him - well he's proving invaluable around the farm. I'm getting quite attached to him really.'

'Auntie Enid was so grateful when he put up those shelves for her.'

'He's good at drawing and painting as well. That picture he painted for the village hall last year looks really nice. It certainly brightens up that side of the room.'

Sandra ticked Robert off for playing a little too roughly with one of the kittens.

'Aunt Lucy. What do you think about Peter and Sylvia's parents wanting them back in London?'

'I'm not at all sure about it. Take their schooling for instance. When the evacuations started, a lot of the schools in the cities shut altogether because the teachers were evacuated with the children. As you know, a lot of those teachers evacuated down here with the children have now just been abandoned here whilst most of their pupils have gone back to London and other cities. Oh I can understand the parents wanting their children back - but the danger is far from over. I think the children would be far better off staying in the country.'

'Yes. Now I've seen what it's like living in the country, I don't ever want to go back to living in London - all the dirt and crowds. Ugh! Robert loves it here as well. I want us all to stay down here.'

'Oh I'm glad Sandra you feel like that. Before you all

first arrived, I was so worried whether you would all be happy here.'

'Did you say you had received a letter from Colin this morning?'

'Yes. It's over there.'

Lucy fetched the letter from the big dresser and handed it to Sandra.

Apart from commenting on one or two points in the letter, Sandra read it in silence. Colin referred to his last home leave with his parents in Ealing. Sandra remembered the kindness Colin's mother had shown her when, well over a year ago now, she and Lucy had stayed with her the day before her father's funeral. Colin had written quite a bit about the times he had spent with the evacuees on the farm. The humorous way in which he described them caused Sandra to smile, as she too recollected some of the happy times they had all shared together. She felt herself blush when he referred specifically to her a couple of times - about how pleased he had been when she, Robert and Enid had moved into Mr Simpson's cottage.

During the latter part of 1940 she and Colin had forged a close friendship - an affinity she couldn't explain. Sandra remembered - as she had laid in her bed at night throughout that time - her body and feelings maturing - realising she had a huge crush on him. Since those early days, since Colin had returned home and then, later, since he had joined the RAF, Sandra had come to realise that it was more than a crush she had felt for him. The feelings she had for him **now** were something much more than that.

The last part of the letter was taken up with news of things he had been doing or, had been involved with, since joining the air force: new friends he had made; names of aircraft she hadn't heard of - Airspeed Oxfords, Ansons, Hampdens.

She finished reading the letter and turned to Lucy. There was an anxiety in her voice.

'Colin's due to join a Heavy Bomber Conversion Unit next week. What does that mean aunt Lucy?'

Lucy paused for a moment before answering. Her own emotions now stirring.

'I presume it means that soon Colin will be flying in attacks over Europe.'

Sandra shivered and was suddenly cold.

'Do you think we'll have a chance to get to see him soon?'

3

In contrast to the previous day the morning had dawned very overcast and grey with a stiff breeze and outbreaks of drizzle. James's interview had been arranged for 10.30 and, after breakfast, they finished off the little amount of packing required and arranged for their luggage to be left at Reception for them to pick up later. Whilst James attended his interview, June would spend the time looking around the shops in Kensington and Knightsbridge and they would meet back at the hotel.

As they kissed, said cheerio on the corner of De Vere Gardens June said: 'I wish you luck darling. I'll be thinking of you. Hope it goes well.'

'Thank you. You enjoy yourself.' Then, teasingly 'Please don't go spending too much money. Remember, we've got to pay for the work on the roof and chimney.'

They kissed again.

'Please James. Promise you won't volunteer for anything dangerous?'

He stroked her cheek affectionately. 'I'll do my best not to.'

They parted. He watched her walk off in the direction of Kensington High Street waving back at him. Yesterday he had thought he would take a taxi but, having spent a little more last night than he had intended, considered it more prudent to get a bus. He crossed the road.

Many of those working in offices or factories had long been at their desks or benches as James waited in the drizzle for the bus. His mind dwelt happily on the previous evening spent with June. In their room before they got ready for dinner they had made love. They had last seen each other at Christmas and now, three month's later, they had been so hungry for each other. With an urgency in her caresses and kissing she had urged him to remove her clothes whilst, at the same time, deftly using her hands she had removed his. After dining in the hotel they had travelled into the West-End and found a place James had heard about from other Officers at his present posting. As well as civilians, there had been a lot of Service Men and Women from all the services. A top-rate band had been playing and Anne Shelton was an excellent main vocalist. The band had played many of his and June's favourite tunes including: *Deep Purple; Paper Doll; A Pair of Silver Wings,* and they had spent much of the evening dancing. Since their marriage, they had not really had an opportunity to attend a dance and for much of their journey back to the hotel they talked about the music and dancing. Back in their hotel room they had danced a slow waltz - one of their favourites they had danced to earlier in the evening - James humming the tune gently in June's ear. Then, sinking onto the bed, they had made love again. On their brief honeymoon June, especially, had been shy at first and their love-making inhibited as he had first seen her coy nakedness, then, shyly she had submitted to him, letting him dictate things. Last night, as she had mounted him, she had shown a growing inventiveness - a lack of inhibition to bring him pleasure - she had dictated the rhythm of their love-making. After, as they had lain in each other's arms, her sweet breath playing on his bare chest, she whispered again and again how she never wanted him to unnecessarily risk his life again.

After getting off the bus, James walked across Horse Guards Parade. It was still drizzling. As he took out the letter to remind himself of the address, the stiff breeze nearly snatched it from his fingers. A little while later he entered a large, mainly unfurnished room, wherein fifteen or so other men and women stood around either talking to others or, solitary - shifting ill-at-ease from foot to foot. Some were in uniform, others in civilian clothes. A nondescript little man asked James his name, looked down a list on a clipboard, eyed him up and down suspiciously and, with a little grunt, ticked his name off on the list. James grew even more mystified - just what was this interview all about? A few minutes elapsed and a woman in her fifties appeared from the doorway. A pair of spectacles were perched on the end of her nose, she wore her hair with a severe, tight bun at the back. She called out eight names, of which James was one, and summoned the eight people to follow her. Out on the landing, she indicated four individuals to another room further down the corridor, the remaining four - including James - to follow her up another couple of stairs and into another room. Inside this room was an arrangement which reminded James of polling station booths. Behind each screened booth sat, what James took to be, an interviewing officer. The one seated at the booth on the far left smiled warmly and beckoned him over. As James sat down on a rather rickety chair they shook hands.

'Miserable day isn't it?' And, without waiting for an answer 'Thank you for coming.' For a moment the man looked at the papers in front of him then, in business-like fashion, asked 'James Graham? Recently, Squadron Leader James Graham?'

James confirmed his identity but wondered why the

man had emphasised "recently". One by one, he confirmed as requested his address, next-of-kin and various points with regard to his Service Record and Postings etcetera. Suddenly the man across the desk cast the paper aside, placed his hands behind his head and leant back in his chair.

'You have a good knowledge of both written and spoken French.' He paused. 'What about other languages - German for instance?'

James reiterated he had a thorough knowledge of French but, had difficulty convincing the interviewer any knowledge he had of German could only be described as very sketchy at best. At last the interviewer seemed convinced and, now, with his hands on the desk in front of him, leant towards James in a rather confidential manner.

'All I can say at the moment is if you're selected for what we have in mind, you'll find the work very interesting - it's something to do with working with Free French airmen. I was also going to say if you were selected, you would get instant promotion to Squadron Leader. However, seeing from your papers you've only fairly recently been promoted, that won't apply in your case.' He extended his hand towards James. 'Good-day to you. Thank you again for coming. Now Squadron Leader Graham, if you would like to go and find Miss Hawthorn - the lady who showed you in - she'll tell you what you have to do next.' James began to move away. 'Oh and by the way. Please don't talk to anyone about anything we've discussed when you get back to the waiting area?'

Agreeing he wouldn't and, even more intrigued than he was before, James went to find Miss Hawthorn. It was all very well the interviewer saying he wasn't to say anything but, what had they discussed - really nothing more than a few personal details about himself and his knowledge of languages. That and something vague about working with

Free French airmen and the work, whatever it was, being very interesting. All very puzzling.

The lady with the severe-looking bun in her hair asked him coldly to wait in yet another room. This one had a hatch cut in the near wall. There were only a few people in the room: two soldiers - one a Lieutenant, the other a Sergeant; a Flight Lieutenant, about the same age as James; a WREN in her early thirties. As they weren't talking to each other or didn't acknowledge his entrance, James assumed their interviewer had also instructed them not to discuss anything. After what seemed ages the bang on the wall, as the hatch doors were opened, startled James. A young man poked his head through the hatch opening - his appearance comically reminiscent to James of the "Aunt Sally" fairground side-shows he and Colin had so loved in their boyhood.

Indicating the door to the side of the hatch the young man said: 'Good morning to you all. Perhaps you would all come through here please?'

The young man stood, shifting his feet from side-to-side, looking nervously at the five persons in front of him. He motioned them to each take a seat at the large, battered and worn table. He scurried around the table distributing sheets of blank paper before returning to his previous position.

'I presume you each have a pen or pencil? I'll be giving some passages of dictation. Some will be in French, which I require you to take down in English; others will be in English which you will take down in French.' He paused dramatically and with relish continued, as if about to deliver the surprise denouement in an Agatha Christie thriller. 'I will dictate slowly and repeat each passage twice. Do you all understand?'

He paused for a moment awaiting their reply. From the others in the room there was no response. The first passage was in French.

James completed the numerous pieces of translation without any difficulty. Replacing his pen in his pocket, he thought was that the best they could come up with? He had mastered more complicated exercises before he had left school. When the others had completed the tasks given, the young man scurried around again collecting all the papers. Whilst he did so he looked cursorily at the candidates' efforts.

'Now, if you would all like to go back next door, you'll find a warm drink waiting for you. Help yourselves and, if you wouldn't mind waiting for a while, either myself or one of my colleagues will come and explain what will be happening next.'

After about twenty minutes, the young man rejoined them and exchanged a few pleasantries before announcing 'WREN Murphy, Squadron Leader Graham and Sergeant Mills could you please wait with me? Flight Lieutenant Armstrong and Lieutenant Carter you are free to return to your units. Someone will be in touch with you. Thank you both for coming. I'm afraid, at the moment, I'm not at liberty to say anything further.' After the two left the room, the young man handed each of those remaining a slip of paper. 'These give an address for you to go to next and a time of appointment. I'm afraid you'll all have to make your own way there. If any of you are not sure of the way, please wait and I'll give you directions.'

The WREN did not know the way so, with the Sergeant looking as bewildered as himself, James and he made their way out of the building.

'I don't know about you sir' said the Sergeant. 'I'm going to get something to eat first. There's an Emergency Feeding Centre just down the road.'

James declined to join him and the two men turned in different directions. From the paper in his hand, James saw he had to head for an address in Northumberland Avenue with an appointment for an hour's time. He had no way of letting June know where he was and was worried the appointment, whatever it was about, might prevent him from meeting her at the time they had arranged. Oh well! He would have to keep his fingers crossed and hope for the best.

In an anonymous-looking building in Northumberland Avenue, he was shown into a large office some floors up. Opposite the door was a desk, backed by a large window. A very large, winged desk chair had its back turned towards him. Partially concealed by the back of the chair, James could see the top of a man's head. The chair's occupant was obviously watching something outside the window. For a moment there was no acknowledgement of his entrance. Suddenly, the chair swivelled around. In the chair sat a man a few years older than James. He sported a stiff, military moustache and wore the uniform of a British Army Major.

'Ah Squadron Leader Graham! Forgive me.' He nodded his head back in the direction of the window behind him. 'I'm a keen ornithologist. Pigeons. Curious creatures. I was watching a pair of them bickering over a particular stretch of coping.'

James crossed the room, his right hand outstretched proffering a handshake. The other man rose to his feet, off-putting James by extending his left hand. He did not have a right hand or arm.

'Thank you for coming. Please, take a seat. Make yourself at home. I'm Pierre Walton.' Seeing James was obviously curious about his name 'My mother was French, father English. As a compromise they agreed my Christian name be of French origin.'

'I see' said James smiling.

'What did my colleagues at the other office tell you James? You don't mind my calling you James?'

'No. Not at all.' He was put at ease by the other man's relaxed and informal manner. 'All they told me was that it was something to do with Free French airmen.'

Walton smiled slightly but didn't say anything. James had the feeling what he had been told earlier was a pretence. The Major slid a file across his desk so that it was in front of him and studied it in silence for a couple of minutes.

'You were in Fighter Command, flying Hurricanes. Shot down and crash-landed after a tally of eight aircraft either destroyed or damaged. Out of action for more than six months. After a period of leave you were selected for transfer to 5 Group HQ Bomber Command. Subsequent training and still currently at this posting.'

Walton did not give James any chance to respond or agree to these abbreviated salient points from his file or, to the other points Walton proceeded to reel off. James simply listened mesmerised as Walton listed other details from the file: details and occupation of his parents and brother; details of his education et cetera. There were even details of his physical characteristics. He thought, surprised and shocked, *God they've been checking up on me pretty thoroughly. Just what is this all about?*

At last Walton paused before asking 'Do you agree with all that James?'

'Well yes. But can I ask what this all for?'

'More of that later. First I would like to compliment you on your knowledge of French. In our little test earlier, you achieved maximum marks. You obviously enjoy languages.'

James agreed he did and went on to say about the translation work he had done for Rosemary Pickering over two years ago.

'Yes. I read about it in the file. Excellent.' Walton rose from his seat and sat on the front edge of the desk swinging his right leg. He was a stocky, well-built man. The shoulder of his tunic, bunched up where his arm would have been, somehow made him look even more stocky. 'I hear you've been frustrated about not being able to fly anymore. Would you agree with that?'

'Yes. I must confess it's taken me a long time to come to terms with - I suppose to be honest, I still haven't really come to believe I will no longer to be able to fly.' Quickly adding 'It's not of course that I'm really hating what I'm doing now - and I like the people I'm working with and everything. It's just so different that's all - at least I feel I'm doing something useful - but it's not ...'.

'... Flying.' Walton had finished the sentence. 'Especially flying Fighters. I would think flying Fighters is the ultimate in excitement.'

'Oh it is. Definitely. Nerve-wracking at times, tiring too but, it was everything to me. Somehow you feel so free up there - somehow you feel at one with the power and movement of the machine around you. Then, the elation, the satisfaction, after you've out-manoeuvred and destroyed an enemy aircraft.'

'Then, a bit of bad luck and all that's gone. You're forced into something more mundane but, nevertheless, just as important in its own way.' Walton pointed to his armless side. 'You feel like I did - still do sometimes. Lost this in a training exercise on Salisbury Plain in August 1939. All I'd wanted to do since I was a boy was to join the Army. I got my wish, was selected for Sandhurst, gained a Commission and got all geared up to fight Hitler. Then, in a tinkling, bang. All that preparation and training for nothing or so it seemed. Since then, a whole range of Army Staff postings, mainly desk-bound jobs.' He paused for a moment. 'So bloody frustrating. I would do anything to get another chance.' He walked back to his chair and, suddenly, became more formal as he referred once more to James's file. 'Now, let me see. James, in French, tell me about your school - the one you attended immediately before joining the RAF. Describe to me as many details about it as you can please? I'll tell you when to stop.'

James had enjoyed his time at St. Edward's, as had Colin after him, and he had no trouble at all in describing it to Walton. He began by explaining the history of the school and when it was founded, the style of its architecture - its great gables and mellow colour of Cotswold stone which blended so well into the Oxfordshire scenery. He described the Principal of the school and the two teachers he remembered best. He went into some detail about the tradition and ceremonies which always marked "Founder's Day". Throughout the ten minutes or so he spoke, he was aware of how closely Walton was watching him and how intently he listened.

'Thank you James' said Walton, suddenly stopping him in mid-flow. 'Yes your spoken French is first-rate too. No doubt about that.' He leant back in his chair. 'Was Mrs Barker still the Matron when you were there?' Walton was grinning broadly at him across the desk.

James was aghast. 'But how did you know - I mean - I never mentioned her.'

Walton was now laughing loudly. 'Oh my dear chap! I've been most unfair. You see I know all about St. Edward's. I went there as well.' He paused. 'It's about time I put you out of your misery. Tell you what all today's business has been about.' He closed James's file decisively, leant back in his chair and rubbed his chin thoughtfully. 'We need to - our organisation need - to be sure the people we select can speak and write French fluently - can relate a story convincingly as though French is their mother tongue. You obviously have that ability. James, would you be interested in special wartime service?'

'What, exactly, do you mean by "special wartime service"?'

'To serve overseas. In your case it would be occupied France.'

James froze. Was unable to speak.

Walton continued. 'There's an urgent need for us in SOE - Special Operations Executive - to have people working as agents in France and, of course, other parts of occupied Europe. The work is primarily to set up and maintain wireless communications between France and England, to gain intelligence of what the enemy is doing, and provide a link with the burgeoning resistance movements over there. I have recently returned from a spell serving there. My own expertise is in wireless communication you see.'

James was amazed. 'You've actually been in France?'

Walton treated the question as rhetorical. 'The people we're seeking would also be expected to make contact with the resistance movements, to engage with them in the planning and execution of various operations of sabotage against the Germans. Also, and I have to be careful here, as the work is really the responsibility of another organisation based in England.' He paused. 'Namely: as our air attacks on the Germans in the occupied countries increase and, will continue to do so, our aircraft will increasingly be shot down. Many of our aircrews will find themselves having to bale out over occupied France and Belgium. It's vital we try and liaise with this other organisation and the resistance movements to get as many of these aircrews - those not captured - back as soon as we can. There are already in existence, various groups of French and Belgians co-operating in this. However, this work is in its very early stages and there is a need to work with the organisation

I've mentioned and the local people over there to extend the networks so far established and to make these networks more secure. The people we're recruiting, we hope, will be able to do this. What do you think James? Would you be interested in joining us?'

'Well - I don't know - it's all come as a bit of a shock. It certainly sounds interesting - exciting I suppose.' He hesitated. 'You've obviously checked up on me very thoroughly.' He tapped his injured leg. 'But what about my injured leg and the injury to my eye? Do you not think these might impair my mobility - my ability in this work?'

Walton smiled thinly.

'In this work, we check our potential recruits **very** thoroughly. You were at Penley Manor. From there we've ascertained fully the effects of your injuries.' James must have looked shocked, as Walton quickly added: 'Don't worry, your Mother-in-Law, Dr Margaret Wilding - a Consultant there I believe - knows nothing of our enquiries.' James was again shocked at just how much the man talking to him knew about him. It was an eerie experience. 'From what we've found out, our Organisation is happy your injuries would not unduly hamper what we need you to accomplish in France.' He paused for a few moments. 'The real question is James - **do you** feel you would be hampered by your injuries?' Walton had expressed this question rather like posing a challenge. He got up from his chair. 'The work, if you choose to accept, will without a doubt, be a great help in the effort to win the war.'

'Of course.'

'I will make no bones about it James. I owe it to you to be honest. It's very dangerous work. Your life will be constantly endangered. If caught, you would be arrested, tortured and almost certainly shot. For us to get you over there, you will be landed either by special aircraft, dropped by parachute, motor boat or fishing vessel. Each of them not without a great risk attached.'

'I see.' James hesitated for a long while. 'How long can I have to think it over?'

'Within the next ten minutes.'

Walton's answer paralysed his senses. He found himself unable to speak, to think. Gradually, the senses returned. He thought of June, their new life together, their new home. He thought of his flying days, the excitement and fear he had experienced then, of what Walton had said and the challenges, excitement and dangers posed. He found himself saying 'Yes'.

'Excellent. Welcome to our organisation James. You will be contacted within the next two to three weeks with further instructions. I'm afraid it will also entail a very intensive period of specialist training.'

'What do I say when I get back to Lincolnshire tomorrow and my CO asks how my interview went?'

'Not your worry. Your commanding officer will be notified *via* our usual channels. In the meantime, if anyone else asks where you've been, you will say you had to see a specialist for a further assessment of your injuries. When your transfer to us comes through, the leaving of your current post will be explained away as an "unexpected" posting. Is that clear?'

'Yes. Understood.'

'Also James. You must not even say anything whatsoever to your wife.' He paused. 'June isn't it? Do I make myself quite clear? A suitable cover story will be developed later.' Abruptly, Walton shook his hand. 'It was nice meeting you James, and thank you.'

Walton returned to the window to continue watching the Pigeons on the roof coping.

Outside the building James took in some welcome gulps

of fresh air. He stood still for a while, still feeling shocked, not really clear in his mind just what he had agreed to. Suddenly, remembering he had to meet June, he looked at his watch. Just enough time to get there. Then, to enjoy a little more sightseeing, go into the buffet on the station where they had first met, then to catch their respective trains. As James began to walk away he grew very anxious. In the interim, what could he tell June to explain away what he then realised would now be prolonged and indefinite absences?

4

Colin finished reading his book and laid it on the locker beside his bed. The novel had been with him throughout all his time of flying training and now, many weeks later, he had finally got to the end of it here at the Operational Training Conversion Flight. There had been too much to learn, both in theory and practice, for him to enjoy the luxury of reading a novel. In this time he had also clocked up some 350 hours flying experience on Tiger Moths, Airspeed Oxfords, Ansons and Hampdens. Before switching off the light, he reflected on his last day of training within the Conversion Flight, the bonds and trust now forged with the rest of his crew, the familiarity and knowledge now gained from flying the wonderful Lancaster Bomber.

Colin had been so eager to reach the end of the novel, he had quite forgotten to put his uniform in the wardrobe provided but, from the comfort of his bed, decided it would do no harm leaving it hanging on its hanger hooked over the top of the wardrobe door. Seeing the pilot's insignia and the ring on the sleeve denoting the rank of Pilot Officer - still both relatively fresh on the tunic - he could still not quite believe he had not only received his Commission but, also, successfully completed his training and had been selected to pilot and captain a Lancaster.

Lancasters had only recently started being delivered

to some squadrons but were already building a wonderful reputation for themselves amongst the crews now flying them. The aircraft was truly remarkable - much better than anything preceding it. Strong and powerful with a cruising speed of 200 mph fully loaded; had a basic weight of 36,000 lbs; carried a maximum bomb load of 20,000 lbs; a safe endurance time of 9 to 10 hours; relatively well-armed. What had really surprised Colin however, the very first time he had clambered into one, was just how cramped and dark the interior of the fuselage was and, manoeuvring oneself along the fuselage was made very awkward - especially in full flying kit - because of the large main spar crossing it roughly halfway along. The sheer bulk of the spar effectively reduced the already limited headroom by about a half. Amongst the many, numerous compliments about flying it and its effectiveness as a heavy bomber, had been some criticism that the Lancaster was one of the most difficult of aeroplanes to get out of in an emergency. Having seen the cramped space and darkness for himself, Colin dreaded to think of the scenario of the aircraft being badly hit by anti-aircraft fire and flak or, by a German Night Fighter and, probably ablaze, with frightened or injured crew members trying desperately to bale out. He did all he could to shut that possibility right out of his mind.

Laying there, now becoming drowsy, he thought again about his fellow crew members and the different roles they would perform. His Navigator - a New Zealander, Pilot Officer Ben Cansdale, who would have to conduct safe and accurate navigation of the aircraft by using information - collected in the past and present - and understood fully the use of all navigational aids and obtained as much information as possible from other crew members whilst using these aids. The Bomb-Aimer was also from the Commonwealth - though the other side of the world - a Canadian, Flight

Sergeant Doug Harvey, the eyes of the Navigator. Visual information was still essential despite the introduction of some radar aids now beginning to be introduced. Doug would report the local weather conditions and work certain radar apparatus and, would carry much of the responsibility for guiding the Lancaster over the last ten miles to target. In the target area he would have to locate the aiming point and guide the aircraft on its bombing run - working closely with Colin and Ben to do this. It was his duty to decide the exact moment for bomb release and would have to man the front gun turret in emergency. Flight Sergeant Michael Richards, the Wireless Operator, by the strangest of coincidences, came from a hamlet in Somerset close to where Colin and James's aunt Lucy had her farm. Because of this, Colin and he had struck up an immediate rapport. In an early conversation it turned out that Michael and Colin had probably first met when they were both about 11-years-old and taking part in a "Sack Race" at Lucy's local Church's Annual Summer Fete. As usual, Colin and his brother had been spending part of their school holidays on the farm. Michael's job in the crew included obtaining certain radar fixes, checking the Distant-Reading-Compass Master Unit when required. He would also be responsible for all recognition signals and to watch for the approach of enemy aircraft on the radar. It would be Michael who informed Colin, as the Captain, of all messages transmitted to the aircraft and transmitting messages from the aircraft. As was usual, the Flight Engineer had not joined the crew until they had been posted to the Heavy Conversion Unit. Once in the crew, Sergeant "Ginger" Toppin, from the West Midlands, had blended in very well. He was very humorous - a big practical joker. "Ginger" was a very tall, lanky individual. Because of his height, on numerous occasions, he had cursed very loudly after banging his head on some part of the fuselage or cabling brackets when getting in or out of the Lancaster. Geoff had been so named "Ginger" because of the unruly mop of ginger, curly hair which sat atop his lanky frame. One night after a heavy session in a local pub, at the end of a day's training, the rest of the crew had wrought revenge on "Ginger" for some of his practical jokes, by putting him to bed semi-conscious complete with a woman's hair-net and curlers adorning his unruly mop of hair. Before setting off on a bombing mission or any flight, Geoff would be the link between Colin and the ground crew, would supervise fuelling, draining and re-filling oil tanks and the application of de-icing paste. During the pre-flight planning he would work out the fuel plan. Once in the air, Geoff was responsible for operation of engine controls such as cooling and fuel cocks, checking fuel consumption and temperatures and for carrying out repairs and adjustments if and when necessary. The two Air Gunners, both Sergeants, were Jack Gaskell - Mid-Upper and, Rear or "Tail-End Charlie" - Dennis Wilson. Jack was a dour Geordie whom, for a while, Colin had not fully taken to. Jack had not joined the crew until after a few days into their training in the Operational Training Unit, hastily replacing a Yorkshireman who mysteriously went missing from the airfield after a session of night-time flying training. At the time, rumours abounded that the Police had arrested the Yorkshireman for some crime committed just before the outbreak of war. Colin remembered that no questions about this rumour would be answered by anyone. However, as the last few weeks of their training continued, Colin had grown to like Jack, respect and value him as a dependable crew member. Besides, within him, Jack had a ruthless streak - could be useful when defending the Lancaster against a hostile German Night Fighter. Dennis Wilson, the oldest member of the crew, was of a very short stature, a cheerful and chirpy Cockney, who had no difficulty whatsoever in getting his body into the cramped and unfriendly rear gun turret. Unlike the rest of the crew, Dennis was married. In fact, a matter of celebration - a few days ago in a pub near the airfield - was the news his wife had given birth to their first child - a son. The skills both gunners had to have attained was a very high standard of aircraft recognition, the theory, knowledge and the use of their guns and sighting. They were both responsible for the defence of the aircraft and its crew and, as such, would advise Colin on combat and evasive manoeuvres.

The crew's long training was now completed and, now having been declared "Fully Operational", any day soon would be taking off on their first real mission. Colin at last fell asleep, hoping against hope their intensive training, different skills attained, teamwork, bonding and growing friendship would get them all successfully and safely through their tour of duty of 30 Op.'s.

5

The bright morning sunshine shafting through the window woke Colin at 7.00. On the roadway which ran beside the accommodation block he heard a vehicle approach and stop, its engine remained idling. Men were talking and laughing and there was a metallic bang as one of the truck's doors was slammed shut. With a grinding crunch of gears and a revving of its engine, the truck moved off. Colin had one last stretch, glanced at his watch and got up. With a bit of luck he might beat most of the others to the bathroom and lavatory which serviced his part of the accommodation block. Walking down the corridor, he blessed his good fortune for serving on a Bomber Station with good facilities and reasonably comfortable. Some of the stories he had heard about the comfort and facilities available on some of the newer Bomber Stations - which had mushroomed in number and built in haste as war progressed - were truly grim. Ablution blocks sometimes as much as 100 hundred yards away from the accommodation - wonderful for character building in the depths of winter!

Returning from the bathroom Colin glanced at the calendar hanging by the locker. Incredible how the weeks had flown by, the time hastened no doubt by the amount of work and training crammed into them. Now, here he was - the training, flying exercises and familiarisation with his crew now behind him. He and his crew were fully operational and ready for their first Op. His Squadron, like many in Bomber Command, tended to nurse their new crews along a bit during their early days. Usually initiating them by including them in the supposed easier missions or "Milk Runs" as they were widely known. He wondered if it would be such a mission tonight. His stomach turned nervously and he reminded himself that he really must write letters to his parents and brother James some time today to tell them his news.

On his way down to the Mess for breakfast, Colin met Ben Cansdale, his Navigator.

'Morning Ben. How are you?'

'Is it really morning?' The New Zealander looked decidedly pale and fragile. 'Surely I didn't drink that much. I feel as if I've done over a month's solid sheep-shearing. Was the beer last night the usual brew we drink?'

To celebrate being declared fully operational, Colin, Ben and the other five of the crew had spent the previous evening in the *Plough,* a delightful, friendly little pub near the airfield.

Colin laughed loudly. 'Yes you did drink that much Ben and, no, it wasn't the usual brew. We - most of us that is - were quite content with the usual ale. You, my old friend, insisted on trying and staying on the local brewery's special brew. We, and the landlord, did try to warn you.'

'God!'

Colin just managed to prevent Ben from walking into the corner of the wall.

'That was not all Ben. The rest of us had a hell of a time finding you before we left the pub.'

'What do you mean?'

'Eventually we tracked you down to the little out-building at the side of the pub. You were in there with that big blonde. Having a whale of a time you were.'

'You don't mean the one with the big ...?' With his hands, Ben illustrated a big bust and hips. 'Oh God no! The last thing I remember is talking to her about her dad's farm.' Suddenly, Ben's complexion grew even paler. 'You don't mean - I was - you know ...? She had such goofy teeth. She was horrible.'

'Yes you were. Well if you weren't, you were giving a pretty good imitation of it. Your trousers were down around your ankles.'

'Oh no! No! Thank heavens I can't remember anything about it.'

They had reached the entrance to the Mess.

'Don't worry about it old chap. You'll feel a whole lot better with a Mess breakfast inside you. Perhaps your memory will return as well.'

'That's what I'm worried about.' He paused. 'But Colin! You don't think she'll ...?'

Colin gave a little laugh. 'Who knows. Nine month's time will tell.'

Ben now looked even paler.

Breakfast brought a bit more colour back to the New Zealander's usual healthy complexion. After leaving the Mess Colin and Ben met up with the rest of the crew and altogether they made their way to assemble for morning parade. Michael Richards and "Ginger" Toppin were especially merciless in their teasing of Ben about his choosing to drink the brewery's "special" ale the previous evening and his time of passion with the big blonde. The morning parade itself was fairly informal, really held to check the availability and fitness of each crew assigned to the Op. scheduled for that night. The parade over, the next thing was for the crew to journey over to their aircraft waiting at the dispersal pan.

The particular pan Colin and his crew had to get to was situated on the far side of the airfield. Sometimes, aircrew members were able to grab bicycles to get to their aircraft after parade. However, as had happened frequently during the last week or so, there were no cycles left by the time Colin and his crew got there. Short of waiting for an MT vehicle to arrive, the only alternative was for them to walk to their aircraft.

'Bloody hell!' Complained the Canadian Bomb-Aimer, Doug Harvey. He kicked a small stone angrily. 'All the bikes have been pinched again.'

Colin laughed. 'Typical. A lot of lazy sods around here. Still, we've got plenty of time to walk it. Nice morning for a walk mind you. The fresh air will do us all good. Especially Ben here. Besides an MT might pass by and we can hitch a lift.'

"Ginger" replied 'One dark night I'm going to steal out and stash a bike away underneath my bed.'

The seven men began to walk along the perimeter track. Personally, Colin was pleased for the opportunity of a walk. The sun still shone brightly and there was something of the freshness of spring in the air. The perpetual breeze, coming from the direction commonly prevailing at the airfield, lightly brushed his face. It was common for this breeze to have the magnitude of a wind. The part of the perimeter track they were on was bordered by huts and other buildings which, in turn, were bounded by ancient hedge and woodland. Rooks chattered raucously and argumentatively in their dense community in the treetops above them. Personnel - groundcrew, mechanics, fitters, armourers - busied themselves in workshops; scurried in and out of the various huts grouped in various sections beside the track. Some personnel walked along clutching files and papers, others rode bicycles along the track or between the various buildings. For a moment Colin and his crew were distracted as three shapely WAAF's crossed the perimeter in front of them, after alighting from a car, before making their way towards the Control Tower. The WAAF's returned warm and friendly smiles. Over to Colin's left, a group of mechanics were noisily assisting in the loading of engine parts onto the back of a truck which faced the direction of one of the maintenance hangars back down the perimeter. Way over on the main runway, a lone Lancaster revved its engines at the take-off point - Colin assumed, about to embark on some test or training flight. For Colin there was a special atmosphere of an airfield - something inspiring, whether it be when all was relatively quiet and not "making ready" for Op.'s or when, as today, all was activity in the preparation of a mission. He found it in some way therapeutic to walk amongst and experience the activity and anticipation. Also, the walk afforded him the opportunity to collect his thoughts, prepare himself for his first ever bombing mission later tonight - to try and assimilate his feelings about it. As the seven men continued to walk along the perimeter, chatting and joking on the way, Colin wondered if his crewmates' fears and apprehension about their first mission were affecting them in the same way as they were him. He was now really beginning to feel the heavy responsibilities of being their Captain, in setting a good example by not showing his own fear outwardly. Glancing at the men around him, not one showed any real outward sign of the fear and uncertainty they must each be experiencing - hiding their apprehension cunningly from each other in the banter and comments they exchanged. Since the seven had been together - apart from the occasional mention in conversation during final training or during a bash at the pub or at other quieter times - Colin could not recall any one of them really talking about their fears.

At last they stood in the shadow of Lancaster "P" for Peter. Colin had never ceased to be in awe of the Lancaster. The aeroplane was big, strong and solid. Its big wheels were thick and immense and, in height, came well above his waist. The bomb doors were open and he gazed up into the vast void which was the bomb bay, currently empty and awaiting its deadly load. He walked out from underneath the starboard wing between the two large propellers. Again he noticed the distinctive smell - a mix of oil, fuel and grease - which always seemed to pervade the area around an aircraft. Coming out of the shadow of the bulky wing into the sunlight, Colin had to shade his eyes as he looked up at the shining side of the cockpit window about fourteen feet above him. He and his crew began to clamber into the aircraft and make their way to their appropriate positions to commence inspection and testing of the aircraft's equipment. Doug, like "Ginger", was tall although heavier built and cursed as he banged the top of his head whilst dropping himself down a foot or so through the opening in front of the pilot's seat to the Bomb-Aimer's position. Colin settled himself in his seat, was briefly anxious as he took in the immense array of dials, compasses, levers and buttons facing him. Then, recovering his thoughts, he familiarised himself again as to what they were and did. "Ginger" pulled down his drop-down seat beside Colin, studied the gauges which monitored the aircraft's engines, fuel consumption, temperatures etc. Michael settled himself in his position almost under the Astradome. Ben patted Michael's shoulder as he passed by on his way to the Navigator's position.

'I've always said Mike. You Wireless Operators have the best position of us all.'

Jack Gaskell and Dennis Wilson set about checking their guns and gunsights. The rear gun turret was really cramped and uncomfortable, difficult to get in and out of.

Being a rear-gunner was one of the few times in his life when Dennis was grateful for being of small stature, it enabled him to attain both tasks with comparative ease. Being short also had other advantages for both the rear-gunner and the rest of his crew. Most Night Fighter attacks on Lancasters came from the gunner's blind spot of dead astern and below. Being short, Dennis discovered during his Lancaster training, he was able to stand up in the turret and look down and astern through the panel cut out of the glass and Perspex.

After Colin and his crew completed all their checks and tests they made their way back to the Squadron Office. A message had been scribbled on the blackboard: "Op.'s tonight confirmed. General Briefing 15.30. Times of detailed briefings to be announced".

The message was read with different responses and outward emotions. From some, muted cheers that at last after all the training and waiting the time for the real thing had arrived - others reacted silently, their feelings and fears kept to themselves. Each one though, without daring to show it to the others, inwardly experienced the very same natural apprehension, doubts and fears. There was now no way back. From this minute until they landed back after the mission - in the very small hours of tomorrow morning - they could now not even leave the airfield for a source of distraction or telephone family and loved ones. Until the time of the briefing, all they would be able to do is return to their billet to rest, to read or write letters; perhaps a game of darts, cards, snooker or billiards. Perhaps, as the weather was good, play a hastily arranged game of tennis, cricket or football.

Before that, however, like the more-seasoned aircrews, Colin and his crew had a desire to try and work out their possible target for tonight. And, like the other crews, would place bets on it.

Ben said: 'Over the last few days I've been putting some spade work in on that pretty little map clerk. I'm going to try and find out what charts and maps are being issued.'

Colin laughed. 'I would have thought Ben, you had enough potential woman trouble on your hands after your escapades with that big, goofy, blonde last night?'

'Ugh! Don't remind me.'

'Well off you go then Ben' continued Colin. 'Do you reckon "Ginger" you could try and find out what sort of fuel load is being planned?'

'Shouldn't be a problem. I've managed to build up quite a friendship with the ground crew fellows.'

Colin turned to his Bomb-Aimer 'Doug could you discover what type of bombs we'll be taking?'

'Sure. I'll take a little wander around the bomb dump and ordnance stores.'

'Right. Say we all meet back here in about an hour?'

'Okay skipper. See you later.'

******

On the morning Colin was declared "fully operational", James waved good-bye to June as his train began to pull out of the station in Sussex. Even though for brief moments their view of each other was obscured by clouds of smoke belching from the engine, they continued to wave and blow kisses. The hastening train rounded the bend. They could see each other no more.

He settled himself in his seat in the crowded compartment. Deliberately, he averted his eyes from his fellow passengers. He had no wish to enter into conversation with anyone. He just wanted to think about and remember his short leave and precious moments spent with his wife.

James now fully understood just what he had volunteered for - it had constantly been on his mind throughout the last few days. He now realised that the odds of seeing June again were steeply stacked against him. Worse, to him, in many ways, was the fact he had lied to her as to what he was about to embark on. Total secrecy, duty to his country dictated it - his signing of documents had reinforced that. He had been given a cover story by the "Organisation" explaining to June and his parents his imminent, prolonged absence. Nevertheless, he really hated the fact he had lied. James also remembered when, in London after his first interview, he had told June of the possibility of him being sent away for a while. When he said he had volunteered she had reacted by being more angry than he could ever remember, had not spoken to him for the rest of the day.

Just over a week ago he had been woken at 06.30 in the morning, having been in a mission de-briefing in the Intelligence Block until 02.30 hours. He had been woken to receive the letter he had been expecting from SOE. Following the instructions given in the letter, James had barely time to wash, pack and breakfast before being driven away. He had not even had the opportunity to say cheerio to fellow and superior officers, friends and colleagues. He was never to find out how his sudden departure was explained away. Graciously, the contents of the letter allowed him to take a few day's leave but, also, re-confirmed in an uncompromising way, his previous commitment by signature that on no account was he to give any indication of what he was about to undertake. The letter also stated a time and date when he was to report to an address in Baker Street, London.

He allowed himself a glance out of the carriage window as the Sussex scenery now sped by.

******

That same morning Derek Pickering put the last few things into his suitcase.

Rosemary entered the bedroom with another of his shirts and clutching Christopher their young son, conceived during the weeks before Robert Thompson had brought her the terrible news of her husband's injuries.

'Here darling. Pack this shirt. It's one of your favourites.'

'Thank you my love. I was looking for that. Nearly finished. I'll be down in a minute. Could I have a cup of tea before I leave?'

'Of course. Just going to change this young man. Then I'll put the kettle on.'

Derek watched his wife with their youngest child leave the room. He shut his suitcase and sat on the bed close to tears. He recalled his agony as he had fought to climb out of his blazing, falling Hurricane. Still vivid in his mind how he had seen flames engulf his hands, arms and thighs then, the flames on and around his face. The agony, as his rescuers finally got to him - then, during the weeks and months after, as he lay in hospital. The burns still caused him frequent pain as the repair and re-construction work on his body and face by the plastic surgeon struggled to keep pace with the changes to the surrounding skin and tissue. This was the reason for his journey today - to return to the hospital in East Grinstead for further treatment by Archie McIndoe and his specialist burn's team. Every so often, Derek had to return for further skin grafts and other modifications to his burnt body and face. Today was to be his third visit. Worse than his agony in many ways had been Rosemary's expression of sheer shock when she first saw him after the initial dressings and bandages had been removed, and his children's first reactions and fear when they saw his burnt face and claw-like hands. Rosemary, bless her, after the initial shock, had soon taken it all in her stride, her love and care coming in abundance. Andrew and Sarah, taking their cue from their mother's lead, soon too, had got used to their largely rebuilt father and he now felt totally at ease with them and they with him. Derek himself, had taken a long time, despite numerous prompting from Rosemary, before he felt confident enough to even kiss her let alone become more intimate. Now, thankfully, they had resumed near-normal marital relations. Now too, all three children were able to enjoy kisses and cuddles with their father. However, he still felt very self-conscious when it came to eating meals and drinking as his mouth tended to exert its own will.

Derek's promotion to Wing Commander, just prior to sustaining his injuries, still stood and, after stringent medical assessments, he had been retained in the RAF - for the time-being anyway. This was thanks to some hefty pulling of strings with the authorities by Robert Thompson, the Station Commander. Derek had taken up the post in charge of Flight Control at the airfield and Sector, replacing "Hearty" Hale now with Coastal Command.

Picking up his suitcase, Derek went downstairs wondering how long he would be at East Grinstead this time. However, it never seemed like being in a hospital. Since establishing the Unit, McIndoe had always insisted it be run more like a social club or an extension of a good airfield Mess. In McIndoe's view, running it in that way helped the victim's recovery and assisted them to integrate themselves more easily into society on discharge. Derek glanced at his watch. Before leaving he might even have some time to play with his young son.

6

The meeting at the building in Baker Street had been fairly brief and terse. James had been disappointed it had not been with Pierre Walton he had met on the previous occasion. He had struck up a bit of rapport with him. The man James did see had a rather dictatorial manner and it seemed as if he had regarded his meeting with James as an aggravating interruption. James had been instructed to arrive at the offices in civilian clothes. The instructions also said he had only to bring with him the minimum of personal effects.

During his meeting James was given an address to go to just around the corner from the office and, a train ticket to Perth with precise information as to a place near Perth Station where he would receive further instructions. After a cursory farewell and a muttered 'Good luck' from the unfriendly official, James made his way around to Montagu Mansions, and found his way into the small "reception-like" area as instructed. A short, bald-headed man, dressed in a shabby jumper, appeared furtively through a doorway clutching a battered holdall.

'Morning. Can I help you?'

'I was told to come here and ask for Arnold. I presume I'm in the right place?'

'Your name please?'

'Squadron Leader James Graham.'

'I'm Arnold. Pleased to meet you Squadron Leader. I've just been told I was to expect you.' He shook James's hand vigorously. 'This holdall is for you. Better check all is correct.' He placed the holdall on a well-worn table in the centre of the room and went over to the window. He looked up and down the street cautiously before returning to the table beside James. 'We have to be careful you know.'

Arnold proceeded to check through the contents of the holdall. Peering over Arnold's shoulder, as the man checked each item out loud to himself, James saw a compass and numerous items of warm, waterproof clothing and footwear.

His checking of the contents completed, Arnold fastened it and said: 'Yes. It appears to be all present and correct.' Then, rather apologetically 'I'm afraid you'll have to sign for these Squadron Leader.' James signed the form proffered. He noticed the man cleverly concealed the title of the form with his hand or, did he imagine that. Arnold shook James's hand vigorously once again. 'Well nice to have met you. Good luck. Hope to meet you again. I assume you know how to get to the station?'

James replied that he did, picked up the holdall and went out into the street, the sense of mystery and trepidation growing still more within him. Arnold's words - 'Hope to meet you again', weren't very reassuring.' He turned his head back to the building he had just left and saw Arnold was once more looking up and down the street as if he was seeing whether anyone was watching. On seeing James look back at the building, Arnold hastily - guiltily withdrew from behind the curtain at the window.

James knew he wouldn't arrive in Perth until late that night at the earliest, subject of course to whether or not the line had been bombed or the result of some other war-time cause. He had been given an address, near the station, where he had been told a room would be available.

Since 1940, travel by rail anywhere had been notoriously slow. Caused either by scheduled services being interrupted by the necessity to prioritise transport of supplies of equipment, machinery, armaments and foodstuffs or, frequently, as the result of air-raid damage to track, rolling stock, signalling equipment and stations. His journey this day had proved to be no exception. Delays had occurred at Preston, Carlisle and Glasgow. It was gone 10.30 that night, in a shabby little turning behind Perth Station, when James knocked on the brown front door of a small, terraced house. The house was next to a rowdy, rough ale-house, a place James would never - even if dying of thirst - have thought of entering. Eventually, he heard the shuffling of feet on the other side of the front door and the sound of a big bolt being slammed open. The wizened face of a little old lady, wearing a shabby shawl, stood blinking at him enquiringly. He was a bit taken aback.

'Oh! I'm sorry to trouble you this late at night. But I was given this address.'

Without any facial expression, the old lady opened the door further, pointing an angry, accusing finger at him.

'I was expecting you earlier. You've interrupted my programme on the wireless and I was just about to go to bed.' She paused and shook her head in disgust. 'Well you'd better come in.'

'I'm sorry but you see the trains …'.

She motioned him towards the dingy and austere stairway. He noticed she had an arthritically-deformed hand.

'…Your room's up there to the left of the landing. I expect you'd like a warm drink?'

'Well yes. Thank you. That would be very nice. But your radio programme …?'

' …Never mind. I've missed the end of it by now anyway. I'll call you when your drink's ready. I can't get up the stairs very easily now. I sleep downstairs.'

'Thank you very much.'

'You'll find the lavatory down the garden, through there.' She pointed vaguely in the direction of the kitchen at the end of the hallway. Then, pointing to a doorway to her right. 'Your breakfast will be in there at 7.30 sharp.'

The bedroom James had been given looked out over the road. Like the rest of the house, it was dreary and dark. Positioned on one side was a dresser. On its top was a large jug of water, a bowl for washing and a towel. The ancient brass bed was clean enough but uncomfortable. This, combined with the noise from the pub next door and, with the noise of shouting, fighting and swearing continuing in the street until well after midnight, resulted in him only sleeping fitfully.

As James ate his breakfast of porridge and toast he felt absolutely shattered but, nevertheless, the food was very welcome. When the time came for him to make his way to his appointed meeting place, he thanked the old lady and asked what he owed for his lodging. With, at last, a friendly smile she replied the payment had been taken care of and bade him farewell.

He had been waiting for about ten minutes on the corner of the road specified in his instructions. He was beginning to feel uneasy that perhaps he had misunderstood where he was meant to be met. Even by looking twice at his instructions and, seeking confirmation from a passing postman he was standing at the correct junction failed to lift his unease. Then, his attention was taken by the sight of a mud-splattered and dented jeep stopping at the roadside opposite. In between referring to a paper he held in his hand, its driver looked across at him twice. The driver got out and crossed the road towards him. James was struck at how powerfully-built the man was. A shock of sandy-coloured hair was visible beneath the tweed cap on his head and he wore a thick "fisherman-knit" jumper. The sleeves of his lived-in jacket bulged with large biceps.

'James Graham?' The man asked in a heavy highland accent.

James confirmed he was.

'I needed to double-check.' The man looked down at the dark yellow label tied to the right-hand side of the holdall handle. 'I couldn't see this at first and sometimes the photographs we're sent don't bear much resemblance to the actual person.'

James remembered the series of photographs taken at his first interview at the Baker Street offices and, how adamant Arnold had been that the dark yellow label should remain in its position on the holdall handle.

The highlander continued 'I'm Dougal MacPherson.' His firm handshake near-paralysed James's hand. 'Pleased to meet you. Sorry to have kept you. Some troop movements just outside town delayed me. Now, please, if you'd like to come with me?'

Dougal helped James put his luggage into the back of the canvas-roofed jeep. Reluctantly the vehicle coughed into life and they began to make their way through a maze of streets.

'Is this your first visit to Scotland?'

'I visited Edinburgh once. Very briefly. With my parents and brother. Years ago now.'

'Och! You'll notice a hell of a difference where we're heading. Right out in the wilds we are. Miles from anywhere. All you'll probably see are mountains, burns, heather and sheep. I better warn you. We have a long and, at times, awkward journey.'

'Sounds interesting' replied James. He tried to ask Dougal as to exactly where they were headed. Dougal swiftly changed the subject.

'How did you enjoy your night's stay?'

James paused slightly before answering. 'Well. It was all right I suppose. The elderly lady there didn't seem too friendly. Gave me a good breakfast though.'

James saw a knowing smile play on the Highlander's weathered and ruddy face.

'Old Moira has a heart of gold really. She is invaluable. She's had a hard old life.'

From his companion's words and facial expression, James realised the elderly lady was well known and respected by Dougal. Had obviously been previously used by the shadowy organisation he himself had now been involved with for some weeks.

The boundaries of Perth now behind them they were now on the open road. The day had dawned grey and miserable. James sensed they were heading in a broadly northerly direction. As they continued, the weather grew even more grey and miserable and it started to rain. Apart from small exchanges of conversation between the two men, the journey was passing in silence. The lack of conversation, a long previous day, the fairly sleepless night which followed and the mesmerising sweep of the windscreen wipers compounded and James fell asleep.

He awoke to find them travelling along a winding, isolated road. The rain was now falling heavily from leaden heavy skies, the constant pitter-pattering of raindrops drummed on the canvas roof. Every so often there was a loud splash as a wave of dirty water hit the windscreen of the jeep as it ploughed through large puddles. The rain was so heavy it was like a mist, near-obscuring the not so distant hills and mountains. Now and again, there were sheep grouped together, sheltered in the lee of strewn outcrops of grey rock. It seemed the foul weather was proving too much for even these the hardiest of beasts. Occasionally along the route, outlines of cottages, walls and farm buildings would appear in the distance. However, as the jeep drew abreast of them, James saw the vast majority of these cottages and farm buildings were uninhabited, neglected and crumbling into disrepair. The mounds of fallen stonework stood in sad testament of an age and lives long since past.

'Where are we Dougal?'

'This is Rannoch Moor. A haunting place you'll agree James.'

'It's certainly bleak. Most of these farms are deserted. Where's everyone gone?'

'Most of these holdings were traditionally handed down from father to son. The slaughter of the last war saw to it that there were not many sons left to pass them on to. Nowadays, with the Government efforts to increase food production, some families are returning to try and make a go of them again. Och though! It's a hell of a place to scrape a living right enough. We'll be driving through Glencoe soon. Sometimes a beautiful place but, in weather like this especially, very bleak. Yet another marker of treachery between men and the bloodshed which follows.'

Hearing Dougal speak, James realised there was perhaps a streak of the philosopher lurking somewhere deep inside the bulky frame of the man sitting beside him. The name Glencoe re-awakened within him one of his school History lessons when he had learnt of the massacre of the MacDonald Clan by the Clan of Campbell.

It was late afternoon when Dougal parked the jeep in a street in Fort William. Dougal looked at his fob watch.

'We've not made bad time considering. I daresay you could do with some refreshment and something to eat?'

'Yes please. I must admit I'm feeling pretty hungry and thirsty.'

'I know just the place. Molly will look after us.'

Dougal led James over the road to an attractive-looking house. The heavy rain had given way to drizzle. To James it also seemed a lot colder here than in Perth. From a sign hanging by the gate, he saw the establishment was a guest house. Something though puzzled James.

As they crossed the road he asked: 'Dougal why didn't they arrange for you to pick me up at the station here?'

The other man smiled slightly and shook his head. 'Here, a stranger would stand out like a sore thumb. Perth is a whole lot bigger. Comings and goings are not so obvious there.'

Something in Dougal's voice told James he would not elaborate further. Besides, by now, Dougal had knocked at the door which, almost immediately, had been opened by a startlingly good-looking woman in her early forties.

'Hello Dougal. I was beginning to wonder where you had got to.' She smiled warmly and reached out towards him. Suddenly, seeing James standing behind Dougal, she retracted her arms.

'Sorry Molly. The weather made it slow going across Rannoch.'

'Come in the pair of you.' She turned, looking enquiringly at James.

Dougal cut in quickly 'Molly. This is James. He's come up to do some bird watching and shooting on the estate.'

Molly shook James's hand lightly.

'Well pleased to meet you James.' She lead the two men into the dining room. 'I've prepared something to eat. It won't be any trouble to prepare for one other. Won't be long and I'll bring it in.' She indicated James to take a seat. 'Now make yourself at home James.'

Molly passed through the door into the kitchen. After a moment, Dougal followed her, leaving the door slightly open. James looked around the room and caught sight of an attractive landscape painting hanging on the wall. He got up to look at it closely. Through the slightly open door, he saw Dougal and Molly standing together. The pair of them were embracing and kissing - Dougal's hand caressing Molly's buttocks. James smiled. The scene confirmed what he had suspected in the way she had reacted on seeing Dougal on the doorstep. He returned to his seat. After a few minutes, Molly and Dougal returned carrying a selection of plates and dishes and another set of cutlery. Between them, they arranged the plates and dishes of food on the table. Molly laid a second place setting on the table. James thought to himself: so she definitely wasn't expecting Dougal to be accompanied.

'Now' said Molly. 'If you'll both excuse me, I must go up and finish getting ready. I've an appointment.'

The two men began to eat their meal.

After she had gone Dougal said: 'Hope you didn't mind my dreaming up about the bird watching and shooting. I've known Molly for a good many years but, even so, we have to be very careful. Where we're heading - the place selected for your training - is very isolated. Although the folk hereabouts know something goes on there - it's designated as a "wartime protected" area - they are traditionally very secretive and wouldn't be given to talking broadly about it. Nevertheless, there's no need to broadcast unnecessarily where individuals are going.'

'I see.' James paused as he completed a mouthful of delicious fresh-baked bread. 'How long have you worked for the organisation Dougal?'

'For a few months now. I help them out from time-to-time with various things. No doubt you'll find out in time exactly how. I'm motivated to do so really out of loyalty to the Laird.'

'The Laird?'

'His estate adjoins the area of land you're going to. I'm his Gillie. The Laird has always invited parties and individuals onto his estate for hunting, fishing - holidays and things. This arrangement has continued during the last few months or so, even though he and his wife have seldom been there. Thus, it is not unusual for the locals or anyone else to see me transporting people like yourself backwards and forwards.'

'You say he and his wife are seldom there?'

'Yes.' Dougal finished mopping up the gravy on his plate. 'Their eldest son - and heir to the estate - he was an officer in the army - was posted as "missing" after Dunkirk. Their daughter - Ailsa - was in the ATS. She was working in London and was killed at the end of 1940 during the blitz. The grief of the Laird and his wife, after the loss of two of their children, was such that they now spend much of their time in Canada. All my life, their family have always been good to me - and my parents before me. I owe them a lot. Doing what I do for your people just seems a way of paying something back to the laird and his wife - helping them get back at the Germans.'

Molly returned wearing a coat and hat.

'Well that's me ready. How are you two getting on?'

'We've just about finished here Molly. Thank you. Just what we needed. You'll have to give me the recipe one day?'

James added 'Yes. Thank you very much. It was very kind of you.'

Dougal said 'When I'm next in town Molly, I'll drop off

some rabbit and venison. I've got some hanging right now. I will probably be taking some more guests to the estate next week. They will be staying first at the hotel down the road.'

'That would be very welcome Dougal. Thank you.' She walked towards the table. Let me clear these away. I'll leave them in the sink till I get back. Then I must away for this appointment.'

'Och! I'll give you a hand taking them out. We must be making tracks soon ourselves.'

James started to help them.

'Och no! We'll manage these James.' Dougal nodded his head in the direction of an occasional table.

'While we're doing this you may be interested in glancing through that fishing magazine?'

James took the hint, suspecting Dougal and Molly were wanting to say farewell to each other properly. After a few minutes Dougal re-entered putting on his jacket and holding James's coat. James took it and the two men followed Molly out into the street. She turned down the road, they crossed the road to the jeep, waving to her and thanking her again as they did so.

During the journey westwards, Dougal pointed out Loch Eil and the tip of Loch Shiel. He also indicated the boundary of the estate to which he was employed as the Gillie. From here the terrain grew ever more rugged. The road became more of a rough track. Rain again began to fall heavily. The going became a lot slower, the ride a lot more uncomfortable as, almost continuously, the vehicle jolted and jumped over the uneven surface. Dusk was falling fast as Dougal pointed to his right, explaining that the dark depths of Loch Morar - reputed to be deeper than Loch Ness - lay over in the distance.

It was fully dark when, some while later, the jeep swept

up a wooded drive, rounded a bend and came to a halt outside what looked, in the gloom, to be an old baronial hall. James stepped out of the jeep onto a gravel surface. Dougal came round to James's side and lifted his luggage out.

'Well here you are at last. Just knock at that large door.' Dougal shook James's hand firmly. 'Well it's been nice meeting you. I may well be seeing you again sometime during the next few weeks. 'Good-bye and good luck.'

James was about to thank him but, before he could, Dougal had left his side and rounded the jeep to the driver's side. James watched as the jeep again coughed into life and turned around an obelisk mounted with some statue. He continued to watch as the jeep gradually disappeared down the drive. The rain continued to fall heavily. James shook a raindrop off his nose and walked towards the building. Now James could make out more easily the lines and architecture of the house. To him it looked like some vampire's castle from a horror story or, an archetypal haunted house. As he approached the large heavy door, he began to feel a strange dread and wondered just what was he letting himself in for. Still, it was now too late for second thoughts - he knew there was no turning back. Apprehensively he pulled the ancient, metal, bell chain.

7

The Briefing times were announced and specified as: Pilots at 17.00; Navigators at 17.15; Air Bombers at 17.15; Wops at 17.30; Flight Engineers at 17.30; Air Gunners at 17.30; Main Briefing at 18.30.

Although the flying meal of bacon and eggs smelt and looked delicious, Colin struggled to eat half of it. His nerves were making his stomach churn and he felt vaguely nauseous. Looking at the others around him he saw many of them were also eating without enthusiasm. It was obvious they were having similar attacks of nerves. Finishing what they could of their meal, Colin and Ben collected flying rations of sandwiches, boiled sweets, bars of plain chocolate and handed their flasks to the steward for filling with a hot drink. The pair of them met up with the other five - also clutching their rations - and they all headed towards the Briefing Room. As a precaution against air attack, the airfield's Technical, Communal Quarters' and Admin. Sites were widely dispersed around the airfield which, although sensible, was inconvenient for personnel moving around. On the way to the Briefing, the seven men again compared and discussed what information they had separately gleaned about the Op. earlier in the day.

'My money is still on the destination being Holland' said Colin.

'Judging by the fuel load, it's either Belgium or somewhere in Northern France' said "Ginger".

'I agree with "Ginger". Probably Northern France' added Doug Harvey.

'No. Mark my words you two. Its going to be the Netherlands' scoffed Colin. 'Make sure you've got your money ready for me when we get back.'

Michael Richards, in the Wops Briefing, on hearing the target was to be in Holland smiled to himself. Like his skipper, he had bet "Ginger" and Doug the target would be Holland. Michael listened intently as the call signs and W/T frequencies were given. He wrote down the designated colours of the day on his piece of rice paper. After listening to one or two questions being answered, he rejoined the six others just as they were trooping into the main Briefing.

The Briefing Room was large and, at the far end, stood Wing Commander Lazenby the Squadron Commander, Burton the Station CO and other Officers who would be contributing to the Briefing. Colin led his crew to a table, where they would be able to collate and discuss what each individual had been briefed previously. Burton read out the Operational Order received from Group HQ then turned to reveal the large map on the wall behind him. The targets were to be railway marshalling yards near Goes in Southwest Holland and Oosterschelde, a large sea inlet and a complex which, from intelligence gathered, were barracks and the administration centre for the training of marine and water-borne landing troops. On the map, were pinned lengths of coloured tape indicating the routes to be followed from base to target and for the return. Routes especially selected to avoid flying over areas known to be heavily defended. Separate boards bore lists of the names of the pilots against the call-sign of each aircraft taking part in the mission; the take-off times for each aircraft; details of the type of bombs being used. Burton proceeded to present his overview of their mission, passing on the special instructions received from Group HQ.

Since first meeting him, Colin had come to admire and respect Lazenby, his Squadron Commander. And now, as he listened to the man relate information and give his advice about the operation so encouragingly and reassuringly, those feelings grew. As a pilot, so new to it all, Colin wondered, from the detailed knowledge Lazenby imparted, just how many times his CO must have flown to or over the area in question. Lazenby moved to one side and the Flying Control Officer informed the intently-listening crews about the designated runway and take-off procedures. The Intelligence Officer, working from his detailed maps, spoke of the landmarks and distinctive geographical features by which to identify the approach to and location of the target. He also emphasised where barrages and enemy air defences could be expected.

With all the detailed information being imparted, Colin's head began to whirl. He hoped against hope he and his crew could remember all that was being said - their lives depended on it.

Using his charts the Met. Officer outlined the weather conditions in the target area, the type of cloud, wind speeds and wind directions which would be encountered on their journey there and back, the degree of icing to be expected and whether there was any possibility of fog or mist awaiting them on their return.

Colin looked around at the sea of faces gathered around the tables in the room. There was something about the more seasoned crews which made them easy to spot. The other new "sprog" crews seated in the room, he could also identify easily.

The Briefing completed, the Station Commander and

the Squadron CO offered more words of encouragement and wished them all good luck.

Ben set to work plotting their course based upon the take-off time and estimated time of arrival over the target. A while later, on their way out of the Briefing Room, they collected their Escape Kits. Quickly, Colin checked his kit contained the relevant maps of Holland and ensuring compass, food tablets, water-purifying tablets and Dutch currency were all included as well.

'Your personal belongings please?' The Intelligence Officer reminded him.

Colin looked at the man vacantly.

'Personal belongings?' Asked the Intelligence Officer again, though this time more sharply.

'Oh sorry. Forgot.' Colin was embarrassed he had forgotten an important bit of his training which stressed - in the event of baling out over occupied territory - the importance of not being caught with anything that would link one with life in England or an Allied country. He turned everything out of his pockets. Amongst his belongings, he reluctantly handed over the watch he had always kept with him since his parents had given it to him as a present on his birthday. He gave the watch one more loving look. It was as if the watch was his last link with his family and normality. Sensing his reluctance, the Intelligence Officer softened somewhat and smiled kindly.

'It's all right. I understand. Don't worry. We'll look after it for you. It will be here when you return.'

In the Crew Room, as Colin hauled his Irving Flying Suit on over his uniform, the rear gunner Dennis Wilson chirped up. 'By the time I've got all this bloody clobber on, the bloody mission will be over.'

Successfully getting on his flying suit, Colin set about putting on his "Mae West".

In his usual dour manner, mid-upper gunner Jack Gaskell said: 'Let's all hope Dennis the trigger of the air bottle on your Mae West doesn't get caught and inflates the damn thing like it did on our last training Op. It took two of us ages to deflate it and get you into the turret.'

'Come on chaps' called out Colin good-naturedly. 'If we don't hurry up, we'll miss the bus out to the kite.'

The bus deposited them at the dispersal pan where Lancaster "P" for Peter waited. There was still plenty of time for full checks before take-off. Ben, Jack and Dennis took the last opportunity for a cigarette before boarding; "Ginger" headed for the latrine located near the dispersal pan calling: 'Won't be long skipper.'

'Honestly "Ginger". You really ought to get those bladder and bowels of yours seen to.'

'Yeah' added Ben. 'Why don't you pee over the wheels of the kite for luck like the rest of us do?'

All last minute pre-take-off rituals observed, Colin led his crew aboard. One by one, they each settled into their positions to commence their individual final checks. Down in the bomb-aimer's compartment Doug looked above his head at the ring-mounted gun turret. At the front of the compartment was a perspex dome with a flat, clear-view panel fitted in its lower half; for anti-icing a glycol spray pipe was installed in the upper rim. The bomb-sight was located above this and, immediately behind, an upholstered body rest where he would kneel on the cover of the escape hatch. After boarding the Lancaster, Doug's first job was to check all the switches. The switch pre-selector panel was to the right-side of the compartment - the bomb-tit incorporated in its housing. To Doug's left was the camera control with, behind it, the camera - its focal lens protruding through the floor. Behind him, and serving as a step up into the cockpit, was a tank containing glycol. If necessary, prior to bombing run, Doug would use the small opening panel above this tank to peer into the bomb bay to check whether there were any problems in the bomb bay or, when returning back home after the raid, to check all the bombs had been released. Doug's only means of illumination in his domain was a tiny length of wire with a small bulb shining through a white, translucent panel - enough light to check his switches, not enough to be seen outside the aircraft. To reassure himself Doug reached to his right - between the bomb switch panel and the glycol tank - to feel if his parachute had been stowed.

The Very light fired from the control tower lit up the sky. "P" for Peter's bomb doors were closed and one by one Colin started the engines. The aircraft began to vibrate noisily, exhaust fumes and smoke drifted into the cockpit through the still open window and temporarily clouded his view of the airfield.

The noise, borne on clear night air, became deafening as, one by one, numerous aero engines roared into life. Rooks took flight from their nestings, ascending away in giant black protesting clouds. Testing the Lancaster's controls and running up the engines, Colin reassured himself everything was working correctly.

He called 'Everyone ready to taxi?'

There was a resounding and unanimous 'Yes skipper.'

Colin yelled down to the ground crew 'Here we go' and waved the chocks away.

He warily taxied his aircraft to the perimeter track to join the queue of others weaving their way along to the holding point at the end of the runway. Lancasters were approaching Runway 1 from both sides. Colin's Squadron from one side, those aircraft being used on the raid from the other Squadron approached it from the other. They would be allowed onto the runway singly and from the perimeter track alternately. Waiting for their turn seemed an eternity for him. Although it must have also seemed like that to the rest of his crew nothing was said about it - no impatience uttered. There was a vocal silence around him in the cockpit and behind in the fuselage. The remainder of his crew sat at their stations, each perhaps making final adjustments to equipment - each, Colin knew full well, alone with their own private fears and thoughts of what lay ahead of them.

Colin watched the aircraft in front of them increase speed down the runway and begin to lift off the ground. His own nerves now manifested themselves terribly, worrying away at his insides so that he felt quite sick and sweaty. An insect, awakened into flight by the engines starting, flitted in front of Colin's face. Idly, aimlessly, he waved it away. Suddenly, there it was, the green light of the Aldis Lamp from the Controller's Caravan - their time to go. He taxied the Lancaster to the end of the runway.

He called 'Okay lads. Here we go. Good luck everyone.'

He applied the brakes, set engines at zero boost. A second green light. He closed the throttles again before slowly building the engines' power. He released the brakes and the aircraft slowly rolled forward.

As was usual at take-off time airfield personnel, from the most senior ranks down to the most junior, crowded along both sides of the first part of the runway to wave their farewells and good wishes. This tradition of affection as always a major boost to morale for the departing air crews. Michael Richards stood in the astradome to acknowledge these good wishes.

The Lancaster slowly gained speed, the hydraulics of the undercarriage - because of the weight of the bomb and fuel load - causing the aircraft to bounce. The roar of the engines and Ben's voice calling out the speeds from the ASI repeater the only sounds to be heard. Colin was sweating with the sheer concentration needed in controlling the aircraft's perturbing usual tendency to swing to the left. They were now rapidly approaching the end of the runway - Colin felt panic building within him - the build-up of speed seemed far too slow. Suddenly, to his relief, "P" for Peter got airborne. Quickly "Undercarriage Retract" was selected and the Lancaster rapidly gained height over the airfield before disappearing in the darkness.

Those watching the departing bombers knew that - barring any emergency - nothing further would be heard from any of them until their Captains sent coded messages that the mission had been completed.

As Lancaster "P" for Peter gained height, Michael tuned in to the squadron transmitter and changed the Very cartridge for the appropriate colour of the day. After they had set course, he tuned in the group transmitter. At specified times along the route, this would be sending a time check and number. As "P" for Peter's crew settled down - each constantly checking for mechanical and electrical faults - Colin and Ben discussed and reviewed their course. "Ginger" checked cooling and fuel cocks, fuel consumption and temperatures; Mike listened out on his frequencies and watched his radar; Doug, Jack and Dennis - in their turrets - kept their eyes searching the dark sky all around them.

They crossed the English coast mid-way between Great Yarmouth and Lowestoft. Down beneath them lapped the waves of the deadly and forbiddingly cold North Sea. Peering downwards momentarily, Colin pondered on the huge numbers of aircraft which already lay with their crew on the sea bed - their graveyard - deep below those treacherous waves.

Ben and Colin referred to the wind speed and direction. As they drew further away from the English coast it began to increase and its direction change. They were having to make more frequent adjustments and corrections to their course. Colin hoped their hastily adjusted calculations were correct - one just had to have faith and confidence. From time to time "Ginger" would confirm reassuringly that fuel and temperatures were as they should be. Under his breath, Colin cursed the Met Officer. He had informed them of 5/10ths cloud. From where he was sitting it looked now more like 8/10ths. He hoped it didn't get worse and would improve closer to the target. On and on through the darkness they continued. So far so good.

'Jack and Dennis. Keep your eyes peeled' called Colin to his gunners at about fifty miles from the Dutch coast.

Not long after, Doug called 'Enemy coast coming up skipper.'

Dead ahead of them Colin saw beams of searchlights and bursts of exploding flak.

'I can see the mouth of the inlet' called Doug.

'You're sure?'

'Positive. Outline of the coast just as they described it.'

'Fighter!' Screamed Dennis suddenly over the intercom. 'From the port quarter! Corkscrew port!'

Instinctively, immediately, Colin threw the Lancaster into a steep spiralling dive. The four Merlin engines screamed in protest. The fighter curved after them. Momentarily, it disappeared from view.

'Can you see him Jack?' Dennis shouted again.

'No. No, not yet' replied the mid-upper gunner.

The Lancaster began to pull out of its dive.

'I see him. I see him Dennis' yelled Jack. Fleetingly, the fighter was in their sights. 'From starboard! From starboard!' Yelled Jack again. 'Corkscrew starboard.'

In his turret, Dennis watched as the night fighter followed the Lancaster through its curves of evasion.

As the bomber pulled up again, Dennis called: 'I've got him again Jack.'

'Yes. So have I.'

The fighter was now well in their range and squirting his cannons at them. The orange flashes streaking just past the rear quarter of the Lancaster as it corkscrewed again.

'Here he is again.'

'Yes I've got him as well. Now together. Ready, ready, let him have it.'

The .303 Brownings from both turrets spat their barrage of defiance. The night fighter gave another burst and disappeared beneath them. Dennis felt the nose of the Lancaster lift up. It was now flying straight and level. His eyes searched the darkness in every direction. There was no further sign of the fighter. Dennis was not a religious man but offered up a quick prayer of thanks. He shivered. Sweat was running cold beneath his clothes.

'Can't see him any more Dennis' called Jack.

'No. he appears to have gone. All clear skipper.'

Colin acknowledged 'Well done you two. Good work.'

Flak was exploding all around them. It was buffeting the aircraft around. During his training Colin had heard all about Flak and the danger it posed. Bursts of it were exploding closer and closer. Very apprehensively he steered and picked the Lancaster's way through it. He couldn't remember being as frightened in his whole life.

'Taking us back up to 19,000. Everyone keep a lookout? Michael. Get up into the astradome and give Jack and Dennis a hand looking out for more fighters? Everyone check for damage and report?'

Between the efforts of Colin, the navigator and bomb-aimer, they got "P" for Peter back on course to their target. Seemingly unscathed, the Lancaster proceeded on its way.

'Ten minutes from target skipper' announced Ben over the intercom.

'Okay Ben. Okay. Ready when you are Doug' said Colin.

'Selecting bomb switches skip.'

'Three minutes to target' called the Navigator.

Doug began to guide Colin to the target. Ben continued to relay their heading.

'Drifting to starboard' Doug called. 'Bomb doors open.'

'Bomb doors open' confirmed Colin.

'That's it. Steady. Steady now. Steady. Hold it there. Bombs gone!'

Simultaneously, relieved of its heavy and deadly load, the Lancaster jumped upwards.

'Photo's taken Doug?' Asked Colin nervously. He knew full well the dangers of flying straight and level over the target whilst waiting for the all-important aiming point photographs to be taken. Agonisingly, it seemed like hours before Doug replied.

'Yes just finished skipper.'

Colin closed the bomb doors as quickly as he could.

'Bomb doors closed. Now. Let's get the hell out of here.'

He put the Lancaster into a full boost turning climb before steering the aircraft away on its course for home. Colin had decided to go for altitude. As "P" for Peter's nose headed for his chosen 26,000 feet, Ben had been working furiously in his dark compartment plotting their course for home, Michael had transmitted the coded message "Mission Accomplished".

For them there was still huge dangers lurking out in the dark of the night sky. If not from a stalking night fighter, the possibility of a collision with a friendly aircraft also fleeing away or, revengeful angry Flak. Colin again stressed the importance for his crew to keep a sharp lookout.

Dennis moved his rear turret through 180 degrees and searched the skies. As the Lancaster continued to climb, he grew colder and colder. By God, he felt cold. The slipstream rushing through his clear vision panel made his eyes smart painfully - burning them - making it hard for him to see anything at all. He thought of his wife tucked up in bed warm and snug with their new-born son - he must contact her as soon as he could after they got back. When they got back - what a lovely thought. He could almost smell and taste the welcoming rum and coffee awaiting them at their de-briefing. No. For now he mustn't allow his mind to wander. For his sake, for the sake of the rest of the crew, he must continue to concentrate, continue to be vigilant.

Doug's voice crackled over the intercom. 'Crossing enemy coast.'

As they carried on, drawing further away from the coast, Colin began to feel more reassured.

'Bloody hell!' Exclaimed "Ginger". 'Over there skipper! A flamer!'

Colin looked in the direction his Flight Engineer indicated. Way over in the distance he saw a Lancaster. Its port wing and both port engines were trailing huge orange flames. As he watched, the stricken aircraft began to go into a dive. Instantly, his reassurance evaporated and he climbed another thousand feet.

'There's nothing we can do for him now I'm afraid. Ben? Get a fix on that Lanc? When we're closer we'll radio its position. Hopefully, some of the crew are able to take to its life-raft.'

'Will do skipper. Then I must pay a visit to the Elson.'

'It's getting bloody cold up here skipper' grumbled Jack over the intercom.

'We'll have to watch the icing skipper' "Ginger" reminded him gently.

'I know "Ginger". I'll watch it.'

The Lancaster drew nearer the English coast by the minute.

Eventually, Colin called 'I'm taking her down to 5,000 feet. All watch your ears. You can take off oxygen masks when I give the word.'

In his rear turret, Dennis felt the tail lift, hear the wind noise increase. He thought his ears were going to burst.

8

The main, big house was set amidst thousands of acres of woodland, moorland, mountains and glens. At a distance from the house, sparsely scattered, were lesser more humble dwellings and buildings. One of these buildings, a former hunting lodge, was James's accommodation - which he shared with others. He had learnt people of other nationalities were also being trained at the establishment and they were accommodated in other buildings. Now, five days into his course, he had not yet come across any of these people. He came to learn later all the different nationalities were deliberately kept separate and always would be.

At the induction meeting, together with the other new British recruits, James had met the Commandant of the place - a severe, tough individual - formerly an instructor at a commando training centre. He and the other newcomers had also been introduced to two of the other instructors working at the complex. All three awesome individuals. Like the Commandant, they were uncompromising and also from very tough military backgrounds. On hearing details of what the training course would comprise, James was filled with trepidation. Much would cover activities totally foreign to anything he had ever experienced before or, normally, would never have envisaged doing.

The last four days had been used to test the recruits'

physical fitness, build on those elements of their fitness which were reasonably good, strengthen those areas needing improvement. James had been one of six recruits in the current intake - four like himself seconded from the military. The two others had been recruited from civilian life: Roger Turner had come from the Diplomatic Service - he had spent a lot of his time in the middle east; Martin Davis's career had been in industrial chemistry. The physical fitness training had been particularly rigorous and James and the three others from the military had fared, perhaps understandably, better. Roger had coped very well and was not far behind them in approaching the fitness demanded by the instructor - a very solidly built ex-Sergeant Major from Northern Ireland. Martin had struggled to keep up and was still struggling - as the tough Irishman Patrick Kennedy, continuously and sometimes cruelly, kept telling him. However, Martin never appeared to get rattled or upset by Kennedy's constant criticism of his poor physical prowess and demonstrated an enthusiasm and an eagerness to do well which James and the others admired. As well as the physical training there had been equally rigorous basic infantry training, again conducted by the uncompromising Patrick Kennedy. In this, to everyone's surprise and pleasure - not least to their instructor, Martin excelled.

With all the physical exertions of the last few days, the sheer dogged efforts of coming up to a standard of proficiency sufficient to provoke some congratulatory response from Kennedy, James should have felt exhausted and with a desire to sleep as long as possible. But he didn't. Whether it was because he was over-tired, whether it was because he kept thinking of June or, whether, it was because he was worried about his ability to succeed in the covert and shadowy existence he had now chosen. It could have been any of these reasons why he had woken early and was standing outside under the porch of the former hunting lodge, watching yet more raindrops ripple the large puddle in front of the doorway. The training centre was nestled in a valley, surrounded on three sides by rugged mountains and hills, the waters of the Cuillin Sound lapping and lashing at its western boundary. As he looked towards the rugged heights around him, heavy cloud was descending further, even more concealing their mysterious peaks.

'There you are James' came a voice from behind. It was Tim Carter, one of the fellow newcomers and recruited from the Royal Corps of Signals. 'We thought you'd absconded.'

James smiled at the pleasant-faced and softly spoken man.

'Morning Tim. Couldn't sleep. I find it rather stuffy in there. Came out for a breath of fresh air.'

Tim looked around at their surroundings.

'What a God-forsaken place this is. I find it bloody depressing. It never seems to stop raining, permanently covered in grey cloud or mist. Such a bloody desolate landscape too.'

'Oh I don't know. It's quite beautiful when its not cloudy or raining.'

'Perhaps.' Tim sounded unconvinced. 'We're about to start getting breakfast.'

'Thanks. I wonder what pleasures Kennedy has lined up for us today?'

'More bloody press-ups and infantry drill I suspect. I don't know about you James but I'm getting pretty bored by all this get fit stuff.'

James nodded in agreement. 'Last night he was saying about starting field work exercises today.'

Forty minutes later, James and the five others assembled as instructed outside the main house. Patrick Kennedy and another man emerged carrying as assortment of ropes and what looked like climbing equipment. They placed it all in the back of a parked truck together with a pile of other equipment already there. Leaving the other man to check the truck's load, Kennedy crossed towards them. As he drew near, it occurred to James he had never seen the Irishman smile - this morning was no exception. After a cursory 'Good morning', Kennedy got the group of six to stand in a horseshoe shape around him and checked each wore the attire and had the kit-bags and other items of equipment as he had instructed.

'Nice to see you all listened to me last night and have not forgotten anything. I hope you've all got a good breakfast inside you? It might be some time before you have a chance of a decent meal.' He turned in the direction of the man still standing by the truck. 'Today, Sergeant Barlow will be joining us. We're taking you for a trip. First up into the mountains around Glen Garry for some climbing practice then, some exercises on survival in the wild. Are there any questions at this stage?'

There was silence. Then, hesitantly, Martin asked: 'We were asked to bring sleeping bags. I presume you're anticipating us being away from here for a day or so?'

'How long, really depends on yourselves - how well you get on. The very point of this exercise is to test you all - to see how you can survive away from civilisation for a time.'

'You say climbing?' Asked Roger. 'What height - exactly - are we talking about?'

There was the first hint of a smile about Kennedy's countenance.

'Just exercises in accessing difficult areas or escaping from difficult situations if necessary. If you're all successful in completing your training here and progress to being selected as agents working in occupied territory, there's no knowing what tasks or assignments you might be expected to undertake. In the limited time available to us we hope to equip you with the basic skills to survive by yourselves if necessary. My job and, that of the other specialists, is to train you to be effective in a wide range of tasks.' He paused. 'Now, if there are no further questions, we must make a move.'

Thankfully, the rain had abated when they arrived at the rugged outcrop of rock selected for climbing and descending. It stood about 250 feet and overlooked Loch Arkaig. They spent the remainder of the day and, a good part of the next, under the skilful instruction of Sergeant Barlow continuously practising scaling and descending the rock with ropes. Don Leonard from the Fleet Air Arm, suffered a nasty gash to his head and slight concussion after falling at one stage but, apart from this and the others suffering an assortment of minor cuts and bruises, the exercises passed off successfully to the two instructors' satisfaction. From the time James had first clambered into the truck he had serious misgivings but, having accomplished the task, he found he had rather enjoyed it. To his surprise, his leg also withstood the test without too many problems. As part of the exercises, Kennedy and Barlow showed the recruits how to construct containers from basic and diverse components to hold different weights and shapes of equipment and, how to lower and lift these bundles.

The worst part of the exercise for all the students was to stretch out their individual meagre rations for an indeterminate time. Also, the overnight accommodation. Odd pieces of canvas, fabric and oddments of wood and metal had been issued to build shelters or tents. The instructors had given each student free reign as to the site to erect their shelters. A vicious wind continuously whipped the top of the hillside where they were based and the rain returned. Apart from the difficulties encountered in erecting their shelters - during the night most of the students discovered the site they had selected was quite unsuitable. Being too exposed their shelters blew apart and they had to resort to sleeping without protection in the lee of cliff overhangs.

With these exercises completed, the truck jolted away once more over rough tracks and what passed as roads. The scenery became familiar to James, he began to recognise some landmarks Dougal had pointed out days ago. After another few minutes the truck turned onto a track which led into a forested area. On reaching a clearing the vehicle stopped and a man James instantly recognised walked towards them. It was Dougal MacPherson. He climbed into the back of the truck.

'Meet Dougal' said Kennedy. 'Some of you may have met him briefly a few days ago. Dougal helps supervise part of our self-survival course.'

The truck moved off and they drove for about another mile before drawing up outside a large log cabin. Dougal assisted the six trainees unload their kit and equipment.

Kennedy called 'Good luck everyone. This will be your base for a few days.'

Before any of the students had a chance to reply, the truck sped off.

'If you'll all follow me?' Asked Dougal as he led the six bewildered men into the cabin.

There was a fire burning in the grate - crackling and welcoming. The six trainees immediately grouped themselves around it. Although sparsely furnished - after what they had experienced in the last three days - the cabin was a haven of cosiness and comfort.

'There's coffee in the pot there and mugs. Help yourselves?' Dougal waited while they did so then continued. 'I apologise for you all feeling hungry. The course has been designed deliberately that way. My job is to train you to obtain your own food. Hopefully, when we go out fishing in a while, you'll be in a position to have your first substantial meal for a day or so.'

'And what if we're not successful? What do we do for food then?' Demanded Dick Edwards.

Dick was a Captain in the Royal Engineers. Of all the others, James found him the most difficult to get on with. There was something about him James didn't like - an attitude about him somehow. At the induction meeting there had been something abrasive in his demeanour. And, during the climbing exercises, although Kennedy and Barlow never gave anything away about their feelings toward any of the six, James sensed both instructors had misgivings about Dick. Strange, because out of the six Dick had seemed to excel.

Dougal replied calmly. 'The river and burns you'll be fishing are teeming with eager fish; in fact, all around there's plenty of wildlife - potentially plenty of meals for you. Provided you all follow the instructions I'll be giving you, I'm confident you will all have something to eat for your supper.'

During the next few hours, Dougal showed them how to construct make-shift fishing equipment, traps for rabbits, hares and birds. The students were able to practice the skills learnt - James was particularly proud of his fish lures and hooks. Dougal spent time explaining how to prepare and cook any potential catch or kill. James felt very squeamish when Dougal demonstrated the best way to skin and prepare a rabbit. The Highlander ended the session emphasising that, once out in the field, with all their training completed, their very survival would depend on what he had said and would continue to teach them in the next few days.

Later in the afternoon Dougal led the way out of the

forest and across the moor pointing out various spots the students may find beneficial areas to stalk, shoot or trap their prey. On reaching a river tumbling and turning its way out of the mountains, he allocated each a stretch in which to fish. At intervals he returned to see how each was getting on - offering tips and advice as to how to hone their new found skills. Between them the six recruits managed to catch a selection of trout and other fish and that night, round a campfire, were able to cook a meal fully satisfying their hunger.

During long forays over the next few days, Dougal demonstrated the techniques of hunting with rifles and deer stalking, gave them more practical exercises on fishing, trapping and hunting. Although very tiring, James found the training enjoyable and fulfilling. There was something about being on the moors and in the mountains which he found invigorating and inspirational. He promised himself when the war was over, he would return with June to explore the area further - its isolation and rugged beauty he found so wonderful.

One night, as they sat around watching the dying embers of the fire, Dougal announced: 'Tomorrow, the six of you will be sent out separately. I'll issue each of you with map references and a geographical point to aim for. The object being for you each to fend for and sustain yourselves using the techniques you've learnt.'

There was a shocked silence.

'Dougal, I take it we use the equipment we've each made so far?' Enquired Don.

The Highlander smiled. 'No such luck I'm afraid. For the purpose of this exercise, you have to imagine you're stranded in enemy territory - having to survive on your own. The only concession being, you can take a rifle and a round of ammunition.'

'I suppose we must be thankful for that' murmured Roger.

Dougal added 'Gentlemen, I don't want you thinking me totally heartless. To assist you - at certain points along each of your routes - you may find certain stores of basic components from which to construct your fishing, trapping and shelter equipment. It's entirely up to you how you approach this exercise. Your departure time from here tomorrow is at 07.00. I'll be expecting you back here at midday on Thursday. As evidence of your success, a wooden baton has been placed at your individual geographical objectives. You are to return with this, together with evidence of your kills - pelt, carcass, bones, etc. Good luck to you all and I recommend you get a good night's sleep.'

The field work with Dougal completed, there followed many days of intensive training within the big house itself. James learnt Morse code and the finer arts of unarmed combat and silent killing. There were talks and demonstrations on how to use explosives and affect sabotage operations. One night the six recruits were set the task of scaling the outside walls of the big house and affecting entry into two bedrooms on the third floor and seizing the hapless and unsuspecting Centre Commandant and one of his instructors.

The house had a well-equipped recreation area and a very well-stocked bar. The rule of keeping the different nationalities of students separate was rigidly enforced. With this in mind, a rota system of use of the bar applied. James enjoyed his evenings in the recreation area, shared with his five colleagues and their instructors. The alcohol flowed freely and the sessions proved a wonderful way of relaxing and letting their hair down.

The lessons in theory were complemented by practical sessions. One of the weapons of choice was a commando knife, ideal for the purpose of plunging into the back of an enemy sentry. The actual weapon itself was so lethal the students used dummy knives. They were also taught the vulnerable points of a human body, the areas to target to enable the killing or disablement of an opponent whilst unarmed. Throughout his lectures and, during practical sessions Askew, the instructor, drilled into them: '...to forget any concept of "fair play". You are fighting a bloody war not taking part in a sport. If you don't kill your opponent first they'll certainly kill you. Unless your orders specifically request your opponent is taken alive, always kill them. A prisoner is not only a handicap to you but also a continual danger.'

The same instructor also taught them how to board and alight a variety of moving vehicles. For the purposes of the practical exercises, a variety of cars, trucks and vans were magically conjured up for a night. Continually, this assortment of vehicles were driven over a selection of pre-arranged routes within the grounds, and the six practised boarding and alighting them whilst they were driven at different speeds. The six were also taken out to an isolated stretch of railway line and practised boarding and leaving a carriage and a goods wagon as a little train puffed its way up and down for hours.

Apart from being given the briefest of information during his flying training, James had no real idea about explosives, let alone using them. Within a few days, the centre's explosives and demolition instructor had turned him into rather an expert on the various types of explosives - the suitability of each for use on a particular target or objective. He learned all about types of fuses and how to set them. All around the complex, various buildings and objects for them to practice on had been erected or placed. Also, a motley collection of disused boilers, turbines, pipelines, sections of railway track and vehicles of all descriptions had been arranged. With boyish glee James and his fellow students set about putting their newly-acquired explosive skills to the test, blowing up a line of telephone wires, other objects and vehicles. James took a great delight, as part of a team, in blowing up a building designed as a German army guardhouse and, one night, when they were driven out to blow up a stone bridge carrying a disused stretch of railway. This exercise gave them valuable experience in climbing to place the charges, and to experiment with different types of fuses and detonators.

Major Lawrence Parkinson-Smith, known as "Park" for short, had been introduced to them as a crack shot. Pre-army and army days, he had represented England in world-wide shooting competitions and was one of the army's top snipers.

'Have either of you used guns for sport or clay-pigeon shooting?' He asked the two civilians, Roger and Martin.

They replied they had.

Nodding to his colleague stood beside him, "Park" continued. 'What Harold and I will be teaching you two - and you chaps from the military - is a different style of using a gun altogether. I'll let Harold explain further.'

After picking up a gun from the table beside him, Harold stood before them.

'This is a Colt .32. A good weapon for using instinctively - with tremendous speed and accuracy - to hit the vital parts of an enemy's body.' Harold struck a pose with the Colt in both his hands, as if he was taking aim. 'This is the way those of you in the Army would have been instructed.'

Dick and Tim nodded in agreement. 'In the situations we're training you for, by using conventional firing technique, you would have been shot yourself.'

'Thank you Harold' acknowledged "Park". 'Our principle is to point your gun instinctively and always fire twice. By the time we've trained you to use instinctive firing properly we would expect you to have achieved the object of hitting your target with accuracy every time. For killing at close quarters, you will need aggression, intense concentration, a very strong survival instinct. For example, imagine you're raiding a building at night occupied by an enemy or enemies. You would approach it with stealth - you're all keyed up, nervous and tense, you could be discovered at any moment, danger could come from anywhere, at anytime. Once inside you start searching - along corridors, in rooms, up stairs, in cellars. You turn a corner. Suddenly, without warning, you see someone in the shadows searching for you. Instantly, you react, you fire and kill them before they can kill you.'

For the practical exercises, the Major and his assistant paired up the six. Countless times, under the instruction of "Park" and Harold, the three pairs faced each other practising pointing their guns quickly at a specified part of their partner's anatomy, perfecting control of the direction and elevation of firing. The six were instructed in how to approach a building or target with stealth - how to enter a building or room and search. The two instructors got them practising, refining their instinctive reactions crouched in concealment, balancing their bodies so as to move swiftly in any direction.

The instructors also familiarised the students with the benefits of using the Sten Gun. Emphasising its main advantages: ammunition for it readily available in the occupied countries; could be simply maintained; when used

in the circumstances in which they would be operating -
easily and quickly assembled, disassembled and concealed.

It was 10 o'clock one night, some days later, when the
six were driven out to a remote part of the estate. There was
only a quarter moon and what light it gave was partially
obscured by cloud. Harold was the first to speak.

'For the purpose of this exercise you will again be issued
with live ammunition. So, for God's sake be careful. It's
taken a lot of time and resources to get you this far on your
course. It would be particularly annoying and inconvenient
to lose any of you at this stage. The objective is as follows. Just
round this copse of trees you'll see a house in the distance
set on a hill. You're required to approach this house unseen,
using any route you choose and what cover is provided to
gain entry undetected.'

"Park" continued 'You're to assume the house is a
farmhouse occupied by some German troops - an obstacle
you need to overcome and eliminate before sabotaging an
important installation. It's important you all remember that
if you don't kill these troops, they will certainly kill you. This
is a "no prisoners to be taken" situation. Consequently, you'll
shoot anything that moves in that building. Understood?'

'But ...?' Martin started to ask.

' ... However, to make it harder for you all' he
continued, testily disregarding this interruption and, with
a hint of sadistic pleasure in his voice. 'Some of our training
colleagues will be patrolling around the area of the exercise.
If any of them see you during your approach to the house
they will shout out. You will then have to start all over again,
using an alternative route if necessary. Also, all around the
area a series of devices have been laid. If you should step on

or trigger them. They will set off an alarm. If this occurs, you'll immediately seek concealment wherever you can, until instructed by megaphone to continue to your objective.'

'After you've gained entry' added Harold. 'Taken out the enemy - eliminating any communications equipment - leave by the back door and cross to the old barn behind the house. Wait there until all six of you complete the mission successfully. A word of caution. In making your escape from the house, there may still be a stray "Jerry" lurking around to kill you.'

"Park" turned to Tim. 'You'll be first to go. Once again remember, all of you, there are people in that house prepared to kill you. They've been trained to do so.'

Almost four hours passed before it was James's turn to go. He was the last to do so. Throughout the whole of his approach, he really worked hard to put into practice the stalking techniques he had learnt. He had just crossed a little gravel track near a small stone bridge and was contemplating how to make his ascent up the hill to the house unseen. Suddenly, making him jump out of his skin, a klaxon concealed in the undergrowth nearby deafened him. James froze. Almost immediately there were voices shouting in German and the sound of boots rushing on the gravel of the track. Instinctively he crawled quickly down the river bank and, after hiding the Colt revolver under a stone by the foot of the bridge, moved under the bridge to submerge himself in the river. As he did so, the strong beam of a torch illuminated the bridge wall above him, and he heard angry German voices. The beam played on the water. Under the surface of the river James's lungs were beginning to burst. At last, he saw the torch beam above him move further down the embankment - play briefly once again on the surface near him - to finally disappear. Gasping for breath, he broke surface but stayed in the cover of the bridge. The water was brackish, unpleasant and cold. After what seemed ages, through a megaphone, came the words: 'Well done James. Continue to your objective.'

The wet clothes clinging to him felt intolerable. Retrieving the gun, he cautiously made his way up the embankment. Even more warily than before, he edged his way towards the house.

About an hour later back at the barn, the six students stood in a group laughing as "Park" and Harold stood before them displaying an assortment of stuffed dummies dressed in German uniforms.

'Meet our version of Hitler's bodyguards' "Park" announced, laughing raucously.

'I must admit' said James 'The scream from the one on the landing was a nice touch. I really thought I'd killed someone.'

'Exactly what you were meant to think' replied "Park". 'Each scene encountered in the house was designed differently for each of you. Particularly specific to what the other instructors, Harold and myself have learnt about each of you during your time here so far.'

Harold added 'We're particularly pleased with how you all did. We will have a little time tomorrow on the firing range to perfect your marksmanship still further. Oh by the way. Martin and Don exacted the most painful deaths on our little German army here. You both managed to shoot some of your targets in the testicles.'

'It was all pretty impressive' observed Roger. 'How were all the dummies operated? They looked and moved so realistically.'

"Park" replied 'For that we have to thank the organisation's engineering workshop and some others of our training staff. See you all tomorrow. Once again, well done all of you. Good luck with what remains of your time here with us in Scotland.'

Whilst the six trainees were spending the last day of their four-week training course on a final compass and map-reading exercise, the Centre's Commandant was sat in his office reading through his final report on their progress and suitability for further, specific, SOE training. He had prepared his report after talking at length and in detail with all his instructors and, after considering their opinions on each trainee.

Drawing heavily on his cigarette, he reflected on his decisions. Martin Davis - the industrial chemist - was considered not physically up to being an Agent in the field. Patrick Kennedy also felt strongly he did not possess enough of the killer, ruthless instinct to be effective or survive in occupied Europe. On the other hand, John Morris - the Centre's explosives' expert - thought his understanding of explosives and their working was better than any of the five other students and, that this should be taken into account. Morris recommended Martin's aptitude for working with explosives should not be wasted by SOE, further recommending he be retained in some way. The Commandant had agreed, deciding his report would commend the organisation to use Martin as an explosives' instructor based within the UK. Roger Turner - formerly of the Diplomatic Service - had matched up to all the qualities required for an Overseas Agent, and should be put into a programme for further training as soon as possible. Also, considering Turner's experience in the Middle East, he, the Commandant, would recommend SOE to assign Roger Turner to their Middle East Section. Don Leonard - the Fleet Air Arm Officer - had performed well in the majority of the exercises, was enthusiastic in all he attempted.

However, when the Commandant had looked back on Don's initial file which Baker Street had forwarded, one or two things concerned him, including his linguistic ability. The Commandant, himself an accomplished linguist, had even personally worked with Don to see if his French could be improved.This was all to no avail and he had concluded the young Fleet Air Arm Officer just did not have the aptitude to speak or communicate in French as a native - essential for him to survive in occupied Europe. Captain Tim Carter from the Royal Corps of Signals - the results of his training at Arisaig had exceeded expectations. His knowledge and use of radio communications was exemplary. The Commandant resolved to recommend Tim be sent to work initially with the communications boffins - so much was being researched and worked on currently with this speciality to aid agents in the field and the emerging Resistance movements. He also strongly recommended that Tim, ultimately, be used in the field by SOE as a radio operator trainer. The Commandant came to the notes he had written about Squadron Leader James Graham. On first seeing James's file from Baker Street, he had had serious misgivings initially that James's "gammy" leg and the injury to his eye would be impairments to success as an agent for SOE. It had proved not to be the case, despite all Patrick Kennedy's efforts to prove otherwise. James's knowledge of French could not be faulted and the results of the former pilot's training exercises had all been first-class. However Dick Edwards, from the Royal Engineers, was a real concern for the Commandant. Apart from the undisputed enjoyment the well-stocked bar in the Recreation Room brought to trainees and instructors alike, it also served as a test for the trainees. Alcohol possesses the ability to loosen tongues. The main reason for the bar being so well stocked, was to see how the trainee Agents' tongues loosened after a few drinks. An Agent in occupied territory, whose tongue was loosened by alcohol or, whose demeanour was changed by it, would be a serious liability to all he worked with or who he worked for. On all these accounts, Edwards failed. To further rule him out, the Commandant had staged a scenario whereby Edwards was given a reason to spend a couple of nights in a little town nearby. A local woman, employed by Arisaig specifically as a temptress for would-be Agents, was used to get Edwards into conversation at the hotel arranged for his stay. Since the training centre had used this woman's services, it had never been discovered by the Commandant whether "Heather", as she was known, actually ever took would-be Agents to bed in the line of duty. Whatever, as far as Edwards was concerned - as Heather's report confirmed: "This candidate has a dangerously loose tongue and is liable to draw attention to himself...".

The Commandant stubbed out his cigarette firmly in the ashtray. Yes, there were also other things as well about Dick Edwards that greatly concerned him, the Commandant, and his instructors. He would send a special message to Baker Street about their deep concerns. How Baker Street would deal with Edwards, the Commandant did not know or care - that wasn't his job. It would be up to some Government Agency how they chose to investigate a suspected enemy agent. Until Arisaig received further instructions the Commandant and his staff would keep Edwards under strict but discrete supervision.

Before finalising his report ready for despatch to London, the Commandant paused in thought for a moment. Baker Street's initial selection procedure for sending trainees to Scotland must be getting better - this time, four candidates out of six passed. Last time, a couple of months back, out of five candidates sent to him, only one was deemed as suitable for being retained by SOE.

9

With the ferocity of Hitler's onslaught now more focused on Russia, the Mediterranean and Middle East things were quieter at the hospital. Though the Luftwaffe still sent aircraft over to attack ports, factories, docks and other targets, the daylight raids were less intense and numerous, so reducing the civilian casualties needing treatment. Although Margaret Wilding and other staff at the hospital still had many patients to treat, the caseload was mainly of a more routine nature - complemented, of course, by an increasing number of cases resulting from dietary insufficiency and also disease prompted by a shortage of habitable housing and polluted water supplies. However, the sheer volume of emergencies being admitted had decreased and Margaret had taken the opportunity to take some leave - her first real leave since her husband had died.

During the last few days at her home she had been busying herself sorting out a lot of Peter's belongings and clothes - a job never pleasant and one she had long put off. Some of his military memorabilia which held no sentimental value for her, she had already sent to his old regiment for their archives. Other non-sentimental detritus accumulated during his life, she had donated to various of the many voluntary organisations still busy with their fund-raising activities for the war effort. Peter's clothes, Margaret had found the most difficult to deal with. Each garment - especially those worn before his Dunkirk injuries - held for her special fond memories of happier times. His army uniforms, she had spent ages looking at before returning to the wardrobe - not bearing to part with. Every garment she sorted through was so indelibly etched with Peter's personality. Having at last completed packaging up his clothes ready to donate to charities, she washed and tidied herself for when June was due to arrive. She was looking forward so much to spending the afternoon with her daughter.

Margaret had constantly harboured intense and painful guilt over her brief, adulterous affair with Robert Thompson. Occasioned, she knew only too well, by her loneliness, her craving for affection and episodes of Peter's totally foreign behaviour towards her. She and Robert had broken off their affair before he had been posted to a training command in Canada. However, whilst in Canada, Robert had been taken seriously ill with some virus and sent back to England in the in the April of 1941. When, eventually, he learnt of Peter's Robert called on Margaret one day. Since then - but more as a friend - he again provided warm and supportive friendship for her. Gradually their love for each other rekindled and, during the last few months, they had been seeing a great deal of each other - once spending three days together in the Peak District.

Margaret had chosen this afternoon to broach the subject of Robert's and her love for each other with June and, as she sat waiting for her to arrive, she rehearsed over and over again in her mind as to what to say. She knew there was no way she could tell June of her affair with Robert whilst Peter had been alive. No, she would concentrate on her last few months with Robert. Even then, would June think the interval between her father's death and her mother having a new man in her life indecently short? Would June be pleased? Would June be angry - critically hostile?

A little later they were sitting in the lounge. Sunshine streamed in the window, its light like a spotlight highlighting the colours of the Chinese rug in the centre of the room. From outside came the occasional clank as Billy's hoe struck a stone as he removed weeds between the rows of vegetables which now replaced the roses in the beds.

'And you've still not heard a thing from James? Not a telephone call, telegram, or anything?'

'No. Only that brief note - about ten day's ago, telling me he was safe and well and not to worry.'

'There was no indication where he was or, where the note came from?'

'No none whatsoever. It was just written on a blank piece of paper.'

'It must be so worrying for you darling.'

'Yes. All James said after the meeting - you know when I went with him to London - was he would be having to go away for a while. On some training course or other.'

Margaret cuddled her daughter.

'That's one of the terrible things about war. It tears families apart, it doesn't take account of those left behind, not knowing what's happening to their loved ones - whether they're safe. Let's hope you'll hear from James soon. It's just the same with Stephen and Richard. Just the very occasional letter - sometimes I know roughly where they are in the world. All one hears on the radio is - in very general terms - what progress is or is not being made by the allies.'

June sighed. 'The last letter I had from Stephen - he was somewhere in the Mediterranean. I haven't heard from Richard for ages now.'

'All I know is what I've read in the newspapers - heard

on the BBC - Rommel and his army are sweeping through Libya. I just pray he's safe.'

'Me too. Stephen has recovered well from his injuries?'

'Yes thankfully. Though, if I'm to be honest, one part of me wishes he hadn't recovered so quickly. Then, perhaps, he may have been given a more safe - land-based posting.'

June took her mother's hand tenderly.

'Did you manage to sort daddy's things out mummy?'

'Yes I did dear. It took me ages. It was something I'd put off for far too long. It was horrible and very upsetting.'

'It must have been. That's why I wanted to help you. It just wasn't possible to get any leave.'

'I understand June. Never mind. Besides, I thought it best I did it myself. In some ways, strangely, I believe its helped me. You know, all the memories.'

'There must have been a lot of stuff?'

'There was. Perhaps you'll come upstairs with me shortly. There are some of daddy's things I've put in the attic which you and James may like for your home. There's things up there I'm also saving for Stephen and Richard.'

June crossed to the window.

'You wouldn't recognise the garden now would you. Usually, this time of year, with all the spring plants and flowers, the garden would have looked so full of colour.'

Margaret joined her at the window.

'I know. I miss the colour dreadfully. Your father would have done as well. Hopefully, when the crops Billy and I sowed start to grow, it won't look quite so bare and desolate.'

'You must have been working really hard out there clearing those beds, preparing the ground for the vegetables.'

'Yes it was hard work - still is. Billy has been wonderful though - he's been a tremendous help. Still, working out there has helped me take my mind off things - kept me occupied and relaxed when I'm not at the hospital.'

June turned to her mother and hugged her.

'Poor mummy. Are you feeling dreadfully lonely?'

'When I'm not at the hospital, there's not a lot of time for me to mope around. With the shortage of doctors and nurses at the moment, I'm kept pretty busy there as well.'

'Yes, I've heard things are still pretty desperate in all the hospitals.'

Margaret led June back to the sofa.

'June there's something I must talk to you about.'

'Mummy what is it?'

'June this is so difficult for me. The thing is - you remember meeting James's Station Commander?'

'Yes at that lunchtime party. Robert - um …?'

'…Thompson.'

'He got you involved with the work at Penley Manor?'

'That's right. Well since then I've got to know him well - we became friends - good friends. He's a widower.' She paused.

'Well what about him? What is it?'

'Robert was posted to Canada at the end of 1940. Well, he became ill and ended up back in England. Since then we've been seeing each other quite a bit. First of all, just as friends.'

'Well, what's wrong with that mummy?'

'Recently though we've become more than just friends - we spent some days away together.' She hesitated. 'You see June, I'm in love with him.'

For a while June didn't utter a word. Margaret went cold.

'Well that's wonderful mummy. And you're happy?'

'Yes very. He's very kind. Understanding.'

'That's all that matters then. I'm very pleased for you. I'm sure Stephen and Richard will be as well.'

The two women cuddled.

'Oh June! I'm so relieved I've been able to tell you. I was so worried you'd be angry.'

'Why should I be?'

'Well it's not so long since daddy passed away...'.

'...Oh mummy! Your happiness is all that matters. Some things are meant to be. I know you and daddy loved each other so deeply - Stephen and Richard know that as well. Your care for daddy - after he came back from Dunkirk - was so devoted and loving. None of us will ever forget him. Ever.' She paused for a while. 'But we all have to try and re-build our lives.'

'You don't object to it or resent me for falling in love again?'

'Of course not. As long as you're happy. That's the main thing.'

This moment of close affection for each other was interrupted by Billy calling desperately from the hallway. 'Dr Wilding! Dr Wilding! I've cut my hand.'

10

Colin and his crew now had three Operations under their belt. Each Op. a typical "Milk Run" but, the missions had proved invaluable in giving them experience and really bonding them together as a crew. Each of the seven now had complete trust and confidence in each other's ability. They were also becoming firm friends. Even the usually stand-offish, dour, Jack Gaskell had mellowed accordingly and blended in fully. The other more seasoned crews too, now seemed to accept them more. It was as if, initially, they had been viewed with some suspicion and that now - having passed their probation period - they had at last been fully welcomed into the fold. Whilst Colin and his crew had never been precluded by the words or actions of the experienced crews it was just somehow a different atmosphere now they had been blooded.

Three day's leave had followed the third Op. and Colin used the time to go down to Lucy's farm, where his mother was staying for a few days.

During and after the blitz on London, Colin's mother had been driving ambulances as a volunteer. Since the blitz there had been a lull in the air raids and she had taken the opportunity to visit her sister-in-law. Working at night had not really agreed with her and, no matter how hard she tried or what she did, she found getting to sleep by day very hard. She felt exhausted and Lucy's invitation to spend a few days in the fresh air of Somerset, had been very welcome. Work too had prevented her husband from joining them but, with Colin also there, it reminded her of the happy times they had spent on the farm as a family before the war. The biggest change on the farm she had noticed straight away was the greater emphasis on arable crops rather than livestock. This, she knew, was as a result of the Agricultural Executive's insistence that this should be so for all farms. The number of Land Army girls working there had also increased. Because of Walter's increasing age, he now only carried out the lighter jobs around the place and John, the once troubled and disagreeable Evacuee, had now taken over Walter's role much to Lucy's delight and pleasure. Another change that had occurred on the farm - one which had saddened Lucy as much as the lessening of the livestock - was the loss of much of the woodland running down to the river. This woodland had once given so much pleasure to Lucy and her late husband and, to her brother and his family during their holidays on the farm. After endless battles with Government officials the previous year, Lucy had eventually bowed to their pressure to have the timber harvested for the war effort.

As soon as Sandra had heard Mrs Graham was staying with Lucy she called in to see her. Knowing her good-looking son was with her was an added incentive to rush from her aunt's cottage to the farm. Sandra often thought of Colin and, on her still frequent visits to the farm, continuously asked Lucy for any news of him. She couldn't wait to see him again.

Colin had been thinking of Sandra too since he had arrived back at the airfield after his leave. Now, as he waited in the crew room for transport to dispersals, he was thinking of her again. In the time since that summer he'd first met her, Sandra had matured into an attractive young woman. Several times during his leave they had gone for long walks, had talked and laughed so much - the conversation and laughter so effortless and uninhibited - so natural. One night they had gone to the cinema in Minehead. They had kissed for the first time. The kiss was so natural and instinctive, would always be remembered by both.

Refreshed after their leave, Colin and his crew had attended the main briefing at 15.00 hours.

Their target was to be a chemicals factory and its distilling and refining installations north of Essen. With an approximate bomb load of 11,000 lbs, the route would be low level over the North Sea to avoid enemy radar. The first rendezvous point would be over King's Lynn, the second being over Tilburg in the Netherlands. The force of 38 Lancasters would bomb at 10,000 feet. The route home to be over Gelsenkirchen, Hertogenbosch, Dordrecht and crossing the coast north of Ouddorp. The crews had been warned about heavy flak and anti-aircraft fire and night fighters around Duisberg. They were to avoid at all costs flying to the east of Essen.

Colin climbed over the main spar of "B" for Baker, passing the Wireless Operator's and Navigator's positions. Moonlight illuminated Colin's seat in the cockpit and the control column in a narrow beam of a ghostly, pale blue light. During the briefing the Met Officer said whilst the east of England would have relatively little cloud, heavier cloud was to be expected over the North Sea, thinning over the coast of Holland until around the area of their second rendezvous point. From there to the target 6/10ths to 7/10ths cloud was expected.

The crew went about their final pre-flight checks. To

Colin, with three Op.'s now under his belt, the checks were now becoming second nature and so familiar and, this had helped his confidence enormously. The glare from the Very light lit up the sky. He closed the bomb doors. Starting the Lancaster was usually a four-handed job and, working with "Ginger", Colin prepared to start the engines. The Engineer controlled the main fuel cocks, booster pump, booster coil switch and starter buttons; whilst Colin operated engine master cocks, magneto switches and throttles.

"Ginger" said 'Let's hope skipper, this time all the engines start first go.'

'Keep your fingers and everything crossed "Ginger".'

With a smile Colin remembered their last trip - to Walcheren - when, at engine start-up stage, the port inner engine refused to start. One of the ground crew, in the usual way to rectify this, had climbed onto the main wheel to reach the appropriate priming pump. Colin had not remained sufficiently alert and had allowed the starboard engines to quietly die. Since Colin had control of the throttles, he had suffered a good-humoured tirade from "Ginger" as the Engineer had to then assist the ground crew to start the engines.

'You got me jumping up and down from the starboard main wheel like a bloody yo-yo' he had complained bitterly.

Colin had defended his actions by replying 'That was just to keep you fit.'

The huge throb of the four engines confirmed reassuringly the situation hadn't arisen this time. Together the pair continued their checks, paying special attention to the brake pressure. Colin tested the engines in pairs - inboards and outboards - to zero pounds boost for CSU and carried out the magneto checks.

Colin called 'Ready for taxi everyone?'

'Yes skipper. All ready and correct. Set for taxi.'

Taxiing was always tricky with the Lancaster. The tail wheel did not lock and there was a degree of hysteresis in the braking system, and the pilot was compelled to run both inboard engines at 800 rpm to preclude them stopping and to keep the plugs clean. However, using the techniques taught - now well-practised - and using large bursts of power from the outboard engines whilst conserving as much brake pressure as possible, Colin steered the aircraft down the perimeter track very competently. He remembered his flying instructors stressing how easy it was to get out of phase with the throttles, due to initial lack of aircraft response and the associated high inertia, and, when a Lancaster taxis, it always appears to weave like a drunk down a narrow pathway. The Lancaster in front of them was piloted by Ray Bateman - like Colin another fairly new pilot. Colin watched nervously as Ray's kite begun to swing progressively erratically and out of control.

'Come on Ray' Colin said to himself. 'Close all throttles - I hope you've got enough brake pressure.'

The only way to get out of the situation Ray was in, was to stop and replenish brake pressure - give himself a breather to sort things out and get back in "synch." with the throttles. Over the radio, the Controller berated the hapless Ray. Then, after a little while, Ray was in control again, set to move off. The winding procession to the runway continued.

Tonight, No. 2 runway was the one in use. Because of the prevailing wind, it was not the one usually used. It was also further away from the main technical, "admin." and communal sites. As such, Colin wondered if the usual hordes of airfield personnel would brave the longer walk through the rather squally winds, to line the runway to wave them off. Again, there was the usual silence of expectancy and anxiety in the fuselage behind and in the darkened cockpit around him. From outside, the steady throb of the four Merlin engines was strangely hypnotic. Finally, "B" for Baker was cleared into their position on the runway. Colin rolled the plane forward slightly so as to straighten the tail wheel.

Colin called 'Okay here we go. Good luck everyone.'

He increased power for a final check on engines externally and by gauge readings. He saw the coolant venting from the engines as sometimes occurred. All temperatures were well within limits so there was nothing to prevent take-off. Colin released the brakes, the aircraft began to move - very slowly at first but gaining in momentum - he then advanced the port outer throttle with an extended thumb, following up steadily with the remaining engines to try and counteract the Lancaster's one main irritation - a tendency to "crab" to the left.

'Bless them' called Michael like an excited child from the astradome. 'They've still bothered to turn up and wave us off.'

Colin smiled to himself. His earlier doubt about the steadfast support and good wishes of the airfield personnel was dispelled. He began to feel the Lancaster's tail rise, the rudder begin to become effective as the aircraft accelerated. There was no need for him to do anything quickly but high inertia meant keen anticipation was required. Suddenly Colin had aerodynamic, directional control and he relinquished the throttles. He asked "Ginger" for full power.

Geoff had been following up on the throttles and now advanced them steadily to the stops. The noise of the engines was almost intolerable, Colin felt the noise vibrating through his backside. The noise of four engines at + 14 lbs boost and 3,000 rpm gave a great impression of power and, at full power, the acceleration was remarkable. The Lancaster eased away from the tarmac. As was usual, the undercarriage took some time to retract, levering itself slowly into the inboard nacelles.

On their very first OTU flights as a crew Colin had briefed Geoff to operate undercarriage and flaps, so he could concentrate on flying the aircraft. Now, he felt confident and competent enough to undertake both operations deftly. The flap lever was equipped with a spade handle at the top and operated in a vertical slide with three positions: "up", "neutral" and "down". Knowing it was only too easy to overshoot the neutral position and move the flaps in the wrong way, he carefully began to retract them in stages of 10 degrees. Noting the safety speed was at 140 knots, he called for climb power.

At a power setting of + 7 lbs boost, 2,650 rpm, the Lancaster was climbing well at 145 knots. This setting made the Merlins sound very sweet, especially when synchronised by the engineer. Geoff achieved this by looking through the two port propellers, continually adjusting them until they strobed, repeating the exercise with the starboard propellers until they were synchronised acoustically with the port pair. It was a tedious job for the Flight Engineer and took time but every Engineer on the Squadron, especially Geoff, prided themselves on eliminating any "beat" or irregularity. His efforts in this respect would produce the characteristic Merlin roar, now becoming so familiar to those on the ground below them, whether they be friend or foe.

Colin banked away from the airfield and set course for the first rendezvous point.

The first rendezvous was made without any difficulty. Michael Richards at the Wireless Operator's desk had tuned in to the group transmitter and would keep listening on this frequency. If no messages were to be passed, the group transmitter would send a check of time and a number every 20 minutes and 50 minutes past the hour. After making the rendezvous, Colin dropped "B" for Baker down to the height briefed and they crossed the coast to start the trip over the North Sea. Ben, the Navigator, confirmed they were still on the right heading. "Ginger" reported all was well with temperatures, oil and fuel. All distress frequencies were on the medium wave and worked on the trailing aerial which Michael now reeled out.

Now and again another Lancaster would appear from nowhere and disappear just as suddenly. Since flying Op.'s Colin had always thought it strange that, despite the number of aeroplanes being despatched on any particular raid, one seldom saw them on route to the target. Some minutes later the weather began to deteriorate. The wind was increasing and worse, beginning to veer from another direction. They also found themselves in heavy rain.

'Damn!' Exclaimed Colin angrily. 'The Met Officer didn't mention this.' He called up Ben. 'Have you a revised heading Ben?'

'Yes skipper. Just worked it out.' He proceeded to give the revised course.

'Yes skipper. From the D-R-C, I would confirm that' added Michael helpfully.

'Fine. Understood. Thank you both' replied Colin.

Ben added 'Skipper, I calculate this will make us about eight minutes late at second rendezvous point.'

'Understood Ben. Thank you. We'll see how it goes.'

Colin became anxious. Being that much delayed to the second rendezvous point could cause some real problems for them. Subject to the wind and fuel restraints, he would have to do his very best to make some of that time up. Thankfully, they got round and through the patch of dodgy weather within a few minutes.

He called up his crew. 'We must be nearing the coast now. Keep a sharp look-out everyone.' To his mid-upper and rear gunners: 'Jack and Dennis. Everything okay with you two?'

The two gunners confirmed it was. A few more minutes passed. Michael received another check of time and number from Group.

'Skipper' called Doug Harvey from his position in the nose. 'Coast about ten miles dead ahead.'

'Thanks. Okay everyone keep your eyes peeled.'

Michael began to reel in the trailing aerial. Suddenly, without warning, beams of strong light appeared out of the blackness ahead of them. In the cockpit, Colin and Geoff shielded their eyes from the dazzling glare. Almost immediately, streaks of orange lights in columns - shells - raced towards them.

'Shit!' Screamed Doug from the nose. 'Anti-aircraft and flak boats.'

Colin yanked back on his stick, the Engineer and he instinctively putting on full climb power. The Lancaster's nose rose responsively. Papers, pens and slide rules slid off Ben's and Michael's desks.

'Christ! When did they move them there!' Exclaimed Colin, cursing the intelligence at the briefing not knowing about the German defensive vessels. Still pulling on the stick, his other hand darted around in front of him adjusting the flying controls. He called urgently 'Oxygen on everyone.'

The noise from the screaming engines was deafening. Dennis in the rear turret was suddenly looking down - near vertically - at the black sea beneath him. Way over to their left, a bright ball of orange illuminated the night sky like daylight.

Jack called out wildly 'Lancaster going down on our port. The bastards have got one.'

Briefly, Colin glanced over his shoulder to see blazing chunks and fragments of a Lancaster spinning and falling down into the coastal waters below. He thought those poor sods, they didn't stand a chance.

He levelled off "B" for Baker. The German gunners were reacting but not quickly enough, the majority of their shells and flak were falling harmlessly and bursting beneath their aircraft. Other aircraft were not quite so lucky.

Geoff glimpsed a Lancaster banking steeply away with one of its starboard engines on fire.

'Another Lanc. On fire.' Hopefully, he added. 'Hope he makes it back.'

They had now crossed the coast, leaving the worst of the anti-aircraft fire behind.

Colin called 'Everyone all right? Report any damage please?'

One by one his crew reported they were okay, had sustained no damage to their equipment and could not detect any damage to the aircraft around their respective positions in it.

'I need something for my vertigo skipper' quipped Dennis cheerfully. 'I thought you were trying to tip me out of the back. Good thing these straps are strong.'

'You owe me a protractor skipper' added Ben. 'I'm buggered if I can find my one. It slid off the table.'

'If it's all right with you skipper. I need to visit the Elsan. That's if you haven't managed to turn it upside down' said Michael laughing.

Colin smiled to himself. The good spirits of his crew were very heartening.

'Quieten down now you lot. Everything's all right up here as well. Settle down and enjoy the rest of the flight. Beware though, I expect "Jerry" has some more nasty surprises. Oxygen on everyone.'

'No evidence of hostile aircraft on the radar skipper' reported Michael.

'Fine' acknowledged Colin. 'Keep a watch on it when you get back.'

'Will do.'

Michael made his way down the fuselage to the Elsan closet, positioned just forward of the tail plane. Ben called out the speed from the ASI and gave the revised course and heading.

Jack, in the mid-upper turret called Colin. 'We're leaving a hell of a Con trail skipper.'

Colin cursed to himself. Leaving a tell-tale vapour trail was dangerous. Flying over enemy territory was hazardous enough without telling them exactly where you were.

'Understood Jack. Thanks. I'll drop her down a bit.'

"B" for Baker carried on towards the second rendezvous point uneventfully but, reaching it late because of the bad weather and enemy fire encountered earlier.

Colin asked his crew the usual question in such a situation 'We're going to be very late over target. Do you wish us to go on?'

It was agreed by all they should. To abort the mission would cancel out a trip on their tour of duty tally and, as one of them added: 'We haven't brought these bombs all this way for nothing'. They seemed to continue on their way for ages. Colin was beginning to feel nervous they were way off course. Michael was still not reporting any sign of night fighters on his screen, the two gunners also reported no sighting of anything to alarm them. To reassure himself a little he asked Geoff as to the fuel situation. The Engineer told him and Colin made a few quick calculations in his head, remembering what was said in the briefing. Fair enough. Fuel levels were roughly what he would have expected at this stage of the mission. Suddenly, his intercom came to life. It was Ben.

'I calculate we're a couple of minutes from the German border skipper.'

The intercom crackled again. This time it was Doug. 'I agree Ben. We've just crossed the River Maas.'

'Aircraft approaching fast from the stern' shouted Michael. 'About three miles away, at 16,000 feet. Looks to be a pair of them on the screen.'

'Very good Mike.' Colin knew a night fighter's favourite approach of attack. 'Jack. Dennis. Keep a look out for those "Jerry's"?'

They were roughly over Krefeld. Jack saw a night fighter coming in for an attack on their rear quarter and yelled: 'Skipper corkscrew starboard. Go.' He fired his guns furiously.

Colin immediately dived the Lancaster to the right, forcing the rest of his crew to hang on desperately to anything they could. The aircraft increasingly gyrating threw everything around in the fuselage.

On the fifth or sixth corkscrew, Dennis yelled: 'Another coming in from the rear starboard quarter.' He gave it a long burst of his guns. Then, screaming: 'Jack. Jack. Can you see it?'

Jack brought his guns to bear and fired a burst. 'Yes. Yes. I've got it.'

Twin streams of orange tracer spat from the fighter and curved inches above Jack's turret.

Their altitude was falling away rapidly. Colin chanced pulling out of the corkscrew and regained another 1,000 or so feet.

Dennis yelled again 'Skipper corkscrew port. Go.'

Colin reacted instantly again, only this time diving "B" for Baker to the left. With a violent judder, the Lancaster protested. For a horrible moment he feared they'd been hit. Throughout the defensive manoeuvre, as the two gunners fired defiantly, they gave a commentary of what was happening. It was like bedlam in the aircraft. Dennis fired again. Whether he hit the night fighter he never knew. It suddenly broke away, curving away steeply above them to the right. Moments later, high above and, far to the right, there was a ball of flame. Judging by the size of the fire ball, it looked more like an unfortunate Lancaster. Dennis prayed it wasn't and it was only the night fighter. Jack saw the explosion too. He presumed it had been a collision between the fighter and a bomber.

All went strangely quiet as Colin levelled out. He hoped for a few moments of peace so as to settle himself and his crew down. Onward to the target they continued.

The heavy flak and anti-aircraft fire they had been told to expect in the Duisberg area came as no surprise in its ferocity, even though they were skirting just north of it. After a few close shaves they got through the worst of what the German defences threw at them. Essen lay dead ahead.

'Ten miles to target' Doug reported.

Colin dropped down to the specified bombing height and commenced their bombing run.

'Over to you Doug.'

The flak became intense. The delay over the North Sea and their various brushes with the enemy had made them late over target. Therefore, the German gunners now had the track and height of the bomber stream and were able to reach them with heavy, medium and light flak. Through it all came Doug's voice feeding Colin with instructions.

'Right, right, steady, steady, right again, hold it there.'

The sky all around was full of shell bursts. The noise of them bursting, combined with the steady throb of the bomber's engines was deafening. The tracer shells fired from the rapidly firing enemy guns streaked towards them. The shells, at first, seemed to climb so slowly into the air. Though, as they climbed higher, appearing to increase in speed before streaking very closely past the Lancaster's cockpit.

'Jeez! They're close' hissed Doug.

With shells and flak exploding, bursting all around it, "B" for Baker began to buck violently. Some of this turbulence, no doubt, attributable to the slipstream of aircraft ahead of them in the bomber stream. Suddenly, alarmingly, the beam of a searchlight penetrated the Lancaster cockpit, illuminating its interior like bright sunlight. The crew knew only too well that once, caught in a beam, it usually meant curtains for a plane and its crew. No matter what he did, Colin couldn't get out of the beam. He tried one last desperate thing.

'3,000 revs, plus 14 boost' he calmly ordered.

They were out of the beam. Doug's voice cut through the fear and tension.

'Left, left, steady, bomb doors open, left, steady. Bombs gone.'

Immediately, now much lighter, the aircraft lifted. For the necessary photo to be taken, another minute or so of straight and level flying was necessary. For all those on board that minute seemed like hours.

'Right' yelled Colin. 'Let's get out of here. Hang on tight everyone. I'm taking her right up.'

There was a responsive roar from the engines as he climbed the bomber in a steeply curving climb towards 20,000 feet and away from the carnage left below. During their bombing run, Michael had reported night fighters swarming on his screen at 6,000 feet.

'Mike? Get up in the astradome. Help Jack and Dennis keep a look out for those bloody night fighters.'

Colin proceeded to issue his instructions for getting out of the area. Ben began to work out the course for Gelsenkirchen and the rest of the way home. Geoff worked out the fuel consumption calculations, checked temperatures and pressure. Everything was working fine. By some miracle, the Lancaster had come through it all apparently unscathed. Flak, although still heavy, was being left further and further behind. Michael returned to his position, signals were exchanged to confirm mission accomplished and he returned to the Group transmitter frequency. Eventually, an air of relief spread through the crew. Coffee from the flask was passed around and everyone congratulated Colin and each other.

'Understood "B" for Baker. Your request confirmed. Continue to circuit 600 feet - six zero zero feet - and await further instructions.'

'I love that one' remarked Michael, referring to the voice of the WAAF he had just spoken to. 'She's got a real come-to-bed voice.'

Colin smiled weakly. He was tired, far from happy at the prospect of doing yet another circuit. Back at the airfield, the weather had deteriorated quickly. It was raining, visibility was poor and the wind speed had increased. If he couldn't get the Lancaster down this time, there was a high chance of having to abort landing and try and get in at another Group's airfield some distance away.

After a while Colin prepared for his final approach. There was another communication from the tower. He looked ahead and all around him. The flares looked so welcoming. Mercifully, in the time it had taken to complete the circuit, the weather had abated slightly. He felt confident he could land safely. Lancaster wheels met concrete with a bump and a bounce. Using every bit of concentration - every ounce of strength and dexterity - he brought "B" for Baker under control. With just yards of runway to spare, landing was complete.

'Well done skipper' said "Ginger" thankfully, looking rather frightened.

It was 02.15 hours when Colin commenced the taxi around to dispersals.

Stepping off the aircraft's ladder and onto the concrete of the dispersal pan, Colin had never realised how good it was to feel *Terra Firma*. He ached all over and was still damp with perspiration. The very keen wind and drizzle on his skin and already-moist clothing made him shiver as he led his crew to the waiting bus that would convey them to the de-briefing room.

They had been one of the last to return and, when entering the room, it was already packed with aircrew milling around as they awaited interrogation. The atmosphere was like entering a room full of a very large and friendly family. Colin supposed it was because they were late back and he perceived a tangible reaction of especial relief and welcome directed toward him and his crew by the others. Someone thrust a mug of coffee - laced with an optional tot of rum - into his hand.

Ben couldn't abide rum and directed his shot of it into Colin's mug. Colin also, was not a great lover of the dark liquid but the warmth of it, together with the coffee, seemed like the best drink he had ever had. As the beverage entered his mouth he savoured every drop.

After a de-briefing, a post-Op meal was always offered in the Mess. Tonight though Colin didn't really feel like it. His six crew members started to clamber aboard the waiting transport.

'Come on skipper' called Ben warmly. 'After getting us through that lot, you deserve to get on first.'

Colin laughed lightly. 'Thanks all the same. I'll think I'll walk. It'll help me unwind.'

'Fair enough skipper. We'll see you in the Mess' said Doug.

'Yes. Save me a seat.'

'Perhaps I'll walk with you' said Michael. 'That's if you don't mind?'

'Course not. I'll be glad of the company.'

Out of all the seven, whether it was because of their links with the West Country, Colin and Michael had become especially good friends. The bus swung away with the other five waving out of its window. As they walked, the two men discussed various aspects of the trip from which they had just returned. Colin's mind kept dwelling on what they had heard at the end of the de-briefing. Nothing had been heard of what happened to Lancaster "M" for Mother. Lancaster "O" for Oboe was missing - although there had been reports some of its crew were preparing to bale out off the coast of Essex.

11

After leaving Scotland the temporary home for James had been *The Gables,* a six-bedroom house which, with various other properties, was once owned by the second Baron Montagu. All originally having been part of his estate of Beaulieu. Each of them was hidden from the other and lay in extensive grounds and could only be approached by private roads or rough tracks. Their concealed seclusion made them perfect for the use of SOE as a training establishment. Each property only housed people of one nationality. The same rule as had applied in Scotland also applied here. Amongst the properties was a rambling, half-timbered mansion called *The Rings* which served as the headquarters building. Further contributing to the suitability of the whole site as a training area, was its mass of footpaths and woodland walks as, was its close proximity to the Beaulieu River.

Beaulieu's whole objective was as the final testing place for whether potential agents could perform and survive behind enemy lines efficiently, effectively, safely, secretly and, most importantly, without compromising the safety and security of others - whether they be as individuals or entire organisations. The sort of things taught, rigorously tested and practised were: how well trainees reacted to every situation they could face and in the way they reacted; their general intelligence, quickness of mind and their ability to put into practice what they had learnt; their temperament - their readiness and ability to fully understand and accept orders and instructions.

James was in the last days of his training there and was in his room at *The Gables,* looking out of its latticed window at the lush growth of foliage on the trees surrounding the building. He smiled as something startled a Fallow Deer and it darted for cover in the trees and ferns beneath them. Rhododendrons of many colours adorned the edges of the house's garden and fringes of the woodland. He thought back over the last few weeks - the training he'd undergone - the activities, tests and exercises. Many of the tasks he had tackled he would never have contemplated in normal times. He looked away from the window at the photograph of June by his bedside. He could never remember his feelings and emotions being in such turmoil. One part of him was pleased and very satisfied with what he had achieved throughout his training, both here at Beaulieu and in Scotland - his instructors, without exception, had voiced their full approval of these achievements and he was eager to put what he had learnt into practice. The other part of him worried what the future weeks, months, even years, held in store for him. It was all so unknown and uncertain and, there was no telling when the war might end - how long he would have to live and survive as an anonymous being cloaked in clandestine obscurity. Yes, a big part of him wanted to run away from Beaulieu, back to an RAF career he knew and understood and, most of all, back to the pretty young woman in the photograph he knew so well and loved so much.

Looking out of the window again James thought of the many diverse topics of instruction he had received at Beaulieu preparing him to be an agent working in France. Much of the time spent in learning what life in France was currently like - information obviously brought back and updated as agents returned to England or, *via* those very few French patriots whom occasionally and against all odds, miraculously had managed to get to England. For instance: the type of identity cards and other forms of identification needed; how the French police force was organised and, how closely it worked with the occupying Germans. It had been stressed that not all the French police were pro the French resistance movement or, were willing to assist agents working in the field. He had learnt about the dangers posed by the many German collaborators and ways which would help him identify them - collaborators bought and bribed by the Germans or motivated by their own political agendas, greed and ambition or self-survival. He had been made aware of the branches of the German security forces and army - how they worked and interacted with each other had been explained thoroughly to him: the Gestapo who, in the main, operated in civilian clothes; the Waffen SS; the ordinary Wehrmacht. There had been some lectures on the Nazi Party: its history; its beliefs; how it operated. Things to do - or not to do - when stopped or challenged by police or German patrols at check points or when randomly stopped in the street. There had been particularly sobering sessions learning about German and Gestapo interrogation and torture techniques - should he have the misfortune to be caught. The importance of giving colleagues and helpers as long as possible after his capture to conceal any evidence and make themselves scarce.

Each section of the training course had concluded with tests, both written and oral. There was certainly much for him to remember.

Apart from the basic principles and techniques, he had also had to absorb specific details of France: its different regions, cities, towns and villages; how to dress inconspicuously; the way to order drinks in a bar or café without raising suspicion or drawing attention by ordering foods that were very scarce or unusual in a particular region; what particular cafes were known to deal in the black market and, subsequently, more likely to be raided by the police. The techniques of disguise, together with various suggested props and accessories, had been another valuable series of lessons. It was best to use simple methods which could be easily altered so as not to arouse suspicion - changing clothes was easiest and quickest. Therefore, he would have to gather a wardrobe of clothes including rough working clothes and good lounge suits tailored in the style common to France. He had noted with interest that a single-breasted suit with stripes downwards made someone appear taller. Hair, cut or combed in different styles, could alter an individual's facial appearance dramatically. A selection of differently-styled spectacles would also be invaluable. Also, interesting to practice, had been the art of making false scars with colloid. A module of instruction James found particularly fascinating was when a convicted crook taught him and his fellow students the criminal skills of burglary, safe-breaking and picking locks - the crook had been particularly adept at unlocking handcuffs.

James got up from his seat by the window and crossed to the door. He still had about seven minutes before his appointment. Ample time to make his way through the grounds to *The Rings*. His appointment was with Beaulieu's Chief Instructor. What was worrying James was he had no idea what had prompted the appointment.

'Come in' boomed a commanding, cultured voice from the other side of the door.

With a feeling of trepidation James entered the large, airy room. Behind a large desk facing the door, sat the large figure of Colonel Rodney Barclay. As he looked up from a file directly at James, his face with its large bushy moustache reminded James of an alert and watchful Walrus.

'Come in, come in Graham? Sit yourself down?'

Since his time at Beaulieu James had discovered from some of the administration staff, that they lived in a degree of awe and fear of Colonel Barclay. This had been James's feeling when he had first met Barclay. However, during lectures Barclay had led or, in the well-stocked bar of *The Rings* on the few evenings Barclay had joined them all, James had grown to believe he was basically a warm-hearted, caring man - though one certainly determined to have his way and was not to be brow-beaten by anyone as to how Beaulieu was run.

'You asked to see me Colonel Barclay?'

'Yes Graham.' Barclay referred briefly to the file again. 'As you know, you're now near the end of your time here with us. There are still a couple of tests for you to complete I'm afraid.'

'So I believe.'

'I'm sending you off to the seaside for three days - to Bournemouth.' James was puzzled. 'All though you'll be paid for two night's accommodation, don't think it's a holiday. Far from it, what you'll be doing is completing a part of your training which, in many ways, is probably one of the most important elements of all.'

'I see.'

'For our purposes, from this very moment, you're to assume the identity of William Dickens. You are an official of a bank in London down in Bournemouth calling on a customer who owns a local factory. The purpose of your visit - to see if the recent expansion of his factory, funded by a loan from the bank, is proving successful and profitable.' Barclay noticed the look of concern on James's face and went on to explain further. 'Don't worry, one of our contacts within the bank's head office in London will back-up the story if your visit is queried at all. In fact, during your meeting with the owner of the factory, you're to request he contacts the head office to clarify a point in the documents you will have with you. In that way our man within the head office will be able to establish if you're suitably convincing the factory owner of your legitimacy.' He handed James a large sealed envelope. 'Open this later. You're to make your own travel arrangements and seek the necessary accommodation for your stay. In that envelope you'll find every detail of your cover story - false papers and documents for your meeting, everything. You've got the rest of the day to familiarise yourself with your new identity. During your stay in Bournemouth, it's absolutely vital that at no time whatsoever do you waver from your new identity and cover story. If you do, everything we strive to do here - the whole essence of SOE's work - could be dangerously compromised. Do I make myself clear?'

There was no mistaking the menace and meaning in Barclay's voice.

'Yes Colonel. Perfectly.'

Barclay handed him a photograph. It was of a young woman in her twenties.

'This is Sally. One of our secretaries. In all probability, you won't have seen her before. For obvious security reasons we like to keep our secretaries and clerical staff shut away from our students. On your first day in Bournemouth, your task will be to follow Sally undetected wherever she goes. Sally's role will be to lose you and vanish from sight. For the purposes of this exercise it is assumed that Sally is a collaborator passing messages to the Gestapo, and you are an agent trying to follow her.'

'Where am I to start following her from?'

'Details of where Sally will first be found are in the

envelope.' The Chief Instructor gave a little chuckle. 'I hope you're fit. You see, we like to give our helpers a free reign as to where they go and how long they take. Some of them have been known to lead our students about for hours through a whole town or city.'

'And this is on the first day you say?' Asked James.

'On the second day, at some time after your business appointment, we've arranged for someone to start following you. Your task is to detect they're following you and shake them off using any means you feel appropriate. After, at a place instructed in the papers in the envelope, you'll wait to rendezvous with another young assistant of ours. By using a certain expression - again given in the papers you have there - and from their reply or response, you will ascertain they belong to our organisation and, when you're absolutely certain they are who you think they are, you will pass them the message included in the stuff you have there. He or she may well leave a message of further instructions for you to act upon. The technique you use to pass on or exchange a message is left entirely to you - the important point being that any message exchange must be done undetected by anyone other than the courier. In order for us to assess your performance as a potential agent, it goes without saying, you will be observed at various times after you leave here tomorrow morning. Now, do you have any questions?'

James had no questions.

'Very good then.' Barclay pointed to the large envelope now in James's hands. 'Now I suggest you go and get down to swatting up that little lot.'

James rose from the chair. It was now lunchtime and he was fearful whether the afternoon and evening would be sufficient enough time to become thoroughly conversant with his new identity and cover story. He crossed to the door.

'Oh Graham' called Barclay suddenly.

As soon as he turned round, James realised what he'd done. Barclay tut-tutted disapprovingly.

'I did say "… from this very moment you are William Dickens". Beware. If I had been a member of the Gestapo, you would now be being placed under arrest and a candidate for torture and interrogation.' He smiled lightly. 'Good luck.'

It was early evening on the last day of his time in Bournemouth and James was walking towards the station to commence his journey back to Beaulieu. On the whole, he felt pleased with how he had accomplished all the tasks set for him by Barclay.

James had managed to follow Sally for a couple of hours, apparently undetected by her, during which time she had called into a house in Yelverton Road, met a friend in a café, and spent ages looking around the ladies' wear department of a large shop. He had finally lost track of Sally in a cinema. During the interval, from his seat in the corner of the auditorium, he had watched her head for the ladies' toilet. The main film had already started when he began to realise Sally had given him the slip. He eventually asked an usherette to enter the toilet "…to see if his girlfriend was unwell". It was after the usherette re-emerged from the toilet announcing no one was in the toilet and, mystified, was holding Sally's hat, coat and glasses in her hands, his suspicion of having lost her was confirmed.

The factory owner had been convinced by the pretence of James's visit and his "an official from the bank" cover story. Even more convinced, by the telephone call to the bank's head office when any remaining doubt the factory owner may have had was dispelled by the person on the other end of the line in the bank's head office.

After his factory visit, James had been aware of a young man who appeared to be following him. James had satisfied himself he had succeeded in shaking off his follower after about twenty minutes near the sea-front.

Then, a little later, as Barclay had instructed, James had successfully identified a young woman as the "message courier" at the bus station and exchanged messages with her. As far as he was aware, their message exchange had taken place unnoticed by anyone.

Now, as James neared the railway station, he became aware of a black Wolseley saloon car moving slowly along the kerbside behind him. A man in his forties standing in the station entrance began to approach him. From out of the car, now at the kerbside beside him, stepped a shorter older man who also approached him.

'Excuse me a moment sir' said the younger man.

The two men now stood either side of James.

'Your ID papers please?' Asked the man who had got out of the car.

James took the papers out of his pocket and handed them to him.

After studying James's ID for a few moments he asked 'William Dickens?'

'Yes.'

The two men either side of James looked at each other. The older man placing a hand on James's arm.

'We would like you to come with us.'

'But ...' James began to protest.

Now both men had a firm hand on each of James's arms and he was being propelled towards the Wolseley.

'But ...' James protested again.

'... We're taking you to the Police Station for questioning' declared the younger man.

12

'It was a bloody uncomfortable night in that cell' remarked James somewhat bitterly.

He was sitting in Rodney Barclay's office completing the Bournemouth exercise de-briefing. It had taken two hours so far and James was tired and irritable. His night in the cell at Bournemouth Police Station and his anxiety whilst there, together with the stiff interrogation conducted by Chief Inspector Lowe had not been conducive to a good night's sleep.

Barclay was laughing. 'Yes I'm sorry you had to endure that discomfort Graham. We don't always enlist the assistance of the police in our training. You should feel flattered really. To be truthful Graham, you did so well in your tests we wanted something a little extra just to try and trip you up. Our old friend Lowe does take his part in our training very seriously when we do call upon his services.'

'He certainly played his part convincingly. I really believed I was going to be charged for holding false ID documents and passing secrets to the enemy.'

Barclay smiled. 'He, in turn, was very impressed with your performance. He says not once did he detect a flaw in your cover story or explanation for being in Bournemouth. Well done Graham. Well done.'

'Thank you very much Colonel.'

Barclay looked through some papers on the desk in front of him.

'Well I'm pleased to inform you Graham you've been successful in the selection process. SOE have been very impressed with the results of your training both in Scotland and here. Now I won't beat around the bush. We need to send you to France within the next couple of weeks.'

'As soon as that?' James was shocked.

'Yes. We originally planned to send you over *via* a fishing vessel. However, somehow the Germans have learnt about the little coastal inlet on the French coast we've been using. Two of our recent drops by that route have run into trouble. You'll now be taken by Lysander. However, by opting to use a Lysander for your transport we're governed very much by the period of the moon. If we miss the next favourable moon, the whole mission we're planning will have to be postponed - we just hope conditions will be right.'

James hesitated before he spoke. 'Can I ask why it's important to get me over there so urgently?'

Barclay studied him closely for a while without speaking. He got up from behind his desk and pressed the bell push on the wall behind him.

'Another drink Graham - coffee - something stronger perhaps?'

'A whisky would be nice please. Thank you.'

Barclay returned to his seat. 'Initially, we were going to use you primarily in a sabotage role - communicating and working with local Resistance groups.' He paused as a young woman entered the room. James recognised her instantly. It was the girl he had followed all over Bournemouth two days ago, had so infuriated him when she shook him off her tail in the cinema. She smiled at him. 'I believe you've met Sally before Graham?'

James returned her smile. 'Yes, but only from a distance.'

'Sally could you please bring us two Scotches? I've some water here.' After she went Barclay continued. 'As I was saying. We were going to use you solely for sabotage operations. However, the game plan has changed somewhat in the last few days. You've now got another urgent task to fulfil.'

'I see.'

'Apart from some sabotage work and making contact with the local Resistance, another problem needs attending to quickly. The "Castle" Resistance Circuit has been infiltrated. During the last few days, dozens of the group's members and supporters have been rounded up by the Gestapo. Others associated with the group have scattered till things settle down. It's still too early really for us to assess the scale of the damage done to our work and what the Gestapo will do with the information they have gleaned.'

'Do we know how the group was infiltrated?'

'At the stage, suffice it to say we have our suspicions. You'll be briefed more fully in due course.'

Sally returned with their drinks.

'Thank you.' Barclay waited for her to leave the room again. 'How are you for water?'

'About the same again. Thank you.'

'Due to the demise of the "Castle" circuit there will now be a big vacuum around the whole Charleville area. As far as Resistance work is concerned, the area is very important to the well-being of the German war machine. There's an urgent need to get a replacement group up and running as soon as possible. We also have to try and find the person or persons responsible for passing information about the "Castle" circuit to the Germans and eliminate them. This is where you come in as well. We want you to take that job on as well.'

'Me Colonel? But ... are you sure? ... I mean I'm so new to all this business.'

'Now don't go all coy on me Graham. Currently, amongst all our students, you've the best ability, both in the French language and your knowledge of France. Throughout your training with us you've proved yourself more than able to take this on. Your RAF background will come in very useful as well - with the planning and selection of drop zones, aircraft pick-up points and so on. I've been discussing it thoroughly with all my training colleagues. We're all agreed, you're the ideal one for us to send.'

James felt a warmth of pride as he heard Barclay's words. A pride tinged though with misgivings. He had agreed to - wanted to join SOE at the outset all those weeks back during his meeting in Baker Street - had commenced his training to perform in some way a small part in defeating Hitler but, he had envisaged playing his part in some backstage way. It all seemed now so much responsibility. He hoped he could live up to the faith and trust placed in him by Barclay and the organisation that was the SOE.

'Thank you for your comments Colonel. I appreciate them.'

'You joined us from Bomber Command. You have a younger brother - Colin - a pilot with Bomber Command I believe?'

'Yes. On Lancasters. Not too long into his first tour of Op.'s.'

'Then you're obviously aware of the constantly increasing number of missions now being flown over occupied Europe.'

'Well, since I've been on SOE training, communications with my family - the outside world in general, has been very limited.' Barclay nodded in agreement. 'In my last job at my Group HQ, we certainly knew the number of sorties being flown and the numbers of aircraft being sent. We were certainly getting concerned about the scale of Bomber losses and were beginning to question the effectiveness of Bomber Command's efforts.'

'Exactly. The top brass have been getting decidedly worried about it. If the total of casualties were not bad enough, there are also worries about the numbers of combat-experienced aircrew being lost by the squadrons. Being a former pilot yourself, you know the huge amount of time and resources needed to train aircrew properly. With the number of raids by Bomber Command -and indeed Fighter Command - set to increase still further, there's an urgent need to expand the existing network of evasion and escape lines in Belgium and France. It's becoming a top priority for MI9 to get as many as possible of those aircrew personnel forced to bale out back to England.'

During his time at Beaulieu, James had learnt something of MI9's work, their responsibility to set up and maintain escape and evasion lines in occupied Europe - was aware of the mutual suspicion between the two organisations.

'MI9 have not succeeded in getting any of their people into the Charleville region - who've survived, for some months now. Not since their principal evasion line was also infiltrated. Unusually, they've asked for SOE's help in setting up another network. James, we want you to see what you can do. On the strict understanding, of course, that as soon as they can get someone established over there, responsibility for maintaining an evasion line will pass back to them.'

'I understand.' James was surprised that Barclay had now started to call him James rather than using his surname.

'Excellent. Well I think that concludes our meeting.' After shoving the files on his desk into a briefcase, Barclay got up and walked towards James. 'There's a person waiting outside to meet you. He's down here from Baker Street.' Suddenly, he extended his hand towards James. 'Welcome to the fold James. I wish you all the best in France. Now, if you wouldn't mind waiting here for a few moments?'

After shaking James's hand firmly and, before James could reply, Barclay swept out of the room. James crossed to the bookcase. On one of the shelves stood a photograph of a group of army officers and two sports shields - one for Rugby, one for Cricket. Studying the photo, James identified Barclay sitting in the front row. There was no date on the photograph but, from Barclay's appearance, he guessed it had been taken at least ten years' previously. James glanced at his watch and returned to where he had been sitting. Suddenly, a startlingly tall man in his fifties dressed in a smart sports jacket entered.

'Pleased to meet you James. I'm simply known as David. I understand Colonel Barclay has told you a little of what you'll be doing for us in France?'

'Yes. Well just touched on it really.'

'Fine. And you also know we need to get you over there quickly?'

'Within the next two weeks.'

'Precisely. The purpose of my coming to see you now, is to allow you as much time as possible to get to know the new identity we've given you. After all your training you'll now understand how important it is for you to be thoroughly conversant with your new identity and cover story.'

'Absolutely.'

David pulled Barclay's chair round so it was positioned next to James. Beginning to unwrap the sealed package he had brought in with him he sat beside James. He placed a document from the package in front of James.

'You will be Edouard Estornel.' James opened up the

document and saw a photograph of himself together with the name and details of one Edouard Estornel. 'We found Edouard's ID papers on a body amongst the wreckage of a French fishing boat beached on the Isle of Wight earlier this year.'

'Has this Edouard Estornel's identity been checked through?' Asked James.

'Yes, as thoroughly as possible. We believe he may have been trying to escape to England with others. As you know, many French people have tried to do the same thing. Many of the boats trying it have either hit stray mines or are shelled by German E-boats.'

James continued to look through the package contents. He held up a photograph of a young woman and a little girl.

'And this photograph are perhaps of his wife and daughter? And were with his belongings?'

'Yes. Our people over in France have been doing some checking up. He and his family used to live in St. Nazaire. His wife Monique and daughter Emilene were both drowned in a boating accident in 1938. Are both buried in a local churchyard. After the tragedy our friend Edouard left the area and moved to Beauvais to begin a new life for himself.'

'But surely there must be some relatives or friends who would recognise Edouard? People - acquaintances in Beauvais?'

'As far as we can ascertain, the only surviving relative was Monique's widowed mother who lived with them in St. Nazaire. Conveniently, for us, she died last year. As far as Edouard's life in Beauvais is concerned, his Landlord - a member of the local Resistance - says Edouard's trade meant he spent a lot of time away from Beauvais. This is why this identity is perfect for you.' From the package David showed James a battered notebook. 'Our forgery specialists have compiled this as Edouard's address book - which you will carry with you. They've excelled themselves I think you'll agree? Should a German or the police in the area you'll be working want to doubly check up on your identity, any of the people listed in the book will say they know you either as a friend of have had work done by you. Those you have supposedly worked for have already been supplied with settled or unpaid invoices. Obviously, Edouard's flat in Beauvais has been "sanitised" to back up every element of your cover story.'

'I see Edouard worked as a bricklayer and handyman' observed James warily. 'You'll know from the notes made during my preliminary interview in Scotland, I'm reasonably competent in carpentry. However, bricklaying! Apart from once when I helped extend the cow shed on my aunt's farm, I've hardly ever done any bricklaying.'

David responded calmly. 'That's precisely why, tomorrow morning, you'll be taken to another of our establishments for a week's very intensive training in that particular trade. I'm confident by the end of the week you will be sufficiently proficient at it to convince any Gestapo passer-by.' David sprung to his feet. 'Now, I recommend you get working on learning your new identity and cover story. It's vital you know them inside out. In a few day's time you'll be issued with full details of your assignment, code names and transport arrangements. There is one other thing I'm afraid. It is policy, at this stage - prior to any agent's departure - that SOE escorts are assigned to them. Two SOE officers are waiting outside now. From now until your departure they'll be spending every minute of every day and every night with you.' David noticed the expression of shock on James's face. 'Don't worry. You'll get used to it. Besides, our staff are usually fairly friendly. If you come with me now I'll introduce you to them.'

13

The target, Hamburg, had been a hellish trip up to now, the worst Colin had experienced so far in his tour of duty. Heavy flak and night fighters had been expected and on both counts the predictions had been understated. The weather too had conspired against the force of more than 100 British raiders. They had encountered far more cloud around the area of Ostfriesische Inseln than the Met Officers had intimated. A violent storm over Cuxhaven had also meant a hazardous re-calculation of their route. On route he witnessed the terrible, blazing destruction of several Lancasters, claimed either by very persistent night fighters or the very numerous pockets of anti-aircraft flak. His Squadron had been briefed to attack the road and rail links to the port and its communication centres.

'Skipper, I estimate we're approaching Stade' came Doug's voice over the intercom. 'I remember from briefing - that bend in the Elbe looks familiar.'

Ben, the Navigator, piped up 'That's what I calculate too skipper.'

'Fine. Thank you both' acknowledged Colin as he headed Lancaster "K" for King to port and climbed her another 2,000 feet. 'Keep a lookout everyone, expect some flak.'

As soon as he spoke, ahead and to starboard, pillars of

light pierced the darkness, flashes of orange mushroomed in the now lightened sky. Like rolling thunder, above the beating throb of the aircraft's engines came the thudding sound of exploding shells. Suddenly the cockpit lit up as a searchlight beam dazzled Colin and illuminated every crevice of the flight deck. Darting streams of orange tracer streaked past the starboard wing tip. After a shout from Colin for power plus boost, they escaped the beam of dazzling light. The scream of the four Merlins vibrated through the bodies of the seven aircrew. There was a loud thud immediately below them as a flak burst exploded. The Lancaster heaved upwards, then immediately another thud, this time to port, which pitched it sideways. Whilst instinctively trying to shield his face, Colin fought to regain control and with rapid adjustments he eventually succeeded. With the turbulence of the explosions all around them it was like being tossed around in a barrel. Now another flak burst, above and to their right - its cascade of burning debris fell just behind the wing. Colin continued to weave the Lancaster around the shellfire and flak bursts. The combined noise of the engine and explosions were deafening; the flashes of shells and flak confusing and frightening. Suddenly, behind in the fuselage, there was a loud crackle and explosion. The Lancaster pitched violently, the control column was snatched from his hands.

'Christ!' exclaimed Jack in his upper turret. 'Bloody flak.'

Ginger was urgently checking pressures and temperatures.

'You and everyone all right back there Jack?' Colin called over the intercom. 'What's the damage?'

'I'm alright back here skipper' replied Dennis from the rear turret.

'I'm OK as well' added Jack. 'We're hit around the

parachute stowage area. As far as I can see from here damage appears minor.' There was a pause, then, agitated he shouted 'No. Sorry. There's a fire just below me.'

Ben and Michael confirmed they were also uninjured.

'Michael! Go and do what you can with that fire' snapped Colin.

'Cooling, temperatures, fuel and oil all seem to be intact' chipped in Ginger, relief very apparent in his voice.

'Thank God for that' said Colin. 'Geoff, you'd better take a look back there just in case. Give Mike a hand with that fire.'

'Will do skipper'.

The engineer got up from his folding seat and disappeared into the blackness of the fuselage behind them.

'Jack, Dennis. Keep your eyes peeled for night fighters.'

As well as flying the aircraft, in the absence of his engineer, Colin was also keeping a wary eye on the temperatures and pressures.

'How far to target?'

'About 16 miles skipper.'

After a while Ginger returned.

'Between us we got the fire out. Bloody close to the oxygen cylinder though and I hope we don't have to use the parachutes.'

'What other damage?'

'Fuselage has got a few holes. By some miracle all cables and lines appear to be still intact.'

'Ten miles to target skipper.' Doug called from his position in the nose.

Colin, Ben and Doug commenced their now well rehearsed procedures for the start of their bombing run. Dead ahead the flak emplacements guarding the target demonstrated their defiance. The flak was very heavy and intense and Colin worried whether they would get through it unscathed. Ahead and just above them, the outline of a Lancaster was vivid and clear in the all-revealing beam of a searchlight. A glow of orange flame flared on its starboard wing, before mushrooming into an all consuming glow of flame and smoke engulfing the whole aircraft. As if in slow motion, blazing fragments fluttered and tumbled to earth. Colin forced all thoughts of the aircraft's vaporised crew from his mind as he steered towards his own target. For him, the next few minutes passed automatically - he reached the target without any real recall of how he got there. Over the intercom, Doug's instructions of guidance to their target sounded in Colin's ears somehow strangely disembodied.

'Bombs gone.'

These two words from the bomb aimer came sharp and clear, galvanising Colin's focus as he kept "K" for King flying straight and level until the all-important aiming photographs were taken. Quickly he closed the bomb doors and, with a full boost turn, dived into the blackness away from the target area, all the time wary of colliding with a friendly aircraft in the crowded sky and, with Jack and Dennis on the lookout for stalking night fighters. Whilst on the last stages of their bombing run, Ben, in his curtained alcove, had been working on their course for home. Now as they sped away he informed Colin of what the heading should be.

Although the miles between the target and them were increasing, every member of the crew was painfully aware of the many perils waiting for them during the miles ahead. There would be more night fighters waiting, more enemy flak batteries to encounter. They all hoped that, during their long journey home, the flak damage sustained would not prove worse in its effect on the aircraft systems and fuselage then envisaged.

They had been flying for some while and, mercifully, not troubled by fighters, had only encountered comparatively light flack which they had managed to skirt round. Colin called up Ben on the intercom.

'I reckon we're drawing close to the Dutch border. What do you think Ben?'

'Agreed skipper.'

'It looks like Emden down there' said Doug. 'There's the shape of that big inlet.'

'About another couple of hours to get home then' replied Colin.

'A bit less then that with this tail wind' said Ben.

Colin could almost taste the warm drink and food awaiting them back at the airfield.

'How's the fuel situation Ginger?' He asked.

The flight engineer reported accordingly. 'Make it back with a little to spare.'

'Night fighter!' Shouted Dennis. 'Corkscrew! Now! Port! Do you see it Jack?'

'Yes - and another coming in above him.'

Colin threw the Lancaster into its evasion manoeuvre. Above the sound of it's engines he heard his gunners firing. Continuing in the downward spiral he heard Dennis and Jack shouting at each other as to the approach of the attacking fighters. He levelled the aircraft out, only to have to put it into an immediate corkscrew to starboard. There was a terrible staccato explosion as cannon shells thudded into the aircraft, followed by a blood-curdling gurgle on the intercom.

Colin shouted at his engineer 'Sounds like one of the gunners has been hit. Get back there Geoff.' As he levelled out again, orange tracer streaked past the cockpit. He called 'Jack. Dennis. Are you alright?'

There was a muffled reply from Dennis. Colin heard him firing his guns.

The Lancaster was weaving, turning and diving all over the place making Geoff's progress difficult. As he clambered over the main spar he tripped, banging his head sickeningly on the rear spar fuselage frame which stopped him in his tracks. He cursed and continued on to the turret step. The step was slippery with blood and glycol leaking from one of the pipes. Jack was a large man and with great difficulty Ginger managed to get him out of the turret. The Lancaster turned again steeply, he heard Dennis firing another quick burst. With horror Ginger saw the fighters' shells had peppered the fuselage around the turret and the turret itself, opening the fuselage in places to the darkness outside. Jack was unconscious making it all the harder for Ginger to move him back towards the rest-bed. Jack was bleeding heavily, the dark fuselage making it hard for Ginger to identify where he was injured. Slipping and slithering on blood and leaked glycol he somehow managed to get Jack onto the bed. At least, it seemed they had succeeded in shaking off the night fighters. Exhausted and sweating profusely from his rescue efforts Ginger went forward to his own position. The port inner engine's temperature was off the clock and oil pressure falling fast. He told Colin he was shutting down and feathering the engine. Instantly Colin made necessary adjustments to the trim.

'How's things back there Ginger?'

'Jack's badly injured I'm afraid and we're riddled with holes. Jack's unable to take oxygen. For him to stand any chance of getting back alive we won't be able to exceed 8,000 feet.'

Colin nodded and looked out of the cockpit. 'There's the coast.' Then, to Ben on the intercom 'Can you give me a position Ben?'

'We're skirting the coast. South of Borkum skipper.'

Colin continued 'Good, I'll do the best I can Ginger.'

'Skipper, can I take Michael back with me to see what we can do for Jack?'

Colin nodded his agreement and Geoff disappeared towards the rest-bed.

Michael was in the habit of writing verse whenever the opportunity arose during a mission. He tore off sheets from the notepad he kept for the purpose and went back with the engineer to help the injured mid-upper gunner. Immediately Michael saw Jack was badly injured and saw two machine gun injuries around the shoulder area. Between the pair of them Geoff and Michael did the best they could to staunch the bleeding with Michael's paper and apply what first-aid they could. Jack was drifting in and out of consciousness. Michael grabbed a blanket to put under Jack's head, lifted Geoff's earphone and whispered as he shook his head.

'He's seriously injured Ginger. I hope he can make it back. I think the best we can do is to make him as comfortable as we can.'

Geoff nodded sadly, took a sheet of paper from Michael and stooped down to speak right into Jack's ear.

'Jack.' After a moment the gunner half-opened his eyes. 'Is there anything you want me to get for you? Whisper and I'll write it down.'

There was a long pause before Jack whispered something which Michael couldn't discern from where he was. Ginger scribbled something down and showed Michael what he had written - it said "A cigarette please?".

'The skipper would have our guts for garters' replied Ginger, smiling.

There was another long pause before Jack pointed to his top pocket and whispered something else to the engineer. Ginger fished around for a moment in the pocket before extricating a blood-stained photograph. Jack drifted back into unconsciousness. The wireless operator and the engineer plumped up the blanket under Jack's head and placed two more over him to keep him as warm as possible. Already very cold in the aircraft's fuselage, the night-fighter's shell holes were making it even colder. The two men drew back from the bed.

'It's a picture of his wife and children.'

'I knew he was married' replied Michael. 'But I didn't know he had any children.'

'No he's always been a cagey individual. Never spoke much about his family life. He wants us to write to his wife and tell her what's happened. Hopefully though he'll make it back.'

Michael shook his head doubtfully. 'I hope so Ginger. I hope so. Perhaps you'd better go back up front to help the skipper. It's not going to be easy for him to get her back with only three engines. I'll go and take a look to check Dennis is alright.'

Back at his position the engineer reported on Jack's condition and set about investigating the erratic readings on the dials and gauges on the panel in front of him.

'We're now over the North Sea' said Colin. 'She's giving me some problems though - please God no stray night-fighters have another pop at us. This poor old kite won't take much more punishment.'

Michael's voice came over the intercom. 'Skipper. I've checked on Dennis. He's received some minor injuries and knocks.'

'Nothing too serious I hope' replied Colin as he made yet more adjustments to trim, rudder and power.

'The poor bloke's freezing. His turret looks a bit like a sieve. I gave him the spare old jacket and gloves he found laying around a few days ago and managed to hoard away. Dennis said at the time they may come in useful one day.'

Michael began to prepare the "colours of the day" for their return across the English coast and settled himself at his desk ready to transmit and receive messages to and from their base.

The darkness of the night was just beginning to lose its intensity as Sergeant Alfie Hammond left his quarters to join the others waiting at the truck for transport to the area they would await the returning Lancasters. He and the others boarding the vehicle were part of the vast team of reception ground crews which, in a short time, would be taking over the bombers from the aircrews to check, repair or, if necessary, partially rebuild the tortured and hard-working aircraft. At this time, the start of their working day, neither he nor the others had any way or knowing just how many Lancasters would be returning to receive their attentive and skilful care.

Alfie Hammond was not properly awake. In fact, he didn't feel at all well. He had felt like this before after a heavy drinking session in the *Red Lion* but, by some miracle, whenever the distinctive smells associated with aircraft met his nostrils his hangovers usually left him.

The truck jolted its way along the roadway towards the maintenance hangars and dispersal pans and passed the old Grange - many years ago requisitioned by the Air Ministry, its house and grounds now totally encompassed and absorbed amongst the acres of concrete and buildings of the airfield. There was another reason Alfie felt like death warmed up and tired. He and George, another "Erk", had met a local girl drinking with a WAAF girl. After the pub closed George and the WAAF had found an old storehouse behind the pub where they got better acquainted. The local girl's parents were away and she had taken Alfie back to her home. With regard to sexual encounters Alfie was a bit of a novice, whereas the local girl was not. In her bedroom Alfie had been well and truly initiated in the joys and pleasures of lovemaking.

Having arrived at the reception point for the returning aircraft, Alfie and the others jumped down from the truck into the chill of the early morning to await the arrival of their charges expected to arrive very soon. Within a few minutes the distinctive and familiar sound of a Lancaster could be heard in the distance.

'Cherrywood from Gauntlet, "K" for King calling.' Michael was talking to Flying Control after they had been given their landing number. 'We have sustained significant damage. Have casualties on board. Permission to come straight in.'

'Message understood "K" for King. Permission granted. Will make arrangements. Continue your approach at current altitude. Wait for further instructions.'

'Understood Cherrywood. Much obliged.'

'Thank goodness for that' said Colin. 'How's Jack?'

'Not too good' replied Ginger, returning to his position.

Colin sighed. 'Time to check the undercarriage. Let's hope for the best.' He proceeded to adjust the Aileron, Elevator and Flaps Selector controls down at his right. He operated the Undercarriage Control Lever. Reassuringly he heard the whirring of the mechanism - felt the wheels leave their housing. 'Phew!'

The grey light of early dawn had begun to yield up the secrets of the landscapes below as they continued onwards. Looking down and ahead of him, Colin now began to make out the familiar landmarks and contours of their approach.

Suddenly, he saw the much-loved, welcoming and reassuring tower of St Stephen's Church.

The wireless chattered again.

'Hello Gauntlet "K" for King from Cherrywood.'

'Hello Cherrywood. "K" for King receiving.'

'Your direct approach for Runway 1 confirmed. Runway cleared for landing. Wind speed 8 mph, direction 090°.

'Thank you very much Cherrywood. Understood.'

'Emergency and rescue vehicles awaiting you on perimeter track to your right of runway. Switch to Channel 2 and keep Channel open.'

'Understood Cherrywood. Now switching to Channel 2.'

Colin selected appropriate flaps. A short while after "K" for King crossed the boundary. With every nerve and muscle tensed in his body he braced himself at the controls, fully prepared for a difficult and problematic landing.

Within seconds of the Lancaster coming to a halt, the crews of the emergency and rescue workers were swarming around it. With Jack on the stretcher, Colin and Michael assisted the ambulance crew in getting him out of the rear entrance door.

'How bad is he?' Colin shouted anxiously as the stretcher bearers got to the ambulance.

There was a long pause before one of them replied gently, sadly shaking his head.

'I'm sorry sir, I'm afraid it's too late for anyone to help him.'

The words carried an extra chill across the crisp early morning air. The six remaining crew members looked numbly at each other.

Dennis was the next to leave the aircraft, assisted by two more medical personnel. He had various deep cuts on his face, was very dazed and cold and had the appearance of being concussed. Colin led the others down the ladder to the ground. Stepping onto the concrete his legs buckled beneath him - caused not only by the realisation of Jack's death and the injuries to Dennis, but also by the stress and exertion of their mission. He could not recall ever before being so exhausted. In a daze he was aware of the ground crews talking to his crew but didn't hear what was being said.

'Do you have the "Aircraft Faults Book" sir?', Colin heard someone ask through the fog of exhaustion and upset.

It was Sergeant Alfie Hammond who had asked. Colin remembered the book he held in his hand. In this was recorded any faults encountered during a flight.

'Oh yes.' He handed the book to Alfie and looked up at the port inner engine. 'She's taken some punishment I'm afraid. Lots of things will need attention and patching up.'

Alfie smiled 'We'll soon get her patched up and rearing to go again. Now you go and get yourself a good night's sleep sir. Goodnight. Take care.'

Colin made his way toward the awaiting transport which would take him and the others to the debriefing. Behind him he heard Alfie Hammond summon his team: 'Right you lot, let's get this one's damage and work assessed. Mind you, if you ask me, a lot of the work will have to be done by the specialists of the Service Flight.'

As the truck moved off, there was an ear-splitting roar of Merlin engines at full power. Colin and the others looked out the back to see an incoming Lancaster low over the runway and obviously in trouble. A moment later it was climbing steeply in a desperate attempt to abort landing. Suddenly, his remaining engines died. For a brief moment it hung motionless about 200 feet above the ground, before plunging vertically to earth. On the ground there was a mass shout of 'Take cover'. The Lancaster hit the ground in a massive explosion - the intensity of flame illuminating all around. For a while all was deathly silent - the shock and horror of what had happened experienced by everyone nearby.

Although after a mission the crew were always exhausted, on the way to the debriefing a degree of good-hearted banter and chat was normal. It was one way for them to unwind, let off steam after all the rigour and tension experienced. However, on this dawn it was so different. They had lost a member of their close-knit team, another had been injured, they knew not how badly. It was all so quiet in the back of the truck. Each man sat silently, deep in their own thoughts. For Colin it was worse. He was the Skipper, he felt responsible for Jack's death. He remembered Ginger saying how Jack had asked him to let his wife and children know what had happened, but as Skipper, he believed it was his responsibility to either write or go and see them. Of course, there would be the usual notification but, even so, as Jack's Captain, he reasoned Jack's widow would appreciate a visit or communication from him personally. Colin determined later in the day he would obtain Jack's address so he could either write or visit. However, what would be especially difficult was that Jack had been an individual who largely kept his private life to himself. Colin only knew his wife's name and nothing else except that they lived in the south of Yorkshire - he didn't even know how old Jack's children were. The other thing playing on his mind was he and the crew still had two-thirds of their tour of 30 Op's to complete. The thought of having to complete their tour with an unfamiliar replacement upper-gunner filled him with horror. And what of Dennis? How serious were his injuries? If he recovered to flying fitness, how long would it be before he could rejoin the crew? Perhaps when he visited him later in the sick bay he would learn more.

The truck stopped with a jerk outside the debriefing room.

Michael spoke to Colin kindly. 'You alright Skipper?' Colin just nodded. 'I know. It's not easy is it.' Michael patted him on the back. 'You mustn't blame yourself, there is nothing you could do that would have prevented it.'

As Colin left the debriefing the CO of his Squadron drew him aside. I understand what you are feeling Colin' he said kindly. 'It's never easy for any of us when we lose a member of the crew. You did well last night. Well done to you and your crew.'

'Thank you sir.' He paused. 'Do you have Jack's address? It's just that I would like to write to his wife.'

His CO smiled 'You don't have to do that. The Commanding Officer will take care of it.'

'I know sir, it's just that .....'.

'.... I'll dig Jack's address out and let you have it.' They started to walk out of the debriefing room. 'I'll walk back to the accommodation block with you. I hate to mention it so soon Colin, but you'll obviously need a new mid-upper gunner.'

'Yes.'

'I'm placing Sergeant Danny Cuthbert with you.' He saw the expression of concern on Colin's face. 'Don't worry Colin, he's a good man. Experienced as well and with a gong for bravery to go with it. He's still got 14 trips to complete his tour. I'm sure he'll blend in fine with you and your crew. Since he bailed out over the North Sea from "O" for Oboe after that Essen trip he's been flying on one or two Op's - making up the numbers. He will be pleased to be given a regular spot in a crew. Of course, I'll arrange a "familiarisation sortie" for you so you can all get to know him.'

Colin felt too exhausted to ask any more questions about his new crew member.

'I don't suppose you've heard any more news of how Dennis is have you sir? He was taken straight off in an ambulance.'

'I'm afraid not. You know what a cagey lot the Medics are.'

'I hope his injuries aren't too serious.'

As they reached the accommodation block, Colin and his CO went their separate ways. Colin met Ben in the corridor.

'It's good news about Dennis' said his navigator cheerfully. 'Some nasty cuts will have to be seen to - and bad concussion. They reckon after a few days off Op's he'll be as right as rain again.'

'Thank goodness for that.' replied Colin, relieved. 'We'll go and visit him in the sick bay later.'

Back in his room, the shroud of exhaustion and strain of the trip to Hamburg finally enveloped him and, without getting undressed, he sank onto the bed and into an immediate and blissful sleep.

14

Sitting in the back of the Lysander, James heard the pilot call up on the radio confirming the course and heading. During the last few days, this particular pilot had been responsible for teaching James the technique and procedure for being dropped in occupied France. Also, explaining how drop and pick-up zones were laid out by the French Resistance, how passenger "loads" had to be exchanged in less than three minutes. James regretted SOE rules forbade agents - known as "Joes" - to enter into deep conversation or get too friendly with the pilots of the Special Duties' Squadrons. The only way these pilots were permitted to address agents was by using the code name issued to the agents for the duration of their pre-flight training and the actual flight.

'We'll be crossing the French coast in about fifteen minutes' the pilot announced over the intercom.

James exchanged a weak smile with the young woman sitting in the back of the Lysander with him. He had first seen the brunette earlier this morning as she arrived at the cottage near the airfield currently used by SOE. Departing agents were always escorted and he presumed her escort, like his, had been an official of SOE's French Section. He had seen her through the bedroom window - watched her ushered into the cottage. She must have been segregated in one of the other rooms as, until the pair of them were driven to the aircraft he had seen no more of her. Even now, apart from exchanging basic pleasantries during the flight, the two of them had not spoken. For a moment James considered whether to her he appeared as nervous as she appeared to him.

It was a clear night and James knew the pilot would have no difficulty in seeing the French coast-line clearly. As the Lysander climbed to avoid any possible light flak, James reflected on the briefing he received that morning in the cottage's living room that served as the Op.'s/Crew Room. By now he knew his cover story and false identity as second nature. His code name to be used during communication by everyone was *Merlin,* the operational name for his drop-off was *Phoenix.* James hoped the message announcing his arrival had been heard by the Resistance. It would have been sent in code *via* the list of "personal messages" broadcast after the BBC French language news programmes this evening. Hopefully they would, this very minute, be preparing for the Lysander's landing. But, SOE and he were all too aware of the German's jamming of radio broadcasts. After landing in the field at Le Mont-St-Adrien near Beauvais, he would be met by members of the local Resistance group. After being hid by them for a short while, arrangements had been made for him to travel first to Rethondes near Compiegne, onwards to Logny-Bogny, then Charleville which he would be using as his base and centre of operations. His first task after landing would be to distribute to the reception party two portable transmitters, some weapons, false papers and ration books the Lysander was also carrying.

The Flight Lieutenant at the controls of the Lysander, an expert now in this type of operation, was unusually apprehensive about the route selected tonight. The routes used for these special duties flights usually took them down south, well away from the heavily flak-defended areas in the north - the routes used mainly by British bombers to and from missions over Germany. However, he had managed to navigate his way through the northerly routes before and, no doubt, would be required to do so in the future, especially as in recent suitable Moon Periods, the traffic in agents was now increasing dramatically. Also - he had learnt in the flight briefing - his mission tonight coincided with a very big bombing raid already laid on. He hoped against hope the German night fighters and flak batteries would be too busily engaged with the bombers to worry about a far smaller blip on their radar. Thankfully, the Lysander was now clear of the coastal flak and he took the aircraft down very low so as not to fall easy prey to radar-controlled interceptions. He began to concentrate fully on the map on his lap and search for the landmarks he knew to look for on their way to the landing field. Again, thankfully, the design of the Lysander permitted pilots an excellent view downwards on both sides to assist but the Mercury engine in front somewhat obscured the forward downward view. Suddenly, way over to his left, he saw an illuminated shape of an inverted "L". From the ground came the light of a torch, flashing the pre-arranged Morse letter. In the prescribed way of acknowledgement, he throttled back momentarily twice. Flying parallel with the long leg of the "L" - noting his heading on the direction gyro - turned onto the down-wind leg. He throttled back to reduce his speed to about 100mph, as he did so, having a good look at the landing area and it's surroundings. There were no tall trees, farm buildings or other large obstructions to cause any problems. At around 400 feet above the ground, he commenced a gentle descent and straightened out at about 70mph with slats out and flaps down and just a little throttle open. Once down on the ground he cut the throttle, applied the brakes gently. As the aircraft got to the second lamp of the flare path, his speed was slow enough to do a sharp U-turn to starboard - inside the third lamp. He began the taxi back to the first lamp. Already members of the reception party were gathering. Quickly the pilot went through his cockpit drill ready for take-off and, as a normal precaution - until he was satisfied the reception committee were genuine, he took the safety catch off the pistol always carried. The Operation Officer of the reception party introduced himself warmly as *Pharoah*. The pilot put the safety catch of his pistol back on.

Pharoah stood at the foot of the ladder. After saying the phrase of greeting she had been briefed to say, the young brunette prepared to leave the aircraft. On hearing the pre-arranged response she descended the ladder. James passed down his and her cases, the parcel of false documents, the container of rifles and pistols and, lastly, the two portable transmitters. James had been informed a returning agent was to be expected. From the group of people standing on the ground a short, tubby man came forward. After a quick farewell to members of the reception party, he thrust his bag upwards toward James. James hastily stowed this under the hinged wooden seat in the aircraft. As soon as the returning agent was aboard, James used his sentence of greeting and after receiving the response expected climbed down from the Lysander. He joined the young woman on the ground and heard the door of the aircraft shut. The operation officer gave a thumbs up sign to the pilot and shouted something. Quickly, those on the ground moved clear of the Lysander as its throttles were opened fully. They watched the aircraft nudge forward and gain speed as it bumped gently over the field, climb and bank away into the night sky.

Pharoah said quickly 'Josephine take the young lady straight to Papon's farm?'

A girl, James thought no older than seventeen, went to his fellow passenger, touched her on the arm in a friendly way and lead her off into the darkness to the right. With quick and precise efficiency members of the reception party gathered together the stuff James had brought with him, whilst others set about extinguishing and collecting the flares that had marked the landing ground and removing any traces of the rendezvous. The rumble of the Lysander's engine could still be heard in the distance. James supposed the whole process of unloading passengers and cargo and re-loading and aircraft take-off, had not taken much longer than two minutes.

Pharaoh called quietly, urgently, to his colleagues: 'You know where to take the radios and weapons?' A man about twenty and an elderly man confirmed they did. Another handed the parcel of false documents to *Pharaoh*. 'Andre and Georges, I'll meet you in the Café Le Bistroy tomorrow morning at 11.00.'

Within seconds, James and *Pharaoh* were left by themselves in the field as the others faded away into the darkness in various directions. Belatedly, the two men shook hands. It had started to drizzle. As they began to walk towards a livestock shelter, *Pharaoh* looked skyward.

'You arrived just in time my friend. The forecast is for heavy rain for the next day or so. I'm afraid we've about a two kilometre walk to where you will be staying for tonight and tomorrow.'

'Don't worry. It'll be nice to stretch my legs. The dear old Lysanders are not the most comfortable forms of transport.'

Just before reaching a livestock shelter they took a path to a gate which they climbed over.

Pharaoh explained 'We'll have to stick to farm tracks for most of the way. If the Germans heard the aircraft they'll be sending out patrols.'

'I must congratulate you and your friends on the efficiency of your pick up' said James.

The other man laughed a little. 'Thank you Monsieur. It was the very first one the group has been called upon to undertake. We're also very pleased to receive the radios and other stuff you brought with you. Badly needed to help our resistance work.'

As they talked, continuing to wend their way along the winding track, in many areas rather overgrown, James discovered *Pharaoh* had a British father and French mother. He was tall, thinly-built and, though he spoke in English, there was a strong French accent. The rain was now beginning to fall more heavily. Suddenly in the distance, from the direction of the road beyond a large orchard, there was the sound of several motor vehicles.

'Germans!' *Pharaoh* yanked James down into a shallow ditch.

The vehicles drew closer. James felt his heart throbbing - could hear his own breathing. Now, very close by, the vehicles stopped. He heard the distinctive guttural sounds of German voices shouting, the sound of boots on the road surface - the sound of vehicle doors slamming. During his time flying Hurricanes he had come pretty close to Germans but that was so different. Then, they had been simply impersonal beings entombed in the fuselage of their aircraft. Now, they were out in the open air, physically close and hunting for him. He could feel his heart throbbing harder, heard his breathing getting louder. There were more shouts and commands. Beams of powerful lights probed the darkened landscape. From the lights and sounds James knew the Germans were splitting into separate little search parties. The strong beam of a light pierced the sky just above their heads, illuminating the scrub and vegetation behind them. For what seemed like ages, the beam seemed fixed on the ditch-side behind them. *Pharaoh* placed a calming hand on his shoulder. Some voices were nearer, the sound of army boots approaching and squelching through the now wet grass beneath the trees of the orchard. To James it sounded as if there were at least three pairs of feet still approaching and only a few yards away.

Suddenly, with a loud shrill, the sound of a whistle cut through the air. There was a distant loud command in German away to the right. After a pause, the troops nearly at the ditch ran off in the direction of the command.

'Sounds like they've discovered where the plane landed' whispered *Pharaoh*. 'One of the reception party couldn't have properly scuffed over the wheel tracks it left.' After waiting another few moments until certain there were no Germans left nearby, he tapped James on his arm. 'Come on, quickly. Whilst they're occupied over there we'll make a run for it. Keep below the line of this ditch and watch out for the uneven ground.'

After running along the ditch for a while, with countless stumbles and painful knocks to their bodies, *Pharaoh* became satisfied they had put enough space between themselves and the search parties.

'Here' he said. 'We'll take this path. It will be safer but take longer.'

The two men were both fit, but probably because of the tension, they took a few moments to gather themselves before setting off on the path to their left. James had banged his arm on the protruding edge of an old brick wall and it was hurting like hell. Worse, the injury to his leg from his air crash was now causing him a lot of pain but he refused to mention it to *Pharaoh*. Eventually, by the side of a small stream, the path began to open out and they passed one or two barn-like buildings. Ahead of them, the path opened out still further and James could see the entrance to a street.

'Here we are. Le-Mont-St-Adrien' said *Pharaoh* quietly.

Cautiously the two men walked on a bit further. There was the sound of boots walking on the roadway and voices. They threw themselves into the porch way of a building. Through a gap in the wall, James saw six German troops pass the entrance to the path, heard them noisily clamber aboard a truck parked in the road just to the right of the path. The noise of the soldiers laughing and shouting and the truck starting up prompted a dog to bark aggressively somewhere nearby outside in his kennel. As the truck moved off noisily it splashed through a large puddle. For a couple of minutes or so the two men hid silently in the porch until they were sure the coast was clear.

'Be careful as we approach the road.'

Rounding the building on the left-hand corner - a little school - they were in the main high street. All was clear. It was only a small town with some shops, a couple of cafes and a church. After walking along the street, quickening their pace and hugging the shadows of the buildings, they crossed the road to a little square dominated by what looked like a town hall. *Pharaoh* led the way curving off from the square down a small road. As the road began to run into countryside again they came across a courtyard fronting a rambling, rather shabby-looking, house. Swiftly but furtively, *Pharaoh* led James across the courtyard. A cat hissed angrily at them out of the darkness and jumped off an old barrel, startling James. *Pharaoh* knocked on the front door three times. The sound of the knocker seemed to reverberate with an echo all round the high-walled courtyard. After what seemed an eternity, they heard the shuffle of footsteps in the hallway on the other side of the door. The door opened and there, framed in the entrance, illuminated by a large hand-held lamp, stood an elderly, bowed man. He greeted them warmly.

'Ah! My good friends. Come in. Come in. We have been expecting you.'

James entered the hallway. Before he himself did so, *Pharaoh* took a careful look towards the street. With a solid bang, the large front door was shut behind them.

Pharaoh introduced Monsieur Maheo to James. The man held out a large hand which he shook. Although bowed, the elderly man was powerfully built and muscular. His big, round, lined face was dominated by an impressive moustache. Monsieur Maheo led them into the sitting room. For James it was like stepping back in time. With all the pictures hung on the wall, ornaments arranged on every available surface, the room had an air of the Victoriana about it. Across the room, an inviting looking fire blazed in the hearth. The hearth itself was set in a huge dark wood surround, atop of which was a large shelf on which stood a variety of other ornaments and bric-a-brac. From out of one of the large armchairs rose a diminutive elderly lady. Madame Maheo had snow-white hair tied back in a tight bun, her smiling little face was as equally wrinkled as her husbands. She wore a dark blue dress with white spots and wore a little apron.

'Welcome, welcome.'

James introduced himself and was aware of Madame Maheo's eyes fixed on his torn and mud-splattered clothes. He caught a glimpse of his mud-grimed face in the mirror above the sideboard and realised what an appearance he presented to his hosts.

'Thank you very much for what you are doing. I apologise for my untidiness.'

'Yes, thank you again' said *Pharaoh*. 'I'm afraid we were nearly caught by the Germans.'

Monsieur Maheo made an aggressive spitting sound. 'Ugh! We hate the Germans for what they have done to France.'

Pharaoh continued 'I'm sorry we're later than we said.'

The elderly couple waved aside their apologies and thanks in a friendly and smiling way.

'Nonsense' said Madame Maheo. 'It's nice to see someone from England.' She then addressed James. 'I will be able to mend and wash your clothes before you leave us. Do not worry. Perhaps you would prefer to wash before you take some supper with us? Or would you like a coffee first?'

'We do not have much to offer you I am afraid' added Monsieur Maheo, 'But you are welcome to have some of Edith's soup, fresh-baked bread and cheese perhaps?'

'That sounds lovely' replied James. 'Thank you. I think I would like to wash first.'

'Certainly. Let me show you where you may wash and will be sleeping.' Monsieur Maheo opened the door to the hallway. By the light of his lamp he led James up the steep staircase and along the landing to a door which creaked on its hinges as he opened it. It was a small room and scantily furnished. The room had a slanting ceiling with an old bed against the wall where the ceiling was at its lowest. On the other wall was a washstand complete with jug and bowl. With a mischievous grin on his face, Monsieur Maheo beckoned James to a battered old bookcase standing to the side of the washstand. He took out an old green leather-bound book from the top shelf. There was a metallic clunk from behind the bookcase. It swung open to reveal a small hatchway and what looked like a "priest hole". Monsieur Maheo chuckled loudly. 'This is our big secret.'

He motioned for James to step inside the cubby-hole. James inspected the pulley mechanism inside and was impressed. 'Incredible.'

'I have just finished this' the elderly Frenchman announced proudly. 'I built it to help our Resistance fighters. Should the Germans pay us a visit whilst you are with us, please hide in here.'

'Of course.' James agreed.

Monsieur Maheo demonstrated how to open the secret door from the inside and showed him once again how to open it from the bedroom.

'Now I will leave you to have a wash and I'll see you downstairs.'

As he freshened and tidied himself he thought of the bravery of the Maheos and the many other French people risking their lives daily to assist the Resistance groups and the allies fight the Germans.

Pharaoh waited for James to come downstairs before taking his leave. The two men went out into the hall and he shook James's hand firmly.

'Well my friend, I have a lot of arrangements to complete. Now the Germans have discovered there was a drop-off, they will be teeming all over the town, searching. I'm surprised they haven't already started. It will be especially dangerous for you to move from here for the next day or so. It is very important you lay low until the intensity of their search lessens. Is that understood?'

'Perfectly. However, I need to get a message back to England that I've arrived here.'

'Don't worry my friend. I will take care of that as soon as I leave here. Monsieur and Madame Maheo's niece will visit here within the next day or so. She will have a message for you with further instructions from me.' He moved towards the door and smiled. 'I'm sure you will sleep well tonight my friend.'

'I'm sure I will.'

It was now raining heavily and as the man, James

knew only as *Pharaoh,* opened the front door the raindrops drummed on the tarpaulin pulled over something stored to the left of the doorway. Back in the room with the Maheos he sat down to the supper prepared. The piping hot vegetable soup and delicious bread and cheese was one of the most welcome meals he had ever had.

15

For over three days the Boche and Milice carried out extensive searches of buildings and land in Le-Mont-St-Adrien and the surrounding area. The Germans failed to find any trace of the passengers or equipment dropped by the Lysander and took their frustration and anger out on some of the residents. Some people had been beaten about, others taken away for further questioning. Hidden in the safety of the cavity in the bedroom of the Maheo's house, James had heard troops storming around the house shouting and searching, throwing about and upturning furniture as they did so. Eventually they left, mercifully leaving Monsieur and Madame Maheo unharmed but, nevertheless, frightened and shaken. After the Germans left, the Maheo's niece had arrived with some freshly-picked flowers from a nearby meadow for her aunt. She also brought the message from *Pharaoh* James was expecting.

The next day, after the majority of German troops had moved on to search further afield, he had travelled with Monsieur Maheo to Beauvais. As it was a market day there was less chance of people travelling arousing suspicion. Though, during their journey the two men were stopped twice at checkpoints. On the first occasion, just outside town, after checking the back of Maheo's little van loaded with vegetable produce and cheeses, the Germans were convinced of their reasons for travelling to Beauvais, the young soldiers appearing to be more interested in questioning three attractive young women waiting in the queue behind them. On the second occasion, however, the officer in charge took extra interest in James - travelling as Edouard Estornel - bricklayer and handyman. James was dressed in the appropriate working clothes, had with him a large canvas bag containing a large collection of the tools appropriate for his work, all meticulously examined by the officer concerned. At last, after extensive questioning, the officer appeared satisfied by his and Maheo's explanation that "Edouard" was simply being given a lift home after working on repairs to the wall surrounding Monsieur and Madame's field. As they drove away from the checkpoint, James was perturbed. The officer had made a note of the address of his "home" in Beauvais given on his identity card.

Monsieur Maheo stopped the van in the shadow of the vast Cathedrale St-Pierre. After thanking his companion again for the assistance and kindness he and his wife had shown, James got out of the vehicle and said his farewell. For a moment, he watched as the van drove off in the direction of the market. It was still fairly early in the morning, people were only just beginning to get about their daily business. The Gothic cathedral standing behind him was truly impressive and, many years previously, whilst at school, he remembered reading about it. How, when building began in 1227, it was designed to soar in height above its predecessors. He remembered reading about its famous astronomical clock assembled in the 1860's. James craned his neck to take in the enormous height of the structure, estimating it to be in excess of 150 feet. He studied the junctions of roads intersecting were he stood. Before departing England, he had done his homework thoroughly and had no difficulty in selecting the narrow road he knew would lead him eventually to the flat - the home of Edouard Estornel. Walking through the streets and avenues, he was surprised at the amount of bomb damage and devastation of buildings already sustained. Whilst working in the office at his Bomber Group's HQ James had seen many intelligence photographs of bomb damage wrought on various towns and cities, but those photographs were impersonal, had to be, but here, right amongst the debris of Beauvais, everything took on a far more personal perspective of the destructive potential of attacks from the air. Along one road he paused at some shops to purchase whatever basic provisions he could obtain. Examining the necessary documents, the various shopkeepers concluded the transactions without any trace of suspicion. He was immensely reassured about the skills of SOE's forgery experts.

After about fifteen minutes, he arrived at the door of the building which housed the flat. The building was located in a shabby-looking road, it's exterior clearly showing the affect of three years of neglect. The area itself, in the main, had been spared the bombing. A wizened old lady, dressed completely in black, wheeling a squeaky old pram piled high with junk, passed on the other side of the street. Further down the street two old men stood talking animatedly. The pair paused in their dialogue only briefly to note his arrival at the front door. Apart from these three people, the street appeared to be deserted. After looking around again, he unlocked the front door and entered the hallway. Apart from a shabby dresser, the hallway was bereft of furniture. The unopened correspondence for the occupants lay in three little piles on the dresser. The biggest pile was for a Monsieur Paulin, a smaller one for a Mademoiselle Touzet, a smaller one still for Monsieur Estornel. Quickly he picked up the envelopes addressed "Monsieur Estornel" and started to climb the stairs to Edouard Estornel's first-floor flat.

He cast his eye around the living room and it's contents. The flat was reasonably furnished and tidy. James crossed to the kitchen, studied it's fittings and other contents briefly before passing into the small bathroom and, lastly, the bedroom. He opened the wardrobe door, looked at the rail of clothing, the shelves of shirts, socks and underwear left for him. Examining each garment carefully, he noted with satisfaction they all originated from Northern France, were in a style and cut obtainable at a cost which would not arouse suspicion about Edouard. After changing out of his work clothes, he returned to the living room and considered carefully the flat which was to be his home. Everything seemed as it should be. The flat had something about it which indicated it had housed a single man - there were no feminine touches whatsoever. He crossed to the window which had a outlook enabling him to see a good way down the street in either direction and would prove invaluable in keeping a lookout for anyone appearing to be watching the building for comings and goings. James busied himself in moving the little settee which occupied the space in front of the window to the adjoining wall, the dining chairs arranged around the table he moved aside so as to move the table in front of the window. The table was heavier than he imagined and he lost his grip. The table slid a few inches away making a thud on the floor and loudly shattering a floor standing ceramic pot containing a fern. He cursed his careless clumsiness and finished moving the table into it's new position, quickly and silently re-arranging the dining chairs. That was better. He would now be able to work at the table whilst keeping a watchful eye on the street.

James sat at the table and opened the correspondence he had picked up downstairs. He knew one of the letters would contain an invoice from a builders' merchant. The invoice heading would give him the contact address of the wireless operator working with the local resistance and enable him to arrange the transmission and receiving of messages. He did not know where the other letters originated from but had to read them should they contain anything he would need to modify his cover story and identity. There was a knock on the door. He quickly concealed the letters in the bookcase and looked at his watch. He had been told to expect a visit from the landlord - a member of the local Resistance, but that wasn't to be for another two hours. He was on his guard.

'Monsieur Estornel!' Called a voice from the other side of the door. 'Edouard, is that you? It's Jules Paulin.'

James was now thinking very quickly. What should he do, or say. Paulin, that was the name on the letters downstairs. Because of his stupid clumsiness with the table, this neighbour must have heard him. To not respond would arouse Paulin's suspicion - he might take his suspicions to the police - that could cause unnecessary problems.

'Alright Monsieur Paulin. I'm coming.'

James opened the door to reveal a short, rotund man.

With surprise at seeing James, Paulin's jaw dropped open. 'But who ....? I was expecting ...'.

James smiled. '... Don't worry, it's alright. Edouard is my cousin, he's allowing me to use his flat for a few days.'

'Oh I see. Only Edouard told me he would be away working in St. Nazaire for about three months - I wondered perhaps if he had returned unexpectedly. I finished my work earlier than expected, I heard a bang from your flat and something breaking. I thought it best to check everything was alright. You see, with all the bombing, there's been a lot of looting. These people doing this are despicable.' He shrugged his shoulders in disbelief. 'War can sometimes bring the worst out in people.'

James shook the man's hand warmly. 'Thank you Monsieur for checking. It was very kind of you. Edouard will be grateful you're keeping an eye on his flat.'

'It's the least I can do for a good friend.'

James paused. He thought carefully. 'You say you are a good friend of Edouard's?'

'Why yes, ever since he moved in here.'

His mind was still racing. 'Please come in Jules, would you like a coffee? My name's Albert by the way. I was just about to make one for myself.'

Jules Paulin gratefully accepted the invitation, settling himself in one of the newly-positioned dining chairs whilst James prepared the coffee. They continued to speak through the open kitchen door.

'I see you have been busy moving the furniture around' observed Paulin.

James laughed. 'Yes, that's how I came to break the plant pot. The light from the window will be better for me to do all the paper work I have to do.'

He returned with the coffee, gesturing Jules toward the armchair.

'Oh yes, the dreaded paperwork. Edouard is always complaining about that' said Paulin laughing as he thanked James for his coffee.

'Is he?'

'The estimates, the invoices, the book-keeping. Letters to the bank, the tax people. When we go fishing together or have a drink in the café, he's always complaining about it.'

'My cousin has always enjoyed his fishing.'

'Yes, very keen, Strange in some ways.'

'Strange?'

'Yes, I think so Albert. Especially as he was fishing when his wife and little daughter drowned.'

James wondered how long Edouard and Jules had been friends.

'Yes it was terribly sad' James agreed. 'A terrible tragedy. You say you became friends when Edouard moved here?'

'Yes, very good friends. Edouard and I really have a lot in common. Because of his work Edouard spends much of his time working away from here. Myself similarly. I am a fabric and tapestry salesman - you will of course know Beauvais has a long and fine tradition of tapestry manufacture.'

'Of course.'

Paulin was now in full flow and continued 'Regrettably, because of the war, business for me is very bad at the moment. However, I am still just able to make a living.' He paused, then hesitantly continued 'Because many of the German officers appreciate fine tapestries, fortunately or unfortunately depending on what way you look at it, I'm able to do some business with them.' He shrugged his shoulders as if to justify his guilt at trading with the occupying forces. 'The other thing Edouard and I have in common is that neither of us have many relatives or family. Also, by a strange coincidence, I do still have one or two relatives and friends in St. Nazaire.'

James felt the hairs rise on the back of his neck. This situation was getting worse. It was the second time Paulin had mentioned St. Nazaire and St. Nazaire was the home town of Edouard Estornel.

Casually he asked 'Do you visit your relatives in St. Nazaire very often?'

'No, not very frequently. Though I am due to go and visit them next week. In fact I had arranged to meet up with Edouard whilst I was there. He's often spoken of an enchanting little café nearby on the estuary. A part of the estuary excellent for fishing apparently. It will be nice to tell him I met you.'

The situation was getting very difficult now. The scenario of it's outcomes were flashing through James's mind. To try to discourage Jules from travelling to St. Nazaire could arouse suspicion, if on arrival there to meet his friend and there was no sign of Edouard, Jules would want to know what had happened, ask God knows who where he was which may trigger some further investigation. And, with his trade, he did have German contacts. Jules could discover there was no cousin Albert - what then?

Paulin paused. Shook his head as if not comprehending something. 'It's strange he's never mentioned you Albert. I was sure Edouard had said he has no living relatives. I even remember - a short while ago - I had to witness some legal document for him as he said he had no living relatives.'

In that instant, James realised he had to do something. He was hearing about a lot of coincidences. Coincidences a lot of the time never added up to anything. On the other hand, sometimes they did. He knew deep down inside, from his SOE training, he couldn't ignore what Paulin was saying. He knew he had to do something. If he didn't, his own cover story and security could be at risk. Worse still, it could compromise the whole point of his being in France. He rose from the table.

'Another coffee Jules?'

'Well yes, thank you. It's so nice talking to you. Usually when I'm here there's no one to talk to all day. Unless, of course, I go for a stroll down to the café. Mademoiselle Touzet upstairs is often away for days on end nursing her mother, as she is at the moment - she will be away now for three days.'

It was just what James wanted to hear. Suddenly, with a lightning reflex, he threw the full weight of his body on Paulin's. His hands and thumbs on either side of the man's neck, on the vital pressure points the instructor in Scotland had shown him. Harder and harder he exerted the pressure. Paulin had no time to even gasp. At first he struggled violently. Gradually, as James exerted all his weight, increased the pressure, the struggles became weaker and weaker until, at last, the struggling ceased and James felt Paulin's legs go limp. He heard the Frenchman's final breath, but still continued to exert pressure, he had to be certain he was dead.

He was sweating. Paulin had struggled strongly and violently. James slumped down off the Frenchman's body onto the floor beside the armchair to gather his thoughts. He felt sick. It was not that he hadn't killed anyone before - he had been a fighter pilot after all - sent many a German pilot or aircrew member to their death. What he had just done was so different though. He had killed another human being with his bare hands. To make matters worse he knew he could have got to like Jules, he seemed such a pleasant man and, by knocking on the flat door, Jules had only wanted to do someone a good turn. Jules had simply had the terrible misfortune to be in the wrong place at the wrong time. James glanced up at the lifeless body in the chair. There was an awful expression of surprise and terror on the lifeless face. James wondered whether what he had just done would change himself as a man forever? Would it result in himself ever regarding human life with the same perspective again?

He got to his feet and gently closed Jules's eyelids. Methodically, professionally, James checked Paulin's pockets, wallet, diary, a letter he was carrying in an inside pocket, his keys. It was a relief not finding anything to indicate a pending appointment within the next few days - the names and addresses of any relatives other than the ones in St. Nazaire Jules had spoken of. The letter James found was simply a thank you note from a former customer of Jules thanking him for some kind words expressed when the customer concerned had been bereaved. Now, he would have to dispose of the body. It would have to be concealed somewhere where it would not be discovered until he was miles away from the area and could not be linked to him in any way. He would think about that problem later. James looked at his watch. The landlord of the flat would be arriving later. Perhaps he would have an idea - would help him conceal the body. He put Jules's keys on the table. He would also have to check his flat. James looked out of the window. There were a lot more people about now, but no one loitering about suspiciously or watching. He dragged the body into the bathroom and shut the door, returning to the living room to tidy around and clear away any evidence of someone else being in the flat.

There was a quiet knock on the door. James froze.

'Who is it?'

'Louis Colbert.'

His contact had arrived earlier than expected but no matter. James opened the door to a smartly-dressed man in his early thirties.

After exchanging pleasantries, Colbert asked 'You have opened the correspondence that awaited you downstairs?'

'Yes I know where to locate the wireless operator. However, before I had a chance to attend to the rest a problem arose.'

Colbert looked questioningly at him. James motioned him to the bathroom.

Seeing the body Colbert exclaimed 'That's Jules Paulin! From downstairs!'

'His friendship with Estornel could have caused real problems for us. I'm afraid I had no alternative.'

After listening to James's explanation and understanding his unease, Colbert replied. 'Yes I agree, you had no alternative. It is sad but these things sometimes cannot be avoided.'

There was a coldness in the way Colbert expressed his last sentence which James found unnerving.

'Mademoiselle Touzet upstairs is away for another couple of days thank goodness. Later on I will arrange for some of my men to remove and dispose of Paulin's body. The Boche are used to my workers going into and out of buildings with large articles and packages without arousing too much suspicion.' He shut the bathroom door and sat himself on the settee. 'Now to business.'

James brought the letters over to the settee and opened them. Two of the letters to Edouard Estornel were of no significance and, apart from the builders' merchant's invoice, there was a hand-delivered letter from the owner of the *Restaurant de la Cathedrale* asking for an estimate.

'Later, I plan to visit the builders merchant to arrange wireless transmissions' said James. 'I need to arrange the rest of my journey.'

'Of course. However, I'm afraid you are going to have to delay your onward journey for a few days.'

'But my instructions are to …'.

'…I know. But something arose last night - a message from England. You must remain in Beauvais to lead and co-ordinate a vital mission. I do not know much about it myself. Now you must get to Monsieur Guimard's yard as soon as possible to arrange your transmission. A van, together with appropriate documentation, has been made available for your use in and around Beauvais. It's parked now around the corner.' He handed James the relevant papers and fuel authorisation for the vehicle. 'At three-thirty this afternoon you have an appointment with the owner of the restaurant

- Emile Levaillant. His restaurant has a good reputation, so good it's used by many of the German officers.' Seeing James raise his eyebrows he went on to clarify. 'As the Germans patronise his restaurant so much, it makes the situation perfect for our work. They wouldn't suspect we would be so bold as to carry on our activities right under their noses.' He gave a large laugh. 'The bloody fools. Monsieur Levaillant stores certain of our supplies for us.'

'From what I learnt back home, everyone would be wise to be always on their guard as far as the Germans are concerned. And not to write off their efficiency.'

Colbert seemed to accept his mild chastisement and mumbled a sort of agreement.

'After you have met up with Guimard and arranged your transmission, you will have ample time to make it back to the restaurant.' He handed James directions to the builders yard for him to memorise. 'Being a regular customer of Guimard - should he be stopped by a road check - Edouard Estornel would be expected to know the way to his yard.'

'Where shall I meet you later?'

'On the second turning on the right, up here, on the corner, you will see a café. We'll meet there - say at five o'clock?' He got to his feet ready to leave. 'My men will be back later for Paulin's body.' He shook James's hand warmly and spoke kindly. 'Do not worry Monsieur. You did the right thing with our friend here. Regrettable as it is, you had no choice.' He opened the door. 'I will go to his flat now to check there's nothing to indicate he will be missed until you are well away from Beauvais.'

After Louis Colbert left, James changed once again into the working clothes of Edouard Estornel.

16

James located Monsieur Guimard's yard without any difficulty. Guimard's obvious dedication to the resistance and intense hatred of the occupying forces was obvious, only equalled in that by his son and daughter who both worked with him in the business, his son Henri as the manager, his daughter Brigitte in charge of accounts. On meeting the three of them he discovered it was Brigitte who was the wireless operator of the local resistance group. Over a coffee he was talking with them in the office at the back of the building.

Brigitte said 'Transmitting and receiving is always difficult. The Boche are around the town frequently with their detector vans. It's far too risky attempting to use the wireless at the moment.'

From his training, James knew only too well the Germans were now perfecting their transmission detection systems and significantly increasing their efforts in this regard. His training had also included lengthy sessions on Morse - wireless transmissions in general and, he knew the severe time constraints for transmitting and receiving messages. He had also learnt what a terribly hazardous, risky job it was for wireless operators in the field.

Brigitte replaced her coffee cup. 'It is good you have a van. We will have to travel a few kilometres into the country.

I know a secluded place near an old quarry where we can transmit in relative safety.'

A few minutes later James reversed the van into a loading bay in the yard. Obscured from any overlooking windows he and Brigitte placed the wireless set in a specially-prepared cavity in the van's floor and placed bags of cement over it.

'Ingenious' observed James.

'Our group obtained the vehicle some weeks ago and adapted it for our needs.'

After shutting the back doors, the two of them got into the van and James drove out of the yard. During the journey Brigitte pointed out the occasional landmark but on the whole she showed a general reluctance to be drawn into any form of conversation, as if it was deliberately to avoid the chance of anyone getting to know her. It had been a long while since he had encountered anyone so difficult to converse with. She was tall and slim, wore large spectacles which partially obscured an attractive face. Now and again, making their way through the outskirts of Beauvais, they passed German vehicles either stationary or in transit. In other places groups of German soldiers stood around talking amongst themselves, on the roadways, in shop or house doorways, questioning and harassing the locals. Occasionally, when Brigitte saw the Germans speaking to a local she would make a little note on a piece of paper. James presumed she was carrying out some form of intelligence gathering but didn't say anything. Whenever his companion spotted the Germans he also noted the sheer hatred she had for them, either demonstrated by her facial expression or some occasional ferocious comment. Her obvious contempt for the occupiers of her country so tangible.

Following the directions Brigitte gave him, James eventually turned off onto a minor road heading towards Therdonne. He couldn't contain his curiosity about the young women beside him any longer. He had a compulsion to break her frosty exterior, to find out more about her, what really motivated her to put her life in real danger by doing what she did for the resistance group.

'Your hatred for the Boche is obvious Brigitte. Is that the main reason you joined the resistance?'

She turned and looked at him thoughtfully. He had anticipated a stern rebuke for his asking.

Instead, after a while, she smiled slightly. It was the first time since he met her he had seen her smile. He realised just how attractive she was.

'Is my hatred that obvious?' She paused. 'Yes it is true, I resent them, I hate them for being in my country. More than that though, I hate them for killing two people I loved very much.'

'I see.' James was sorry he had asked.

The quality of the road surface was beginning to deteriorate. The van began to jolt as the road began to climb slightly.

'In the December of 1940 there was a demonstration outside the town hall. About yet more restrictions the Germans had imposed on us. The demonstration was loud yes, but peaceful. My fiance Pierre and my nephew Benoit were just passing by. Benoit, Henri's son, was only thirteen. The Germans opened fire. Along with many others - young and old alike - Benoit was killed instantly. Completely ignoring Pierre's grief he was rounded up by the Germans and along with others was dragged away for questioning. Two days later Pierre and six others were shot by an execution squad. The Germans said Pierre was one of the organisers. He wasn't. Pierre and Benoit were just passing by, they were just on their way to visit one of Benoit's school friends.'

Brigitte began to tremble. James noticed tears begin to

form in the corner of her eyes. He felt an urge to reach out and comfort her in some way.

'Oh I'm so sorry Brigitte …'. He wanted to say more.

She said urgently '… Just up here on the left. Turn off onto a track.'

He did as he was instructed. The track was unmade, lined on either side by trees and thick scrub. A bit later on, where the track forked, she told him to go towards the right. After a few yards, there was a break in the line of trees and bushes and they were overlooking a disused quarry.

'Stop here.'

The quarry was oval shaped and from where they had stopped they were afforded a good view of it's whole boundary.

'Wait here a moment.'

Brigitte got out of the van and walked a few steps. James watched her take a look around. The wind pinned her skirt to her upper legs. For a moment, James enjoyed the shapely form of her thighs. Brigitte rushed back to the van. He was about to open it's back door when there was a distant sound of a vehicle.

'Quickly!' She shouted and they ran back and sat in the front. Through the windscreen they saw a jeep appear over a brow on the other side of the quarry. She spoke rapidly and purposefully.

'You are a customer of my father - we're lovers and have sneaked out as he doesn't approve of you.'

The jeep drew nearer and they could make out it's three occupants. 'Now quickly, kiss me, hold me close.' He drew her close to him and began to kiss her. She hastily undid the top few buttons of her dress, exposing a good part of her breast. 'Make it look real - place your hand on my breast.'

He thought of June with an intense pang of guilt, but began kissing Brigitte passionately, as he did so placing his hand on her breast. She responded fully. There was no disguising the fact, he was enjoying her sensuous kiss, the feel of her body in his hands. James was aware of the jeep stopping a short distance away, he heard the first booted footfalls on the gravel, the sound of footsteps approaching the van. Two of the soldiers stood by the front window. Suddenly, Brigitte shoved James away from her, hurriedly doing up her dress and tidying her hair feigning embarrassment brilliantly. She opened the van door.

'You startled us.'

James saw the two Germans smirk. One was a young Lieutenant, the other a Corporal.

'What are you doing this distance from the road?' Asked the Lieutenant in perfect French. Then, very politely 'May I see your papers Mademoiselle?' Brigitte rummaged in her bag and presented them to him. He carefully checked these, lingering rather as he compared her photograph on them with her actual face. 'You are both from Beauvais?' He enquired, again not impolitely.

'This is my fiance, he … we … well, you see we don't have much time to ourselves. It's difficult. You see, my father doesn't approve.'

The Lieutenant nodded. 'I see ….'

'…Please, please, if my father were to find out….'

The officer leant into the car and looked at James with piercing eyes. 'And you are?'

'Edouard Estornel' he answered. 'I am a customer of Brigitte's father.'

'Your papers?' He asked, but no so politely as he had asked of Brigitte. 'You're a builder I see' he observed after a while.

James nodded agreement. 'I was at Monsieur Guimard's yard today picking up some supplies. He was away on business and we - Brigitte and I - decided to have a ride out in the country. Because of work we haven't been able to see much of each other recently.' He wasn't sure the Lieutenant was convinced.

The Officer ordered his corporal - a huge, rough-looking ungainly man - to check the back of the vehicle. James felt the van sink as the corporal lumbered into it. He felt an intense desire to kill the two Germans there and then, but seeing the third soldier in the jeep watching events, gripping his rifle menacingly, knew it would be foolhardy. He must keep his cool. Anyway, judging by the heavy breathing and wheezing of the man behind him in the confined space of the van, he was sure he wouldn't attempt to move the bags of cement. Sure enough, the corporal's search was cursory and he reported to his officer there was nothing untoward to be found. After a closer examination of James's ID papers and another look around the van, the Lieutenant handed back the documents. 'Very well you two. I must ask you to move on.'

With a polite touch of his peaked cap to Brigitte he and the Corporal exchanged another smirk and moved back to the jeep. The Germans waited as James reversed back, making to manoeuvre up the track. He began to drive away. In the mirror, he saw the jeep start up and drive off down the track.

'Phew! That was close.' Embarrassed, he added 'I'm sorry - about - you know...'

Brigitte smiled broadly. 'Do not worry. We were both acting after all.' There was something in her voice which indicated to him he had at last cut through that frosty exterior of hers. There had also been something in the way she had responded to his kiss, indicating it hadn't all been an act on her part. 'Stop please. Just up here. They won't bother to come back. It will be lunchtime now back at their base. Far more important to them than us' she added with contempt.

He stopped the van once more.

'Brigitte I must congratulate you on the way you dealt with that officer.'

She laughed lightly. 'Since they've been in occupation, many of us young women have discovered when they stop and question us, we can get away with things easier than our men can. Now we must be as quick as we can with the transmission in case another patrol turns up.'

Together they got out the radio and set it up. In between scouring the surrounding countryside for any sign of Germans, James watched Brigitte as she worked the radio. Her proficiency was obvious. She was well-practised. She sent the message asking for instructions. The wait for the reply seemed endless. At last the set crackled into life. It was an extraordinarily long message. They grew impatient and edgy. The golden rule was to make all transmissions as brief as possible to avoid detection. At least, where they were positioned, miles from anywhere with a good vantage point, there was not as much risk as in a town, where the Gestapo could sneak up unseen to the area of a transmission. As soon as the message had been received and acknowledged, James withdrew the aerial and Brigitte slammed shut the case containing the set.

As they rushed back to the van he said 'Now, I suggest we get right away from here as soon as possible. Transcribe the message in a village or town where it won't look too out of place for a couple to be seen sitting in a vehicle.'

Therdonne was a quiet little place. Sitting in the van in a side street they set about working on the message. It's contents made James's spine tingle.

'Three days doesn't give us much time for the planning and co-ordination of such an attack' observed Brigitte.

The message was about a meeting scheduled by German High Command. The meeting would be held in the *Hotel de Ville* in Beauvais in three days time, was to be attended by local high ranking commanders of the Army, Navy and Luftwaffe.

'I'll start by getting to know my way around Beauvais. I have some time before my appointment with Monsieur Levaillant.' He started the van and turned towards Beauvais.

Shortly after the invasion of France, the Germans had set up their Divisional Military Headquarters in a country house a couple of kilometres or so outside Beauvais. The Gestapo and Milice shared the accommodation. Although standing amidst large grounds, isolated from other habitation, the house had the disadvantages of being on the small side and away from the centre of Beauvais. This caused the Germans occasional problems in administration and keeping their hands on the pulse of what was happening amongst the local population. As the Germans continued to tighten their grip of occupation, they had outgrown the accommodation and space available - the reason why they were increasingly using the *Hotel de Ville* for meetings, it's bedrooms as billets for many of their officers.

The message received by Brigitte and James required only one objective - kill as many German officers as possible. The local resistance's role was to be an invaluable part of a simultaneous attack on both the Divisional Headquarters and the *Hotel de Ville.* The resistance were to trap and kill the officers of the Divisional High Command at the hotel during their meeting as the RAF attacked the Divisional Headquarters. Unusually a daytime attack by the RAF was planned and the RAF needed accurate details and descriptions of the headquarters building and it's surroundings and of the hotel, both of which James was to supply.

Before making his way to the *Restaurant de la Cathedrale* on rue de Malherbe, he spent time familiarising himself with the streets and landmarks around the *Hotel de Ville*. As he went, making mental notes of the layout of the adjacent streets, avenues and squares and the network of alleyways running behind it. As much as he dared, without arousing suspicion, he studied details of the hotel building, noting it's main entrance, routes of approach and all its other entrances and routes of access. He was aware of a German sentry positioned by the delivery entrance beginning to watch him. Behind the hotel, a brick wall ran around what James took to be a garden. He would like to have studied the garden more, but the sentry was watching him more closely now and he believed he would be pushing his luck too far to linger longer, so he turned and walked away up rue St-Nicolas to where the van was parked.

The restaurant was a double-fronted building situated on a square. It had an impressive façade, its windows lavishly draped with lace curtains. Either side of the doorway were positioned ornate tubs each containing shrubs shaped with skilful topiary. Looking through the door, James saw four German officers sitting round a table. At another table sat three middle-aged women, at another sat two men and a young woman. He entered. It was a large room, furnished in a Chateau style with, perhaps, twenty tables. In one corner was positioned a raised area - obviously used as a stage - with a grand piano; in the other corner a staircase. A highly-polished bar, backed by mirrored shelving, ran along the back wall between these two features. Various paintings of agricultural scenes adorned the walls. The restaurant patrons were partaking of afternoon refreshment. As James hovered in the entrance, two of the officers looked towards him briefly before returning to their conversation intermingled with raucous laughter. A pretty little waitress, dressed neatly in a white blouse and black skirt, placed a tray on the bar and came towards him smiling.

'Good afternoon Monsieur.'

'Hello Mademoiselle. I am a few minutes early but I have an appointment with Monsieur Levaillant.'

'Of course. I'll go and call him. He's in the kitchen. Can I say who is calling please?'

'Edouard Estornel. Monsieur Levaillant has asked me to prepare an estimate for some work he requires.'

He watched as the waitress went towards a door to the side of the bar, pausing as she did so, to check everything was well with the three middle-aged women. Conscious of one of the German officers looking towards him, James smiled and turned to study a painting hanging just inside the door. After a few moments he heard a man's voice calling some instructions and turned to see a portly man dressed in a dark waistcoat close the kitchen door and acknowledge him. On his way over to greet James, Levaillant stopped to exchange a few words with the officers. Nicely done, noted James. Levaillant was obviously practised in suppressing German suspicion of unfamiliar faces.

'Monsieur Estornel.' The restaurant proprietor shook James's hand firmly. 'Thank you for coming so punctually.'

'My pleasure' answered James. He explained away his wearing of working clothes 'I apologise for entering your restaurant dressed like this. But I'm on my way from a job.'

Levaillant brushed aside his apology with a wave of his hand and a broad smile. 'Not at all. I am grateful for you coming. If you follow me, I can show you the work I want done.'

After exchanging some more pleasantries with the

Germans, Levaillant led James through into the kitchen. A cook was finishing off cleaning the oven. The waitress who had greeted him was putting away some plates, another was wiping down a work surface.

'Bernard?' Levaillant asked the cook. 'Could you go to Chevaliers now please? I told him earlier you would be down shortly as we have quite a few table reservations tonight to prepare for. Edith, you can go now. I'll finish off here. I hope your mother is better. Anna, could you attend to the bar please? Those officers appear to be very thirsty this afternoon. If you need me I'm through in the store room with Monsieur Estornel.' After his staff left, Levaillant led James to the store room which lay off the kitchen. He spoke but left the door open. 'Colbert requested I acquaint you with the sort of supplies I store. For authenticity he suggested I wrote to request you visit me to estimate for extending this store room.'

'Yes Monsieur Levaillant...'.

'...Please. My name is Emile.'

'Emile I presume these stores include weapons - ammunition - explosives?'

'Indeed. We have gathered together so far about thirty rifles, some Sten Guns and pistols. Some of them stolen from the Germans' he added proudly. 'We also have several hundred rounds of ammunition, and some grenades.'

'Right. What explosives have you?'

'Half a case of dynamite. Some plastic explosive and timers brought by a predecessor of yours some weeks ago.'

'Good. And you have these munitions stored close to here Emile?'

Levaillant paused before answering as Anna came in to the kitchen briefly to return a coffee pot before disappearing again into the restaurant.

'All my staff are sympathetic to our work - help us in

various ways. However, to be on the safe side, I am careful to limit their knowledge to certain things. Oh yes. They are stored and hidden well but we can lay our hands on them within minutes.'

'Excellent. We will have need to use all of them within the next few days. We will also need to have some men in your Group on standby. With your Group's co-operation I have got to plan something big.'

Levaillant smiled excitedly and shot a questioning expression at James.

James continued 'I'm afraid I can't say too much before I've met Colbert a little later. Suffice it to say is what I'm asking your Group to co-operate in will enable us to hit the Germans hard. I will speak to you again soon.'

Levaillant was looking very excited now. He was grasping his hands in delight.

'Wonderful, wonderful. The members of our Group are getting very anxious to do something to get back at the Boche.'

Knowing the German officers were out in the restaurant, James was conscious the prolonged absence of Emile from the restaurant could arouse suspicion.

'I understand from Colbert the Germans patronise your restaurant frequently?'

'Oh yes. We find it hard to serve them. However, one must be realistic in these things. They spend a lot of money - very welcome these days. And also their custom helps us to build up their trust. There are two benefits for us - the Group. Now and again the drink loosens their tongues, we can pick up snippets of information and by coming here regularly they get a bit complacent allowing us to go about our resistance efforts without overly arousing their suspicions.' Then, with hatred in his voice, he added 'Mind you, all the time we suppress a strong temptation to poison the lot of them!'

James smiled. 'Now I think it best we finish our conversation.' He moved into the kitchen. 'Just before I go Emile, do you know much about the *Hotel de Ville*?'

Levaillant gestured expansively with his hands. 'Monsieur! I know every part of it! I did my training there. I was Assistant Manager there for several years.'

James, realising just how opportune this was, said 'Wonderful. Emile could you supply me with a rough map of its interior and grounds by this evening?'

'Of course. I'll start on it immediately.'

As they returned to the restaurant the German officers were preparing to leave. Loudly, James said 'I will prepare the estimate within the next day or so, will that be alright?'

'Of course. Of course. Thank you for coming so quickly' replied Levaillant convincingly.

James followed the Germans out of the door. For a moment they stood talking. He purposefully strode back to his van.

As much as Emile's restaurant was of a good class, the café Colbert had chosen for their meeting was the opposite. It obviously catered more for manual workers and market traders. There was no obvious sign of a German. The café was busy, noisy and very smoky. Colbert checked quickly there were no strangers in the room and they found a table tucked away in a corner. On the grubby table in front of him Colbert opened a plan of one of his properties and a notebook. Colbert was a well known landlord in this area of Beauvais and anyone seeing him sitting there talking with James would just assume he was merely discussing some maintenance work required on one of his properties.

Colbert began by saying 'Some friends of mine disposed

of Paulin's body a little earlier. If it's discovered at all, it won't be for many weeks yet. Your transmissions took place without too many hitches? And your meeting with Levaillant was satisfactory?' Colbert fired these two questions in quick, staccato fashion.

James briefly recounted his experience with Brigitte and the German patrol. Colbert laughed heartily.

'Yes, Brigitte is one of our most dedicated members.'

'The plans are for simultaneous attacks on the Divisional German Headquarters and the *Hotel de Ville* this Friday' said James.

'Their Headquarters and the hotel?'

'Yes, the intelligence is that a meeting of the top brass in the area is scheduled to be held at the *de Ville.'*

'This Friday!'

The attacks are to be carried out during daylight. I've already started to familiarise myself with the surroundings of the hotel. Emile has promised to provide details of its interior. I have also been requested to supply the RAF with details of the house the Boche are using. I need to spend some time to survey the house and its locality from as close as I can.'

Colbert looked doubtful.

'That will be difficult without arousing suspicion. The boundary, its perimeter, is regularly patrolled. In some places there are lookout posts continually manned.' He took a long pause. 'Perhaps one of our men can be of assistance. He was born and raised in the area, knows it inside out. He's a charcoal burner and spends most days working in and around the woods surrounding the estate. He would be able to get you as close as possible. I'll speak to him - put you in touch with him.'

'Excellent.'

Colbert again looked concerned, a concern reflected

in his voice. 'But the hotel is right in the middle of homes, shops!'

'It is the wish to limit casualties amongst the local population. This is why the plan is to get into the *de Ville* and strategically place explosives - planned to detonate to trap and kill the Germans inside just prior to the air strike on their Headquarters.'

'But the attack on the hotel will need a large team.'

'Yes, I'll need your best people with me. Prior to both attacks, all communication, telephone and road, to both buildings and to Beauvais, will need to be cut and blocked. I presume your Group have the local knowledge and manpower to take care of that side of things?'

'The whole plan will stretch our resources to the full.' Colbert rubbed his chin thoughtfully. 'With regard to the telephone system, one of our people is a telephone engineer. I'll place him in charge of that.'

James took another drink of his ersatz coffee.

'Now Colbert. Emile tells me your Group has ready access to some thirty or more guns, dynamite, plastic explosives and timers. Forgive me asking but what training do members of your Group have in the use of these?'

'Use of the pistols and rifles is no problem. Whenever we can we do give them practice. Our members have used them successfully on various occasions against the Boche. But I admit this is by far the biggest operation we have been called upon to perform.'

James persisted with the other part of his question 'And the explosives and timers?'

Colbert paused. 'Limited experience with the dynamite. Plastic explosives and timers we have never used before.'

'I see. Tomorrow, if you can arrange some time and a suitable venue, I will give them some basic instruction.'

'Understood. I will arrange something with those I think best suited.'

'Lastly, how many people do you believe you can recruit in the time available?'

Colbert thought for a moment and doodled in his notebook, marking ticks, as if he was ticking off a shopping list. 'I believe I can have about 25 good, reliable people available for the actual active part of the operation. Perhaps another five or so I can depend on to take care of the necessary background work.'

'Good. That should be sufficient. As you know I've only just arrived in Beauvais and have had no time to plan and co-ordinate as I would like. Proper co-ordination is going to be vital. We need to arrange a venue somewhere out of the way where you, your team and myself could meet up.'

Colbert rubbed his chin thoughtfully once again. 'A family - very sympathetic to us - have a farm, a few kilometres away. Perhaps we can all meet up there. Before the curfew starts this evening I will bring some details to the flat.'

'Right. Now we both have much to do.' James rose from the table and seeing some German troops walking slowly up the street added 'It's best we leave separately.'

As James walked up the street towards his flat he was tortured with anxiety. He didn't really know Colbert's Resistance Group, their capabilities. They didn't know him and his capability. In truth, his capability had not been really tested as yet, apart from his killing of Paulin that is. Had Colbert's members really been as successful with their guns against the Boche as he had claimed?

17

In one of the banqueting rooms on the first floor of the *Hotel de Ville,* Bartels looked at his watch surreptitiously. He was hungry, relieved to see it was only about half an hour to the time allocated for lunch. How he hated these meetings of Divisional Heads of staff - in recent months they were being held with increasing frequency. One of the reasons he hated them was, nowadays, since the abject failure of Operation Sea Lion, Luftwaffe personnel always seemed to be in a minority. Officers like him from the Lufwaffe always seemed to be outnumbered by Army and Naval Officers. Also, like other brother Officers of the Luftwaffe, he now sensed, since the failure of Operation Sea Lion, Officers of the other services regarded them as having individually and collectively somehow let the side down. As if it was their fault - not that of their boss, the bungling, fat, vain oaf Reichsmarschall Goering - the whole thing had failed. Bartels pondered for a moment on the many brave Luftwaffe comrades he had seen perish at the hands of the British Spitfires and Hurricanes. Today's meeting he was hating the more so because he had left his bed very early yesterday morning to attend. He had been staying in a chateau near the French/German border and, in order to get to this meeting on time, had left before sunrise without breakfasting properly and he was tired. That lovely cosy warm bed had been awash with the delicious perfume of his gorgeous French mistress. He had got to bed late anyway the evening before and Monique had kept him active most of the night satisfying her insatiable sexual appetite. Yes, he has hating this meeting. Bartels looked once again around the others in the room. Most of them of a rank equal to his or higher.

At this same time, on the lower ground level of the hotel, three German sentries watched the dark blue and white truck reverse into the driveway of the loading bay. Although a little later than usual, the arrival of the vehicle did not arouse any suspicion with the sentries. It looked like the same vehicle which delivered provisions four days a week to the hotel. Though, for the young man reversing the truck, Jacques, this delivery was a nervous ordeal. His nerves troubled him so. Not only because he had never delivered provisions before, but because this occasion was the first time he had been called upon by Monsieur Colbert to take part in a Resistance Group operation of real significance. A German sentry guided Jacques to the appropriate bay to off load the delivery, motioned him to stop and approached the driver's side of the vehicle. On seeing Jacques, he expressed surprise.

'You are not the usual driver - who are you?' he demanded abruptly.

Jacques remembered the story he had been briefed to say: that he was a nephew of the owner of the provisions merchant and as the owner had been taken ill, was helping out in the family business.

'Your papers?' demanded the sentry, thrusting his open hand through the truck's open window. For a while he studied the ID papers Jacques handed him. 'These say you are a student' he said suspiciously.

'Yes, but as I explained, I am helping my uncle by making his deliveries.'

After a while the sentry appeared satisfied with Jacques' explanation but instructed his two other colleagues to search the back of the truck. As they moved towards the vehicle Jacques remembered the sack of food on the seat beside him and how members of the Resistance Group said that "sweeteners" or bribes to Germans were sometimes successful in causing them to lose their usual diligence at checkpoints and so forth. Colbert had gleaned from the provisions merchant the sentries at the *Hotel de Ville* were especially favourable to certain inducements from time to time.

'I have some nice cuts of ham and beef here' Jacques said, quickly lifting the sack and stepping out of the truck.

'No. No. Not here.' The sentry looked up anxiously at the hotel windows overlooking the loading bay, at the same time motioning his colleagues away from the van. 'Come into the office' he added slyly. Inside the truck, James and the other men had listened to the conversation and breathed a sigh of relief as they heard Jacques and the three Germans scrunching their way across the driveway towards the goods-in office at right angles to where the truck was parked. Through a hole in the side of the truck, James saw Jacques, as instructed, positioning himself in the office so that the sentries had their backs to the window. He watched as the Germans got busy dividing out the contents of Jacques' sack between themselves.

'Right. Let's go' said James.

He and three others slid out the side door of the truck and rushed towards the goods-in office, James hoping the Group's person inside the hotel had locked the doors to the two rooms overlooking the loading bay. Within seconds, before the sentries realised what was happening, they were bursting through the door, their weapons ready. James garrotted a Corporal. Claude took care of another with an upward stab to the chest. One of the sentries standing slightly to one side dived for the alarm button. Before he reached it, Jacques brought him down with a rugby tackle, another of the team jumped on his back, stabbing him through the heart. The sentries had hardly gasped their last gurgling breaths as James began barking his instructions.

'Henri go and get the others? Claude and Albert, go and keep lookout by the door from the hotel onto the loading bay? You'll see it across on the right as you go out of this office.' He indicated the dead Corporal. 'He's about the same size as Jacques. Get his uniform off, and we'll lock the bodies in the store room just to the left here?' Henri returned with three others from the van. 'Jacques, slip the Corporal's tunic and helmet on and sit in this seat? Hopefully, any German passing by on the road will not notice anything unusual. Any moment now Jacques you will see a Citroen stop opposite the driveway. There will also be three men on bicycles who'll stop and talk on the bench over there - the people in the car and on the bicycles are members of the Group. The cyclists are there to look after any German patrol who get too interested in this back entrance.'

As the German's bodies were concealed, Jacques spotted a Citroen park as James had said. Moments later a cyclist dismounted, rolled a cigarette and walked to the bench. Two other cyclists appeared from the opposite direction, waved at the first cyclist, stopped, dismounted and joined him on the bench.

James looked out of the window. 'Good, the others have arrived.' He referred to the diagram Emile had provided. From the window he beckoned to the driver of the Citroen. Immediately, it moved into the opening of the driveway. He turned to Jacques. 'Now go out and speak to the driver of the car? Make a big show of inspecting their ID papers. From a distance, from the sentry point on the corner of the road, the uniform won't look too bad on you. The sentries posted there will assume you're checking in some members of the Gestapo. In ten minutes get out of that uniform, return to the truck and drive as far away as you can. Understood? One of the people from the car will lock the gates after you. Henri, you and another man keep a lookout here. And, when Claude has finished, make your way with him to the Reception lounge. Apparently, the top two floors contain only bedrooms. At this time of day, they should all be empty - the Boche using them will be away for the day with their units - but there could be some locals cleaning etcetera. The whole of the second floor is scheduled to be taken over by the Germans as an addition to their headquarters a few kilometres away.' James cast his eye around the group of men and gave them each a copy of his hotel plan. 'You three. I want you to ensure the top two floors are cleared of civilians and the second floor is still unoccupied. Here we go then.' He looked at his watch. 'We have sixteen minutes.'

Warily they made their way up the stairs to the corridor leading to the hotel reception area. Emile had told James that along this corridor, located just behind the reception desk, was the room which served as the hotel's telephone exchange. They entered the corridor. The guttural sound of a German voice answering a telephone at the far end of the corridor confirmed the existence of the exchange - but now manned by a German operator. James was relieved to hear the exchange still operable. It was not planned for the telephones to be cut-off for another few minutes. A few steps from where they stood, another corridor joined from the right. This was the one leading to a staircase to where the meeting was being held.

After driving the Citroen into the loading bay, Colbert and his team made their way to place time-fused explosives at the entrance to the hotel's air-raid shelter and rear exit from the hotel.

In the small square, opposite the main entrance of the hotel, several people from the Resistance Group lingered singly or in small groups talking. Others of them mingled and chatted in the café or in the shops. Every one of them watching the hotel entrance - waiting for the appointed time and signal to play their part in the plot that was, by now, by the minute, unfolding.

As Emile had told James, the first room on the left of the right corridor was formerly the office of the assistant manager. As James and his team turned into this corridor the unmistakable crackle of radio transmission equipment came from the room. The faint sound of Bavarian music could also be heard. The intruders stopped dead in their tracks. James cursed silently. Emile had not been inside the hotel since the fall of France, obviously not knowing the Germans had established their signals room in this former office. He beckoned to Jules. A few minutes earlier on the loading bay, by stabbing one of the sentries, Jules had proved himself able to kill someone in cold blood. James put a silencer on his pistol and motioned Jules to do the same, signalling for the others to wait in the corridor. Stealthily the two men entered the room - two Germans sat at the transmission equipment with their backs to the door. Taking another step forward, a floor-board creaked loudly. One of the radio operators spun round smiling - no doubt expecting to welcome someone. Immediately the smile turned to shock. James shot him clean between the eyes. As the other soldier turned, Jules reacted instantly and shot him in the heart. James closed the door, immediately he and Jules set about disabling the transmission equipment. In the corridor, the lavatory door almost opposite opened. A soldier came out doing up his trousers. Instantly, Robert lunged at him plunging his knife deep into his stomach. Stepping over the body, Robert rushed into the lavatory to ensure no one else was in there. Hearing the commotion James left Jules to finish off demolishing the transmitter.

'Drag him in here with the others and lock the door' ordered James on seeing the body. 'We won't have much time now. We must get up to that room as quick as we can.' His team re-grouped. 'Right here we go. Be prepared to shoot at anyone who gets in our way.'

He led the group along the corridor and up the staircase. According to Colbert's informant at the hotel, there was still some minutes to go before the meeting was scheduled to break for lunch. James and his team had to seal the doors of the meeting room and place the explosives outside before the meeting adjourned. Other floors had to be cleared and secured.

As Colbert and another made their way to place the explosives downstairs, another two - Georges and Paul - found the engineering and maintenance store. They were already wearing overalls and had selected a tool box and a broom before making their way towards the service passageway also leading to the hotel reception.

Perhaps a dozen or so German officers of more junior ranks sat dotted around in little groups chatting, drinking or reading in the armchairs and sofas. Two "maintenance staff" passing through the reception hall towards the big main staircase did not arouse suspicion. After all, many local people worked in the hotel - as cleaners, waitresses, maintenance staff - each of them vetted and checked rigorously every day by the sentries. Georges and Paul joked and talked as they began to ascend the staircase. On reaching the main landing, they saw two sentries patrolling the corridor. The sentry nearest to them at once barred their way, menacingly pointing his rifle.

'Entry to this corridor is forbidden.'

For much of his forty or so years, Georges had been something of a small-time villain and convincing "Con-man". Because of his present shady occupation dealing in various merchandise, he had found it convenient to learn a few words of German - so much easier to sell various items to them. Now, facing the sentry, he used his limited knowledge of German and finely-honed skills as a Con-man to full effect. He held out a form.

'But we have a docket of authorisation, signed by Major Huber, to carry out some urgent work.' Major Huber was the officer charged with the general running of the hotel, the recruiting and vetting of its French staff. To the sentry, it certainly looked like Huber's signature on the docket. The sentry snatched the docket from Georges. 'There's a dangerous electrical fault to a fitting along this corridor.' He pointed towards one of the light fittings on the ceiling hanging unlit a few yards down the hallway - made inoperable in the early hours by Colbert's man on the hotel staff. 'There could be a fire if it's not fixed.'

The sentry beckoned to his colleague at the other end of the hallway to seek his opinion.

Georges persisted - did not waver in his insistence on the importance of the work having to be done. He put his hand in his pocket. Paul already had his hand on the knife in his pocket. The two sentries now stood together as Georges began to explain again the reason they were there. Eventually, the sentries seemed convinced but, for extra reassurance, walked to look up at the light fitting for themselves. Immediately, Georges and Paul seized their opportunity - both were powerfully built - and in the way James had instructed them, plunged their knives into the sentries killing them instantly. Relieving the Germans of their weapons, the two Frenchman dragged their bodies toward an unoccupied room on their left. Paul draped a length of red fabric out of a window overlooking the square. Seeing this signal, Georges and Paul's countrymen out in the square now knew they would soon be needed.

After locking the door, Georges and Paul returned to the top of the stairs and waited.

The telephone in the meeting room rung. Myer, the German General turned from his chart angrily and cursed. He had ordered that the meeting was not to be interrupted. He snatched the receiver from the clerk.

'Myer. What ... the transmitter? ...'. Angrily, repeatedly, he pressed the telephone button to bring it back to life. A little earlier than planned, the Resistance had completed cutting the phone lines. Again, Myer cursed loudly. 'Bridel. Go and see what's happening. One of my officers has not been able to get a response from the transmitter. Now the telephone has gone dead.'

Bridel rushed out of the room to investigate and was faced by James and his team completing setting the explosives. He started to shout a warning as James killed him with one shot to the head. Before the rest of those gathered in the room knew what was happening, James and his team burst in firing - felling Bartels and at least four others instantly. Hearing shots from the floors above, James guessed the corridors had not been totally unoccupied and hoped the resistance encountered by the men up there wasn't too heavy.

Hearing the gunfire upstairs, the officers in the Reception area were now reacting. Some rushed to the stairs and were met by fire from Georges and Paul, others were met by fire from Colbert and Claude as they entered from the service passageway.

Now was the time for those of the Group waiting in the square. Suddenly, a man dressed as a beggar threw a grenade, silencing a machine-gun position outside the hotel. Other sentries were totally unprepared and, before they could fire, were cut down by the guns from across the square. Other sentries from around the corner of the hotel appeared - they too were not spared.

On the first floor, hearing the gunfire outside, James had finished setting the explosives and left two of his team to relieve the dead officers of their pistols and to seal the door of the room with chains. After saying they would meet up downstairs, he raced away with the others to investigate what was happening on the floors above. They met the other three men as they rounded the landing. They were ushering six female cleaners and three men down the stairs.

'What happened?'

'These three Gestapo were on the second floor' replied one of the Frenchmen.

Back in the Reception lounge James saw Colbert, Claude, Georges, Paul and the others guarding the surviving German officers bunched together in a corner - their hands and legs firmly tied. On the floor lay the bodies of others. Some local workers stood in the corner nervously. James saw the entrance doors had been blocked as instructed. From the first floor came the continual sound of those officers locked in shouting and trying to get out. The three Gestapo men were pushed unceremoniously towards the cowering German officers.

Indicating the local hotel staff, James turned to Colbert. 'Release the locals. Quickly, out through the back.'

'The majority yes' replied Colbert. He then pointed to a man dressed as a waiter and a young woman. 'These two though, we know are German informers. They stay here. Tie them up with the others' he ordered.

James didn't argue and instructed Henri to lead the rest of the staff out the back way. He began to place explosives at the entrance to the corridors.

Without warning, Claude fired a shot at one of the Gestapo prisoners who fell dead. 'That's for my sister ...'.

' ...Enough' shouted James. 'They'll all get what they deserve shortly.' There was a sound of vehicles screeching to a halt outside. 'The Boche! Let's go! We've got four minutes before the back entrance blows.'

As they made their way out into the gardens, the air-raid sirens were already sounding and the explosive charges inside began to explode. Gunfire sounded from the front of the hotel as German troops hunted down those of the Resistance formerly positioned in the square. James and the Resistance members with him were already separating and scattering throughout the maze of alleyways and lanes behind the hotel as the rest of the explosives began to detonate. In the distance, he heard the throbbing of the RAF Bombers.

Some while later and miles away, James boarded a train for Rethondes near the Foret de Compiegne. Although pleased and satisfied by the sight of the smoking rubble of the *Hotel de Ville,* and the news of the complete destruction of the Divisional Headquarters, he had been greatly saddened by the grisly sight of many Beauvais residents being rounded up by soldiers and the Gestapo. Greatly saddened too by the screams - the numerous shots being fired in various streets - no doubt the Germans exacting their revenge. As

James settled himself in the seat, he contemplated with great grief how many innocent residents of Beauvais and gallant members of the Resistance Group would fall victim to this vengeance.

18

Since the Hamburg trip, several days of bad weather had prevented Colin's Squadron undertaking missions. This temporary lull in activity meant he and his crew had only flown one mission without Dennis, their usual rear gunner, before he was declared fit for flying again. This trip had been to Kiel. The stand-in gunner had proved himself capable enough but, even so, Colin and the others had been pleased to welcome back Dennis the cheerful cockney for their next trip to Duisberg.

Colin's anxiety about the permanent replacement for Jack Gaskell had proved unfounded. Danny Cuthbert, from the Isle of Wight, had blended in well with his new crew from the minute he introduced himself to them. He enjoyed a beer like the rest of them - being as willing as they were to stand a round. As far as Colin and the others were concerned, Danny's main vice apart from beer was that he was an avid Chess player. Before joining them, Danny had the experience of sixteen trips under his belt. His sixteenth ending in his baling out of a blazing Lancaster over the North Sea and being the sole survivor of its crew. During the trips to Kiel and Duisberg, Danny had won their confidence and respect as a very reliable and capable mid-upper. The Squadron had returned from Duisberg at 01.30 without the loss of a single aircraft.

****

Much later that same morning, James was woken by the clock striking the hour. Reluctant to stir from his bed, he lay for another few minutes listening to the sounds of the street drifting up through the open window of his room in the top of the house just off Place Ducale. His tiredness was as a result of his six days' journey from Beauvais to Charleville which had ended about 33 hours previously.

The train journey to Rethondes had been largely uneventful. However, during it, James discovered from a fellow passenger that the Germans had changed the format of the "cartes d'identitie" - something they were in the habit of doing at short notice to make it harder for foreign agents working in France to travel. Hearing this had forced him to drastically re-think and change his travel plans. It would have been far too hazardous for him to travel the majority of the way by train. James had sought alternative means of transport. He began this by getting off the train and scrambling down the embankment, just outside Soissons, whilst the train was halted at signals. The days following comprised walking or cycling on stolen bikes along tracks and minor roads - frequently having to hide from German patrols; hiding and resting up for prolonged periods; boarding trains and alighting from them before ID checks could be made. On two occasions he managed to obtain lifts, firstly from a Baker near Rozoy-s-Serre, then a cabinet-maker passing through Logny-Bogny. The cabinet-maker had dropped James off just outside Charleville and he had made his way to the house of Dr and Madame Fouquet just before curfew.

After washing and dressing, James sat in the Fouquet's kitchen enjoying the breakfast Madame Fouquet had prepared. She entered from the garden. Madame Fouquet was a tall slim woman, with what could be described as fine, classical facial features - reminiscent to James of portraits hanging in art galleries of aristocratic ladies of the Regency period.

'I hope the washing has a chance to dry before the rain arrives. Your breakfast is all right?' She asked.

'Wonderful. Thank you very much Madame Fouquet.'

'More toast - coffee?'

'More coffee if I may please.'

'Of course.' She picked up the pot and turned towards the stove.

'I do apologise for not coming down earlier…'.

'…No, no. Please do not worry. You are tired and looked exhausted when you arrived. The sleep would have done you good. Hopefully, my husband will be back very soon.' She turned to refill his cup. 'He was called away early this morning to attend to a difficult birth - at a house just outside the town.'

'I see.'

'Yes. Rupert was particularly anxious about this lady. She has lost two babies before.'

'Oh dear.'

There was a sound of a car pulling up at the side of the house.

'Ah! Here he is now.'

James spread some more fruit preserve on his last slice of toast and enjoyed another mouthful of coffee.

'Does your husband get called out frequently Madame Fouquet?'

In a resigned way she nodded her head. 'Oh yes. Increasingly nowadays I'm afraid. Especially since two other local doctors were taken away by the Nazis. They were Jewish you see.'

Dr Fouquet entered the kitchen hurriedly, crossing

to his wife to embrace and kiss her warmly. The affection between the two of them was obvious. Rupert Fouquet was a tall, distinguished-looking man, bespectacled, with silver hair and a neatly trimmed beard. He appeared some years older than his wife.

'How is Madame Galle - everything all right?' His wife asked with concern.

'A lovely baby girl. And Madame Galle is fine.'

'That's excellent. Wonderful. I'm so pleased. You look exhausted Rupert. Coffee?'

'Yes please Isobel. Thank you.' He crossed to James and patted him warmly on the back. 'And how are you my friend? Better for a good night's rest no doubt? I'm glad to see Isobel has given you a good breakfast.'

'Yes lovely thank you Dr Fouquet. This fruit preserve is delicious.'

'Oh yes!' The Doctor laughed and turned affectionately to his wife. 'Isobel's preserves and jams are much-envied by all.'

Isobel, embarrassed, laughed. 'Oh Rupert!'

Fouquet patted James on the shoulder again, before taking the coffee from his wife.

'Please my friend. Call me Rupert.' He sat at the table and looked at his fob watch. 'The first of my patients will be arriving shortly. Never a moment's rest.'

'Forgive me' said Isobel. 'I must get down to the shops quickly. I hope there is more available today. I will see you both later.'

'Of course my dear.'

She rushed out, putting on her hat as she did so. There was a pause whilst Rupert took a drink from his cup.

'Now my friend I have some things to tell you, and good news as well. Regarding your "cartes d'identitie". On the way back from my patient I called in to see one of our group

- a much-trusted member - the Group's forgery specialist. He reckons by this afternoon he will have a new set of papers ready for you.'

'Excellent.'

'In this area of France you now also require an "ausweis". The Boche now insist on them. They're being extra vigilant nowadays. This man is also preparing one of these for you. They will be delivered later.'

'Wonderful. Soon then I'll be able to get out and about and down to work.'

'Yes my friend. It has been unfortunate you have had to remain confined here. I apologise.'

'Not to worry. I have been using the opportunity to study more about this area. The books Madame Fouquet gave me were very detailed and helpful.'

'Good. Good. I am pleased.'

'You are fully aware of my cover story Rupert?'

'Perfectly. It is fortunate that Isobel and myself have been in the habit of taking in lodgers for the past few years. This will help explain your presence in our house. The forger and I have drawn up a list of people we know need odd building and repair jobs done - people we know sympathise with what we are trying to achieve. All you have to do is introduce yourself to them. You can come and go from here as you please. Treat it as your own home.'

'That is very kind of you. I'll take a look at your list of potential customers shortly. I think it would be wise for me to spend a day or so getting myself acquainted with the area, roads, routes, modes of transport. Familiarising myself with places and local customs - how people go about their daily lives.'

'You are very thorough my friend' observed Rupert, impressed. 'I would also like to congratulate you on your language skills. I would never know you weren't French - your intonation, accent, gestures, all just perfect.'

'I just hope any Germans - Gestapo - I come across are equally convinced.' James paused as if in his mind he was ticking off a list. 'Clothes. I obviously brought various items, however I noticed on my way into this region there are some variations in the styling of clothing to that around the Beauvais region. It is absolutely vital I blend in totally. I can't foretell at this stage what sort of situations or occasions I might find myself involved in.'

Rupert laughed lightly. 'Don't worry by friend, leave it all with me. I can arrange things so you will have a wardrobe to suit all eventualities. Just give me a day or so. With regard to transport, there will be many occasions when I can drive you about. Fortunately, for the time being anyway, my profession as a Doctor allows me a degree of freedom in getting about the local countryside without arousing suspicion. This freedom will be useful when you need to use your radio.'

'The radio was meant to have been dropped by now. Before I left England I was told it would be brought on a later flight and delivered here *via* a Resistance courier.'

The door bell clanged in the hallway. Rupert looked at his watch. 'Ah! That must be my first patient. Please, you will have to excuse me. Now, as I say, make yourself at home. We will talk later.'

James poured himself another coffee as he watched the doctor hurry out of the kitchen. He was sure Rupert did not suspect his mission in Charleville was two-fold - not only to set up and train a new Resistance group but also to discover the infiltrator of the now destroyed *Castle* Resistance Group.

19

Before leaving the house James spent several minutes again scrutinising the ID documents he had received the previous day. He didn't know who the Group's forger was but, there was no doubt about it, he was good - a real craftsman. They were some of the best forgeries he had seen. The clothes Rupert had obtained for him were also a near-perfect fit. For today, James had opted to wear a brown jacket and trousers - not new but with just the right amount of wear and tear and, of a material and cut befitting a workman on his day off. The promised transmitter had arrived at last yesterday afternoon *via* a Resistance courier in the guise of a man delivering surgical equipment and surgical dressings. Now, at last, James could get down to work. He had sent his first message back to England to acknowledge safe receipt of the set. Sending and receiving radio messages was one part of his work in Charleville James knew he wouldn't enjoy. However, as the former Radio Operator of the Group - along with many fellow Resistance colleagues and friends - had been rounded up, interrogated, tortured, imprisoned or executed, he had no alternative.

Once out on the street James stopped for a few moments gulping in a lungful of fresh air, the infusion of fresh air instantly invigorating his senses. He had been within four walls for several days and had never enjoyed being confined indoors. Now he felt a huge sense of relief at being able to feel the slight breeze on his body, to observe again the outside sights and sounds around him in a 3-dimensional way. James began to walk along Rue Beregovoy where, at No. 12, the poet Arthur Rimbaud had been born. He passed little knots of people - mostly of an older age group - talking and greeting each other; others, individually, went about their daily tasks. Observing them all carefully, he noticed many people had a cowering, haunted and impoverished appearance. In many of them, the look of fear, oppression or suppressed anger was all the more tangible whenever German troops were nearby. By the minute, James grew more confident the clothes he wore afforded him an appearance matching perfectly with the people around him - a confidence heightened whenever he passed German soldiers either unnoticed or lightly acknowledged. Now and again, he came across children on doorsteps or the pavements playing in the innocence of childhood. At one point he paused briefly as a tall, young, German soldier - in a smiling, friendly way - passed a runaway football back to a small boy. Startled and amazed, the little boy thanked the young soldier in childish fashion and smiled back. This brief incident brought a glimmer of hope to James. Perhaps, in a simple, symbolic way - between two younger people - amongst all the horror of war and occupation, there was some hope for the future.

James was now standing on the quay-side looking across the River Meuse. Close by was the town house *Vieux Moulin,* which he had read somewhere, had the view which inspired Rimbaud's greatest poem "Le Bateau". James was aware of a man dressed in a grey suit sitting on a nearby bench watching him. James's keen instinct told him the watching man in all probability was Gestapo. For a moment he froze inwardly. Then boldly, unperturbed, James called in perfect French: 'Rimbaud was right. This is certainly a lovely view.'

The grey-suited man was momentarily taken aback and simply nodded his agreement.

James said good-bye and turned casually away. Unhurriedly he walked towards a side street. A few yards up the street he stopped, studied the sparse contents of a bookshop window - an expectant shop assistant looked out hopefully towards him. With relief James saw the man in the grey suit had not entered the street after him. He lingered for a few more moments to make absolutely sure and continued up the street. James took the next turning right, then right again and he was in Quai du Moulinet. After a few yards he saw the shop he was looking for - a Chandlers. After quickly looking around again, checking there was no sign of the man in the grey suit, he entered. A bell rang as the door opened.

The shop was empty of customers, had a bare wooden floor and flanked on one side with a solidly-built counter with wooden shelves rising to the ceiling behind it. The other side was packed with various arrangements of canal barge and boating paraphernalia stored on the floor and in display units. The place pervaded with the not unpleasant smell of hardware shops James had known back in England. At the far end of the store, behind another counter bordered by hanging basket ware and various pots for various uses, James saw the white rolled-up sleeve of someone. An unusually rounded face and near-bald head peeped round the hanging basket ware. The big eyes behind the spectacles looking at him reminded James of a wise old owl.

'Good morning Monsieur. Can I help you?'

'I hope so Monsieur. I need another lamp. One of those authorised for use during black-outs.'

'Of course.' The shop owner gestured expressively and

proudly at the array of lamps over to his right. 'As you see Monsieur, considering the shortages, we have a large selection to choose from.'

'I need it for my barge "Merlins Flight".'

As briefed in England, James had utilised his code name to identify himself to the Chandler. On hearing the two-word phrase a flicker of recognition was barely discernable on the Chandler's face. He glanced anxiously over James's shoulder as a man and woman hovered around the shop's doorway as if they were about to enter.

'A lovely little bird of prey' observed the Chandler in the pre-arranged way.

Hearing the other man's response, James knew this was the contact he sought.

'I'm afraid I am a few days later than planned getting here. The Boche interrupted my travel arrangements somewhat. I had to lay low whilst new identification papers were prepared.'

'Never mind. Travel is always awkward now' replied the Chandler in a friendly way. 'Welcome. We may not have much time to talk. My assistant is making a delivery but will be back shortly.'

James came straight to the point. 'With its network of canals, roads, rail and the River Meuse, you're obviously aware of the strategic importance of this whole area to the Germans. The freedom they have in moving troops, equipment and raw materials allows them easy access for supporting their whole occupation of France. It's a freedom causing increasing concern back in England, especially since the *Castle* Resistance Group was infiltrated and broken up.'

A look of great sadness showed on the Chandler's face. 'I lost many good friends and relatives then - men and women - all good, brave people. It is because of their bravery

I and just one or two others survived.' There was anger and resentment in his voice as he continued. 'With the supplies we had, we did all we could to attack the Boche. There were times we felt let down. We kept requesting more weapons, more equipment, more funding. We could have done much more if only these had been more forthcoming.'

Hearing the man speak, James realised it was not going to be easy to set in train what he had been briefed to do. He knew he would have his work cut out to convince and to prove to this man and others they wouldn't be let down again in their efforts.

'Please believe me when I say how sorry we are things turned out the way they did. Also, please believe me when I say this is the reason I'm here now. To work with you. To train your people. To help set up a reliable supply of funds and equipment. Back in England things are changing. There is now a greater understanding of the importance of keeping you and your compatriots adequately supplied with what you need. A lot more resources and better planning are now in place. Please believe me. You have my word.'

The man on the other side of the counter was sitting on his stool, thinking over what James was telling him. He paused before speaking. 'I know of various people still keen to carry on the struggle. But to ask them after all that happened - it may be difficult to convince them…'.

'…Our intelligence network tells us you have a successful business - wholesale and retail.' The Chandler looked at James suspiciously. 'To finance the running of a new Resistance Group in this area, it would be possible to arrange regular payments from England under the cover of your business. How does that sound?'

'Well if that can be done - but how?'

'At this stage I am not at liberty to say. But you have my assurance it will be organised.' Seeing the renewed look of interest on the man's face and drawing his attention to the map hanging at the side of the counter, James pressed on. 'Monsieur, everyday your business must bring you into contact with barge and boat owners, delivery people?'

'But of course!'

'It should not be too hard then, by using the canals north of Reims - the rivers and roads, for us to organise a whole delivery network for the weapons and equipment we will need. The RAF already lay on drops of supplies as far as Compiegne and beyond.' James studied the map again. 'If we were also to look for suitable dropping zones or landing grounds near Rethel…'.

'…I have a customer of long-standing who knows the area very well. And he can be trusted.'

James was sensing a renewed enthusiasm in the other man's voice. 'Excellent. It's important he knows the requirements needed and the size of area required? Pilot's favourite landmarks for night-time navigation are rivers, waterways and lakes?'

'I know these things and will stress the requirements when I see him.'

'Also emphasise the importance of good entry and exit routes around the dropping zones. The suitability of woods, buildings for cover and for hiding containers?'

'Rest assured Monsieur. I will take care of all this.'

'The key thing is to recruit suitable people.' He paused for a moment. 'You said you know of people still willing to work with us? How many would that be?'

'Six who I know we can trust.'

James shook his head doubtfully. 'I know of two others. That would make eight. We need more. We must try and recruit others. Are there others I might be able to approach?'

'I will do all I can. Leave it with me. You might find it

advantageous to spend some time in the *Café des Ramparts* on Rue Dubois. It tends to attract mostly young people - of the sort we need - angry and eager to attack the Germans. Also, the Germans themselves tend not to frequent it.'

James made a mental note of the Café's name and its location. The Chandler saw his delivery van pull up outside.

'There is my assistant back.' Quickly the Chandler wrote something down on a notepad in front of him and handed it to James. 'This is my private address - I live in Mezieres across the ford. I suggest we meet there one evening in a few day's time.'

An extremely thin, greasy-skinned, spotty youth entered carrying a heavy box and said: 'Again Monsieur Lambert did not have the money to pay for his delivery. So, as you instructed, I've brought this back.'

'Oh honestly! Very well Bernard. Leave it in the stockroom. I will have to write him another letter.' The youth struggled round the counter with the box and disappeared from view. Through the still-opened flap of the counter the Chandler came and shook James's hand, adding in a business-like manner 'Well thank you for your enquiry Monsieur. I will get a quotation to you within the next day or so.' After ushering James to the doorway, out of earshot of the stockroom, he said 'I will see you at my home - shall we say on Saturday evening at six?'

The door behind James shut. Using the bit of paper with the Chandler's address as a Spill, James lit a cigarette. He looked at his watch. He had about two hours before he was due at the house on Avenue Forest where, as Edouard Estornel, he would be starting work on a damaged garden wall. Time enough to start investigating one of the things which had been niggling in his mind for a day or so.

Walking along Avenue G. Gailly, James was aware of a

black car driving slowly behind him. He went into a nearby café and sat at a table by the window. Drinking his coffee, occasionally looking up from his newspaper, he saw the car had pulled up on the opposite side of the road. In it sat two men. His instincts told him they were watching him and his worst fears appeared to be happening. Someone had told the Gestapo he had arrived in Charleville - but who? He hoped he would be able to shake off these two men in time to commence his investigations into that. Carefully, from his pocket, he took out the list of bus routes and timetables he had compiled. Conveniently, there was a bus stop right outside the café on a route that would take him near where he wanted to go. He saw from his list a bus would be due any minute. As he paid his bill the black car was still parked opposite.

Hurriedly, James joined the small group of people boarding the bus. Quickly he glanced over his shoulder as the bus pulled away. He was delighted and relieved that a horse-drawn cart coming out of a side street had hampered the car from pulling away from the kerb. After a short while, the bus turned a corner. Again, James looked over his shoulder - there was no sign of the car. Alighting from the bus at the next stop, he made for a shop doorway. In the safety of the cover the doorway offered, James waited. Sure enough, after a few moments, in the reflection of the window, he saw the car with its two occupants pass by following the route of the bus. Losing himself in the crowds on the street James made his way past a building, formerly Charleville's town hall. Then, halfway along the tree-lined Boulevard Gambetta, he saw the shop he was looking for. A gentleman's outfitters. Behind him stood a monument with half a dozen stone steps atop of which , on a plinth, stood an impressive sculpture. James climbed the steps. The large monument allowed him a reasonable view over the wall, embracing a small garden, to the side of the shop. He went around to the back of the sculpture and this half-obscured him from the shop entrance. Suddenly, from out of a side door into the shop's garden emerged a man dressed in a raincoat. He was accompanied by another, dressed in the black uniform of an "SS" officer. James watched as they made their way through the garden to a car waiting in a side alleyway. A few minutes later, from the main doorway, appeared someone James instantly recognised. He went numb. Was it just a horrifying coincidence he was witnessing or something far more sinister?

20

For as long as anyone could remember, the Smith's family shop had traded in furniture and soft-furnishings in the High Street. This family business had served the little town in Somerset for generations. This continuity had ended some three month's previously when Leonard Smith had passed away in his seventieth year. After Leonard Smith's passing, all legal formalities finalised and the shop having been cleared of remaining stock, negotiations had commenced for a temporary transfer of the lease to be granted.

For some months Mrs Appleford had harboured the dream of wanting to set up a shop in the town as a base for the local WVS, where second-hand goods, refreshments and light lunches could be served - the income generated going towards the war effort. A semi-permanent premises like this could also be used as a command centre for the collection point of goods to be used in Red Cross parcels for shipment to British Prisoners-of-War - of which, after almost two year's of war - there was a great number. Premises like this would also be valuable for WVS Committee meetings and from where various other of their activities they were involved with could be co-ordinated.

Almost two weeks had passed now since the WVS had taken over occupancy. A team of volunteers and tradesmen had been very busy and given of their time to convert what had been Mr Smith's office into a kitchen. Mr Marchant, the local builder, with the help of John Evans, had started on the shop's upstairs rooms converting them for use as a committee room and a workshop where the ladies of the WVS and others could knit, sew, renovate clothes and put together the Red Cross parcels. Although John was busy working on the farm, Lucy had no hesitation in letting him help Mrs Appleford in her efforts to get the Centre up and running.

John came into the kitchen as Sandra, her aunt Enid and Mrs Appleford were opening boxes of unwanted crockery and other kitchen utensils they had obtained from a now-closed hotel in Taunton.

'Mrs Appleford, is it all right if I come in and get a second coat of paint on these shelves and cupboards?'

'Right now?' Replied a rather flustered Mrs Appleford.

'Well Mr Marchant has had to go off for a couple of hours and I can't get on with anymore upstairs until he returns.'

'We have the curtains to do upstairs Mrs Appleford' interjected Sandra helpfully.

'Yes. They're now ready' added Enid. Since moving down to Somerset she had involved herself as much as she could with events and happenings in the area.

John continued 'If I give the shelves a coat of paint now, they should be dry by tomorrow.'

'But I won't be able to be here…'.

'…Don't worry. Sandra and I can finish unpacking these and put them away later' said Enid.

'Well we'll go and see what we can do with those curtains then.' Mrs Appleford began to follow Sandra and Enid out. She turned to John. 'I hear your mother was down here for a couple of days? How is she John?'

'I saw her back on the train this morning. She's fine

thank you. She's now got herself a nice little job with a nice little flat that goes with it.'

'Oh I am pleased. Pleased for both of you. And thank you John for all the help you're giving us.'

'I quite enjoying it really.' He paused. 'Mrs Appleford, when this place is open - am I right in thinking you'll be selling things?'

'Yes. All proceeds going to the war effort.'

'It's just that - since I've been down in Somerset I've been doing some drawing and paintings.'

'Yes. Mrs Hughes was telling me how good they are.'

'Thanks.' He seemed embarrassed. 'I wonder - if you thought them good enough - whether you would like to sell some of them - you know to help raise money.'

'Oh John what a lovely idea! Thank you very much. That's very kind of you.'

Mrs Appleford was about to ascend the stairs when four other women arrived. She greeted them as they came in. 'Thank you all for coming. We were about to get the rooms upstairs sorted out.' The four all appeared upset, two of them had tears in their eyes. 'What's happened? Where's Mrs Dawson?' Asked Mrs Appleford.

One of them, Mrs Hawkins, replied. 'I called for her as usual. Earlier this morning she learnt her son's ship has been torpedoed in the Atlantic - lost with all hands.'

'Oh no! Her only son.' No one spoke for a moment. 'How dreadful. I must go and see her later.'

Numbed, pre-occupied with their thoughts and sympathy for one of their fellow helpers, the women busied themselves upstairs with the curtains, arranging large tables which would serve as benches for needlework, knitting and the making up of welfare packs.

****

With the lessening of mass air attacks on London and, against Government advice, many of the Evacuees from London had begun moving back to the capital. It was now a source of irritation to Alec Graham that the Government steadfastly refused to move some of its Departments and their staff back to London - from all the ends of the country to which they had been dispersed - on the outbreak of war. However, at the beginning of the year, his office had moved back to Buckinghamshire, not too far from his home in Ealing, which meant at least some evenings he could return home. Not the case when he had been located near the Welsh borders.

Like many of their neighbours, Alec and Joyce Graham had given over much of their garden for growing vegetables. More of their garden had been taken over, a few months back, after they took possession of a cockerel and four chickens when old Mr Burke, a neighbour, had passed away.

'But they'll attract mice and rats' had protested Alec half-heartedly at the time.

Although the temperature was on the fresh side it was a beautiful morning and, after feeding the chickens, Joyce was sitting on the terrace at the back of their house. She was really enjoying this rare day off from her ambulance driving duties. The terrace was fronted by a garden bed remaining well stocked with rose and favourite shrubs and, although she and her husband fully subscribed to the concept of the "Dig for Victory" campaign, they had firmly resisted digging this flower bed up for vegetables as they viewed it as "their little oasis of fragrance and colour". On the little pile of correspondence on the table beside her, Joyce instantly recognised the handwriting on the top two envelopes as Colin's. She eagerly opened the first one and began to read. Alec emerged from the house carrying two cups of tea and sat beside her. For the first time in many, many years Alec had been forced to take time off work sick. He had been laid low at home for over a week with Influenza.

'Thank you' said Joyce taking her cup. 'It's a bit chilly out here. Make sure your not too cold. I don't want you suffering a relapse. How are you feeling this morning?'

He smiled. 'It is so nice to be out in the fresh air. Besides, I've got this thick jumper which Lucy knitted for Christmas. I'm feeling a lot better thank you. I might go back to work tomorrow, I expect there's a lot piling up on the desk.'

'As long as you're sure you are well enough…'.

'…Letters from Colin I see' cut in Alec eagerly. 'The post arrived whilst I was making the tea. What does he say? Is he well?'

'Yes he is. It's strange though how the letters come in little batches.'

'Well, that's the war for you. Probably because of the censorship process at the airfield as well.'

Joyce continued 'Bless him. Like all his letters, he puts in as much detail as he can about each trip. In some ways I wish he wouldn't. Some of the things he's experiencing sound so terrifying and dreadful - and what with all that noise and searchlights. He says how upset he was after speaking to the widow of his mid-upper gunner. Colin says he drowned his sorrows in the pub afterwards and felt ghastly the next morning. The replacement gunner seems to have fitted in well though. From what he says Colin and his crew all get on very well together. Remember me saying Alec, I met Michael - his Wireless Operator - during Colin's last leave. We couldn't get over the coincidence of Michael and Colin knowing each other from when they were small boys when we had those family holidays on Lucy's farm.'

Alec smiled. 'It looks as if you've got about five pages there.' He picked up Colin's other letter. 'This one looks as long. I will start reading this one.' After a few moments he observed 'Colin says he and a girl called Sandra have been writing to each other quite often.'

'Oh that's the girl evacuated to Lucy's. You know, she came here with Lucy before having to go to her father's funeral in London. Lucy thinks the world of her. And she and Colin have been writing to each other? I must admit when I was last down in Somerset they did seem to be getting on well together.' She finished reading the letter, adding wistfully 'I do wish James would write. It seems ages since we've heard from him. I do hope he is safe. All June as had is a short note saying he was on some sort of course somewhere. She telephoned yesterday by the way, to say we might be able to meet up in the next day or so. I do hope so.'

Alec took his wife's hand reassuringly. 'Try not to worry dear. I'm sure we'll hear from James soon.'

****

At the same time Joyce and Alec were sitting in their garden, Margaret was sitting in her home in Sussex. She was in the kitchen finishing off looking through some papers and documents from the Ministry of Health sent periodically to all doctors advising them of various outbreaks of different illnesses being diagnosed in various parts of the country. She tapped the papers on their ends before placing them in her briefcase. Ruth Fuller was busy at the sink washing up Margaret's breakfast things and some plates and a bowl used for her supper the previous evening.

'Thanks for doing that Ruth. I was so tired when I got home last night I just had to get to bed.'

Ruth turned and, adopting the tone she did when worrying about Margaret's welfare, said 'I'm not surprised you were tired Dr Wilding. Working the hours you've been the last few weeks. I've said before, these long hours and irregular meals are not good for anyone - even doctors.'

Margaret smiled. 'I know. Sadly, it's these Diphtheria and TB outbreaks occurring at the moment. The outbreaks had abated up until a few weeks ago. Still, I have managed to swap some duties with another doctor for the next few days. I shouldn't be home too late this evening. Robert is coming to dinner tonight as well.'

'The Group Captain is coming...?'.

'Oh heavens Ruth! I'm so sorry! I forgot to mention it. He's been in London for a meeting. Something to do with Coastal Command and U-boats. On his way back to Cornwall he said he will be able to call in for a few hours.'

'Oh don't worry Dr Wilding. There's no problem. I'll be able to rustle up something. Tom dropped off some pigeons and rabbits earlier.'

'But you wanted to go early today?'

'It's all right Dr Wilding. I was only going to visit my sister-in-law. She won't mind me being a little late.'

'Oh thank you Ruth.'

Ruth spoke hesitantly. 'I'm glad the Group Captain is coming.' Margaret glanced quizzically at her housekeeper. 'Forgive me for saying so Dr Wilding but, I am pleased you've started seeing him again.' She paused. 'Obviously, after Major Wilding's passing and, during all that time before, when you were caring for him - it was all a ghastly, horrible time for you - for your whole family. Now though, especially during the last few weeks, you seem more your old happy self.'

'Dear Ruth. Yes. It was a terrible time. Of course I miss Peter dreadfully. Still grieve for him. However, with Robert in my life now. I feel my life has -well begun again. I certainly am very fond of Robert - I've fallen in love with him. With Robert I really feel I've turned a corner.'

'I'm so pleased for you. You deserve it Dr Wilding.'

Margaret smiled. 'I had been tortured with guilt about my feelings for Robert for some time. Eventually, I plucked up courage and talked to June, have spoken about it with her again. I was so relieved when I told her, whenever we've spoken about it since. She's happy for me as well.'

'Of course she is. June and your sons, all they would want is your happiness.' She continued with the drying up. 'Has the Group Captain fully recovered from that virus he caught in Canada? It took him a long time to get over it didn't it?'

'Yes. He seems to have settled in to his new posting. I'm looking forward to seeing him. With him based in Cornwall, it's difficult to see each other very often.' She glanced at the clock. 'Goodness. Is that the time. I must be going.' Margaret finished packing her briefcase.

There was a loud knock at the door. Ruth hurried out of the kitchen.

Margaret was just finishing her cup of tea when Ruth returned. The colour had drained from her face. There were tears in her eyes.

'What is it Ruth? Whatever's happened?'

Margaret saw the piece of paper in Ruth's hand. She instantly recognised it as a Telegram. She went numb, shivered, as she took it and turned back towards the centre of the room. Slowly, bracing herself, she began to read it. It concerned her son in the Army. Richard. Ruth came to her side and embraced her.

****

June looked at her watch. She had now been waiting in the corridor for half-an-hour. She did not know why her commanding officer had asked to see her and, the longer she waited the more anxious she became. June's mind went back to an incident which had occurred a week ago, and she grew more and more convinced it was as a result of this her commanding officer had summoned her. The incident in question had been particularly unsavoury and upsetting. One evening, after coming off duty, she had been in the shower room. A woman, two ranks above June, had made sexual advances. With great difficulty and a struggle, June had managed to get away from her. So angry at being rejected, the woman had pulled rank, accusing June of making the advances and of stealing from her bag. Accusations, completely unfounded, which had deeply upset and worried June ever since. Accusations had been levelled against her! It was June's word against the other woman's word! How could she prove she hadn't stolen anything - how could she prove it was the other woman who had made the sexual advances. June looked at the office door opposite. She was now feeling sick with worry as to what was about to happen to her.

Laughing girlishly, two other ATS girls came along the corridor. One of them asking June for a light as they passed.

'Sorry. I don't smoke.'

For something to occupy herself, June wandered a few steps to read a notice advising of the latest air-raid evacuation procedures, reminding personnel of the importance of still carrying their gas masks. She returned to her seat. The door opposite opened. On seeing who came out June froze. It was the woman from the shower room. She paused for a moment and looked menacingly at June. June started shaking. The woman turned on her heels and went off down the corridor. A voice from within the room called out for June to enter. 'Sorry to have kept you Senior Leader Graham. Please stand at ease?' The Company Commander smiled. 'I have been studying your file. You have been on anti-aircraft installations for about two years now?'

'Yes. Two years next week.'

'How do you find that role?'

'I've enjoyed the posting - I still enjoy it. It's very noisy and cold of course. My superior always seems to be pleased with my contribution - I get on well with the other members of my battery.'

The officer studied June's file for a while. 'Yes indeed. Your report is very favourable. Very commendable. Well done.'

June's nerves were now very frayed and wished, if she was to be questioned or disciplined, her superior would get on with it.

'Thank you.'

'Two years is a long time performing one task - especially in an anti-aircraft battery. Would you appreciate a new challenge?'

'Well I can't deny it would be nice to do something different.'

'Good. What I have in mind is certainly different from what you have been doing. As you are aware, with the current manpower shortages affecting everything nowadays - the emergency services, offices, factories and so forth, we're being called on to work with the Police as well. Especially with anything connected to the war and the military. A post has come up at the police headquarters in Brighton. I've recommended you to be seconded to them with immediate effect.'

'Well thank you very much. I...'.

'...Is everything all right Senior Leader Graham? You seem rather - pre-occupied? I thought you would jump at the chance?'

'Oh I'm sorry. Yes. Thank you very much. I would love to do it. I've just got things on my mind at the moment. I apologise.'

'Nothing serious I hope?'

'No.' June thought quickly. 'Just like the majority of people now - worried. My husband in the RAF, my brothers both serving in the forces.'

'Of course.' There was a brief smile of understanding. 'Well, very well then. That's all for now. You may go. When I hear more from the Constabulary, probably this afternoon, we'll talk about it in more detail. And very well done by the way for what you've achieved so far.'

June lingered for a moment, stunned and surprised there had been nothing said about the Shower Room incident.

'Was there anything else Senior Leader Graham?'

'Er! No. Thank you again.'

June hurried out of the room. Her superior officer had said nothing whatsoever about anything else - had heaped nothing but praise on her. Her sense of relief was immense. She had also been offered a new job, one which sounded exciting and challenging. June couldn't wait to get away. Well away from the woman who had frightened and upset her so.

****

It was well into the evening when Derek Pickering parked his car and opened the front door of *Coppice Cottage*. Rosemary greeted him affectionately. The latest operation on his face at East Grinstead had been successful, re-built his features to something more approaching normal. It had certainly helped Derek's confidence when kissing and cuddling Rosemary or when making a fuss of his children.

'The children in bed?' He asked as they walked into the kitchen.

'Yes. Haven't heard anything from them for over half-an-hour now. Christopher wanted you to read him a story but I promised you'll read him one tomorrow. I hope your dinner isn't ruined.'

He picked up the newspaper, went into the dining room and started to read. The paper was full of pictures and stories of American forces arriving in England, anecdotes and reports of a myriad of local initiatives being staged up and down the country to welcome them and make them feel at home.

'What was your meeting with Rogers about?' Rosemary asked as they began to eat.

'To tell me I will continue to be stationed here for the rest of the year at least.'

'Oh Derek that is good news' she replied excitedly. There had been talk recently her husband may well be posted overseas.

'With the Americans now arriving in force, the emphasis for our Fighter Squadrons is shifting to an attacking role. For a while now, the priority for two of the squadrons at the airfield has been for Bomber escort duties on missions to France. In all probability this commitment will increase dramatically. Rogers said if I didn't have any objections to my posting being deferred for a while, he could make out a case for my remaining here as Controller. Especially as I still have to make periodic visits to East Grinstead.'

'Oh Derek I'm so pleased. The children will be thrilled as well. Sarah was only saying this afternoon how glad she is being able to see you most days. Some of the children in her class haven't seen their fathers for two years or more now. I feel so sorry for them. I was hanging some washing on the line this morning and I saw a squadron taking off. As I always have, I wondered where they were going.'

'There was a big Op. on. In spite of our best efforts though, four bombers were lost I'm afraid. We also lost a Spitfire - a Squadron CO.'

21

So far, James's time in Charleville had been largely fruitful. The amount of repair required on the garden wall on Avenue Forest was more extensive than expected. Repairing it had kept him occupied for about four days and, after that, Monsieur Dubock had requested he build a lean-to which his large family could use as extra storage space and wherein Madame Dubock could dry the endless mounds of washing created by their large family. All in all, it resulted in James being at their property for just over a week, allowing him the chance to get to know something of the Dubock family. In fact, Dubock became James's first recruit to the new resistance group. The time spent there had also afforded him the opportunity of becoming a familiar sight in the area for passing Gendarmes and the Germans. It was advantageous for any agent working behind enemy lines to be accepted or viewed as a member of the local community. James had also busied himself liaising with a network of SOE-known and trusted banking contacts in the region, setting up accounts for the fledgling resistance group. After finishing the job at the Dubock's he used the list of contacts of people needing odd jobs done, supplied by Dr Fouquet and found employment for the next few weeks at least. Using this time, whenever he could, James busily groomed and recruited more volunteers. Every evening, on his way home, he would also call into the *Café des Ramparts* and, mixing freely with a group who met in there to play cards regularly, had earmarked at least six potential resistance group members. After checking up on them as thoroughly as he could, he then recruited them.

Travelling sometimes with Dr Fouquet on his patient calls, James would investigate the potential of a house or farm for use as a "safe house" or, as a place for the use by the resistance group for storage of supplies or concealment of resistance workers. James also used these opportunities to familiarise himself with alternative routes for transport or escape. Whenever their route took them close to the River Meuse or the canal network north of Reims, he would spend time studying boat or barge traffic. In his role of odd-job man he had a certain freedom to travel around without arousing suspicion and this he exploited to the full. With a mixture of cycling, rail and bus travel he managed to venture around a large area.

In the weeks since James's initial contact with Didier, the Chandler, many things had happened. Between the two of them they recruited over 24 to the group - more than enough to make the group viable. SOE had finally acquired authority to be independent of SIS in using its own wireless codes, its own networks and home stations. James had joyfully used the earliest opportunity of this greater freedom to signal the group's code name "Heron" in readiness for action. Dideret's contact had researched and identified two possible landing/dropping zones: Biermes, near Rethel and at Vouziers. Using an isolated farm belonging to one of Fouquet's patients, a nearby disused quarry and the forests of Ardennes, James managed to conduct some basic training of their recruits using what weapons and equipment already scraped together.

Tonight, the first drop of supplies from England was

scheduled. It was a pleasant evening as James headed for Dideret's home in Mezieres. Dr Fouquet's wife had announced yesterday they would be out for most of the day and evening visiting old friends in Donchery. Dr Fouquet, separately, expressed great regret at missing the opportunity of being amongst those of the new resistance group to await their first drop of supplies. James had set out from the house by cycle and, in the way trained, had used a circuitous route so as to check he was not being followed and navigated his way through the side streets of Charleville. Typically of a lot of French towns, Saturday evening, prior to curfew, was the time people chose to have a stroll, socialise with friends and relatives. This would assist him in being absorbed in the crowds. On Cours A. Briand, two officious Gendarmes stopped him demanding to see his papers. As they checked these, he tried to enter into good-humoured banter with them but to no avail. They questioned him on where he was going and whom he was going to see. Eventually he satisfied their enquiries, saying it was the only convenient time for Monsieur Dideret for discussions about some alteration work required at his shop.

The higgledy-piggledy, slate-covered buildings and houses of Mezieres huddled around a bend in the Meuse. Re-acquainting himself with the place, James rounded the sombre-coloured wall of the Gothic *Notre-Dame de l'Esperance* tucked in the ancient ramparts of the battered fortifications. On arriving at the house in Avenue de St-Julien and awaiting the heavy door to open, he looked cautiously back down the road. The front door opened with a creak.

'Come in? Come in quickly?' Urged Dideret.

James was instantly on his guard. Dideret seemed very nervy.

As he wheeled the cycle into the hallway he asked 'What is it? What's happened?'

Dideret showed him into the lounge. It had small windows which precluded much of the evening sunshine. James noticed cushions, papers and books were strewn over the floor.

'The Germans were here asking questions. They searched the house from top to bottom.'

'Gestapo!' James helped pick up things from the floor.

'No. An officer and soldiers of the Wehrmacht.'

Alarmed, James asked. 'Did they search neighbouring houses?'

'Yes. One or two others.'

James was aware the Germans were in the habit of randomly searching homes and businesses. It was their way of making everyone nervous about helping enemy agents, resistance groups and people being passed *via* various evasion lines. For some time now, he believed the Germans somehow knew he was in Charleville. Their searching of Dideret's home may not be a coincidence. He remained calm, attempted to reassure the other man as he spoke. 'It was probably just one of their routine searches. If it hadn't been, the Gestapo would almost certainly have been present.' The Chandler seemed more reassured. 'We must still go ahead tonight. Calling the mission off now could have a disastrous effect on the Group's morale. Besides, by now many of them will be on their way. When we arrive at the rendezvous with the others, we'll just have to be especially careful. Have an extra thorough check of the whole area of the drop for any indications of the Huns setting a trap.'

'I know we must still go ahead. It's just, I still remember the things that happened a few months' ago.'

James was concerned. The last thing he wanted was a leading member of the new Group being edgy and hesitant. He let his thoughts of concern pass. 'Is everything ready?'

'Yes. All loaded in the van, hidden in the boat spares.'

They left by the back door where Dideret's van was parked. First checking no one appeared to be watching they drove off down the narrow roadway. Having to use minor roads and tracks, it was almost dark by the time they reached the outskirts of the Foret de la Croix-aux-Bois. South of Mezieres - at Villers-Semeus - they had been stopped for a roadside check then, again, by a patrol near Le Chesne. Mercifully, on both occasions, the Germans were convinced by their forged documents backing up Dideret's story of taking boat spares urgently to a "German-requisitioned-craft" stranded on the River Aisne. They turned off onto a little road heading towards Falaise, close to Vouziers, and the selected drop zone. Many of those selected to meet the drop had arrived by the time the two men entered the disused factory. Others arrived in dribs and drabs during the next few minutes.

James re-briefed the group on the procedure for signalling the aircraft by torches and marking the perimeter of the drop zone; the procedures for retrieving, storing, transport and dispersal of the canisters and their contents; what to do should the Boche turn up. He spent some time answering questions from the group - all eager to ensure they performed their respective roles correctly. James was greatly heartened by the keenness and enthusiasm of the group, their pleasure that, at last, they were being given the opportunity to do something to throw the invaders out of their country.

'Because of operational reasons, the drop has been delayed by 1 hour' announced James after the questions ceased. A general moan of disappointment echoed around the otherwise empty building. He explained briefly the sort of things which could affect an aircraft drop before saying 'However, it will be a good use of this extra time to have another check of the surrounding area. Ensure there was no sign of Boche movements or of them lurking somewhere.'

A tubby little man - whom Dideret had previously told James - had been one of the original "Castle" Group, called out 'My wife's brother owns a nearby farm. Their son was in Monthois a little earlier - the Germans have a small garrison there. He said it all seemed normal and there didn't appear to be any patrols out.'

'Let's hope it stays that way then' replied James smiling. Dideret called out some names, paired them off and gave instructions as to where each pair should check. James added 'The rest of us will wait here. The individual search parties are to be back here by 21.45.'

All but one pair had returned by the time specified. James looked at his watch impatiently and turned to Dideret. 'Where the hell are they?'

'Do not worry. I know Emile well. He's very reliable. He will be here shortly.'

'He better be. Otherwise we'll be leaving ourselves short of time to get into position.'

As soon as he finished his sentence, a breathless Emile and another man burst in. 'To be on the safe side' he gasped out. 'I thought we would check in the woods on the far side over there. It's swarming with Boche. Hugo and I were careful they didn't see us. We just raced back.'

'You both did well' said James. Emile's words had caused confusion, anxiety and noise amongst the others. James took instant command of the situation and shouted 'Silence! All keep calm. Thanks to these two we have a bit of time. Obviously, the Germans are waiting until the actual drop before springing their trap. The pick-up will have to be abandoned. Quickly as you can - without panic and in small groups - leave here, disperse and head home. Hopefully, before they realise, most of us will be gone.'

Instantly, Dideret marshalled the dispersal. Within a minute, a motley collection of vehicles and bikes began to exit the factory yard before the waiting Germans realised anything was happening. Suddenly, searchlights were switched on in the woods, their strong beams illuminating the wasteland and the factory. Machine guns opened up a deadly fire. As James and Dideret headed for the van, James saw raking gunfire cut down a retreating cyclist - a friend stopping in his own retreat to see what he could do for him. Dideret sped over in the van to see if the downed man was dead or injured. James and the other cyclist put the hapless individual into the back. After throwing his own cycle in the back of the van, the uninjured man clambered in as it screeched out of the yard. By now, jeeps and trucks were tearing across the wasteland in hot pursuit. The gunfire was now ceaseless. Dideret crashed through the fence of a field opposite the factory. James and the other man hung on for dear life as the van jolted and jumped crazily over the uneven ground of the field.

'I know the way to some back lanes' shouted Dideret as he drove furiously.

Above the noise of the van, from the skies, could be heard the distant throb of a Whitley bomber with its cargo of supplies. The aircraft's pilot searching the darkness below in vain for torch-light signals.

After a while they emerged onto a farm track. Apart from worrying about the extent of casualties the team had sustained, James's main concern was if some of them had been taken prisoner. Under interrogation they may well talk and, all that had been achieved since he had been in Charleville would be wasted. He hoped they all would make it safely back to their homes unscathed.

'I hope to God they all got away' said James.

The man in the back of the van spoke. 'Norbert and

I were two of the last to get away. I didn't see anyone else fall.'

After putting another few miles between themselves and the pursuers, Dideret stopped the van next to a little country cemetery. James climbed into the back where Norbert lay.

'How is he?' He asked the man hunched over him.

'I have managed to slow the bleeding. He keeps drifting in and out of consciousness. Keeps murmuring his wife's name.'

'Bullets in his leg and shoulder' observed James as he examined the casualty by the light of his torch. 'This will be a job for Dr Fouquet. We must get him back as soon as we can.'

As he drove off, Dideret demanded 'How the hell did the Germans know we would be there?'

'I wonder' replied James thoughtfully. 'Thank goodness Emile was thorough in his search. By now we could all be dead or facing interrogation by the Gestapo. At least it happened before the aircraft dropped the supplies.'

'When do you think another drop can be attempted?'

'One thing is certain. We won't be able to use that drop zone for a while. If ever. The RAF will not be happy either about making a wasted journey.'

As they continued on their way James's head was full of his own theories about how the Germans had known their plans. He was determined that as soon as they got back he would investigate and discover who had told them. By using very minor roads and farm tracks they managed to avoid road blocks or checks. The circuitous route added considerably to the journey time back to Charleville and it was the early hours of the morning before they reached the outskirts of the town. Because of the night-time curfew it would have been foolhardy to attempt to drive into Charleville. They had pre-planned to park the vehicle in the yard of a Mill well outside the town. The location also gave James the earliest opportunity to transmit to England as to what had happened. But, after parking the van, they now had the added problem of getting Norbert medical attention. If James had been alone, he knew he would have taken the distressing decision to finish off Norbert, rather than chance being caught by the Germans with a man with gunshot wounds. However, he considered it not wise to risk shocking the fledgling resistance group by this action.

'We've got no alternative but to carry him back between us' James said. 'If we leave him here a German patrol could find him and - under questioning - well.'

It was a decision not without risks and difficulty. But, by keeping to side streets and alleyways and utilising what cover they could, the three men got Norbert back to his house another hour later.

To the two other men James said 'I don't want more people than necessary knowing whose involved with our Group. You two get off home. I'll get Norbert's wife up and get him into the house.' Then, directly to Dideret 'We must meet up later. Urgently, we need to know if everyone did get away. I will check with those of my recruits, if you can check on the others? We'll meet at 09.00 on the corner of Av. G. Gailly and Av. C. Boutet.'

'Very well.'

The two other men melted away into the darkness. James banged on Norbert's door. To him, in the darkness and stillness of the back street, the knock seemed extra loud. He peered around at the surrounding buildings - there were no signs of him having disturbed anyone. A window above opened.

'What is it? What do you want?' Called a woman's voice.

'I have Norbert with me. Quick. Let us in?' He heard

someone rushing down the stairs. The door opened to reveal a woman pulling a dressing gown round her shoulders. Seeing her injured husband she began to scream. James put his hand over her mouth, pushing her aside and levering himself and Norbert into the hallway. He kicked the door shut behind him. 'Sorry - I had to get inside...'.

'...Norbert! Norbert!' She wailed. James snapped on the light switch beside her. In the dim light he saw she was a petite, pretty young woman in her twenties. 'What's happened? What's happened?'

She continued to scream and cradled her husband in her arms.

'He's been shot. Have you somewhere for him to lay?'

She threw open a door to her left, rushed back and with James they got Norbert onto a divan. A little boy of about five rushed down the stairs screaming. 'Papa!' His screaming increased as he saw the huge blood-stain on his father's clothes.

As they went into the room, out of the corner of his eye, James saw a little toddler standing bewildered and blinking at the top of the stairs.

'Your little girl is on the stairs.'

The young woman rushed out. 'Miriam. No. Stay there. You'll fall.'

By the time she returned hugging her little girl, her son was cowering in the corner shocked and frightened and James had ripped off Norbert's clothes.

'We won't be able to get a doctor to your husband until dawn at the earliest. All we can do at the moment is to stop this bleeding and keep the wounds clean. We need sheets, clothes, anything. Plenty of hot water as well.'

22

As soon as the night curfew ended James made his way back to the Fouquet's house. Letting himself in through the back door, he was surprised to find Dr Fouquet in the kitchen.

'What happened?' Asked the Doctor anxiously. 'I thought you said you would be back at the house last night?'

'It was a shambles. The Boche were there waiting for us. It could have been a bloodbath. Apart from one casualty, somehow everyone seemed to get away. I am meeting some others later to confirm that no one was captured.'

'One casualty you say?'

'Yes. Norbert Champenois. I was with his wife through the night doing what we could for him. I promised I would get a doctor as soon as I could. He has bullet wounds in his shoulder and leg.'

'The family are patients of mine. I will go and see him straightaway.' James followed him into his surgery. Fouquet began to get his medicine bag together. 'Who the hell tipped the Boche off? This is what happened last time - we lost dozens of helpers then. Something's got to be done quickly to find out who is tipping them off. Did the drop take place?'

'Fortunately no. I had received a message earlier the drop was delayed by an hour.'

'I assume there will be no further drops arranged until we find out who is responsible for this?'

'Probably not.'

'Isobel is still asleep. Our friends in Donchery were very generous with the wine.'

'I expect they were pleased to see you. Isobel said your friend had been very ill.'

'Yes. Although it was a bit embarrassing. We were not expected until next weekend. Somehow we got our dates mixed up. He shook his head as he closed his bag. 'Now I must get round to Norbert. I hope I don't wake Isobel as I leave.'

James followed Fouquet into the hall and whispered 'I have time for a doze before I leave to meet the others.' He watched the Doctor walk down the garden path before making his way upstairs. He suddenly felt very tired.

As he slipped off his outside clothes he thought about the people, apart from the Doctor, who knew he was in Charleville. Those who had known about last night's planned drop. He must find an opportunity as soon as possible to radio England.

He had managed to rest for about an hour and was washing at the wash-stand when there was a knock on the door. After a moment it opened and Madame Fouquet entered with a steaming drink in her hand. Her dressing gown hung open revealing a flimsy negligee underneath.

'I thought you might like a hot drink?' She handed him the mug.

James was taken aback. He was more surprised when, as he sat on the bed to put his boots on, she sat beside him. She made no attempt to cover herself more and sat very close to him. She wore an attractive perfume. During the last day or so she had begun to flirt with him - not outrageously - just little things - the looks she gave him - occasions when she had brushed against him almost deliberately.

'I woke to find Rupert has gone out. It's strange he usually leaves a note for me.'

'Perhaps he's been called out to a patient?' Replied James. 'I was awoken earlier - a dog barking. I heard a knock at the door and voices outside.'

'Perhaps that's what it is then.' She moved even closer to him. 'Honestly these people. I keep telling Rupert he makes himself too available. He just laughs it off, saying it is what he's here for, to look after his patients.' Her face was now very close to his. Her eyes looked directly into his. She paused before speaking. 'You don't know who it was that called then?'

'No I don't. I didn't see anyone.'

'I will go and get your breakfast.'

'No, thank you Madame Fouquet…'.

'…Please. Call me Isobel.' She touched his arm affectionately. 'You don't want breakfast?'

'No thank you. I've promised to meet someone shortly to discuss an estimate. I will get something in a café afterwards.'

Her thighs now brushed his. She seemed reluctant to leave the room. Suddenly, she said 'I had to get up earlier - just as it was getting light. I was sure I saw you in the back garden? Perhaps you had trouble sleeping yes - needed some fresh air?'

For a moment he froze. 'As I said, a dog's barking woke me. There was a knock and I heard voices. I couldn't get back to sleep. It was a nice morning, as you said I thought I would get some fresh air.'

She smiled. 'I was worried there was something wrong. You find the room - the bed uncomfortable?'

'No Isobel, everything is fine. Thanks.'

She lingered for another moment. Almost as if she was willing him to stop her leaving.

'Well I suppose I better go and get dressed.'

Suddenly, she took James's face in her hands and kissed him generously, her tongue seeking his. She pushed him back on the bed, urging him to take her.

23

The earlier infiltration and destruction of the "Castle" Resistance Group happened just as SOE began to suspect radio transmissions between them and Charleville were being intercepted or falsified. A disastrous drop of supplies into German hands and the murder of a French Army Captain working with the Group as he was *en route* to the pick-up point for a trip back to England, confirmed SOE were being fed false information and intelligence. In the last transmission to England, there had also been something different about the signalling touch of the operator which alerted SOE to the possibility of a problem in Charleville. More alarmingly, weeks of investigation had confirmed suspicions about Jean-Louis Moreaux - an SOE operative working within their French Section.

It had just turned 22.00 hours when the SOE Officer known as "David" leant back in his chair in his Baker Street office. The rain beat heavily on the window pane behind him. There was a knock on the door.

'Come in?'

'Moreaux has been picked up in St. John's Wood' announced Major Rene Walton triumphantly as he crossed the room.

'Did he give any trouble?'

'He was asleep when they stormed in. The officers seizing him said a near-empty bottle of Brandy lay beside him.'

'Moreaux always did like a drink if he had a chance.'

'Two officers are now searching the flat from top to bottom. They'll bag-up anything of relevance for us to examine. As you instructed, Moreaux has been taken to "Building S" for interrogation.'

David shook his head almost sadly. 'Despite his occasional love of drink, Moreaux was always one of our best - thorough and disciplined. I bet he's been very careful not to leave any trace of anything - documents that could be of any use to us. It will be a real bonus if the officers can find a note of codes or some of his German contacts.' He took a file from the top of a tray on his desk, opened it and studied it deeply for a while before replacing it in his desk drawer. After conclusively slamming the drawer shut, he said 'I'll visit Building S tomorrow. When the interrogation is completed we will have to decide how to dispose of him.'

'I have something else to report' said Walton. 'Something that Moreaux had no knowledge of. We've at last received news that Edouard Estornel no longer exists.'

'Thank goodness for that. They certainly took their time about it over there.'

'I know. Apparently, our people in Beauvais experienced some local difficulties in selecting a body and placing it where the Gestapo would take an interest. They executed a known German collaborator for the purpose.'

'Let's hope they have made it convincing?'

'We're assured there will be no possibility of a physical identification.' Walton selected a cigarette and tapped its end on his silver cigarette case. 'As you're already aware, our agent adopted his new identity before arriving at the "safe house" in Charleville.'

'Excellent.' "David" got up from his chair and turned

off his desk lamp. 'I'm going to adjourn to my Club for a drink. Care to join me?'

'Well yes. Thank you.'

The two men were about to go out the door when the telephone rang.

'Damn!' David cursed. 'I suppose I better answer that.' He snatched up the receiver. 'Yes, speaking. I see. Thank you for letting me know - that's marvellous news. Excellent. Yes. I'll meet you at Building S tomorrow at 08.00 hours.' He replaced the receiver and with a broad smile said 'We now have good reason to celebrate with a drink. That was one of the officers searching Moreaux's flat. Hidden behind a panel they've found a paper, complete with a code and de-coding guide. And of a code style known to be used by the Gestapo. At last we may now have a chance to get back at the Gestapo by playing them at their own game. Start feeding them false intelligence.'

****

Two days after the near-disastrous drop at Vouziers, the RAF managed to lay on another drop. For this drop of supplies, an area of heathland near Biermes had been selected. Deliberately, James had personally selected the bare minimum of helpers to receive the drop. He had also gone to extraordinary lengths to preclude certain members of the Group from knowing anything whatsoever about it or where the supplies were to be hidden. The actual drop, pick-up and dispersal of the weapons and supplies went completely undetected by the Germans. He and the Group felt a great triumph and the effect on morale was tremendous. The total success of the drop also helped him to whittle down his list of suspected traitors.

In the days after this drop - amidst the seclusion of the wilderness, forests and slopes of the Ardennes - James continued to organise some training sessions in weaponry and the preparation and placing of explosives. Certain members of the Group, especially selected by him, were trained to function competently as team leaders. By the time these sessions were completed, James felt confident any specific sabotage requests from England or, any opportunistic objective for disrupting the German war machine in the area, could be mounted with a significant degree of success. All the new Group could do now was wait for an opportunity to arise to put what had been learnt into practice.

It was still James's top priority to detect and eliminate the person or persons who had infiltrated the "Castle" Group **and** the new Group as evidenced by the aborted Vouziers drop. A person or persons were still feeding information to the Germans. He was positive it was the same individual or individuals. His process of detection was assisted some days later by one bit of extreme good fortune. James had happened to be at a farm near Nouzonville, repairing a barn for a young widow struggling to keep the family farm going after her husband's death. Her youngest son, at play on the farm, had returned to the house hurriedly saying a car had left the nearby road and crashed down an embankment into a wooded valley. James and the widow raced to the scene of the accident, to see what they could do. With some difficulty, James clambered down the valley side and reached the car now wedged against a tree. The driver was dead. James recognised him instantly as the man leaving the Gent's outfitters on Boulevard Gambetta with the uniformed SS Officer. Searching through the man's scattered belongings, James couldn't believe his luck when he found a notebook containing contact details of Gestapo officials and collaborators in the Charleville area. These details would be like gold-dust. On one page one name shocked him especially and he knew instantly what he had to do. James gathered up some other papers which would be useful in the future and bundled them in his pocket together with the notebook. He thought quickly. The road above the valley was remote. He had no idea where the car had travelled from but, almost certainly, it was heading back to Charleville. Where the car rested now was secluded from view but, if it was further down in the valley bottom, it would be even harder to spot from the road above and extend the time before it was discovered after its occupant was posted missing. This could give him extra time to work on the information he had found.

'I'm going to try and get the driver out' he shouted up to the waiting woman and boy, doubting they were able to see him clearly.

Picking up the axe and crowbar he had brought from the farm, James started working on the bough of the tree wedging the car. After working furiously for a while the bough gave way. He threw aside his tools and with his shoulder and hands and, no small muscular effort, levered the car over a small rock which still held it. There was a tearing of metal, a crack of timber and the car hurtled down the steep valley side with a crashing and tumbling of vegetation and boulders.

'What's happened?' Screamed the woman waiting above.

'I was just about to get him out' he called back in feigned horror.

There was a loud thump and explosion many feet below him. James struggled back up to the roadside. The woman and her son were cuddling each other in shock.

Again, faking sorrow, he said 'By the time I got to him he was dead. I was just trying to get his body out of the car when - suddenly - it went over the edge.'

'But what are we to do? I have no way of letting anyone know what has happened' she sobbed out.

'Don't worry. I will come back to the house with you. Then go and report the accident to a Gendarme. I have to go back to Charleville anyway to pick up some more materials for the barn.' The woman was still inconsolable. 'It was a dreadful accident Madame but please try and understand, there was nothing else we could have done to help the poor man.'

On returning to Charleville, James went straight to the Group's forger with a sample of stationery he had found amongst the car driver's scattered belongings. This would be priceless for the forger for future use in any plans the Group may have.

It was mid-morning the next day and James was working in his room at the Fouquet's. He was putting the finishing touches to his diagram of the abandoned farm at St-Menges - a few miles south-east of Charleville, ideal for the storage of the supplies dropped at Biermes. The farm was also ideal as an assembly point for the members of the Resistance Group. James checked his diagram again, ensuring the pig-sties, the old farmhouse and its other out-buildings were clearly marked and depicted; that the routes to and from the farm were clearly marked. Satisfied with his handy-work, James put the diagram to one side. On another sheet of paper he wrote down the details of the planned Resistance attack to destroy the railway bridge and so sever the main rail link into Charleville which the Germans relied on to bring in equipment and fuel. Picking up the leather-bound book on the table - the writings of the Philosopher Pascal - he turned the spine towards him. Days previously he had re-bound the volume, increasing the space between the spine and the stitched pages, enabling a larger gap wherein a couple of carefully folded sheets of paper could be concealed and later extricated by tweezers. With the care of a surgeon, he squeezed the spine for easier access and fed the tightly folded two sheets of paper down between the spine and the pages.

There was the sound of footsteps on the landing. Isobel Fouquet was bringing in his coffee. He noticed there were two cups on the tray.

'I will put this on the table?'

'Please. Thank you Isobel.'

She saw his suitcase on the settee. 'You are getting ready to leave already?' She asked with surprise. He took her into his arms and they kissed. 'But you said you didn't have to go to Reims until tomorrow.'

'Someone in Sedan contacted me. They need a job done urgently. I'll travel directly to Reims from Sedan.'

'When will you be returning?'

He sat in the chair drinking his coffee. She stood behind him, her arms around his shoulders. She began to run her fingers through his hair and caress his neck and throat.

'In about four days.'

Disappointedly she said 'Oh! And Rupert is due to be away for two days at his medical meeting. It would have been just the two of us here. I so dislike being by myself in this house.'

She kissed the side of his face and began to undo his shirt.

He stopped her gently. 'No Isobel. I can't now - I have to go - I'm sorry.' He got up and kissed her. 'I will be back soon.'

'Very well. Hurry back won't you? Please?'

'I promise.' He returned the book to the bookshelf, picked up his suitcase and kissed her again. 'Isobel I don't know the area around Sedan very well. Do you think it would be best to use the road which passes St-Menges?'

She paused and thought for a moment. 'Yes definitely. Yes that would be the best route.'

'Thanks.' He moved towards the door. 'Oh! I nearly forgot.' He rushed back to the table to get his raincoat folded over the back of a chair. As he did so an envelope dropped out of an inside pocket and landed, unnoticed by him, under the table. 'I think I may well need this. The forecast is for some heavy rain.' He rushed back to the doorway and blew her a kiss. 'See you in a few days.'

He was running down the stairs by the time Isobel saw the old envelope laying on the floor. Picking it up she noticed it had long been opened and contained a settled invoice. It was headed at the top "Edouard Estornel - Building and Decorating" with an address in Beauvais. She looked long and hard at the paper in her hand. She crossed to the bookshelf where James had replaced the leather-bound volume of Pascal's writings. She took the book out and studied it carefully. Strange, it was not the type of work she imagined her lodger would be interested in.

****

Two days later a young teenager was hidden in a wood, looking through his binoculars at a disused farm near St-Menges. He saw a group of German soldiers and some men in civvies drive into the old farmyard and make straight for a group of structures which looked like pig-sties.

24

Isobel Fouquet had been in bed for an hour but, try as she might, she had found it hard to get to sleep. Her head was full of so many thoughts. Over and over turned the thoughts in her mind. For one, she never liked being alone at night in this big rambling house. It had so many rooms and passages and, being old, it was prone to lots of unexplained creaks and noises. Secondly, the house, also serving as her husband's surgery, had been the target for break-ins on several occasions in the past - the intruders after drugs, medicaments and money. Also, this time tomorrow night, Rupert would be back in this bed doing his best to satisfy her, his sexual efforts more often than not ending in frustration for both of them. Still, when she had accepted his proposal of marriage three years ago she knew, with the age difference between them, how her appetite for sexual satisfaction might - in future years - not be matched by her husband's lack of vigour. She also thought back to the heavy petting session a few days ago with their lodger. This had thrilled her so, promised much before he had resisted when she had wanted to take it further. Also, how disappointed she had been when he announced suddenly he had to go to Reims. Isobel had been so sure, during the days Rupert was away, she could have finally enticed her handsome lodger to succumb to her desire for him - to fully enjoy her body and her to enjoy his. Now, as a result of her meeting with someone earlier, she knew almost certainly she would not see him ever again. Isobel also knew that as the result of that earlier meeting it would help lead eventually to the greater good of Charleville and France in general.

As she turned in her bed for the umpteenth time, outside her house a man silently cut the telephone line. The figure was dressed from head to foot in dark clothing and a balaclava. Stealthily he made his way to the back of the house. Carefully he taped the window, skilfully cut the glass before removing a portion of the pane - enough to allow him to slip his hand in and unlock the window. Silently, after leaning the cut glass against the wall, he climbed into the kitchen.

Pausing first, listening for any sound from upstairs, he made his way across the kitchen, into the hallway. He crept towards the front door to ensure it was locked from the inside and saw the key was hanging on its hook on the dresser. After putting down the long-handled heavy hammer from Fouquet's shed and the jemmy he had brought with him, he began to ascend the stairs.

Isobel heard a creak on the staircase. It was not the usual creaking sound she was used to, it was longer - as though there was a weight on it - the weight of a foot perhaps. She froze with fear. There was someone coming up the stairs. She started to call out - thought better of it. She snapped on her lamp and reached for the telephone. Her trembling fingers tried to dial - silence - the line was dead. A dark figure was in the doorway. She started to scream and grabbed a brass candlestick. The man was upon her preventing the blow to his head. She felt his breath on her face. The man was powerful and fit. They fell to the floor, his hands like a grip of steel bent her arm back. Her wrist now limp her weapon fell to one side. The man now lifted her and propelled her onto the bed and his weight was upon her. Isobel was summoning all her strength as she fought and struggled - she tried to kick out. It was all to no avail, he was too strong. Her nightdress fell from her shoulders. She felt him snatch the pillow at her side. Fighting for her life she tried to lever his body off her with her thighs and knees. It all went dark as the pillow was pressed hard against her face as she was smothered. The man felt her struggles lessen, growing weaker and weaker, heard her fighting to breathe. At last she was still and lifeless. Slowly he lifted the pillow - lifted himself off her body. Her eyes were wide open, her face contorted. Isobel was dead. Unhurried, the man stood up. For a moment he stared at her laying there like a broken doll. She had been stronger than he anticipated.

Unhurriedly, methodically, the man searched the room. All the time he was careful to replace things as he found them. At last, in a packet behind a panel at the back of Isobel's wardrobe, he found what he was looking for. Calmly he left the room and descended the stairs.

After unlocking the front door from the inside, the man turned towards the room Fouquet used as his surgery. The man knew he had to act quickly. The Fouquet's house stood by itself on the road, the nearest neighbours were around the corner in another road and, possibly, wouldn't hear any disturbance at the front of the house but he would have to be quick and before the next scheduled German patrol was due. He would have to take a chance. He picked up the hammer and smashed open the surgery door. He proceeded to ransack the room, smashing open storage and filing cabinets. Swiftly he moved out of the surgery, opened the front door and started to work on it and its surround with the jemmy hoping the noise didn't disturb the neighbours. After satisfying himself the damage looked convincing the man discarded the jemmy in the garden, re-entered the hallway - picking up the hammer as he did so - and locked the smashed front door before replacing the key on the hook. He made for the kitchen to leave by whence he entered.

Outside in the garden he was careful to wipe the hammer clean of splinters and paintwork from the surgery door before replacing it where he had found it in the shed. Picking up the pane of glass so carefully removed before he now peeled off the masking tape, then threw the pane through the empty frame so it smashed into pieces on the granite worktop inside. A dog in a nearby kennel began barking. For a moment the man froze. Once satisfied the dog's bark had been ignored by its owner he melted away into the darkness and shadows.

Sitting in the grounds man's hut in a nearby park James looked through the contents of the packet he had found in Isobel's wardrobe: signalling code books; guides to code-breaking; Gestapo contacts; names and addresses of local people - some of whom James knew were previous members of the "Castle" circuit - and their known contacts; the plans of the old farm at St-Menges; the false plans of a Resistance attack on the railway bridge, he had deliberately hidden in the book of Pascal's writings. James's suspicions about Isobel had all started when he saw her leave the shop on Boulevard Gambetta, fully confirmed when he saw her name in the notebook belonging to the driver of the crashed car near Nouzonville.

James allowed himself a smile at the prospect of the Germans laying a trap for the Resistance at the railway bridge, whilst the Group attacked the railway sidings and warehouses a few miles further down the line. It also gave him great satisfaction to know, by now, the Gestapo would be heavily involved in tracking down the British Agent they still believed was active in Beauvais and Charleville - a certain

"Edouard Estornel". Isobel couldn't have believed her luck when she saw Estornel's address on the invoice James had deliberately dropped out of his raincoat! On his transmitter he started to signal London: 'The main infiltrator of the "Castle" Group eliminated'.

After he hid the transmitter again and left the park, James now focused his full concentration on the Group's attack on the railway sidings and warehouses scheduled for later today.

25

Karl Neumann the local Gestapo Chief Intelligence Officer sat behind his desk.

'There is still no news of Berger?' He asked his assistant sitting opposite.

'No, not a thing. According to our office in Charleroi he left there as arranged. There's been no sign of him or any communication since then. We have a team searching, making enquiries between Belgium and here.'

Although Neumann didn't show it he was growing concerned. During the last few weeks there had been isolated incidents across France of Gestapo staff being captured by local Resistance Groups despite the revenge they knew would be exacted on their fellow compatriots. Before execution, Gestapo staff had been tortured, in some cases information and intelligence had been obtained by the Resistance. Damn the Resistance - they were the bane of his life. Besides, as Neumann saw it, gaining information under torture was the sole province and speciality of the Gestapo and no one else.

'Damn Berger! He's always been a maverick - done things his own way.' He laughed. 'Knowing him he has probably found himself some country peasant girl and is shafting her silly.' He lit yet another cigarette and exhaled a large cloud of smoke towards the ceiling. 'How long did you say you and Bremer's troops were at the farm at St-Menges?'

'Over three hours.'

'And not a single person showed up' said Neumann thoughtfully. 'And nothing hidden in the pigsties as shown on that plan - in the other outbuildings - anywhere?'

'Nothing whatsoever.'

'My source was so right about the drop of supplies at Vouziers for the Resistance. Has been correct as well with other information supplied. I will investigate what went wrong this time, ensure my informant's loyalties are not wavering or, has not been found out.' He thumped the desk angrily with his fist. 'Also, when we were all waiting by that damned railway bridge expecting an attack by the Resistance. What happens - the French bastards attack the sidings miles away and destroy weeks of supplies in the warehouse. Berlin is angry. Very angry. Even our source in London indicated an attack on that bridge was imminent.'

'The damned Resistance have many spies working for them Herr Neumann. No matter what we do to deter them, they're everywhere - in the towns - in the country.'

Neumann erupted angrily. 'I do not need you to tell me that!' He paused. 'Perhaps then, it's time we gave the locals another reminder they will not beat us' he added chillingly. The clock he had brought with him from his home near the Black Forest chimed the hour melodically. 'I've been cooped up for hours in this office. Come Fritz. Let us take a walk in the town and take some refreshment. Perhaps we might be able to pick up some clues as to those behind all this.'

His colleague hesitated before speaking. 'I presume our informant in London is still secure?'

Neumann brushed the suggestion aside arrogantly. 'Of course. Moreaux is far too clever to be caught.'

Before they left the room Neumann picked up the

telephone and ordered men to the nursing home around the corner. He ordered the man on the other end of the line to pick ten patients at random and shoot them as a reprisal for the attack on the railway siding.

The two men crossed Place Ducale towards the café they frequented. Neumann despised the café's slimy little proprietor and his wife with her horse-like features and build. However, now and again they had been useful to him and his team, passing on occasional little snippets of information about the pro-resistance activities of their fellow compatriots. They were nearing Dr Fouquet's house and saw a Gendarme entering the premises and another standing outside, and recognised a car parked outside as a Gestapo staff car.

'What's happened?' Neumann demanded of the Gendarme standing outside.

'There has been a death. One of your staff has just arrived.'

The Gendarme hardly finished speaking as Neumann pushed his way past him. With Fritz following close at his heels he entered the hallway where Spiegel, newly-arrived on his staff from Berlin, was talking to a French detective.

Spiegel greeted his superior and, before the detective could speak, added 'There's a female's body upstairs.'

'And the body is?'

'Madame Fouquet. The Doctor's wife.'

'Yes. Yes I know she was the Doctor's wife' snapped Neumann impatiently. Frostily he asked the detective 'Who found the body?'

'The housekeeper. Dr Fouquet returned home shortly after. He had been away at a meeting.' He nodded his head toward the sitting room. 'The pair of them are in there talking to one of my Gendarmes.'

Neumann crossed to the open doorway, cursorily

observed the two of them comforting each other. A Gendarme stood before them making some notes. Neumann turned on his heels and began to stride up the stairs. Angrily but, unable to stop him, the detective protested and chased after him.

'But you can't. We are…'.

Completely ignoring the detective's protests, Neumann swept along the landing and into the Fouquet's bedroom. Isobel still lay on the bed where she died, her nightdress disarranged, the top half of her body bare.

'Any idea how and when she died?' Neumann demanded.

Reluctantly the detective answered. 'Sometime late last night and it was definitely murder.' He pointed to the crumpled pillow beside her head. 'We are certain she was suffocated with that pillow. It strikes us as strange there are no other marks of violence on the top half of her body, no signs of bruising or finger pressure points on her neck and throat area. We're not sure yet whether she was raped.'

'Do you have any theories as to another motive?'

The detective despised the Germans and the Gestapo in particular. Detested the way the Gestapo always wanted to interfere with French Police matters, resented being forced to have to work with them. However, he knew by reputation what Neumann was like, that once he had shown some interest in a case the local Police were working on it would be futile not to co-operate with him. Grudgingly, he answered.

'We believe Madame Fouquet disturbed an intruder looking for drugs or money. This house is also used as a surgery and has been targeted before for the same reason.'

'So that is your theory' replied Neumann in a dismissive and patronising tone.

Neumann stood silently, observing the candlestick on

the floor, the dishevelled bed, the signs of a violent struggle. His eyes fell on the dead woman on the bed, took in the contours of her naked breasts. Isobel's body, even in death, remained beautiful. He thought of the times they had spent together, the times he had been inside that gorgeous body. At least he now knew why her telephone line had been unobtainable last night. Then, more clinically, he considered the many valuable pieces of information on Resistance activities she had fed him and, now, what would be the ramifications for the Gestapo's work in Charleville now such a reliable source of information had been stopped? He walked out of the room, making his way downstairs to join Fritz and Spiegel.

He had demanded of the Gendarme standing outside the front door that the jemmy found in the garden be handed over to him and his trained "Intelligence" eyes studied this and the damage to the front door. He knew Isobel was always fastidious about locking the front door. He checked - yes the key was hanging on its hook which suggested the front door had been forced open from outside to gain entry. Somehow though, Neumann's instinct was that this had not been the case. He turned his attention to the smashed surgery door and surveyed the extent of the ransacking but had no idea yet, what if anything, had been stolen.

The detective was standing behind him, fuming silently. Neumann turned to face him, saying 'I will need a list of what has been stolen by the end of the day?' It was not a question but a command.

Neumann then examined inside the kitchen and around outside. There had been no shards of glass or any evidence of someone being outside the kitchen. Back inside the kitchen again, he picked up a piece of window glass and looked at it carefully. He was sure the window pane had been taped before it was taken out. The intruder, whoever it was, when entering, had been extremely careful not to have made a noise. But then, why did the intruder not worry too much about noise whilst smashing in the front door and ransacking the surgery? Could it have been two separate incidents? To him, the whole thing no matter what conclusions the French police may come to, indicated it was not a common or desperate crook looking for drugs or money but a professional job. But a professional job to achieve what? His instincts told him this had been the work of the Agent he was now sure was in Charleville and had broken in to silence Isobel for ever. Neumann was going to make it his main business to track this Agent down.

Turning to the detective he ordered 'A list of what has been stolen by the end of the day and I will expect your full report on this incident soon after.' He ignored the expression of anger on the detective's face. 'I understand the Doctor and his wife recently took in a lodger. I also want to see your notes after you have questioned him and Dr Fouquet. Is that understood?'

It wasn't that Neumann suspected the Doctor was implicated with the Resistance. He was confident Isobel would have told him if he had been. Besides, there had been occasions when Fouquet himself had passed on bits and pieces of valuable information. It was a top priority of his now to investigate Isobel's theory about their lodger's presence in Charleville.

He turned to his two staff 'Come you two. We will leave the Gendarmes to continue their work.' Once outside he asked Spiegel 'Spiegel I want you to contact Beauvais. I want to know everything about an Edouard Estornel?'

26

'Thank you for letting me know.'

Neumann replaced the receiver. He sat behind his desk staring at the telephone in disbelief. Absolutely dumbfounded by what his opposite number in Beauvais had just told him, for one of the few times in his life he was at a loss as to what to do. On the day of Isobel's murder, a man's body had been found laying unrecognisable on the main rail line to Beauvais. There was evidence the man had been in the process of sabotaging the track. The ID papers found, parts of letters and photographs of a woman and child indicated the body was that of an Edouard Estornel. All the information collected from the scene in Beauvais and, what was left of the body, matched up with the subsequent Gestapo checks. Investigations had confirmed Estornel had lost his wife and child in a boating accident some years previously. When questioned, the landlord of his flat and fellow tenants, confirmed that although they hadn't seen him for some while - assuming he was away working - the ID material recovered was indeed that of the Edouard Estornel they knew. Moreaux in England had also confirmed Edouard Estornel was the identity the agent was using. Isobel had also said she was positive their new lodger was Estornel, the agent Neumann was seeking.

The other telephone on his desk jangled. He answered it 'Neumann.'

The call was to inform him his car was waiting downstairs. After summoning Spiegel, the two men left the building.

Although the streets were crowded with market-day vehicles and people, their Staff Car drew up outside the Fouquet's house within a few minutes. Whilst waiting for the front door to open, Neumann cast his practised eye over the property and its boundaries, checking whether there were any features warranting further investigation. The door was opened by the elderly woman dressed in black he saw the other day sharing her grief and shock with the doctor. The two men strode over the threshold without speaking to her or acknowledging her presence. Fouquet was sitting in the lounge with another man. Neumann noted the obvious unease of the Doctor as they entered the room. He motioned the other man menacingly to remain where he was.

'Dr Fouquet we are from Gestapo headquarters in Charleville' announced Neumann with uncharacteristic pleasantness.

'I know who you are' replied Fouquet in an unwelcoming tone. 'You're intruding on my grief.'

Neumann ignored this. 'Yes I realise you've lost your wife. Sorry.' He said the last word without sincerity. 'However, there are one or two things connected with her death I wish to clarify.'

'The local police are dealing with the investigation' replied Fouquet dismissively.

'Quite so.' Then, with a hint of threat 'I will remind you Doctor, we are the occupying authority in Charleville. You would be wise to co-operate with me. Is that understood?'

'Perfectly' replied Fouquet, still with a hint of bitterness, as he slumped back in his chair.

'Do you know of anyone who would have a motive for killing your wife?'

'The Police are working on the theory it was someone who broke in looking for cash or drugs and, perhaps, Isobel disturbed them. The records at the Gendarmerie will show the house has been burgled on previous occasions for the same reason.'

'But do you not think it strange that if your wife disturbed them, why her body was found in your bedroom?'

Fouquet shrugged his shoulders slightly. 'Perhaps the intruder - the murderer chased her back upstairs.'

'I see.' Neumann took a few steps around the room, observing various furnishings and pictures.

'The other day, after the Police had arrived, myself and other colleagues visited the house. I noticed one or two things suggesting it may not have been a casual crook chancing his arm. The glass in the kitchen window - through which the intruder entered - may not have been smashed initially but smashed after entry. Do you think Doctor this would be the action of a casual crook? And, why should he go to so much trouble to be quiet then go on to make such a noisy disturbance of smashing in the front door and surgery door and all the noisy ransacking of the surgery?'

'Surely, the Gendarmes would have observed these same things? The front door was locked as usual from the inside, its key on the hook as usual. The murderer simply battered it open.'

'Perhaps. Perhaps. However, I think the door was locked after it had been forced open.'

'What things were stolen?' Asked Spiegel, to check the answer would agree with what the Police had told them.

'Some medical instruments. Petty cash. A cup I won for Boulle. The Gendarmerie has all the details.' Then, impatiently 'Why are you asking all these questions?'

'We think break-in was staged for some other reason.'

'What other reason - what are you…?'

'…We believe your wife was involved with the Resistance in some way' said Neumann. 'Perhaps for some reason there had been some disagreement, some argument amongst these friends of hers.'

'Isobel! Why that's impossible! Isobel involved with the Resistance - the idea is ridiculous. Neither she or myself would have anything to do with them. We both have - had too much to lose.'

'I'm very glad to hear that. You know how we view collaboration with the Resistance. The penalties for doing so.'

'I'm a Doctor for God's sake. The people of Charleville need me now more than anything.'

Uninvited, Neumann sat himself in a chair opposite Fouquet. 'Remind me Doctor? You were away on the night of your wife's death?'

'Yes. At a medical meeting in Paris.'

'Did you and your wife speak at all by telephone in the evening before she died?'

'No. Throughout the whole duration of the meeting the telephones in Paris were not working.'

'We understand that recently you and your wife took in a lodger?'

'Yes. It is something we have done for several years now.' He gestured expansively with his arms. 'This is a big house to run. It helps with the costs.' He indicated James sitting in the chair to his right. 'This is that lodger.'

Neumann fixed James in a frosty, penetrating stare. 'Your name is?'

'Jean-Paul Guyot.'

Neumann and Spiegel exchanged a glance. 'You were in Charleville at the time of Madame Fouquet's death?'

'No I was in Reims. I travelled there during the afternoon prior to her murder. I finished my business there sooner than I expected, but I was still in Reims until two days after. I learnt of Madame Fouquet's tragic death on my return.'

'Show us your papers?' Demanded Spiegel sharply. James held them out in front of him. Spiegel snatched them. 'I see from these you come from Troyes?'

'Yes.'

Neumann seized on this. 'Ah Troyes! I know it well. Is that delightful little hotel - the Chamois - still there next to the church? I remember it well. Such a lovely setting.'

James wasn't going to fall into the trap. He knew his cover story too well. 'Yes it is a lovely setting - lovely hotel. But it is not next to the church, it's opposite the school about a kilometre away.'

There was just a flicker in Neumann's expression. James knew the man was disappointed with his reply.

Neumann laughed. 'Of course. I must have got confused. It is a while since I was there.'

Spiegel was still studying James's ID papers closely. He compared the photographs on them with the man opposite him several times. 'How did you get that injury to your eye?'

Without a pause James answered. 'Two years ago. An accident whilst I was working on a lathe.'

'It must make it difficult for your work. When you need to take measurements and things like that?'

'Yes it can prove difficult sometimes. However, I've got used to it. It's the same with this leg I injured some years back.'

Spiegel studied the documents for a while longer before nodding to Neumann they appeared to be in order. He more or less threw the papers back at James.

'Can you prove you were in Reims on the night of

Madame Fouquet's death?' Neumann was confident the question would defy a satisfactory explanation.

'I'm not sure - let me think.' James paused and, rather embarrassed, continued. 'Of course.' He looked sheepish. 'Yes, I'm afraid to say I spent the night in the cell in the Gendarmerie on Rue. de Talleyrand.' The other three men threw a questioning glance in his direction. 'I am ashamed to say I got rather drunk. I was arrested.' He began to fumble in his jacket pocket and retrieved a crumpled piece of paper. 'Yes. Here it is. This was my written caution.'

Neumann looked at it and very deflated handed it to his assistant. 'Spiegel. Use the telephone in the surgery to check this.'

'How long have you been lodging here?'

'Just about six weeks.'

'How did you learn of the room vacancy here with Dr Fouquet and his wife?'

James answered and then had to answer a whole series of questions: about where he had been working in and around Charleville; about his time in Reims and how he had travelled there. The Gestapo Officer seemed satisfied with his answers. Spiegel returned looking somewhat disappointed. James watched as Spiegel whispered something in Neumann's ear.

Looking at James and Fouquet, Neumann said 'That is all for now. We will need to come back again.' He and Spiegel turned towards the door. 'We will show ourselves out.'

Through the window, Fouquet watched the two men get into their car. He turned to James. 'Who on earth in our Group would want to murder Isobel? She had always been one of the most brave and loyal of our couriers. The last thing she would do, either carelessly or deliberately, is to help the Boche in any way.' He began to cry. 'No. All I want is the Police to find the animal who broke in here and murdered my Isobel. Now, if you will excuse me, I would like to be alone for a while.'

'Of course.'

Back in his room James thought of the increasing network of Resistance groups across France now working to defeat the Germans. Inspector Roux of the Reims Police had long been a trusted supporter of the local Reims Resistance Group and had been delighted to give James his alibi for the time of Isobel's removal. After a few moments he set about planning the transfer of equipment, weapons and explosives from their temporary place of concealment to a more permanent, safer place of storage.

During the journey back to their office, Neumann struggled to clarify his thoughts. He had first met Isobel in the mid 1930's, when they had both been studying in Berlin. Their romance had begun shortly after they first met. Although she was French, Isobel and he had attended many of the mass rallies Hitler held at that time. And, like himself, Isobel had been swept along with Hitler's oratory as he expounded his theories and dreams of a different type of society and shared Neumann's fervour for Hitler's ideas. With her studies completed, Isobel had returned to France and, with his own growing involvement and commitment with the Nazi Party, the months and years had rolled on without them seeing each other and their romance had waned. Isobel had met Fouquet at the hospital where they both worked and subsequently married. Two years ago, as a rising star in the Gestapo, Neumann had been posted to Charleville and by accident they met each other again. It wasn't long after this meeting, their romance re-kindled and he discovered Isobel still held many of the views they had shared in Berlin. She began to give him little snippets of information on the activities of the then burgeoning local Resistance Group. In no time at all, Isobel had become one of his most trusted, reliable sources of information in this regard. It was her information in the main which had enabled him and his fellow Gestapo Officers to destroy the "Castle" Resistance Group.

Two facts really troubled Neumann. In the last eighteen months or so, Isobel had been so reliable and accurate with the information she had given him. How could she have got the identity of her lodger so wrong? Also, was it Edouard Estornel - Moreaux their agent in England had told them about - found lying dead by the railway track in Beauvais?

One thing was certain. Neumann knew somewhere in Charleville there was an English agent on the loose. He would make it his business to hunt him or her down no matter who had to be tortured or executed for him to do so.

Later on in the day as James made his way to Dideret's shop, he dwelt deeply on the grief he had brought upon his host Dr Fouquet. He hoped against hope Rupert would never find out why Isobel was killed and who it was that killed her.

27

'Bombs gone' called Doug Harvey.

Colin held the course steady whilst the all-important photograph was taken. 'Well done Doug. Now let's get the hell out of here.'

Colin closed the bomb doors and swung Lancaster "F" for Freddie to port and away from Koblenz. As the bomber curved steeply away he could see all was ablaze beneath them. Great mushrooms of flame sprouted from the overall glare of orange as more bombs fed the inferno. All of a sudden they were in the midst of bedlam and hell. Heavy flak bursts on their port side illuminated the sky all around them. Fragments of shrapnel showered and clattered down on the wings and fuselage, the noise clearly audible above the sound of the engines, only lessening as Colin put full power on and threw the Lancaster into a violent evasive manoeuvre. The beam of a searchlight lit up the rear half of the aircraft and threads of ack-ack shells curved up towards them. Michael, the wireless operator, held onto his desk tightly to stay in his seat as the Lancaster twisted and turned violently. He knew this is what one got for being towards the back of the bomber stream, late over the target and, the German ack-ack crews down below well and truly woken up and obtaining good fixes on the aircraft above them.

Colin tried yet more violent evasive tactics. Great clouds

of flak surrounded them - anti-aircraft shells dazzled them. The tortured scream of the four Merlins was deafening, the whole aircraft shook and vibrated as he tried yet another violent manoeuvre. "Ginger" ducked instinctively as shells slammed into the fuselage just to his right. Colin fought to keep control of the aircraft. Suddenly they were in thick cloud. The Lancaster rolled, twisted and turned. With nothing but cloud surrounding them Colin couldn't orientate himself. It was frightening. Sheer panic welled within him. Doug in the bomb-aimer's position was thrown backwards and cracked his head on the glycol tank behind with a sickening thud. Try as he might he couldn't get up - he was pinned down by the "G" force, its effects stretching and twisting the skin on his face and cheeks.

Between them Colin and "Ginger" fought with all their strength to regain control. "F" for Freddie was now in a steep banked turn. The Lancaster rolled, spun crazily and plunged like a stone out of control. Ben the navigator, whom amongst all the crew, had the strongest of stomachs, vomited explosively all over his desk. Danny, in his mid-upper turret, hung "bat-like" from his strapped seat, was choking on his own vomit. He felt a warm vomit stream trickle down his face into his goggles and down his forehead into his hair.

Still the Lancaster plunged downwards. Seven voices shouted and screamed in confused unison over the intercom.

Sweat streamed down Colin's face, the fight with the controls causing every muscle and nerve in his body to ache and hurt. Slowly, gradually, "F" for Freddie was responding - he was regaining control. Using the artificial horizon dial, Colin recovered his orientation. Gently, gingerly, he climbed the Lancaster to 19,000 feet. His flight engineer began resetting controls, the familiar constant purr of the engines began to return.

'My God! That was close!' Exclaimed Colin turning to his flight engineer.

'Well done skipper. And thank you.'

Ben, a badly-lapsed Catholic, crossed himself thankfully and started to wipe the vomit from his desk and navigational implements.

Little isolated bursts of flak continued to balloon, occasional streaks of shells streamed up harmlessly in their vicinity but they were through the worst.

'Apologies for that everyone' called Colin over the intercom. 'Everyone okay? Report damage please?'

'Bloody draughty around here' called Michael. 'Shell holes in the fuselage beside me. Lines and cables seem largely intact.'

'Same here skipper' added Ben.

Danny was next. 'Some flak or shell damage to turret fairing and turret mounting ring.' Over the intercom Colin heard a whirring sound as Danny tested the turret. 'Movement of the turret limited. I'll see if there is some way I can fix it.'

Expecting visits from night fighters later in the journey back, Colin hoped he succeeded.

'Everything seems okay back here skipper' called Dennis. 'Although the starboard rudder and rudder tab are a bit shredded.' This confirmed to Colin the various changes to the aircraft's handling. After a pause, Dennis added 'I think I might have to change my pants and trousers when I get back. It doesn't smell too good in here.'

'Working out the course for the way home skipper.'

'Thanks Ben. Everyone keep a lookout, be on your guard for night fighters.' Colin turned to "Ginger" busy checking his dials, gauges, pressures and levels and enquired about the fuel level. Within seconds they were out of the cloud and Colin saw the twinkling stars again. He took "F" for

Freddie up further and they headed homeward through the velvety night sky.

After about ten minutes Doug called over the intercom. 'Skipper. Below us. At 11 o'clock.'

Colin looked down. He saw an orange glow about 4,000 feet below them. 'I see it Doug.' As he watched, the glow suddenly flared and spread in both directions. It was a returning Lancaster and fire was spreading rapidly along its starboard wing and engines. 'It's a blazing Lanc.' Flames engulfed its fuselage. He saw an explosion. The stricken bomber rolled on its back and fell earthward in a mass of flame. 'See anyone bale out Doug?'

'No skipper.'

Colin called his wireless operator and navigator. 'Take a fix Mike and Ben? We'll tell Intelligence when we get back.'

For a moment Colin dwelt on the hapless crew of the downed aircraft. He hoped if none of them had the chance to bale out, at least they died instantly.

Somewhere over and near Wittlich - his eyes aching with the concentration of endlessly searching the dark sky all around him - Dennis, in his rear turret, suddenly caught a glimpse of a menacing black shape closing from the starboard quarter and slightly below. It was about 700 yards away and closing fast. He gripped the trigger of the four .303 Brownings and shouted over the intercom. 'Fighter! Fighter starboard quarter! Prepare to corkscrew starboard. Can you see him Danny?'

'Not yet. This bloody turret is jamming.'

'Ready to corkscrew' called Colin calmly.

Dennis watched the night fighter curving in towards them. 'Corkscrew! Go!'

The Lancaster's nose dropped sharply in its evasive action. For a few seconds Dennis lost sight of the fighter.

Colin pulled the Lancaster out of its dive and Dennis saw it closing in again.

'I see him Dennis. I see him' called Danny.

'Fire together' called back Dennis. 'Ready, ready. Fire!'

Simultaneously they fired. Their tracer streaked towards the German. Still he closed on them.

'Bloody hell Danny!' Shouted Dennis. 'You're firing was well out.'

'It's this bloody turret.'

Dennis gave another brief burst. The Lancaster continued to corkscrew. The night fighter held off, biding his time. Dennis was giving a commentary as the bomber continued its evasive manoeuvres. The fighter began to close again.

Danny called 'The turret's moved a bit. Let's have another go together. Ready, ready. Fire!'

Again the two sets of Brownings spat forth ferociously. The fighter's nose dipped and he disappeared from view.

Dennis called 'I think he's gone Danny' then, to Colin. 'Seems all clear behind skipper.'

Colin levelled off and began to climb again. 'Well done you two. Thanks.'

Suddenly Dennis shouted over the intercom. 'He's coming back fast. Port quarter, port quarter! Corkscrew port. Corkscrew! Go!'

Instantly Colin threw "F" for Freddie into another evasive manoeuvre. The fighter curved towards them. He was only about 100 yards away. Simultaneously, the guns of the Lancaster and those of the fighter fired. Dennis watched his tracer fly towards the fighter. The fighter's tracer curved directly towards him. Dennis awaited death - briefly a clear vision of his wife and new-born son flashed in his mind. Opening his eyes there was no further sign of the fighter in the darkness around him. He was suddenly aware of Colin's voice calling over the intercom.

'All right back there Dennis?'

'Oh yes. Sorry skipper.' He peered into the darkness. 'All clear behind.' He felt cold sweat freezing under his flying clothing. He was looking near-vertically down his gun barrels as his captain climbed the bomber steeply for greater safety.

"Ginger" reported again on temperatures, pressures and fuel consumption.

Colin replied 'Thank goodness for that. Keep watching those gauges though "Ginger". We've sustained yet more damage and still got miles to go. I don't know how much more this kite can take. It's hard enough flying her as it is with the damage to her rudder.'

Danny, in his mid-upper turret, was getting increasingly concerned as he looked at the dangerous tell-tale con trails left by the engine exhausts in the now crystal clear night sky. 'Skipper, what height are we?'

'20,000. Why?'

'We're leaving dirty big con trails.'

'Only to be expected when it's minus 35 degrees outside' observed Ben over the intercom.

'I'll drop her a bit' said Colin. After a while he called up Danny again. 'How are those con trails now?'

'A bit better skipper.'

'Where do you reckon we are now Ben?' Colin asked his navigator some minutes later.

'About thirty miles south west of Bastogne.'

'Very well. There's heavy flak batteries dotted all around Neufchateau. I'm going to have to take her up higher as we approach that area. We're going to have to take our chances with the con trails I'm afraid. Danny and Dennis keep your eyes peeled for fighters.'

There was not too much trouble from Neufchateau's flak batteries and "F" for Freddie continued homeward.

'Fighter! Fighter!' Shouted Dennis. 'Below us starboard quarter.' He fired his guns. 'Corkscrew starboard!'

Colin had just started to respond as shells slammed into the aircraft, exploding all around the fuselage. The control column was snatched violently out of his hands. 'Christ!' He grabbed the stick and fought to regain control. More shells raked the port side of the aircraft. He was still fighting to regain control. The Lancaster was spinning wildly. 'Bloody hell! The control cables have gone!'

'Port inner engine on fire' shouted "Ginger". 'Shutting down and feathering.'

Colin attempted to make the necessary adjustments. The Lancaster continued to spin wildly.

'Fire spreading along wing to port outer!' Screamed the flight engineer.

"F" for Freddie was beginning to roll on its back. The whole outer half of the port wing was disintegrating.

Colin called 'Attention crew, attention crew. Abandon aircraft. I repeat abandon aircraft.'

Michael looked up to see Ben clutching his parachute and trying to right himself - his body shape silhouetted against the glare of flame outside the cockpit canopy. Over the intercom he heard a confusion of frightened voices. Dennis was shouting: 'I can't budge the bloody door!' Michael yanked off his helmet and clipped on his parachute before scrambling to the rear of the fuselage to help him. Suddenly, there was an explosion and he was thrown on his back and pinned inside the fuselage. Michael felt the glow of searing heat, there was the rushing sound and chill of racing, whirring air.

The Lancaster was gyrating crazily and spinning downwards. Doug, "Ginger" and Ben had already made their way down towards the escape hatch in the Bomb Aimer's compartment. But, try as he might, because of the violent spinning, Colin was finding it impossible to get down after them. His limbs felt heavy like lead - he was being pressed against the step. There was a massive explosion behind him and the whole of the cockpit area tore apart from the fuselage. As if by a mighty, invisible hand, Colin was snatched out into the freezing night air. The rushing air current was hammering and beating against his face.

28

Beautiful birdsong awoke Colin as the first grey light of dawn spread slowly over the countryside. A thin blanket of mist hung dreamily above the ground, loosely enveloping the trees of the wood and covering the meadow beyond like a frothy cake topping. Colin shivered. He was still dressed in full flying gear and had used his parachute as a blanket but, in the chill of the early morning, felt freezing cold. After his 'chute had delivered him safely to the ground in a meadow, he had made for the cover of the wood and found a hollow ringed by trees. Thankfully, apart from aching ankles and a few minor scratches he was uninjured. Now, without darkness to aid his concealment, he knew he must get as far away as possible from the area. The Germans would be sending patrols, renewing their efforts in searching for the crew of the downed Lancaster. A small spiral of smoke away to the north, forcibly reminded Colin where most of the smouldering wreckage of "F" for Freddie lay, adding urgency to the fact he must now seek an alternative - more distant hideout. By using a stout branch lying on the ground he dug a hole to bury his parachute.

Colin tore away the top half of his flying boots to leave the bottom portion to suffice as shoes at least for the short term. As he also buried these, he admired the ingenuity of the person who designed this aid to evasion. Hurriedly he checked the contents of his Escape Kit: maps; compass; food tablets; water-purifying tablets; chewing gum; chocolate; appropriate currency. Apart from knowing he was somewhere in the Ardennes area, Colin had no idea where he was. He began to study his map and compass. Suddenly, on the other side of the rise in the ground behind him, he heard a noise in the undergrowth. He spread-eagled himself on the damp ground. Although he was breathing normally, Colin was sure it would be heard. Footsteps grew closer - were at the rim of the hollow. He heard leaf-mould displaced, was aware of someone slipping down the slope.

'Skipper?' A shocked voice called quietly but urgently. The voice sounded familiar. Whoever it was rushed down the incline.

'Skipper! Are you okay?' It was Michael.

Colin jumped up. The two men grabbed each other's shoulder's warmly.

'Mike! Am I pleased to see you! I'm fine - are you?' He laughed nervously.

'Fine. Good to see you too.' Michael nodded behind him. 'I thought when I first saw you from up there - laying so still - you were - you know.'

'I thought you were a bloody "Jerry" out searching. Where have you been lying low?'

'Really not far from here. I've just been wandering around a bit in the woods. Trying to get my bearings.'

'You've hidden your 'chute?'

'All taken care of.'

'Have you seen anything of the others?'

The wireless operator shook his head. 'No. Not a sign.'

Colin nodded towards where the thin column of smoke still rose. 'As far as I am aware, everyone baled out. Let's just hope they all got down safely and in one piece. Just before you arrived I was trying to find my whereabouts as well. One thing is certain. Now dawn is breaking, there will be "Jerry" search parties out and we must get as far away as possible. We need a place we can lay low for a while. Any ideas?'

Mike pointed vaguely south-eastwards. 'From where I was in the woods, I could see a farm or something about a mile in that direction.'

Colin shook his head doubtfully. 'I'd rather get further away.' He looked at his map. 'According to this there should be a road, about three miles directly to the south. I reckon, by sticking to these woods, we head in that direction.'

'Sounds all right to me.'

They had been walking for about twenty minutes, the breaking of dawn seemed to have accelerated alarmingly. The wood had become more like a forest now and began to clad the lower slopes of steep cliffs, now and again its density broken by rocky gorges and stony outcrops. The noise of several vehicles drifted up from the valley floor. A few steps away, a stony outcrop stood like a gigantic doorstep. Colin and Mike went towards it. The position afforded a superb view and as they laid down on the stone, observed in the near distance, several hundred feet below them, German vehicles and troops on foot - some with dogs at their side - fanning out searching the surrounding area.

'The bloody Huns are on their way to the crash site.' Colin looked around before referring to the map again. 'If I'm not mistaken they're on this road - the opposite end of the road we need to keep parallel to. If I am correct the road should lead to Montherme.'

Mike was looking over Colin's shoulder. 'That river in the distance must be the Meuse then.'

'Looks like it. Well we better get away before they start sending men up here into the woods.'

'Skipper look!' Mike exclaimed, pointing to his right.

'Oh God!' Colin was horrified by what Mike was pointing at.

Just above them, on the other side of the rough track, wedged amongst the twisted boughs of a tree, hung a man's body dressed in RAF flying clothes. The body was still harnessed to the tangled cords of the remains of a burnt parachute.

Colin struggled to reach the part of the tree in which the body was lodged. It was obvious that most of the bones in the poor unfortunate's body had been broken, his facial features unrecognisable. Colin looked at the man's ID disc and called down. 'It's Danny. The flames from the Lanc. must have caught his 'chute as he baled out and he was unable to open it.'

'God. Poor Danny.'

'There is no way we can move him. If I can, I'll try and retrieve his ID disc.'

After a while Colin managed to scramble back down and began to share out Danny's issue of foreign currency and his escape kit contents between himself and Mike. He then buried Danny's ID disc. Both felt a dreadful numbness.

Some while later, still keeping to the wooded slopes they neared the valley floor. Much of the walk had been through a very difficult terrain of rocky gorges, fast-flowing streams and waterfalls. Neither of them had rested or slept properly since prior to their bombing mission. They were exhausted. It was just before ten when, off to their left, mostly obscured by trees and scrub, they glimpsed the slate roof of a building. Cautiously, they went to investigate.

'What do you reckon?' Asked Mike as they stood surveying the old stone-built hut facing them.

A door almost off its hinges, hung half-open. Approaching the doorway, they observed the large heaps of rotting branches, old rusting tools and machinery laying in the clearing fronting the hut. On the far side of the clearing were the remains of a kiln-like structure.

'Looks like the site of an old charcoal-burners camp' said Colin. He and Mike stood in the doorway looking into the dark, dank void formerly both a simple home and workplace. A stove stood by the far wall with cob-webbed kettle, pots and pans still standing on its top. Either side of the stove was an alcove, in each of these was a stone platform on which old sacks were folded. 'Those platforms would suffice for us to rest on for a while. Can't be any worse than spending the night in the woods.'

'I suppose not' replied Mike looking at them and their piles of sacking dubiously. 'Do you think it will be safe to stay here for a while?'

'Well, for a while. "Jerry's" search efforts seem to be being concentrated round the other side of the escarpment - near the crash site. One thing's certain. I'm feeling worn out and I am sure you are as well. We must rest. I'm sure we will have a couple of hours before they start searching around this side.' He paused. 'As you know the Squadron lectures on evasion all stressed the importance of wherever possible, only moving about at night. However, coming down where we did - we don't have much choice - we're miles from anywhere.'

Despite their serious misgivings they agreed to rest up for a while and did what they could to make themselves comfortable.

Mike shivered, looked longingly at the kettles and pots on the stove. 'I wish those things looked more desirable to use. I'm dying for a hot drink. Though I suppose it would be too chancy to kindle up the old stove - with all the smoke it would create.'

Outside there was a noise. Colin was the first to hear

it. He had slept very deeply and it took him a few seconds to gather himself. He leapt up from his makeshift bed and shook Mike awake.

'Someone outside!'

Nervously, keeping away from the open doorway and edging along the wall - both numb with fear - they peeped out the broken window. On the far side of the clearing a youth was moving some old sheets of corrugated iron sheeting. Beside him on the ground lay a large, empty canvas sack. As he worked, picking up shovel-loads of charcoal, he whistled tunefully what could have been a local folk song. Colin glanced at his watch. The pair of them had been asleep for about four hours.

'What do you think?' Whispered Mike. 'What shall we do?'

They continued to watch the youth.

Eventually Colin said 'I think we're going to have to take our chances. Hopefully, he'll be sympathetic to us, manage to get us fixed up with a more secure hiding place.' As far as he could see there was nobody else around. He went to the doorway and called to the youth: *'Aviateur anglais.'*

Hearing Colin's voice so startled the youth he dropped his shovel, nearly tumbling into the pile of charcoal in front of him. He stood facing them frozen to the spot. Colin and Mike emerged fully from the doorway and began to approach him. He stooped to pick up his shovel and held it in front of him defensively. They continued to approach him slowly. Unlike his older brother, Colin was not so gifted with languages and did his best to make himself understood. Out of the shadow of the hut, the youth was better able to identify Colin and Mike's flying clothes. Realising now the two men were not Germans, the youth at last relaxed. Again, as best he could, Colin explained who they were and what they were doing there.

'*Anglais?* You're from the plane crash over there?' Asked the youth in broken English, pointing generally in the direction from which Colin and Mike had scrambled and fought their way down the hillside. He threw his shovel down and embraced them. 'The Germans are all around that side of the cliff searching.'

'Could you help us please?' Asked Colin. 'We want to get away from this area. Could you tell us where we are?'

'About two kilometres from Joigny-s-Meuse. In that direction' replied the youth. 'You will need to wait here for a while. I will be back in about an hour - I promise. I will come back with some friends who will be able to help you.'

'But we're worried about the Germans finding us' said Mike anxiously.

The youth did his best to reassure them. 'They will not think you are over this side.' Adding calmly 'It will be ages yet before they start searching this area. Trust me.'

With that, the youth got his cycle and hurried off down the track resuming his tuneful whistling. Colin and Mike turned and went back into the hut, hoping against hope the youth would be as good as his word and would not share his discovery with the Germans or a non-sympathetic local person.

29

It was now well over an hour since the youth had cycled off.

'I said we shouldn't have trusted him' snapped Mike angrily.

'I know.' Colin looked at the map again. 'He said we were about two kilometres from Joigny-s-Meuse.'

'Yes' replied Mike again angrily. Adding cynically 'If we can believe him.' The whinnying of a horse and the sound of wheels on gravel made the two men rush to the window. A large working horse pulling a cart full of hedge cuttings and cleared scrub entered the clearing. Two men sat at the front, behind them in the cart atop its load sat the youth. He waved at Colin and Mike enthusiastically. With obvious relief Mike said 'Take back what I just said.'

The cart came to a halt in front of the hut and the two men climbed down from it and approached. They were both in their thirties and dressed shabbily. One was tall and slim, the other built like a bear and, to the two airmen's consternation, carried an ancient but effective-looking rifle.

'Anglais? RAF?' Asked the slimmer man, though not in an overly friendly way.

Colin and Mike answered in the affirmative but were taken aback by the Frenchmen's unfriendly attitude.

Especially, as in the past few weeks, words had percolated back *via* the Bomber Command grapevine just how friendly and welcoming most French people had been to those RAF evaders repatriated thus far.

The bigger man spoke in reasonably good English. 'Shall we go inside?' It seemed more like an order than a request.

Leaving the youth outside with the horse, the two Frenchmen followed Colin and Mike back into the hut. Immediately, the bigger man asked them their names, rank and number. After obtaining these he turned to his friend, saying quickly something in French. The other man left the hut. Colin and Mike watched him walk back towards the cart.

Sharply, the bear of a man snapped 'You two over by that wall.'

The two airmen presumed this was to prevent them seeing what was going on outside. The Frenchman began questioning them ceaselessly about where their plane had crashed, what type of aircraft it was. Tried to prize out of them technical details of the aircraft, details of their mission. Each time Colin and Mike replied simply by giving their name, rank and number.

After a while and borne out of a mixture of tiredness, frustration and anxiety, Colin snapped back: 'Until we know who you are, this is the only information you'll get.'

Menacingly, the man opposite levelled his rifle at them. 'Messieurs you are forgetting, I am the one holding the rifle. And, if you do not give me the answers I want - have no doubt I will use it.'

The cold manner in which the Frenchman threatened them, left Colin and Mike in no doubt he meant what he said. They shifted uncomfortably and a silent stalemate ensued. After a while the other man returned and nodded to his colleague. Instantly, Colin and Mike sensed an improvement in the demeanour of the man with the rifle. For the first time a smile broke on his face.

'Raymond and I belong to the local Resistance. England have just signalled us on our wireless hidden out there. They have confirmed you are who you say you are.' He paused. 'However, just to be sure. The address of the Savoy Hotel?' Thick and fast there followed other questions about various London streets, hotels and landmarks. 'Who are the Beefeaters - what does their uniform look like? Where is the Tower of London?' It was obvious the two Frenchmen needed still more convincing.

'Would you both like a 295?' Asked Raymond suddenly.

'Forty-eight hour's leave? Yes we would. Right now.' Answered Mike, knowing Raymond was referring to the current designation for an RAF leave pass.

'What colour are they and where do you get them from?' Asked the big man. On hearing their reply he shouted joyously 'It's all right. They are RAF.' He dropped his rifle and suddenly embraced both airmen warmly. Raymond followed his example. 'As I said this is Raymond, I am Albert. Now we must get away from here.' He grabbed his rifle again and with Raymond ushered Colin and Mike towards the cart.

Colin said 'You had us worried Albert. Now we just want to get as far away as possible from the Germans.'

'We understand my friends. I apologise for our behaviour. We have to be so careful. Now we still have some time before the Boche start searching around here. They do not know the territory as we do.'

Albert and Raymond began to conceal the two airmen under the mound of hedge and scrub cuttings in the cart. Once this was done the youth sat himself on the top of the mound and the cart jerked away.

Colin wasn't sorry when the cart at last came to a halt. It was now early evening. The discomfort had been immense. They had journeyed *via* rough track ways and across untamed land, the floor of the cart was hard and ridged and its load of cuttings was hefty and prickly. Insects, enraged at their habitat being disturbed, had taken out their revenge on the two airmen by constantly biting them. The fresh air was wonderful and refreshing as Albert, Raymond and the youth began to remove the material which had entombed them. Dusting himself down and looking around them, Colin saw they were outside a rambling farmhouse of an architectural style of perhaps 100 years previously.

'This is my brother's farm' said Albert, warmly placing his huge arms on the shoulders of Colin and Mike standing either side of him. Since he and Raymond had confirmed they were genuine evaders, the Frenchmen's friendliness and warmth had become very tangible. 'My friends you will be fed and looked after here and will be able to rest.'

Albert's brother Georges emerged from the doorway to greet them. Like his brother, Georges was a big man though not quite so tall.

'Welcome. Welcome. It is a privilege to meet you. Come in? Come in?'

Colin and Mike were ushered into the large kitchen. Four children, two boys and two girls - ranging in age from about 4 to 11 - stood shyly by a big dresser to the left of the door. The two little girls especially had angelic faces reminding Colin of little china dolls. Georges introduced the children to them. Almost in wonder the four children fixed fascinated eyes on the two unfamiliar uniforms.

'Claude, Charles, Emilene and Mime. Don't stare - it's rude' chided their father gently.

Mike laughed. 'That is all right Monsieur…'.

'...Please. Call me Georges.'

Colin ruffled Charles's hair playfully. 'With all this dust and dirt on us. We must look very strange to them.'

A woman appeared through the scullery door opposite. She had a plain but, nevertheless, pleasant face and was dressed in a floral smock.

'Messieurs. This is my wife Angeline. Angeline, come and meet two of our very good friends from England. They are of the RAF' he continued proudly.

Angeline smiled with a smile which illuminated her face. She shook Colin and Mike's hands warmly and almost curtsied with a humbleness which made Colin feel embarrassed.

'Pleased to meet you. We are so grateful for what our allies are doing to help us. You must eat with us.'

Colin, aware of what he had learnt in Squadron escape lectures, about how short the French people were of food, hesitated. 'Please Madame. Do not go to too much trouble. Some bread and soup will be fine.'

Angeline raised her hands in horror. 'Nonsense. Nonsense. It is the least we can do. Georges and I keep aside things for special occasions. Some soup and ham perhaps?'

'Well if you are sure. That would be wonderful' said Mike. 'Thank you very much.'

'Come children. Help me in the cellar? These gentlemen will want to talk.' Ushering her children before her, Angeline disappeared through a low door and down some steps.

Raymond turned to the youth who - it turned out - was his brother. 'Jean-Claude, we must go and arrange for civilian clothes for our two friends here.' Addressing Colin and Mike 'Do not worry, but it may be late afternoon tomorrow before we can return with them.'

Georges stopped them. 'Before you go Raymond, you must try some of my very best Calvados.'

Raymond laughed devilishly. 'Very well then. How can we refuse that offer.'

Colin and Mike watched fascinated as Georges drew back a rug, lifted a floorboard and held high a bottle of liquid. He got some glasses from the dresser and poured the drinks. When they lifted their glasses standing around the huge kitchen table, the Frenchmen uttered the French equivalent of "Cheers" which Colin and Mike gallantly tried to mimic.

There was a pause in the laughter and merriment and Albert looked at Colin and Mike. So penetrating his look, Colin feared what he was about to hear.

'I was working near the area of your crashed Lancaster this morning. Through my telescope - I am sorry - but I saw the Boche standing over a body near the rear of the wreck. It was difficult to see but it seemed to be a small figure laying there. From how I describe it do you know who of your crew it may have been?'

Colin and Mike glanced at each other. Colin murmured 'Sounds like Dennis, our rear gunner.' A chill ran through him as he thought of the cheerful cockney's wife, how proud Dennis had been of his recently-born son - a son he had never seen.

Angeline returned carrying the best looking joint of ham Colin had seen for years. The four children followed her excitedly.

'I have a loaf of fresh bread. Would potato soup and some ham be all right?' Colin and Mike were touched by how generous their French hosts were. 'Now children. Could you please go and shut the chickens in?'

With squeals of delight the children ran out into the yard. Their mother began to busy herself preparing the meal.

Raymond and Jean-Claude finished their drinks. 'Right. We must go.' Raymond turned to the two airmen. 'Farewell for now Messieurs. I will be back tomorrow afternoon.'

The four remaining men continued talking and getting acquainted. They had another drink, discussed and compared how things were in France and England. After a while Angeline turned from the sink.

'Honestly Georges. You are impolite. Think of our guests. Haven't you thought, they may like a wash before supper? Go and draw some water from the well so I might boil it up for them.'

'Oh of course. Yes. Forgive me Messieurs.'

Something about the way Angeline had spoken to her husband indicated it was she who wore the trousers in the house. Colin smiled to himself.

'I am so sorry my friends. Please forgive me. Please though come with me first?' He lead them to the door and, then to his wife 'I will also check the livestock.'

It was now dark and by the light of his lamp, Georges filled two large buckets of water from the well. 'Messieurs, please wait here while I take these in. Then, I will show you where you must hide.' He returned carrying a tall step-ladder and a bundle and lead Colin and Mike toward a big pigeon loft sitting on top of a tower-like structure. 'I am afraid it is not very elegant accommodation but I am sure it will be secret enough.' As Georges shone his lamp upwards, Colin saw there were entrances for the pigeons on five levels or storeys with, in one wall of the loft, a hatch for access. Georges explained he had modified the loft to act as a storage facility for the local Resistance. In fact, only its lower portions were able to be used by the birds. 'Inside the loft - above the lower levels - is a false ceiling concealing an area just big enough for the two of you to sleep. In the false ceiling is a hidden panel I will show you presently.' After opening the ladder to reach the hatch, he picked up the bundle and climbed up. From the top of the ladder he unfolded the bundle. It was a stoutly constructed rope ladder which he looped over two hooks before descending again. Georges explained how to open the hatch, locate, open and close the hidden panel. He turned to Colin. 'Now Monsieur ensure you are satisfied how to conceal yourselves?'

Colin climbed the rope ladder and did as he was requested. Although a tight squeeze he got through the outside hatch and located the secret panel. The void above the false ceiling was dark but, by the light of the lamp, he could see it was clean and dry and just large enough for him and Mike to lie down and, by stooping, it would be possible to move around a bit. After practising opening and closing the secret panel a couple of times, he descended to the ground.

'It's ingenious Georges' he said laughing.

'Obviously Messieurs, before you close the outside hatch you will pull the rope ladder up behind you. After supper I will give you some bedding.'

'Thank you Georges for all you and your family are doing for us' said Mike.

As Georges checked on a young calf and its mother in the barn he said 'We are fortunate this yard is enclosed and can't be seen from the lane or surrounding fields. But, please Messieurs, if there is any hint of Germans in the area, you will hide straightaway in the loft? I beg of you. It is not for myself I worry - it is Angeline and the children. The Boche are doing such terrible things to families caught concealing allied soldiers and airmen.' Georges fear for the safety of his family was so very obvious. The risks they were prepared to run on the airmen's behalf - a bravery Colin and Mike found very humbling. 'Hopefully, after Raymond returns with clothes for the two of you and, later, documents and papers, you will not have to endure the discomfort of the loft for too long.'

Angeline had laughed at Colin and Mike's modesty as they bathed in a big tin bath in the kitchen whilst she finished preparing the meal, had assured them she had seen naked men before and would be having her back to them anyway whilst they bathed. The gloriously warm water had been wonderful, banishing their muscular aches and refreshing them completely. After, as expected, the soup and ham had been delicious. The children had gone to bed and Colin and Mike remained sitting around the table with Albert, Georges and Angeline drinking and talking. The only pause in their conversation, when Angeline switched on the radio to listen to the BBC French Service broadcast the news and seemingly endless coded messages. As it was totally forbidden by the Germans for French homes to possess radios, this was an exercise in itself. It entailed moving the heavy metal utensil stand on the hearth of the big kitchen fireplace and, lifting the radio set out of the concealed cavity housing it.

'On behalf of all of us Messieurs' said Albert, as Georges poured their guests another Calvados 'I would like to apologise for my hostile behaviour when I met you this afternoon. We have to be so careful.'

'I must admit Albert' replied Colin 'We were mighty scared when you pointed your gun at us.'

'Rest assured my friends, if you had not turned out to be who you claimed you were, I would not have hesitated to use it. The damned Boche are so clever at infiltrating the evasion lines and Resistance networks. Mercifully, I was one of the few to escape with my life when our local organisation was infiltrated only a few months back. I still have many bad memories - bad dreams of that time. It was just terrible. So many men, women, even children taken away to be tortured, imprisoned - killed.'

Hearing Albert speak reminded Colin again of the aircrew's escape and evasion lectures. They had been told of countless stories of Nazi brutality and reprisals metered out on local people daring to or, attempting to, assist allied servicemen in occupied territory.

Angeline noticed Mike was having difficulty in keeping awake. 'Now Georges, Albert. I think we must let our guests get some sleep. They are exhausted.'

Immediately her husband got to his feet. 'Of course. Of course. Pardon Messieurs.' Rounding the table, he slapped their backs warmly. 'We will continue our talk tomorrow.' Fetching the bedding Angeline had left on a chair, he lead them towards the door. 'Here, take my lamp.' As they crossed the yard he said 'I do hope my little hiding place will not be too uncomfortable for you. Tomorrow morning, when I am sure there are no Germans about, I will come over and call you for breakfast.'

The wine and Calvados had affected the two airmen. After ensuring they had climbed the rope ladder safely, were competent at accessing their hiding place, had pulled up the ladder after them, Georges turned back towards the house. High up in the night sky above him he heard the distant but distinctive sound of a solitary bomber heading back towards England. Georges hoped they would make it back safely, wondered just how many more downed allied airmen might find themselves in his part of France during the coming months or years.

Once in their hiding place Mike said 'My, this is cosy isn't it?'

Colin replied 'Yes. Let's hope neither of us farts too much.'

The pair of them arranged their bedding and within moments were sound asleep.

30

It had been some time since Margaret had been to the coast and was relishing this opportunity for some rare time off and, to be walking along the Brighton sea-front with her daughter. Similarly, for June, since her secondment to the Sussex Constabulary, days off had been a rarity too. Last night on the telephone they had hastily arranged to meet for lunch, agreeing they would meet in good enough time for a walk beforehand.

It was a pleasantly warm day with sunny spells. Thankfully, the heavy rain of yesterday had moved away. A breeze from the sea brushed their faces, bringing with it a faint fragrance of seaweed left stranded on the beach by a fast-retreating tide. The noise of seagulls squabbling loudly as they flew overhead, caused Margaret to look up. Puffy white clouds drifted lazily inland. It was the sort of day when, well over two years ago now, the beach and promenade would have been busy with people of all ages relaxing, playing with their children and enjoying themselves. Now though, barred to the public, the beaches lay bereft of people. The unending waves of tide uninterrupted by people splashing, paddling and swimming but, now, interrupted by the ironwork of anti-invasion devices. More ironwork and barbed wire was positioned higher up the beaches in unsightly continuous lines stretching as far as the eye could see. Barbed wire and ironwork defences also lined the seaward side of the promenade, the ugly rusty line occasionally punctuated by some anti-aircraft or anti-personnel emplacement. Since the immediate threat of invasion had passed Margaret had heard or read occasional stories of talk by seaside councils it was being considered that coastal defences could be lessened somewhat to permit limited access for the public to the beaches. However, like many stories at this time, the rumours never came to anything. She glanced up at the sky again remembering that, under two years ago, the skies above would have been streaked - near constantly - with aircraft vapour trails and reverberating with the sound of duelling aircraft fighting for victory. Now, aircraft still did fly back and forth but with nowhere near the same intensity.

'And it was yesterday evening you heard about James's brother?

'Yes, James's parents told me on the telephone. Colin's CO wrote to them but wasn't able to say much more than he was alive and well. He promised to let them have more information when he could.'

'What a relief for them. I know how we felt when I finally heard Richard had been taken a prisoner-of-war in North Africa. You remember, the weeks after receiving the Telegram saying he was missing, believed killed, were absolutely terrible.'

'I wonder when we will hear from Richard again.'

'Goodness knows.'

'He's alive and uninjured thank goodness. I hope at last he's received a Red Cross parcel.'

'One thing is certain though. I doubt if he and the other prisoners are being fed anywhere enough. I just hope and pray he's not being too badly treated in that Oflag something or other.'

'Let us hope we get some more news from him very soon mummy.'

'I really feel so sorry for you too June. Not knowing what James is doing or where he is.'

The two women stopped to look out over the sea. An elderly woman passed by walking her dog. June bent down to make a fuss of the little mongrel.

'Yes I'm so worried. I've received one or two short notes telling me he is well but that is all.' She paused. 'It is so strange though. Somehow the notes just don't seem to have been written by James - and they're all typewritten. I realise everything nowadays is censored but, somehow, they are not newsy, there doesn't seem to be any warmth in them. It's all very strange.'

'Please June. Try not to worry. What you're going through is being experienced by the majority of people in the country at the moment. He's, in all probability, closeted away somewhere very top secret, doing something also very top secret.'

'Oh I suppose so. Though I do wish his letters would say more about how he is. I just can't wait to see him again safe and well.'

Margaret saw tears trickling down her daughter's cheeks and cuddled her. 'You will my love. You will.' Desperately wanting to change the subject, she asked. 'So how is this secondment of yours going? How are you enjoying working with your Inspector Cavendish?'

They started to walk again.

'I'm enjoying it. It is certainly different - less noisy - than working on the anti-aircraft installations. The Inspector is really an old sweetie, old fashioned - a bit of a stickler but, nevertheless, very pleasant to work with. He's very kind really. He is due to retire soon but not looking forward to it. I think he's frightened of being lonely. His wife is very ill in a nursing home, unlikely she will ever be coming home. Their son died during the fall of Singapore.'

'Oh how sad.'

'Yes very.' An ambulance, its bell ringing, tore urgently past them. 'The work is very varied.'

'Is it ordinary crime you help investigate June?'

'Goodness me! Not personally. I just drive the Inspector around - help with some of his clerical work and so on. Sometimes I may make some routine enquiries for him or, sometimes, help in comforting relatives and that sort of thing. At the moment we spend most of the time investigating Black Market operations or cases mainly allied to the military.'

'It still sounds very interesting.'

'You're looking very tired mummy. Are things still as bad at the hospital as you said they were the other week?'

'I'm afraid so. The hours seem to be getting longer and longer. We are down to just three Registrars now and two Consultants. Luckily, now the work at Penley Manor has been passed to military medics, I don't have that as well. Supplies and equipment are getting harder and harder to obtain. Unfortunately, for the foreseeable future, things are not going to get any better either.'

'Please mummy. Take care of yourself. Try not to overdo things.'

'June do you think you will be able to get a few hours off on the weekend?'

'When Stephen is home? I'll certainly try. Perhaps if I speak to the Inspector nicely. He's usually very understanding. It depends on how investigations are going. We're heavily involved with an enquiry into bogus ration books at the moment.'

'I hope you can, even for just a few hours. It will be so

nice to have two of you at least at home for a while. It all seems so long since we have all been together at Oakfield.'

'Ages. Stephen told you I managed to see him about a month ago? The Inspector and I were in Plymouth in connection with a case. As we were so near to where Stephen is based, Cavendish allowed me to go and see him. We only had a few minutes together though. Stephen was saying he was due to go before a medical board. He seems so frustrated at having to be shore-based.'

An expression of concern showed on Margaret's face. 'I know he is. He's desperate to get back to sea. To be perfectly honest, I hope he fails the medical board. Oh don't get me wrong. Obviously, I was thankful Stephen's injuries weren't any worse but, in some ways, I hope the results prove to be just bad enough for him to fail the board. I just feel he would be safer being shore-based.'

'Do you see the Group Captain - Robert - much?'

'Only when he has to travel up to London for some meeting. With Robert down in Cornwall and me working long hours at the hospital, it's difficult. I managed to see him a week ago - he was in Portsmouth - we were able to see each other for an evening.'

'You're very fond of him aren't you mummy?'

'Yes June I am. Very.'

A few yards ahead of them, the ambulance racing past a few minutes earlier was parked with its doors open. Margaret was looking across the road at the burnt out ruins of a hotel.

'The poor old Majestic. Still in ruins after two years. I remember going to some big function there with your father before the war.' June sensed her mother had abruptly changed the subject for some reason. Margaret looked directly into June's face. Words were on her lips but she hesitated a long time before speaking. 'June ... I was going to tell you over lunch … I must tell you something.' She held her daughter's arms. 'I don't know how to tell you…'.

'…Mummy what is it? What's wrong..?'

'…There's nothing wrong. It's just that. Well - Robert has asked me to marry him.'

For a moment June was lost for words. Every kind of emotion raced through her - all confused and mixed up.

Ahead of them a voice shouted up from the beach. 'Give us some help to get him over the wire? He's still alive - just.'

Margaret and June saw an ambulance man with a stretcher trying to get round the barbed wire. Bystanders and a policeman went to assist the ambulance crew.

Margaret raced towards the group calling out 'I'm a doctor. I'll help.'

June heard the voice of one of the ambulance crew. 'He's an airman of some sort - came down in the sea..'

Quickly June followed her mother. Her mind though full of what Margaret had told her. It wasn't that June wasn't happy for her, it had just been a bit of a shock. So much had seemed to have happened in the last few years.

Standing a bit back from the group huddled around the stretcher, June watched the tender and caring way her mother attended to the figure laying unconscious and bleeding. Looking down at the pale, moribund face of the casualty she saw it was a very young man - perhaps even younger than James when she first met him. She began to cry.

31

It was early afternoon of their third day on the farm. For the most part of their first day there Colin and Mike had been entombed in the pigeon loft, only leaving it to relieve themselves and, to receive and change into the clothes Raymond had obtained for them. However, after dark, they had been invited to share the hospitality of their hosts. Now, two days on, they were pleased to have had the friendly restrictions imposed by Georges and Albert lifted somewhat. In part the result, as Georges had informed them, of a scaling down of the numbers of German troops in the area searching for survivors of Lancaster "F" for Freddie.

Although very grateful for the given sanctuary of the loft, Colin and Mike were relieved to be spending more time outside its confines. It hadn't been as uncomfortable in there as feared but, nevertheless, it was cramped, dark and smelly and the time had dragged so. Always leaving the rope ladder hanging, prepared in case a German patrol approached the farm, Colin and Mike were now venturing around the farmyard and spent time helping Georges with the everyday chores required. They were grateful for the physical exercise and to be doing something meaningful and helpful. By helping Georges and Angeline they also felt it repaid in some way the hospitality shown - the risks being undertaken by their hosts on their behalf. There had been a scare the previous day when a German patrol had been spotted approaching the farm and had stopped to check and search the farm and question Georges, Angeline and Albert. Colin and Mike had just managed to secret themselves in the loft as the Germans drove up the lane. The patrol remained at the farm for ages searching everywhere and questioning intensively. At one stage, a soldier started to investigate the pigeon loft more closely - so closely Colin believed he would surely hear him breathing. Colin contemplated whether they should give themselves up, try and plead their presence in the loft was unknown to the owners of the farm. On reflection though, he doubted this would have been believed and the whole of the family could suffer horrific punishment. Fortunately, something else distracted the soldier and he moved away. It had been a chillingly close shave. Also fortunately, Colin learnt later, the patrol's commanding officer was unusually civil in the manner in which he led his patrol's search and questioning, did not demonstrate the usual thuggish and destructive methods typical of such an event and the four children were away for the day at a relatives. Angeline had said previously how skilled German officers were at exploiting children's naivety in coaxing from them whether there had been any strangers in their parent's home or hiding nearby.

On this their third day at the farm, Albert had left at first light. From the pigeon loft, Colin and Mike had seen him leave after appearing furtively from the barn. He had been carrying what looked like guns wrapped in sacking. During the previous evening, Colin thought he had been acting somewhat mysteriously. On occasions when they had entered or left the kitchen, Albert had hurriedly concealed things in a drawer or bag or had stopped abruptly in what he had been saying to Georges. Colin and Mike wondered if Albert was about to embark on some sort of Resistance activity and, if that was the case, they hoped he would return safely. However, such was their worry and anxiety of being caught by the Germans, they hoped these people they were staying with were who they said they were and not enacting some elaborate charade before ultimately turning them over to the Gestapo. Colin and Mike and all aircrew had been told back in England that this sort of thing was not unknown in occupied France. In the pigeon loft, Colin and Mike looked at each other with uncertainty.

Later on when Raymond cycled into the yard, Colin and Mike were herding the young calf and its mother from the barn.

As Raymond leant his cycle against the wall he greeted them. 'Good morning Messieurs.' Georges emerged from the barn. 'I have brought your papers' he continued and handed them to the two airmen. 'There was a delay in getting them. The Boche have changed the format of travel documents again. In the next day or so instructions will arrive for your move from here.'

'Thank you very much. I take it you don't have any news of other members of my crew Raymond?' Enquired Colin.

'I believe so. A Canadian - Doug Harvey - is being sheltered at a house just outside Nouzonville. He has no serious injuries. There have also been reports that, near to where you were found, the Germans captured someone we believe is a member of your crew. If I get more news I will let you know. As far as I am aware he was also uninjured when captured.'

'It's good news then about Doug' said Mike. 'I wonder who it was "Jerry" captured?'

Georges turned to Colin and Mike. 'Excuse us a moment please.'

The two Frenchmen headed towards the farmhouse leaving Colin and Mike to practice their newly-acquired husbandry skills in getting the cow and calf into the nearby field.

Raymond asked Georges. 'Did Albert get away in good time this morning?'

'As soon as it was light. He left a message for you in the kitchen.'

Raymond nodded his head back towards the two airmen and asked 'And those two are not aware of our plans?'

32

Since Isobel's murder Karl Neumann had not lost his suspicion that Fouquet's lodger, the man calling himself Jean-Paul Guyot, was in some way implicated in her death. True, he had an alibi for the night of her death - the custody officer of the Gendarmerie in Reims no less. This particular officer too was on Gestapo files as being of help to them in passing information on the activities of the Resistance, so why should he lie now to the Gestapo about Guyot being in his cells. It was all very strange. Still, Neumann was always strongly guided by his instincts and his instincts told him Jean-Paul Guyot was implicated in Isobel's murder and, in some way involved with the Resistance. He had determined to watch him very closely.

Also, although he had no evidence - had never found anything in his files to suggest the Doctor was involved in the Resistance, of late he had been increasing his intelligence team's vigilance and surveillance of the physician. In all the occupied countries the Gestapo kept a close watch on all Doctor's movements and contacts. Neumann prided himself of working in a different way to many of his Gestapo colleagues. He preferred to watch and study from afar, wait as long as possible before interrogating suspected helpers of the Resistance. He had found by delaying taking suspects for questioning until the last possible moment, they invariably led him to yet more Resistance workers. This is why, up to now, he had allowed Dr Fouquet more freedom than perhaps others would have.

Neumann paused to reflect for a moment, took a cigarette, lit it, leant back in his chair and watched the blue smoke swirl in rings above him. Surely though, if Fouquet was involved with the Resistance, Isobel would have known and informed him of his involvement - unless of course the Doctor had been especially careful and cunning in keeping his involvement from her. Still Isobel had got it wrong when she told him she believed her lodger was the Edouard Estornel he was trying to hunt down - perhaps she hadn't been as reliable as he thought. No, he decided he would bide his time until Guyot and Fouquet made their first mistake as they surely would. Besides he had other pressing things to occupy himself with at the moment. Inhabitants of Charleville and Mezieres and the surrounding area were getting increasingly troublesome, their activities had to be quelled. Also, news had arrived that some Jewish people were being sheltered in the area and these and their helpers had to be tracked down.

Since the night he executed Isobel, James was aware he was now being watched very closely. Although this extra attention was forcing him to be more careful than usual and thus slowing down the time it took him to do things, these problems had not proved insurmountable. He had just found new techniques and methods for doing things - there was no alternative. With the assistance of various residents sympathetic to the Resistance, he had organised various "safe" establishments wherein he had left disguise outfits into which he could change and false ID papers he could use before emerging again later from a different exit with a different appearance and ID. James had begun using this ploy whenever there was a particularly persistent Gestapo agent following him or, to be seen as Jean-Paul Guyot, could seriously compromise a member of the Resistance network or an assignment he was working on. And today was one of those occasions. He had arranged to meet Monsieur Dideret, the Chandler. Disguised as a Priest, James sat on the bench agreed for their meeting in a part of the cemetery furthest from its entrance on Avenue de Flandre. The cemetery was very large and as he waited for Dideret he cast his eyes over the acres of tombstones, stone monoliths and massed statuary of angels and cherubs all around him. To the back of him, not much distant from where he sat, were the huge and ugly barracks - once occupied by French forces but since purloined by the Germans. Occasionally, James glanced back toward the barracks watching troops parading, vehicles arriving and leaving, the sound of incessant, guttural orders and commands carried through the air as a raucous background. Once more he looked impatiently at the fob watch which made up part of his disguise. James and Dideret had chosen to meet in the cemetery as it was the anniversary of the death of Dideret's brother, and the Chandler visiting it today would not arouse any suspicion. Dideret's brother had died in 1917 as a result of injuries sustained in the bloodbath of the Great War and, since then, every year as far as anyone could remember, come rain or shine, Dideret had visited his grave - the Dideret family tomb. For generations the family had lived in Charleville and generations of them were buried in the cemetery. It was only after Dideret's wife passed away four years ago that he had moved to Mezieres, wanting to shed all his memories of the former family home. Suddenly, James saw Dideret appear on the path. Saw him stop and look toward him uncertainly - look around uncertainly. As no other bench nearby was occupied, Dideret moved slowly towards him. James smiled to himself, at least from a distance his disguise must look convincing.

Dideret greeted James with the usual respectful greeting reserved for addressing Priests and settled himself uneasily on the far end of the bench. James waited a moment before speaking.

'You are late Monsieur Dideret. I thought perhaps something had happened.'

The Frenchman, recognising the voice, nearly fell off the bench with surprise. 'Why Monsieur I did not recognise you! Magnificent! Magnificent! I would never have known you.'

'Did you have a problem getting here?'

'I apologise for keeping you. The Boche closed Rue du Molinet. Their thugs were arresting a family. Jewish I think and the family sheltering them; they just dragged them down the stairs - dragging them through the street and threw them into the back of their trucks. It was terrible. One of the little children went to defend his mother - one of the soldiers just smashed the child's head with his rifle butt. Another of the women - she was struggling also - the soldiers were ripping her clothes from her body. Some of the Nazis were firing at the crowd - it was truly awful.'

'Bastards!' Exclaimed James angrily. He paused for a moment. 'Our friends in Chaumont are ready to ship the next consignment. Is everything ready at the abattoir to receive it?'

'Yes. I checked first thing this morning. All is ready.'

'Good. I will despatch a courier to Chaumont to tell them.' He paused as a woman pushing a pram passed by, nodding reverently at him as she did so. 'And a team is in place to distribute the consignment?'

'All arranged, all hand-picked. Some of our best members.'

'Excellent. Tonight I am expecting confirmation of our target from London during the BBC broadcasts. People will be notified tomorrow. Do you have any other news for me?'

'There is word that two English airmen are being sheltered by relatives of one of our group.'

'Whereabouts?'

'On a farm near Joigny-s-Meuse. Their identities have been checked and are authentic. Other checks were satisfactory - the English style of placing their knife and fork after a meal - everything. They were members of a Lancaster crew.' From the direction of the town centre there was the sound of rifle-fire. 'They have been there about five days. The family sheltering them are getting increasingly anxious for them to be moved. It has just been too risky in the last day or so to attempt it. Hopefully, something will be able to be arranged shortly.'

'I may be able to help. I have some contacts who may assist with getting them moved. With the Group about to be involved in the operation we're planning, I am reluctant to stir the Boche up too much. However, I will see what I can do. Now if there is nothing else, I suggest we meet again tomorrow afternoon. Shall we say 15.00 hours by the fountain in the Square de la Gare?'

'Yes.'

The two men got up from the bench.

'Before we go, I think it best we visit your family's tomb together to pay our respects. I can't see anyone around but just in case we are being watched.'

Together they made their way towards the Dideret family tomb, stood in front of it in due reverence and prayer, then left the cemetery in opposite directions.

33

Knowing the consignment of explosives, weapons and ammunition from Chaumont was now on its way down the Meuse toward Charleville and, confirmation of the Group's target having been received the previous night *via* the BBC French Service, James watched Dideret make his way out of the gate off Square de la Gare.

Before leaving the square himself James thought of the target - the factory on the Av. Louis Tirman in Mezieres. This, which all going well, he and members of the Resistance Group would attack within the next four days. It was to be the biggest, potentially most important target the fledgling Group had attempted so far. The Germans had been using the factory to assemble and repair gear boxes and engines of tanks and armoured vehicles and, as a storage facility for components, lubricants, fuel and other supplies. By using the River Meuse, the rail and canal networks of the area, they transported the materials to other parts of western Europe. As James turned to follow Dideret out of the square, his thoughts switched to the two airmen in hiding at the farm near Joigny-s-Meuse.

****

As Monsieur Chaillot watched the last of his pupils walk out of the playground of the school on Rue Carnot, he saw the man enter the playground and walk towards him. Monsieur Chaillot was pleased to see the man arrive and that the repair to the window in the school hall would be completed within the next hour or so. Thus, allowing him to get home in good time to start marking the mathematics homework set that day. He greeted his visitor loudly, aware his nosy school secretary in the office behind him had her window open.

'Ah! Monsieur Guyot. Thank you for coming so promptly.'

'No problem Monsieur Chaillot. I was able to fit your job in after finishing another' James replied equally loudly. 'Now where is this broken window?'

'In the school hall. I will show you.'

In the hall, out of earshot of the Headmaster's office, James began to take his tools out of his box. 'You received my message?'

'Yes. You require passes for the factory. I will have them ready in good time.'

Hearing the cleaners arriving in the passageway, James started removing the broken window. After they had passed by he said: 'I need your daughter's help?'

'Of course. What is it you require?'

James told him about the two airmen needing to be moved and whereabouts the farm was located.

'Madeleine knows where that is' replied the Headmaster nodding his head. 'She will probably set-off before curfew. If she thinks it necessary, she may arrange to transport them by river. Her boyfriend's family own boats…'. Chaillot saw the expression of concern on James's face. '…Do not worry Monsieur. He can be trusted.'

Within an hour the window was repaired and, after making arrangements for delivery of the factory passes, James left the school and headed towards Coups d'Orleans.

From one of the local workers used in the factory, James had already ascertained the times the German sentries changed guard, the time it took for sentries to patrol the factory's perimeter, the position of their machine-gun posts and other check-points along its approach road and within the factory itself. However, he wanted to double-check as much as he could, his SOE training had taught him to be thorough in everything planned. The old, run-down flat above the equally run-down shop almost opposite the factory entrance was just perfect for this requirement. The dingy flat enjoyed a good vantage point, where James could observe the main factory entrance and a good part of its approach road and he could also study and time the routines of the sentries and main checkpoint. From the window, he noted the average time it took for the sentries to patrol up and down the eastern wall of the factory, calculating how long it would take a man to emerge from a culvert - running parallel to the wall at a distance of about 50 yards from it - and make it to the shadows of the high wall in between sweeps of the two searchlights mounted on each corner of the wall. He had been using the flat during the last few days and had spent some of the mornings, some of the late afternoons/early evenings, observing routine deliveries and despatches by vehicles of goods and supplies - also noting the routine arrival and departure of local workers. There was always a consistency about the Germans, they were always methodical, always observing strict adherence to times and schedules.

Within the factory the skilled workers - the engineers, specialists and supervisors - were German. However all the menial, dirty, labouring and laborious tasks were carried out by enforced workers from either the immediate locality or from further afield. It was from within the ranks of the local workforce in the factory that the success of James's plan of sabotage would so much depend. He just hoped the workers amongst this workforce, recruited by the Resistance, would measure up to the task. Throughout his observations of the factory, particular factors had especially interested James: the clockwork regularity of the morning arrival and early evening departure of the waste-disposal vehicle - and the cursory inspection of it afforded by the sentries; the constant times of the mass arrival and departure of the workforce.

Suddenly, James was distracted by the din of vehicles arriving and stopping down the street and German voices shouting. Troops began storming buildings on either side of the road, breaking doors down. Quickly he fled from the room and sprinted down the steep staircase to the back door.

James shouted to the proprietor of the shop, an old man. 'The Boche are down the road. Starting a check all the way along. Don't resist them - just let them check around. There is nothing upstairs to indicate I was ever here.'

At the back of the shop there was an area of wasteland. Making his way across this, taking out an old sack he had with him, James nonchalantly began picking up firewood. Eventually, he emerged on the Avenue de St Julien.

'Halt!' Came a shouted command from a German soldier across the road.

James stopped dead in his tracks, turned to face the two soldiers crossing the road towards him.

'Papers?' The older one demanded.

James put down his tool box and sack of firewood and reached in his pocket. The soldier snatched the document from him and examined it before passing it to his colleague.

'Open this box?' Barked the younger soldier after studying the document and looking at the tool box.

The older soldier was looking through the sack. 'What are you doing here?'

'I was working at a shop on Avenue Louis Tirman and I am on my way home.' The younger soldier looked enquiringly at the waste ground behind them. Quickly, James continued 'This area is good for collecting firewood. I needed some for my stove.'

For what seemed like ages the two soldiers closely studied his ID again. Eventually they said he could go. Calmly, James closed his tool box, picked it and the sack up and began to walk away. A feeling of relief flooded through him. Suddenly, one of the soldiers shouted after him.

'Stop!' With a feeling of dread James turned towards them. 'You have a light?' The older soldier had a cigarette in his lips and was trying to get his lighter to work.

With forced courtesy James replied 'Of course.'

34

The tall, slim girl had arrived at the farm at dusk the previous evening. Together with those at the farm she had supper and, as she sat across the table from him, outlining her plan for his and Mike's departure, Colin had reckoned she was about nineteen years of age.

Madeleine Chaillot, Colin and Mike left the farmhouse before dawn. The rain which had fallen through much of the night had turned into a persistent drizzle. Last night Madeleine had been dressed in a floral-patterned dress but, now, as she led them purposefully across wet and muddy meadows, she wore grey dungarees which accentuated the slimness of her figure. Wherever possible they kept close to hedge and tree lines and walls. Eventually, the trio climbed over a gate onto a rough track with embankments up to about head height. The track was slippery and stony, made more unpleasant and hazardous by puddles formed by rain run-off from the fields. Colin believed they had walked for over a mile when they entered a wooded area. The drizzle had stopped but water dripped down Colin's neck from the leaves above him. They walked for a while further then, suddenly, through a gap in the trees, the new dawning-light glistened on an expanse of water. Nearby, they heard a startled water-bird take off noisily from its surface. To his left, some way distant, Colin could make out the still dark outline of what looked like a vessel of some sort.

'Careful!' Said Madeleine suddenly. 'The ground drops steeply to the river.' Mike just stopped in time before slipping down the steep incline. 'Wait here a moment.'

She disappeared off to the left. After a while they heard her call out a name, then a reply from the direction of the river. Colin and Mike couldn't make out what was said. Within a few minutes Madeleine returned.

'Quickly, this way.' She led them down the path from whence she had come. 'Didier is there. Unfortunately there is a submerged old landing stage, so he is moored offshore. We will have to swim out to him. I hope you can both swim?'

The path turned sharply to the right and, directly in front of them, moored about 50 yards out, they saw a barge. From just around the bend, getting louder and louder, closer and closer, there was a noise upstream. It was the unmistakable sound of a powerful motor-boat engine.

'Back into the trees! Quickly!' She ordered. 'It is a German patrol boat.'

The trio just made it as the patrol boat rounded the bend, slowed its engine and pulled alongside the barge. The boat's searchlight scanned the barge, lighting it and the surrounding river as if it were full daylight. Another of its searchlights sent a finger of light towards the shore, its brilliance illuminating and penetrating the still darkish undergrowth above their heads. From their hiding place they heard German commands, saw a figure emerge from the barge's cabin, approaching three figures who by now were boarding it. There were some animated exchanges of conversation. Colin saw two figures begin to search the barge. At one stage, one of the boarding party appeared to use threatening tones and gestures. The searchlight shining on the shore began to move - up and down the shoreline it played its beam. Colin thought to himself surely now their game was up - they would be discovered. Should they give themselves up now before the Germans sprayed their hiding place with shells from the machine-gun positioned menacingly on the patrol boat's deck? Eventually, after what seemed an eternity, the searchlight on the shore was switched off and, by the light of the searchlight still shining on the barge, Colin saw the three-man boarding party climb back onto their vessel. The relief of the three hiding amongst the trees and undergrowth was immense. With a roar the patrol boat's engine surged into life and the vessel pulled away from the barge. The waves of its large wash lapped noisily against the shore causing the barge to rock at its mooring. As the sound of the departing patrol boat diminished in the distance, quiet returned. Except for the lowing of a cow in a field on the far side of the river, all was silent. Madeleine signalled the barge with her torch. Within a moment her signal was acknowledged.

'Right here we go. I warn you though the water is cold.'

It was an understatement. The water was absolutely freezing, like getting into a bath of ice. With a lamp, one of the men on the barge lit a passage through the water for them.

'Follow the beam of this light' he shouted. 'Either side of this is submerged debris from the landing stage. You could injure yourselves.'

A muscular young man assisted the three as they scrambled aboard the barge one by one. 'There are dry clothes for each of you and towels in the cabin. The stove has been alight for some while now, so you can warm yourselves up.'

Colin and Mike insisted Madeleine dried herself and

got changed first. She disappeared into the far end of the cabin.

Didier spoke. 'Make yourselves a hot drink? There is some ersatz stuff and mugs in the cupboard there. We must move away from here quickly. That patrol boat will be turning back after it reaches Braux. Now if you will excuse me.'

Colin and Mike watched as he went up the steps to the deck and heard the engine cough into life. Within a few moments the barge was chugging away down river.

The two airmen were already being warmed by the steaming coffee when Madeleine returned. She was dressed in dry dungarees, with a thick blanket draped around her shoulders and was still drying her hair. Something about the way her raven-black hair hung down over the side of her face created a Romany-like mystery and wild beauty in her features, exaggerating the intensity and passion of her brown eyes. Before going to dry themselves and change, Mike poured a mug of coffee and handed it to her. When they returned she had combed her hair back into the previous style. She was huddled close to the stove. Shafts of strong sunlight were filtering through the curtains at the windows. The chugging of the barge's engine drummed out a regular beat.

'It was a close thing with that patrol boat turning up' said Colin as he sat down opposite Madeleine.

'Yes. They have increased their river patrols. Luckily, Didier's family have a licence from the Germans as they carry goods for them. You will have seen, this barge is carrying timber. He had documents to prove the cargo was for them. They wanted to know why he had moored there. He told them he had become unwell during the night.'

Colin asked 'Where are we heading for Madeleine?'

'Charleville. You will be hidden there for a few days.

More instructions will follow.' She looked at the two airmen, an amused smile on her face. 'I apologise for those clothes. They are all Didier had available. I expect your friends back in England would laugh if they could see you.'

Mike looked at Colin laughing. 'Yes. Colin can you imagine what they would say back in the Mess?'

'Mess? What is the Mess?' She asked puzzled.

He answered 'Forgive us. Mess in our jargon - language - means the place where soldiers and airmen eat, relax.'

She giggled girlishly. 'I see. Language is a funny thing, yes?'

'Your English is very good Madeleine' said Colin. 'Much better than our French.'

'Thank you. You are very kind. Would you both like some more Coffee?' She refilled their mugs and her own and returned to her seat. 'My father is a teacher. Throughout my childhood he insisted I studied - still does even now I am older. He has always said how important it is to learn all the time.' She paused, almost as if she shouldn't say anymore. 'In what part of England do you live?'

'I was born in Somerset, in the south west of England' replied Mike. 'My parents still live there. It's a lovely part of England. In fact, after Colin and I teamed up in the same crew, we realised we had known each other when we were boys.'

Colin added 'My aunt has a farm in Somerset. I used to spend most of my school holidays there. With my parents and brother. I first got to know Mike then. My home though is in Ealing - a town outside London. My older brother is also in the RAF. He was a pilot too - Fighters. He got injured in 1940.'

'I have a brother also.' Her expression changed. 'He is in England. He fled there just as the war started. He managed to get a message to us last year. He is with DeGaulle - the

Free French forces. Many times I look at an atlas. Wonder just where he is in England.' There was a flicker of desperation in her look. 'Hopefully, one day when the war is over, I will be able to visit England.'

'Do you live in Charleville Madeleine?' Asked Colin.

'Yes. I have lived there all my life.'

'How long have you been helping the Resistance?'

Suddenly she became embarrassed, anxious. 'I must not say anymore. I have said too much already.'

Both she and the two airmen had found it so easy to talk to each other. But Colin and Mike also realised they had probably said too much about themselves, realising just how easy it can be to fall into a trap set by a German agent. The conversation between the three of them, whilst still friendly, became more stilted, more guarded.

'Madeleine! Madeleine!' Didier called urgently. She went to the steps. 'Boche patrol boat ahead' he shouted urgently again.

She beckoned to Colin and Mike. 'Quick! Quick! Up here.' They followed her to the deck and, as previously planned, crawled towards the stacked timber cargo. Quickly Madeleine lifted the tarpaulin and moved some small-size timber. Urgently she ushered Colin and Mike into a small void left between two stacks of large-planked timber. 'In there quickly.'

Once they were concealed Madeleine moved the smaller timber back and re-tied the tarpaulin. Colin and Mike, horribly cramped between the timber, heard the throb of the patrol boat drawing very close. To their horror, heard the boat pull alongside the barge, heard a German voice. They were fearful not only for themselves but for Madeleine, Didier and the crew. Their earlier conversations with Georges and Angeline had really brought home to them what the Nazis did to anyone found assisting escaping aircrew.

'You need help?' Asked one of the Germans.

'No. No. Thank you' replied Didier. 'The tarpaulin became loose. We did not want to chance the timber getting wet. All is fine now.'

Colin and Mike heard a boot-step on the deck.

The German said 'I will make sure. Just in case.'

Colin admired the calm of Didier as he replied. 'No. It is fine. Besides, I have had to use some old rope - it has got oil and grease on it. Your hands will get covered.'

There was an agonising pause before the German said 'Well very well then.'

There was another agonising pause, a command Colin couldn't properly hear, and the patrol boat began to move away.

When the boat was a distance away Didier turned to Madeleine. 'Luckily he knows me, knows my family. Until we reach Charleville the two airmen must remain where they are.'

Madeleine conveyed Didier's instructions to Colin and Mike. They looked at each other, thought of the weight of timber either side and above their tiny hiding place, looked at each other again, hoping against hope the cargo didn't shift.

Just before reaching Charleville, Didier lifted the tarpaulin and spoke urgently to Colin and Mike. 'Quickly, back to the cabin.' He spoke incisively, with Madeleine providing some translation. 'We will be docking in Charleville shortly. When returning from the sawmill, it is nothing unusual for my family to be transporting workers on our barges. As a way of paying their fare, the workers often help us unload the cargo. The Germans know this and accept it, so their suspicions should not be aroused when they see you get off the barge. However, we cannot take any chances. It is vital you do exactly as I say. Understood?

We will be docking at the Quai du Moulinet, the usual one for unloading timber. To the left of where we dock, you will see two long sheds. The furthest one is where timber is stored. When I say so you will begin to assist the people on the quay to unload. Across the road, directly opposite the sheds, is an office with a big grey and white sign above the door. After you have unloaded and re-stacked two lots of timber, a man will be in the office doorway with a file in his hand and holding a handkerchief. This man will call you over to the office and you will wait inside with him for a while. The office has a side entrance with a window beside it.' Suddenly he stopped. 'Now Madeleine will continue.' He went up to the deck.

Madeleine spoke in the same incisive way as Didier. 'After twenty minutes you will see me outside the window Didier mentioned. I will pause for a moment. After I start walking again, one of you will follow me - but from a distance of a few metres. The next one will wait a few moments before also following. I must stress to you the importance of keeping a distance behind me and between yourselves. It is absolutely vital people do not realise we are together. The route will take about forty minutes to complete. When we reach the safe house, where the first one of you will be staying, I will stop at a newspaper stand. The place you will be staying will be directly behind me. Without any acknowledgement between us you will go directly into the courtyard - a door on your right will be open. The remaining one of you will have paused to look in a shop window. Only when the courtyard has been entered, is the second man to proceed to follow me. At the next safe house you will see me stop to look in my diary. The place you will be staying is the home of a Dentist, his name plaque is beside the front door. Again, there must be no acknowledgement between us. Is that all understood?' She paused. 'Now do you have any questions?'

'What if any Germans are waiting around outside these places?' Asked Mike.

'Just keep on walking. If that should be the case or, I do not think it safe, I will not use either of the signals I have explained. Also, if for any reason Boche soldiers stop me, you are to walk past ignoring the situation. If any of these things happen, you are to head for the Square du Petit Bois and wait by the statue just inside the entrance. Either I or one of our Group will meet you there at 11 o'clock. They will identify themselves by asking for directions to the Courthouse.'

'Understood' said Colin.

She told them what phrases of recognition and response were to be used when they arrived at their respective safe houses or, if they had to wait in the Square. The barge began to slow.

'We are about to dock. Now if there are no more questions I suggest you wait here, get ready to help unload and do exactly as Didier has instructed.' She paused. When she spoke again, there was a hint of sadness - a real sincerity and kindness in her voice. 'This will probably be the last time we ever speak. I wish you both well and hope you have a continued safe trip back to England.'

Colin and Mike thanked her for what she had done. She left them as she went to help prepare to tie the barge to the quay.

To their horror, as the barge was tied up, German soldiers were standing on the quay. In the main though, they simply watched as the unloading progressed, only occasionally showing more than a passing interest in what was going on and randomly speaking to the workers. Mercifully, none of them showed any interest in the two airmen.

Unloading the timber was hard work. It had been some time since either Colin or Mike had done manual labour of this sort. Despite their unspoken misgivings about how they would blend in with the dockyard workers, they seemed to be accepted amongst them. Another of their reservations had been because of their very basic knowledge of French - how to avoid being drawn into conversation. Thankfully, they managed to avoid this and got by only using simple words and phrases - making knowing gestures and noises when appropriate. Nevertheless, it was with a huge sense of relief when, just as Didier had said, a man holding a file and a handkerchief emerged from the office doorway and summoned them over to him. Colin and Mike followed the man into his office.

'Make sure you shut the door' he called back.

Cursorily the man greeted them. His manner was dour - a man of few words. It was immediately obvious he was on edge and uneasy and, almost blatantly, gave the impression he wished they weren't there at all.

'You will be all right here for a while. I have told my staff I do not want to be disturbed for at least half-an-hour.' He sat behind his desk, motioning them to sit in two battered chairs over by the wall facing the window and side door Didier had mentioned. He did not offer them a drink or anything at all but said they could smoke if they wanted to. 'A German officer is due sometime this morning for a routine check of our work schedules and manifests. If he arrives or, for any reason, one of the staff does come to the office, you are both to go and hide in that cupboard.' He pointed to a door to the right of them. He looked over the top of his spectacles and studied them for another moment. His eyes returned to the papers on his desk.

The difference in warmth and friendliness towards them demonstrated by the man sitting opposite and, that extended to them by the family on the farm and by Madeleine and Didier, could not be more marked. The three men continued to sit in a silence broken only by short spells of awkward conversation when the man behind his desk chose to pontificate on the state of commerce and trade, shortages and unavailability of materials and supplies.

Colin looked at the clock hanging on the wall. Madeleine had said she would appear outside the window after twenty minutes of them entering the office. They had now been waiting over half-an-hour. Had something happened to her? Had she been caught by the Gestapo and taken for interrogation? Had it all been a ploy - a charade just to get them away from the farm? And, if any of these things were the case, what should he and Mike do - where should they go? He began to get more and more anxious. Then, suddenly, he saw her pause outside the window. He nudged Mike who had fallen asleep.

'Mike. There she is, outside. Whose going first?'

'Skipper's privilege. You go first. I'll follow on.'

They thanked the man behind the desk who mumbled a reply. Madeleine was already a few yards down Rue de Conde by the time Colin got outside. She had changed and wore a skirt and blouse, a beret atop her head of raven-black hair. Not once did she turn to ensure he was following her. As instructed, he remained all the time at a distance of about fifty yards. She turned left. Colin saw from a battered sign they had turned into Rue Baron Ouinart. After a short while, Madeleine turned into Rue du Moulin. He had a moment of panic when, just round the corner, he lost all sight of her. A German motorbike and sidecar had collided with a cart laden with fruit and vegetables. The overturned cart and its load almost completely blocked the road, its owner - between extricating and calming the injured horse - was arguing and gesticulating furiously with the

German rider and his passenger also being harangued by the gathering crowd as they sat bemused amongst a spreading mound of produce. One of the soldiers got to his feet and brutally beat the owner of the cart with the butt of his rifle. With relief Colin saw Madeleine emerge beyond the scene of chaos, and quickened his pace slightly to recover lost ground. They crossed Place Ducale, thronged with people, towards the City Hall. To his horror the square was heavily populated with German troops, especially near the Hall. His heart sank, he just hoped he wasn't stopped. He sensed Madeleine put more purpose into her steps as, rather than try to avoid the groups of soldiers, she passed very close to them. Thankfully, the purposeful and confident way she walked seemed to avert any suspicion. He determined to emulate her attitude and he passed dozens of them - within inches in some cases - without arousing a glimmer of interest. Colin hoped Mike would be equally successful. They passed Place Carnot where, in the corner opposite, stood the austere, grey, depressing-looking walls of a building - the main prison of Charleville. During their stay on the farm, Angeline and Georges had mentioned that it was behind those prison walls the Gestapo revelled in exacting their foul deeds of extreme cruelty and torture on people daring to defy and work against them. Angeline and Georges themselves had had many friends and relatives of theirs taken there, only one or two surviving the experience. It was not until he followed Madeleine into Rue de L'Arquebuse and the cheery and warming sounds of the innocence of young children, playing in a school playground, partly expunged from his mind what he had heard about the prison. A left turn, then a right and Madeleine led him into a narrow and dingy street - Rue Couvelet - Colin read on a sign. On the wall above the sign was a drawing of a knife being plunged into a cartoon-like image of Hitler, with a swastika above his head. Colin saw what looked like a dried pool of blood on the footpath nearby. He wondered whether the dark red stain was evidence of the execution of the perpetrator of the graffiti. Madeleine stopped for a moment to look at a poster-board leaning against a newspaper stand and, without a glance back at him, began walking away down the street. Colin got to the spot where she had stood. Sure enough there was a little courtyard set between two buildings. Just into the courtyard a door on the right stood open. Before entering the building he glanced over his shoulder to see Mike walk past the courtyard entrance following Madeleine.

A large buxom woman in her fifties appeared along the hallway. There was something hard and coarse about her, her cheeks heavy with cheap make-up applied without subtlety, her large lips shone with crimson lipstick. Her straw-coloured hair was scragged back tightly and accentuated her coarse features. A bright pink dressing gown was gathered loosely around her but did not really conceal her ample body and bust squeezed into black and red underwear. A sight she did not seem concerned to hide.

'You have just arrived from Sedan?'

Colin was lost for words. The woman looked questioningly at him. Suddenly he remembered the phrase Madeleine had told him would be used as a form of recognition.

'Oh! Oui! Oui! Phoebe's expecting me.'

With her hand on his shoulder she guided him towards the staircase with her body pressed close to his. It appeared to be a four-storey house, everywhere seemed awash with a heavy, sweet scent. From somewhere soft music drifted out from a room. At the top of each flight of stairs were positioned aspidistras or ferns. From a door on the first landing, emerged a weasel-like old man, fiddling with his trousers and turning back towards a room, waving at a young, scantily-clad woman standing within. On the next landing an older but very shapely woman with long auburn hair hurried out of what Colin took to be a bathroom. She scurried into the next door along the landing calling: 'There my Cheri, I promised I would be back soon.'

Arriving on the top landing, the woman showed Colin into a bedroom. A bed dominated the centre of the room, a *chez lounge* was positioned by the far wall - both were adorned with crimson and pink cushions. One wall and the ceiling were completely covered with mirrors fully reflecting the bed.

'I am expecting someone very soon' she said. 'I will come up in about an hour with some coffee. Make yourself comfortable.'

As she disappeared out the door, Colin looked around the room again before sitting on the *chez lounge*. He wondered how long the brothel was to be his shelter and hiding place.

To his right, as Madeleine turned left, Mike looked across to the Square de la Gare. Further over to the right and beyond, he could make out the unmistakable outline of a railway station and its associated buildings, sheds and sidings. For most of the walk along Rue de la Graviere, the road followed the curve of the railway line. He had heard a train whistle, heard it start to move - its wheels spin on the track as it gained traction, saw the plumes of smoke and steam above the sheds in the siding. Continuing to follow Madeleine along the road, the goods train began to pass him. He looked across at the passing engine and its long train of enclosed wagons. Each wagon top was mounted by a German soldier holding a rifle. No doubt each wagon contained weaponry and supplies for front-line troops to strengthen still further their grip on occupied Europe. He saw Madeleine ahead of him, stop at a corner and take a small book out of her pocket. Mike immediately slowed his step and looked at a tabby cat grooming its whiskers contentedly on a wall. Within a few moments, Madeleine returned the little book to her pocket and continued on her way. Walking to where she had stopped, an impressive-looking house with a shining front door and attractive portico stood on a corner. To the side of the door was a shiny metal plaque, from which the morning sun reflected. Looking back down the street Mike saw two German army officers walking towards him. He pulled the metal bell pull. As he awaited anxiously for the door to be opened, the officers drew close. 'Come on! Come on open this door!' He murmured nervously to himself. In the hallway on the other side of the door there were footsteps and someone began to open the door.

35

Jules Vadim was born in Mezieres, had lived there all his 59 years. He was a man of simple pleasures and very few interests, had been happy enough to work as a tailor in his outfitter's shop on Rue Monge for the majority of his working life. His simple, uncomplicated but, hard-working existence had ceased a few months after the invasion of his country, when there was a resulting lack of demand and finance for his service and products and had been forced to close his shop. For the past eighteen months Jules had been one of many people in the enforced labour programme imposed by the Germans. As a consequence, he had been working as a labourer in the engineering factory and warehouse - off Avenue Louis Tirman - before eventually contriving for himself a job as a kitchen porter in the German officers' staff canteen there. It was partly because of his hatred and bitterness toward the Germans, partly because - at last - he had decided to have some excitement in his life, Jules had agreed to help the Resistance. He had agreed to be one of "their people" inside the factory for the operation of sabotage James and the Resistance had been planning. Part of Jules's role as kitchen porter was to sign for the factory's supply of animal carcasses delivered from the abattoir. Once butchered this meat was destined to be enjoyed only by the Germans working or stationed at the factory. However, there was something different about this particular day's delivery. Inside the carcasses were concealed packets of nails and explosives.

Jules watched the van draw out from the delivery yard. He turned to the lamb and pork carcasses stacked beside him. The fat soldier standing on the loading bay with Jules, grinned cunningly as his eyes took in the array of juicy lamb and pork laying before them.

'What is it you would like this week?' Asked Jules.

'Lamb I think' replied the German curtly.

Jules looked around furtively. There was no one else within sight. Quickly he searched inside one of the carcasses, retrieved some kidney and liver and handed it to the soldier who, with deft hands, put them into a bag concealed inside his tunic.

Waiting for the German to move away Jules turned his attention to the delivery. He loaded some carcasses onto his trolley and headed towards the kitchen. The kitchen and canteen were located along a corridor behind the delivery bay. Just off this corridor was a cloakroom with a row of lockers. At this time of day Jules knew the corridor would not be busy with people and, arriving outside the cloakroom, he stopped. Looking around carefully, ensuring he was alone, Jules began to examine the carcasses. The top one did not contain what he was looking for so he lifted it on to the floor. He was about to search the second one when one of the cooks appeared in the canteen doorway. Jules froze.

The cook shouted 'What are you doing?'

'These damn things slipped off the trolley. I will be bringing them through in a moment.'

'Well be quick about it' ordered the cook angrily. Appearing to be satisfied with Jules's answer, he disappeared.

Breathing a sigh of relief, Jules quickly searched the

second carcass. He found the packets of nails. He put these on the floor and lifted the third carcass. Again he found what he was looking for: bundles of what he took to be the plastic explosives. Hurriedly, he took the nails and the other bundles into the cloakroom and concealed them as best he could, hoping in the interim nobody entered the cloakroom. He had just reloaded the trolley when the cook emerged again.

'What have you been doing?' He shouted angrily again. 'Why can't you be more careful? Now hurry up, we have a very busy day. If this happens again, I will have you sent back working in the factory.'

'Sorry. Just coming. Just coming.' Almost running with the trolley Jules headed towards the kitchen.

After unloading and storing the pork, Jules returned for the lamb. He stopped again outside the cloakroom. He was relieved no one had appeared to have been in there. As quietly as possible he dragged the first locker away from the wall. Behind it, for a few days now, he had busied himself removing masonry, creating a fairly large cavity in the wall. Into this cavity, he placed the packages and bundles. Getting really nervous now, he replaced the locker and returned to his trolley. Just as he did so, two German officers passed him - it had been a close call. Jules hoped the beads of sweat on his brow brought on by his fear, had not been noticed. When he had volunteered to help the Resistance, he had no idea the excitement he had secretly yearned would be so dangerously, frighteningly earned. Now, content to have done his bit, Jules returned to the delivery bay for the lamb.

Earlier in the morning Albert, Claude and Jacque had started one of the most uncomfortable journeys of their lives. Out in the countryside, to the west of Mezieres, they had clambered into three rubbish bins in the middle of the refuse lorry destined for the factory. Its driver and mate were known and familiar to the guards and sentries at the factory. They had undertaken the delivery of empty bins and the evening collection of the full bins every day for the past year or more. The driver knew full well, because of this familiarity, the guards only ever cursorily checked the empty bins loaded to the rear of the lorry - if they checked them at all. This had been borne out by James's observation of the factory.

In their stinking, foul hideaways, the three men felt the lorry stop, heard the voices of the guards and the driver. To their horror they heard the sound of someone climbing on the back of the lorry, the metallic clanks as the person proceeded to move and examine the empty containers. As the guard's search grew dangerously close, the guard's colleague standing beside the lorry called up to him to attend to another vehicle which had stopped behind. It was a merciful relief to the men hiding in the bins as they felt a jerk and their conveyance started to move away. After a while they heard the big metal inner gates of the factory yard slam shut behind them. There was now no turning back for them, their fate laid in others' hands. They hoped the next part of the plan worked. Their lives depended on it.

After what seemed ages Albert felt himself being lifted, his legs jarred as the bin was deposited heavily on concrete. He became dizzy as the bin was rolled on its end for several metres. The bin was tipped on its side, its lid lifted.

'Quickly. Behind this wall' urged the driver of the lorry. Albert began to crawl on his hands and knees to where the driver indicated. Looking around he realised the high wall bordering the dustbin storage area was not overlooked by any windows, the area itself tucked away in a quiet corner of the yard. 'Wait there until we bring the others' said the driver. He pointed to a door set at right-angles to the wall.

'Someone will come from that door shortly and collect the three of you.'

Albert waited in the shadow of the wall for Claude and Jacque to join him. Claude was the last to be unloaded from the lorry and had just joined his two friends when, from the door, appeared a man hauling an over-laden barrow. With the lorry affording extra cover for the four men, the man with the barrow, introduced himself as Emile.

He commanded 'Each of you take some of these things.' Albert, Claude and Jacque each took some hand tools, building and plastering materials from the barrow. 'We must be quick. Guards will be on patrol around here any minute. The three of you walk with me. Act naturally, talk with each other. We have to give the impression you are regular workers here. You must do and act exactly as I say. Understand? When we turn left here we will enter the main part of the factory yard. It is absolutely vital you behave naturally, appear to know where we are going. If we are stopped by any of the guards leave the talking to me.'

The four men started to walk as the lorry moved off. They had just rounded the corner into the main yard when two guards appeared a few metres in front of them. Emile nodded a good morning to the two which they ignored and cast an uninterested glance at the four Frenchmen before passing on by without saying anything or challenging their presence.

After the guards were out of earshot, Emile said 'After my slaving in this damn place since 1940, my face is familiar to many of the Boche. I can get away with many things without question.'

The quartet continued walking along the yard, the apprehension of the three newcomers increasing each time they saw a German guard - each guard with watchful and suspicious eyes - supervising the many local workers scurrying frantically about the yard. They were now by the southern wall of the factory when Emile turned to the right, towards a big pair of brown sliding doors.

'We need to go in here. I will deal with the guards by the doors. Just show your permits when asked. These two do not speak any French. Just make out you can't understand them. I know a few words and phrases of German and I will do the talking.'

'Halt!' Demanded one of the two guards standing by the doors.

The other examined Emile's permit, turned to the three others to examine theirs. Emile explained in French what was required of his three compatriots. He was glad the Germans only checked the full ID papers of local workers when they first entered the factory complex and, once inside it, sight of permits was usually all that was necessary to satisfy them.

'Schnell! Schnell!' Demanded the German impatiently, snatching their forged permits before scrutinising each one.

The first guard began to look through the barrow's contents, whilst his colleague checked what the three other Frenchman were carrying. 'What have you all come to do?' He enquired after a while.

Understanding what he had asked, Emile replied casually in reasonably good German 'To continue working on the new wall in the corridor near the warehouse.'

'All four of you?' The guard asked suspiciously.

'As you know the factory commandant requires the job finished by next week. He has deployed extra labour to get it finished.'

'I see. I will need to check this first.' The guard turned towards the telephone hanging on the wall outside the doors.

Emile fought to remain calm. 'The commandant ordered the re-deployment early this morning.' He was now really chancing his arm. 'He has also demanded an explanation for any delay in executing his orders.'

There was a frightening pause as the guard continued towards the telephone. Then, thinking of the repercussions should he be the one found delaying his superior's orders, he at last said 'Very well then' and nodded to the other guard to open the doors.

The wall in question was being built, floor to ceiling, to sub-divide an area of the factory to provide a separate workshop of significant proportions with a dust-free environment. Large scaffolding was in place at the site, and the whole area was seething with people working on the construction. German guards stood in attendance barking out instructions and orders, bullying and beating those they considered weren't working quickly enough.

After parking his barrow at the far end of the new wall around the corner, Emile spoke to the other three. 'This is where we will be working. At first, two of you will be mixing the cement and mortar, the other will be collecting bricks from over there. In ten minutes, the guards will be changing over. Just as they are changing, a distraction will be staged around the corner. When I say so, the three of you are to go down this corridor.' He pointed to his left. 'You will see large double doors to the warehouse. A man will be waiting there to unlock them and to hand over the packets and enough food and drink to last you till tomorrow morning.'

Albert, Claude and Jacque did not have any questions. They had been briefed thoroughly the previous evening and knew exactly what they had to do. Each one of them had studied the layout of the warehouse; knew just where the crates were stored; knew whereabouts within the warehouse they could hide; knew they would have to remain in there until the following morning long after they had opened and re-sealed the crates.

Pierre Papon had worked in the despatch office of the factory since leaving school, long before the Germans had requisitioned it for their needs. There was nothing about the despatch and transportation of goods Pierre did not know. During the years working in the despatch office, he had accumulated a thorough, in-depth knowledge of the rail, road and canal networks of France. A knowledge invaluable to the Germans when they took over the factory and, realising this, they had retained his services. Pierre had always been shrewd. Using this shrewdness he realised, if on occasions, he could slip the Boche snippets of information about activities designed to thwart them in any way he could gain their trust, retain his job in the despatch office where the more important information he had access to would be useful to his compatriots in the Resistance. This ploy had worked and, two years later, he still worked in the despatch office, *albeit* with a German Lieutenant and an uninterested Corporal supervising. There were various times, however, when these two would leave Pierre alone in the office. He used these opportunities to quickly read or copy despatch instructions or manifests and, risking his life, pass the information to the Resistance. This is how James had come to learn of the very next very large consignment of engine parts, lubricants and fuel to be despatched from the factory, finally destined for Rommel's Army in North Africa. It was this consignment James had decided the Resistance were going to target.

The German's trust in him and, the job itself, allowed Pierre a degree of liberty - necessitated his getting about the factory without arousing suspicion. He even had a key to the warehouse. This particular morning he had made an excuse for leaving the office. The Corporal had been too busy resting his fat legs on the desk reading a German magazine, whilst listening to a broadcast about an RAF raid on Frankfurt, to worry about where Pierre was going. Pierre had made his way to the cloakroom near the canteen, retrieved the packets hidden by Jules and, after hiding them in a box of files, headed for the warehouse. He was just approaching the warehouse when he heard a commotion around the corner. German guards ran shouting along the corridor at right angles to the one he was walking along.

Pierre waited by the doors to the now unguarded warehouse. He saw three men heading towards him. One of the three gave the agreed phrase of recognition. Quickly Pierre unlocked the doors and re-confirmed the time he would unlock the doors tomorrow and Albert, Claude and Jacque entered the warehouse. Pierre locked the doors after them and turned back towards his office.

36

James's wish for a dark night had been granted. Dense cloud completely covered the half-moon. It was perfect conditions for what he and the Resistance Group had been planning for days.

To avoid the curfew James had hidden in the Square Mialaret during the late afternoon. From the Square to the culvert by the factory's eastern wall, it had been very slow going. Part of the way crawling along ditches, part of the way dashing between the cover of what trees and bushes there were and, whatever other cover he could find. Now in that filthy, muddy culvert he had a good view - through scraggy and sparse scrub - of the eastern wall. He put down the holdall of explosives, fuses and timing devices and dismantled sten gun and yet again checked its contents and the pistol beneath his jacket.

James had selected one other man to accompany him. Francois Lurcat had impressed him from the time they first met at the very first training session James had held in the forests and wildness of the Ardennes. Francois had been born and raised in a little village near the southern part of the River Rhone - had spent most of his life living there. That is, until the establishment of Vichy France had angered and revolted him so much he had fled north to unite with whom he termed "Real French People". Such was Francois's anger at Vichy's unpalatable bargain with the German's and, his hatred of the Germans, it had not been too long before he had fulfilled an eagerness to join the Resistance. What had impressed James most about Francois was, firstly, his feelings about the Boche, his patriotism and, his determination to do everything he could to rid his country of them. Secondly, he was trustworthy, had been a very willing, intelligent pupil - picking up things quickly; he was precise, eager to learn and anxious to thoroughly understand the Resistance aims and objectives and the right way to achieve them. He was also dependable, very brave and a very pleasant man - easy to like. James was confident he could not have picked anyone better to go with him into the factory.

Francois had arrived at the culvert *via* a different route than James. He too had skilfully avoided the start of the curfew by hiding in the Church on Rue de l'Eglise before approaching the area from the Rue du Mess. He had cut through the southern part of the Square Mialaret, entered a manhole on the Av. Louis Tirman, then along an old sewer which led into the southern part of the culvert. Using the culvert's shallow bank as cover he had arrived beside James at exactly the agreed time. He also had a heavy bag with him.

'Francois! You stink a bit!' Proclaimed James quietly with mock disdain.

'You do not smell so good yourself' retorted Francois with equal mock disdain.

'All set? Double-checked you have everything you will need?'

'Yes. I had a final check in the Church.'

The sweeping, penetrating beams of the searchlights on each corner of the factory wall lit up the area all around them. Both men ducked further down in the culvert. As the beam moved away, by the dim light of his cigarette lighter, James checked his watch.

'We will allow for one more complete sweep of those lights and then I'll go. You will follow after the next sweep. Get ready.'

Francois nodded his acknowledgement. Knowing Francois's capabilities, James knew he didn't have to re-cap anything but, it was a habit he had picked up during his SOE training.

'The old grille lays directly ahead. It's partially below ground level, has been sawn through by one of our men inside and will just push in. I will replace it when I'm in there. Then, when you get over there, you push it in and replace it in the same way. I will wait for you there.'

It seemed like ages as they waited for the lights to finish their cycle and the sentries to meet and turn in opposite directions. James was about to break cover when a dog barked. Another sentry with a dog had rounded the far corner of the wall. Thankful he and Francois were downwind, James cursed again as the sentry with the dog stopped and chatted with the other two patrolling sentries. James and Francois could hear their voices clearly.

Ducking back down in the culvert James whispered angrily 'Sod it! Now we will have to wait for the whole cycle again.'

James glanced anxiously at his watch. Eventually, the sentries continued their patrol, the sentry with the dog entering a door in the wall James had been told was now never used.

As the searchlight beams moved away again James said 'Here I go. See you over there.'

Francois watched him disappear into the darkness and awaited his turn.

At the foot of the wall James slithered into the depression

in the ground by the grille. Rain water had been laying in the depression for ages, it was dank and foul. After placing his holdall on the drier ground above him he kicked in the grille. The grille gave way without too much resistance but, the sound of the metallic clank as it fell was exaggerated by the quietness all around. He looked quickly over the depression. There was no sign the sentries had heard anything. James grabbed the holdall and dived into the old drainage outlet. Before he lifted the grille back into place the searchlights illuminated the outside of the wall like daylight. He hoped the sentries returning on their patrol didn't notice the grille was missing - booted footsteps now told him they were mere feet away. It seemed an age until James heard them turn and move away. Quickly he replaced the grille.

Pierre Papon had smuggled detailed plans to him of the site and James knew he was now under the oldest part of the factory. These plans also included details of the plumbing and drainage, electrical circuits, trunking and cabling routes. He also knew from here he and Francois would get into an old pumping house, up old iron steps and into a disused, narrow mezzanine maintenance corridor - all no longer patrolled. The corridor led into a boiler-house now seldom used. Access into the old pumping house would be through a door locked from the corridor side. James hoped Pierre had managed to unlock the door to the old pumping house but, at the moment, he had no way of knowing. Outside the grille, the dazzling searchlight gradually faded.

There was the sound of someone slithering down the sloping ground. The grille came hurtling inwards and Francois was beside him. After ensuring the grille was back in place the two men crawled along the tunnel.

'When we're further in we can use our torches' whispered James. Shortly, they found themselves in the old pumping

343

room. The big shape of the ancient machinery loomed in the torch light. 'Right we will change our clothes here.'

Their change of clothes were those of German soldiers. The uniforms had been faked and carefully detailed by a seamstress in Charleville. James took the one of a Corporal, Francois the one of a Private. After hiding the discarded clothes, they made their way up the steps. James tried the door. It budged marginally but didn't open. He cursed. Perhaps Pierre had been unable to lock it. They both put their weight against the door. Reluctantly, noisily, it opened a jar but wouldn't move any further. They tried again. With a disturbingly loud creak and a grating sound on the concrete floor it opened sufficient for them to squeeze through. After eventually closing it behind them they were now in the low corridor. James looked around.

'This way' he whispered and led Francois to the right.

They found their way to the old boiler-house, passed through it and up the stairs onto the ground floor. Outside this block of the factory, a yard ran along its entire length separating it from the main, newer factory block.

James looked out of a window across the yard and could see the factory's electrical sub-station, a single light illuminating its entrance. He ducked down beneath the window. 'A sentry with a dog!' A beam of light from the sentry's torch shafted through the window above their heads and played all along the wall behind them as the sentry passed. They heard the sentry talking to his dog. Waiting for the sound of the sentry's footsteps to disappear in the distance, James went to work on breaking the lock. The lock and the wooden door were old and caused him no problem.

Calculating the distance across the yard to the sub-station, James said 'After I have gone, count to ten and join me over there.' He was already starting to disarm the alarm on the door of the sub-station when Francois joined him. The alarm was of a similar type he had practised on at Beaulieu. Leaving Francois watching out from the shadows, he placed the explosives in the sub-station where they would not be readily discovered and would be most effective. He closed and locked the door, re-arming the alarm so as no one would realise he had ever been there. 'Now we need to go to the far end of this yard. There are sentries guarding the back entrance just beyond the door we need to enter. If one of the sentries speaks to us, leave the explaining to me...'.

'...But what if...?'

'...Just act German. The sten guns we've got are the same sort as the Germans. We will get them assembled and carry them. If anyone challenges us I will brazen it out.'

Francois didn't question him further. He had complete trust James would carry it off. Quickly, they assembled the guns and, keeping close to the wall, began to walk along the long yard towards the sentry post. Not one of the soldiers in the building noticed the two men approaching. The loud sound of metal-pressing machinery and lathes carried on the night air from within the factory. They had almost reached the door they were heading for when a soldier appeared from the guardhouse exchanging raucous laughter and words with those remaining in the hut.

'Leave this to me' whispered James.

James saw he was a Corporal and knew by the manner he approached he was going to start a conversation.

'At last the rain has stopped' observed the German stopping right in front of them. He was looking at their bags closely.

'Yes at last' replied James without hesitation and in perfect German. 'I hope we get to the station before it starts again. We have 72-hour leave passes.'

'Back to Germany?'

'Yes' answered James. 'One good thing about this damn place. It is not too far from the Fatherland.'

'As you say that is the one good thing about it.' The Corporal paused. 'But why are you walking this way?'

James was very relieved he had studied Pierre's plan of the factory thoroughly and knew the door they were aiming for also lead to the soldier's sleeping quarters. Laughing, he slapped Francois's shoulder warmly. 'Willie here forgot something. A little present he has bought for his children.'

Fortunately, Francois took his cue correctly, laughed heartily and shook his head as if mocking himself for being so forgetful.

'I see' said the German. 'Where are your homes?'

'Kaiserslautern.'

'Kaiserslautern! My home is in Neunkirchen, just a few kilometres away!'

'I know it well.'

'I will be going back there on my next leave. To see my wife and children.' The Corporal looked at his watch. 'I must not detain you. Your train will be leaving in 30 minutes.'

The German carried on his way. James and Francois hurried through the door, finding themselves in a corridor. Just beyond the door was the entrance to a room containing the emergency generators. Pierre had supplied them with a set of duplicate keys to enable them to enter the necessary areas - each key tagged so James could identify them quickly. Within seconds, the two men were inside the room. Between them they placed the explosives carefully and cleverly and set the timing devices.

'That's taken care of that' said James locking the door. 'Now for the main power room and cabling.' He quickly referred to the plans of the factory. 'This way.' They moved further down the corridor, James looking up at the metal housing encasing the huge run of cabling. Suddenly he stopped. Above them was a ventilation inspection hatch with a metal ladder cemented into the wall beneath it. 'Stand by that corner and keep a look-out.'

James took out some more explosive and a timer. Within a short time he had placed the explosive, set the timer and screwed back the inspection hatch. He descended the ladder.

The corridor they were in ran round three sides of the factory, separating the outer wall from the inner wall and enclosing the workshops, assembly lines, some offices, packing and finishing areas. Along the outer wall, at periodic intervals, there were toilets, shower and changing rooms for the German workers and soldiers, more offices and doorways to the outside. At certain other points, metal stairways led up to wide, "minstrel-gallery-like" walkways giving access to other offices. Now, about halfway along the corridor, they came to a door to the shower and changing room assigned for the use of the German Officers. Suddenly, two young Lieutenants came out of the door tidying themselves, laughing and talking. It looked as if they were about to go off-duty.

'Yours is a blonde Kurt? My French Fraulein is a brunette. She's not a whore but she goes at it in bed like an over-sexed rabbit.'

James's reaction was instant. He fumbled to put the holdall into his other hand to salute, in the process deliberately dropping his sten gun on the concrete floor. Apart from not dropping his gun Francois followed James's lead and also saluted.

With a withering look, one of the Officers rebuked James loudly and sternly. 'That weapon Corporal is the property of the Third Reich. Treat your equipment with more respect or I will put you on a charge.'

'Yes. Sorry Herr Lieutenant. Sorry. You just surprised me by coming out of the door suddenly.'

With a look of disgust and shaking their heads, the two Officers carried on their way along the corridor. In case they glanced back, James made much of re-arranging his holdall. When the two Officers disappeared from view he stood upright and checked the coast was clear. He put his ear to the door to hear if anyone else was in the room. Opening the door he peered in.

'Quick in here.' As they entered he hung a notice on the door. The notice was in German, informing that the room was "temporarily out of use". James grabbed a nearby bench and wedged it against the door. 'According to the plan, the principal water main to the whole factory comes in through here.' He looked up to the ceiling just above the door. 'And, conveniently, the cable runs feed through here as well.' He lead Francois to the far end of the room and a row of wash basins.

Francois looked around at the recently fitted plush fixtures and fittings. 'The Boche Officers look after themselves' he observed bitterly. 'I bet the local workers are not provided with anything like this.'

James smiled but didn't reply and began to examine the man-hole set in the floor. 'Pass me that jemmy in your bag?'

He put the tool under the lip of the man-hole cover. As it lifted, Francois pulled it up and leant it against a basin. He returned to James's holdall and selected the explosive and timer assigned for the task. He handed these to James and watched over James's shoulder as he carefully placed and set the large charge. Francois marvelled at the skilled dexterity with which he did so. James was grooming Francois to lead further sabotage missions and, like an apprentice watching a master craftsman, Francois observed every move and technique he made and used. As James worked, he explained everything he was doing.

At last James got to his feet. 'That will take care of the mains well and truly. Right Francois. Put the cover back?' He stooped again to look at the underside of the basins. 'I put some extra explosives in the bags just in case. We might as well make as big a mess as we can. I will also place a charge under these sinks. This whole section of the exterior wall will also be destroyed then.' Within a few moments he had placed a charge under two of the sinks, concealing it behind the pipe work. 'Now for the cabling.' In the same way he had placed explosive in the cable trunking in the corridor, he placed another charge above the door.

Someone tried the door from the outside. The two men froze. The door handle rattled loudly again and someone cursed angrily outside. At last the person moved away.

After the footsteps died away James whispered 'Can't these Krauts read?' He waited a few more moments. 'See if the coast is clear?'

They moved the bench away silently. Francois looked out into the corridor handing the sign back to James as he did so. 'All clear.'

They turned right into the corridor. After just a short walk they came to a door leading to the washrooms and toilets for the non-commissioned soldiers. Talk, banter and laughter could be heard clearly from within the room. Hearing this Francois hesitated anxiously.

Before they entered, James spoke quietly. 'We have no alternative. They won't be in here for long. If any of them speak to us leave the talking to me. We will not be familiar to them and if one of them says anything, I will say we are newly-arrived from a posting in Belgium - ahead of others being brought in from Germany to strengthen the number of guards and sentries. We may need to stall for time if one of them lingers a while. That is why I included shaving kits and towels in the bags.'

Francois had admired the Englishman from when they had first met. And, now, from the very first minutes of this particular operation, observing the ice cool way James had led them around the factory and the unflappable, methodical and efficient way he dealt with the possible pitfalls encountered, that admiration had grown. Entering the room it was immediately obvious it was a lot more basic than the facility just down the corridor set aside for the officers. There were three soldiers in there. Two were finishing off washing, talking to the third in a cubicle. James and Francois were greeted with a friendly nod but, otherwise, no comment was made about them not being recognised.

'What are you doing in there Klaus? My broody hens at home do not take so long laying eggs' called one of the soldiers over the cubicle door.

A gruff voice from within the cubicle called back 'These damned army rations make me constipated. I will meet you both in the recreation hall shortly.'

James motioned to Francois to take out his shaving kit and towel.

'Very well. See you there Klaus' answered one of the other two laughing.

The two Germans nodded goodnight to James and Francois before departing the room. The two saboteurs had almost finished shaving, were beginning to wonder what other "stall for time" tactic to adopt when the toilet flushed and the bolt of the cubicle slammed back. A huge man's frame filled the cubicle doorway. Like the other two Germans this man was also a Private.

'Evening. You two are new here?' James answered as he had told Francois he would. 'Posted from Belgium –

Charleroi? My younger brother is there, with a Panzer Division. How are things there?'

Thinking off the top of his head, James replied 'The RAF have been paying the area a lot of attention. Most of all though, the damned local people have been causing us a lot of trouble. I would shoot the whole damned lot of them.'

'I agree.' The German spat with contempt into a wash basin. 'It is the same here. Here in Mezieres we try to be friendly with them, but it's hopeless. I do not know why we bother trying. The local workers in this factory are all useless and lazy. However my friends, I will probably be seeing you around here a lot. You must excuse me now, I must go and join the others.' He went out into the corridor.

After waiting a few moments James said 'Francois keep a lookout outside? Like the previous toilet I will be placing charges in the cable trunking and underneath the sinks.'

Within a short while the work was done and they headed for the workers' toilet. If the toilet and washroom for the German NCOs and troops was basic, the area set aside for the use of the local workers was hard to imagine. It was a pre-fabricated annexe through a gap in the wall off a small blind corridor. A great stretch of flapping canvas served as its roof. Instead of urinals there were large buckets sunk in the ground. The cubicles as such were screened from each other by sheets of canvas strung between wooden posts and contained larger, metal, dustbin-like bins, two-thirds sunk in the ground. The only thing serving as a tap for washing was a solitary standpipe. A taller, standpipe-like arrangement, James guessed, was a device for de-lousing the local workforce.

'There's obviously nowhere in here to conceal explosives' said James. 'But we can use it for you to change again into worker's clothes. I will keep a lookout. Remember Francois,

I am going to bully and knock you about as a Boche soldier would. I will try not to hurt you too much.'

'Do not worry Monsieur. As long as our plan to disrupt the bastards works as it should, I don't care how hard you knock me about.'

After Francois had changed James immediately started their well-rehearsed act of abuser on abused.

'Schnell! Schnell! You idol peasant.' And so his physical abuse and bullying of the Frenchmen continued. It continued as James pushed and manhandled him through the double doors of the assembly line area. The sight of the mistreatment was so familiar to the workers slaving in there, none of them even bothered to look up. After a sufficient enough time to convince workers and soldiers alike, James dragged and pushed Francois back into the corridor propelling him towards a line of factory barrows. One of them was piled high with new chairs, linen and other supplies for the senior officers' offices situated along the landing above them. James was still shouting aggressively. 'This needs to be taken upstairs immediately. Bring it now.'

With James still harassing him, Francois pushed the barrow along the corridor towards a goods lift.

Once inside the lift James said 'Well I think that convinced everyone.' The blood from an injury on Francois's cheek was evidence of this. 'The communications room is to the left. We need to go to the door to its right.'

James checked their holdalls were hidden amongst the supplies in the barrow. Coming out of the lift he continued with his abuse toward Francois. As Pierre had said, a sentry stood guard outside the communications room. The sentry challenged them.

James replied 'Supplies for the officers. We have instructions to put them in the storeroom until tomorrow as their offices are locked.'

In a disinterested way the sentry waved them past.

Unseen by the sentry, Francois took the bags out of the barrow and placed them in the storeroom. The room was spacious. Stationery, bottles of German wine and beer and an assortment of other material and supplies were stacked on shelving running along the wall. A new desk - partially unwrapped - stood against the far wall. Whilst Francois unloaded the new supplies and furniture, deliberately slowly and laboriously, James continued to harangue his colleague very loudly. After entering the room, James began to conceal and time the explosives behind the stored materials. The wall of shelving adjoined the communications room. The explosives would obliterate most of the corridor, including the communications room and offices. The sentry had begun to get curious about what they were doing and, as James concealed the last charge, he appeared in the doorway.

James shook his head in disgust. 'Some idiot left this room in a terrible mess.'

The sentry appeared to be satisfied with his explanation. Francois emerged and James closed the door.

Back in the lift James explained what destruction would be caused were they to place more explosives. As they had a little more time than anticipated they decided they would. This would also provide James's protégé with some useful practice in the art of sabotage. With the lift now back on the ground floor and, ensuring there was no one about, he handed Francois more packs of explosive, explaining where to place them for most affect. Under James's tutoring and ever-watchful supervision the Frenchman did as he was instructed. After final checks of his work, they returned the barrow to its place and walked toward the far end of the factory where the warehouse and despatch area was located and where Albert, Claude and Jacque had now been working and hiding for over thirteen hours. James looked at his watch. Pierre had told him what time the warehouse sentries changed shifts. Francois and he were bang on schedule.

James handed a sentry the forged stores requisition for a lathe sprocket and turned to Francois. 'He has come for this.'

The sentry looked at the docket, grunted something and unlocked the door for their entry, leaving it unlocked.

Hiding behind a stack of pallets just inside the door, James quickly changed out of the Corporal's uniform into ordinary working clothes. Albert and Claude approached them from the far end of the dimly-lit warehouse, Albert carrying what looked like a machine component.

'The crates have all been opened and are ready for you' Albert announced. 'How did things go?' He asked anxiously, taking the Private's uniform from Francois's bag and hiding it within the box containing the sprocket.

'No real problems' answered James. 'The explosives are all in place and timed.'

'Magnificent!' Exclaimed Claude as he changed into the Corporal's uniform.

On the other side of the door the change of sentries could be heard. James could just about make out one of them saying a worker had entered the warehouse with a requisition.

James turned to Albert and Claude. 'Just wait a while before going out there. You are both absolutely clear how to get back to where the refuse bins are and, the procedure for the pick-up tomorrow morning?' Both men confirmed they were. He went over one or two bits of the plan for their exit from the factory, adding 'Well done you two. Now off you go. Take care.'

Outside the warehouse, the replacement sentry marked Albert and Claude off his list of warehouse entrants. He was none the wiser - all he was aware a local worker and a

German Corporal had come to take out a lathe sprocket. Inside the warehouse James and Francois hurried to join Jacque. It was nearly 11 O'clock. Within nine hours, a convoy of trucks would begin to transport the supplies to the local railway yard, for onward transportation down towards Marseille. The explosives to be placed in the crates of spares and supplies would be timed to explode as the train neared Troyes. The consignment of vehicle spares and lubricants the Resistance group were targeting were destined for Rommel's army in North Africa.

'Where are the explosives and nails Jacque?' asked James. 'You and I will concentrate on placing the explosives and timers. After we have made a good start, I want you Francois to begin sealing the crates.' Having spent much of his working life in the quarries around Vallee de la Meuse, Jacque was no stranger to working with explosives. James examined the nails. 'What a stroke of luck obtaining these nails from that army truck. Once we have finished, they will never know the crates have been tampered with.'

The trio commenced work.

In his bed in his flat on the Rue Monge, Pierre Papon could not sleep. He tossed and turned, thinking of how things were going in the warehouse, worrying whether the plan would fail and the group in the factory caught and, in turn, whether any time now his front door could be smashed down by the Gestapo after they discovered his implication in the plan. He was also worried about his journey to safety in Switzerland with forged documents. Anywhere before the border - his absence from the factory already noted - he could be apprehended by the Gestapo.

James had taken a decision. Because of Pierre's position in the factory and his access to the transport schedules and knowledge of the factory and its workings, he would be a prime suspect for the feeding of information to the outside. The risk of Pierre being arrested, surrendering to the inevitable interrogation, was too great a risk to take. It could result in another near-annihilation of the Resistance movement in the Charleville and Mezieres area and, that was something the allies would wish to avoid at this stage of the war.

The two refuse bins in which Albert and Claude hid were used for general waste - soiled rags, floor sweepings and the usual debris of a workplace. Emile had contrived to have them covered with the least obnoxious, lightest waste possible without arousing too much suspicion. At last, with the usual German obsession for routine and punctuality, the morning refuse lorry arrived. Its driver ensured the bins, in which Claude and Albert were concealed, were loaded where they were least likely to be checked.

After loading and, as the lorry stopped at the factory gate, Claude and Albert heard the sentries exchanging words with the driver and his mate as identity documents were checked. There was the sound of a sentry scrambling onto the back of the lorry. To Albert and Claude's horror this particular sentry appeared to be very diligent in his search. Claude heard the sentry's boots scrunch on the lorry's floor beside his bin - heard the buttons of his tunic scrape the side of it. Suddenly, just inches away from Claude's head, a razor sharp bayonet pierced a wodge of an old overall and probed around. The impaled, old smelly garment brushed his face and there was a brief pause as the sentry shook it free from his weapon. Almost immediately, the bayonet probed again, this time just missing Claude's thigh by a fraction. Claude fought to control his fear, very nearly shouted out before the next sharp probe could well end his life. Thankfully, the sentry was satisfied and another probe never came. Claude heard the sentry turn his attention to another bin, heard the bayonet go in again. He heard no scream of pain but could not be certain - when eventually off-loaded in the countryside - whether he would discover Albert speared to death. Finally, he heard the sentry shout all was clear then clamber off the lorry. Still anxious about Albert, he felt the lorry begin to move.

After another hour, with no real problems besetting their leaving the factory, James, Francois and Jacque stowed aboard a truck collecting bales of new German uniforms from the warehouse. Being a German vehicle it was not subject to such rigorous checking as the refuse lorry. Realising what the truck was transporting, James was tempted to break into one of the bales to take some of the uniforms for Resistance stock but decided not to chance his luck. It would also be more for them to carry and thus multiply the chances of their being caught.

Eventually the lorry stopped. Peeping out from beneath the tarpaulin, James realised they were in a little village near Sedan. He saw the driver and his mate disappear inside a café. Some old men sat outside it smoking their pipes and quietly passing the time. James crawled across to the other side of the vehicle and looked out. There were no dwellings or people to be seen, only pasture land, bordered by a low wall and, beyond, a belt of trees.

'Quick. One at a time out this side. Using the truck for cover, we will make for the wall and head for that line of trees. Avoid anyone seeing your feet from the other side of the truck. Keep in line with the wheels.'

Crouching behind the wall he explained to the others that, by keeping to the fields and woods, they would make for the station in Sedan separately and return to the Mezieres area by rail.

Walking through pleasant meadows and woods James was pre-occupied. The time to the destruction of the factory, the blowing apart of the train, had now decreased by some seven hours.

37

'Jean-Paul. Jean-Paul.' Someone was shaking him.

James awoke to see Dr Fouquet standing beside his bed. After arriving back at the house, James had gone straight to bed and had slept deeply.

'What is it? What's the time?' He asked, fighting to open his eyes.

'Eleven. Sorry to wake you but there's someone downstairs who must see you urgently.'

'Give me a couple of minutes' James replied irritably.

The Doctor disappeared out of the door. James rubbed his eyes, swept his fingers through his hair as he swung his legs out of bed. Quickly pulling on his clothes and, after splashing water over his face, he looked out of the window. There was no sign of any vehicle parked outside or any person hanging around suspiciously. Going down the stairs he saw a young woman waiting in the hallway. He recognised her straightaway as Miriam, one of the Group's couriers. There was a look of concern on her face.

'What is it Miriam?'

'I have only just managed to get out of Mezieres - I was visiting my grandparents. The Gestapo have sealed off the whole town. There has been an explosion at their factory. They are searching everywhere for those responsible.'

James feigned surprise. 'Has there been much damage?'

'A large part of it totally destroyed.' James was finding it hard to conceal his pleasure. Miriam was now speaking quickly, anxiously. 'More and more Germans are arriving by the minute. Roland is worried that they will be searching Charleville as well. His organisation has two British airmen hidden away and wants them moved straightaway. He has asked for your help.'

James knew the man known as Roland well, had worked with him to get the local evasion line going. Between them they had established a good network of "safe" houses and local helpers. It had been very hard work to establish all this from amongst a frightened local population. He knew he had to do all he could to help Roland's organisation get the two airmen away from the Charleville and Mezieres area immediately. To chance the Gestapo catching two airmen being sheltered by members of his team could destroy all their earlier efforts in setting up the evasion line, compromise the valuable work it did in getting allied servicemen back.

'Miriam can you get a message to Roland now?'

'Of course.'

'I will meet him in an hour in Eglise de Saint Remi. I will be on the right, fifth pew back from the chancel. Can he bring details of the two airmen and where they are being hidden?'

She left by the front door. Quickly, he went into the room on the left and watched as she turned down Rue du Petit Bois. No one appeared to be following her. He went to find Dr Fouquet.

'When she knocked I thought it was my next patient - late yet again for her appointment.' Fouquet had been tending to his house plants in the conservatory, and put down some dead leaves as James entered. 'Is there a problem?'

'No. The operation has been a great success. However, there is something I must attend to urgently. I must try and get to the south of the town. I need to get an accurate idea of the damage done to the factory for the transmission to London tonight. I will be back later.'

Over the last few weeks James had been doing some odd jobs for an elderly couple, Monsieur and Madame Corot. The jobs had not been very big, just simple repairs and routine maintenance to their property - too much for the arthritic Monsieur Corot to undertake. The couple's little house was located on the northern bank of the Meuse, on the Charleville side. From it there was a good view of the factory on the Meziere's side of the river. A fact which hadn't escaped James's attention. Better still, at the bottom of the Corot's garden was a boathouse from which James could easily assess the damage to the factory. Conveniently, the Corots had mentioned they were worried the boathouse was unsafe. Their youngest grand-daughter often stayed with them and, as she loved to play in the garden, they wanted it repaired for her safety. Working at the Corot's property provided a wonderful opportunity and a feasible reason for James to travel to the south of the town.

As James cycled across Place Ducale into Rue du Palais, there was already a large presence of German soldiers, their jeeps and trucks parked over by the City Hall. Miriam had told him the numbers of Boche were increasing by the minute. Not much longer and their search for the perpetrators of the attack on the factory would be spreading throughout the whole area. As he turned into Rue du Theatre there was a roadblock. He knew that to turn back would arouse suspicion. Two soldiers sat with a motorbike and sidecar - its engine running - ready to give chase should anyone turn back away from the roadblock. There was no alternative, he would have to go through the checkpoint, brazen it out, hope his ID papers and explanation of why he was travelling would bear scrutiny.

They made him turn out his toolbox on the ground and questioned him incessantly as to why he was travelling, why he was in that area. Eventually they seemed satisfied with his ID papers and explanation but, with some words of abuse, directed not only at James but at the French in general, one of the soldiers took a sadistic pleasure in scattering the tools with his boot. He laughed as James crawled around on the ground collecting them together. James would dearly have loved to garrotte the sneering soldiers.

James continued on his way, turning right onto the Boulevard Gambetta and cycled down it for a short distance, intending to turn left into Rue Leon Renier. However, troop activity on the corner made James think there could well be another roadblock. His instinct was right, there was, a few metres down it. James cycled on till just after the next turning on the left - Rue Dubois - where an alleyway ran all the way down behind flats and apartments to the Avenue Nationale. The Avenue Nationale ran almost parallel to the railway. At a certain point, he knew he could cut across some waste ground to the railway. Suitably far enough away from the road bridge crossing it, he would cross the track and make his way across another area of waste land to the minor road near the Meuse where the Corot's house stood.

When James reached a point where the rail line rounded a bend and no sentry stationed on the bridge would be able to see him, he crossed the railway and entered an area of dense scrub. Shortly, this gave way to an expanse of open, very rough ground and he hoped the ancient cycle he was using would stand up to the task. Once across this ground he emerged onto a narrow road and turned left towards the Corot's house a few metres away.

Eventually Monsieur Corot opened the door. He held the hand of a little girl beside him.

'Monsieur Guyot! We were not expecting you today.' The elderly man cuddled the little girl. 'We were playing with our grand-daughter in the garden.'

'I know but I wanted to take some measurements, see what materials are required.'

'Of course. Come through.' James followed Corot through to the garden. Madame Corot sat on a seat sifting through a wooden chest of what looked like children's dressing up clothes. She smiled pleasantly and the little girl joined her on the seat. The garden and orchard sloped steeply down to the river. Beyond the far bank of the Meuse, a huge plume of black smoke arose from a large building. Corot pointed towards it. 'It looks like the German factory. There were some explosions. At first, we thought the RAF had bombed it but we had not seen or heard any planes. We do not know what has happened over there.'

James shrugged. 'I wonder' and passed the incident off. 'Well, if you will excuse me Monsieur. I better go and see what needs to be done.' Corot moved to follow him. 'It's all right Monsieur. There is no need for you to come. I will only be a few minutes.'

'Would you like a drink?'

'No. No thank you. I have to get to another appointment.'

From the boathouse, the damage to the factory looked far more extensive than he had anticipated. Perhaps there had been more explosive and inflammable materials in the factory than even Pierre had known about. James was elated with the results obtained and knew the damage would take the Germans weeks or months to put right. After he had sufficient details of the devastation imbedded in his mind for his report to London, he looked at his watch. Soon, the next part of the sabotage plan would unfold - when, just before Troyes, the train carrying components, lubricants and supplies for Rommel's army would be blown apart.

James took the measurements, noted what materials would be required for the boathouse repairs, and made his way up the garden. After exchanging a few words with the Corots and their grand-daughter he cycled off.

Using a different route back, he made his way to the Church and his meeting with Roland. The way he chose was deliberately circuitous. Checking he hadn't been followed, James entered the Eglise de Saint Remi. Immediately, the chill and silence of the building was apparent. It was of huge dimensions and dimly-lit, the main source of light coming from its huge windows but, allowing him to see a number of sanctuaries set off to the right and left, each screened off with ornate, gilt iron-work. He noted the Church was largely devoid of the rich and precious ornamentation usual in normal times. Though, like so many Churches in occupied Europe, all precious objects probably removed and hidden by Church authorities from the plundering of the Nazis on realising invasion and occupation were inevitable. The pews either side of the main nave were sparsely dotted with individuals, either crouched in silent prayer or contemplation. One or two people stood in due reverence in front of stands holding lit candles of remembrance. In the right pew, five rows back from the main chancel, James saw the solitary figure of a man hunched. Aware of an elderly woman observing him as she silently cleaned just inside the entrance, James bowed before proceeding up the aisle. Cautiously he took a seat in the pew, one space away from the hunched man. It was Roland. James slid surreptitiously closer, knelt and spoke in a whisper.

'Sorry I am late. I had to avoid road-blocks. What details do you have for me?'

Warily, the man beside him slid across a scrap of paper. On it was scribbled the names and ranks of the two airmen and where they were hidden. On seeing one of the names, his whole body froze. The name belonged to none other than his brother: "Pilot Officer Colin Graham".

Quickly regaining his composure he whispered 'And these names and ranks have been verified?'

'Twice now' Roland whispered back. 'By my people in the Joigny-s-Meuse area and by myself when they arrived in Charleville.'

Although shocked and numbed his younger brother had been shot down, James was ecstatic he was safe and well. However, he could not admit to anyone one of the evaders was his brother. Nor could he let the strength of blood ties impair his judgement and decision-making. Too much would be at risk for that. Until Colin and his fellow evader were well on their way down the Escape Lines and, indeed, hopefully safely back in England, James knew he would have to remain completely detached and impartial, put natural emotion to the back of his mind.

Screwing the piece of paper up and putting it in his pocket for disposal, James asked 'Can you arrange for a female courier - one of your best - to meet me in one hour by the pond in the Square du Petit Bois? To identify myself I will be holding a small, basket ware sandwich hamper in my left hand. She is to ask: "Why has that statue been moved"?' He paused. 'This house - the Dentist's house. Do you know the Dentist well?'

'Why of course. He is my own Dentist. He is also a close friend of my wife and I.'

'Good. Would he agree to help you move the airmen?'

'Yes. And he can be trusted.'

'Leave the other safe house to me' said James. 'We need to meet later. Shall we say in about two hours in the Bank on Rue de Cleves.' He looked towards the Confessionals on their right. 'Now I am going over there. Wait for a while before you leave the pew.'

A middle-aged woman had gone in to the Confession booth some minutes before him. James patiently awaited his turn. All the time, various ideas about how to move the two RAF evaders came and went in his mind. The woman seemed to be taking ages. He mused she must have a lot of wrong deeds or actions to expunge from her soul. At last she came out - she was crying. At last the little light above the Confessional indicated he was able to enter. James hoped the Priest the other side of the screen was one of several based in this Church helpful to the Resistance. Many Priests were, would endanger their own lives to assist, others were not quite so dependable. A voice from the side of the screen invited James to commence his Confession. Using a few carefully selected words and phrases James explained the help he needed. From the Priest's responses, he quickly ascertained this Priest was one of those who would help with no consideration for the risks involved. James received the necessary promise of help and they planned what could be done.

Karl Neumann, for the second time that day, stood at the end of Rue des Usines in Mezieres looking at the still-smouldering factory. He turned to Spiegel.

'How many do we have under arrest now?'

'Over thirty. There is another vehicle due with another ten.'

'Excellent. We will start our interrogations when we get back.'

A motor-cycle courier stopped. He held a message and

approached them urgently. 'Heil Hitler!' He handed the envelope to Neumann.

After Neumann read the message, he screwed it up furiously and flung it at Spiegel. 'Damn them all in hell!'

'What is it?' Asked Spiegel.

'The train which left this morning has been blown up and destroyed. There were over two month's of supplies for Rommel on that train.' His driver opened the car door for them. As Neumann slammed the car door in a rage he said 'As soon as we get back, the suspects brought in already are to be taken out in the yard. Select ten of them at random and shoot them while the others watch.' Their car began to move off. 'First though, there is a visit we must make. I have a theory I want to test. There are some people whom I hope will lead us to Fouquet's so-called lodger.'

Neumann snapped at the driver, ordering him to a house right on the banks of the Meuse. Inside his astute mind were thoughts and memories which kept recurring. As their car sped toward Rue Voltaire Neumann was gratified to see so many troops searching streets and buildings with vigour, was especially impressed with the beatings they were giving to the hapless victims they encountered. He determined he must order a suitable reward and promotion for the Corporal who had alerted him to a certain builder and handyman - Jean-Paul Guyot - making his way to visit a house on the bank of the Meuse.

Neumann's car drew up outside the Corot's house. Neumann recognised it straightaway. It had been just over a week since he was being driven along this very road, had seen the man known as Jean-Paul Guyot working at the side of the house. The house they were parked outside was on a slope, partially below the level of the road. Over its roof Neumann could clearly see the still-burning factory on the far side of the Meuse. He realised just what a good view the rear of the house had of the far river bank. What he wanted to discover was why, this very morning after the explosion, Guyot had chosen to pay another visit to this house.

Before getting out of the car Neumann turned to Spiegel. 'Fritz, in our experience of dealing with enemy agents, what do we find one of the first things they have to do after committing their acts of sabotage?'

'To try and get a message to England to report their operation has been completed and what the results were.'

'Precisely.'

Pushing Corot aside as he opened the door, the two men strode down the hall. In vain, the elderly man tried to protest.

'We have some questions for you' snapped Spiegel.

In the kitchen, Madame Corot was making bread. Her little grand-daughter sat on the kitchen table watching her. The shock of seeing two strange men bursting into the room made her cry. Neumann and Spiegel forced the elderly couple into the chairs but, prevented the little girl from joining them, so causing her even more distress.

Bullying, Neumann asked 'I believe you had a visitor this morning?'

Corot paused before answering. 'No. No one has been here.'

Neumann stood above the cowering couple threateningly. Suddenly, with terrible force, he smashed Corot across the face with the back of his hand. Such was the force, it knocked the old man off his chair sending his spectacles across the floor and smashing them. His wife screamed.

'You will tell me the truth.' Neumann delivered another blow to the other side of Corot's face.

'I am sorry Monsieur' Corot whimpered. 'Forgive me. It is my age - my memory - I forgot. A man did call here. He has now gone. He just came to measure up for some repairs he is making to our boathouse - down the garden.'

Neumann told Spiegel to take a look at the boathouse and round the house. 'Who is this man?' He moved menacingly to Corot's grand-daughter.

'A builder. He has done some work for us before.'

Neumann began to run his hand gently through the little girl's hair. His voice was quieter now. There was no mistaking though the terrible menace in its tone. 'Who is this lovely little girl?'

'Our grand-daughter' answered Madame Corot desperately.

'What is her name?'

'Emilene.'

'Emilene! Such a pretty name. She is such a pretty little girl. She reminds me of my niece. About the same age I would say.' He began to stroke her face. 'It would be so terrible if anything should happen to her.'

Suddenly, coldly, he took a pistol out of his pocket and held it right against Emilene's temple. The Corots both screamed. Emilene was now near-hysterical.

'Please Monsieur. We beg of you. She is only a child' screamed and pleaded the Corots.

'Emilene' continued Neumann. 'You would not want to be hurt would you? I need your grandparents to tell me some things.' He turned back to the Corots. 'What is this man's name - this builder?'

'Guyot' answered Madame Corot.

'The truth?' Hissed Neumann.

'Yes. Guyot. That is his name' answered her husband. 'We are honestly not sure of his first name.'

'What was he doing here this morning?'

Corot pointed in the direction of the garden. 'As I said, he is repairing the boathouse. To make it safe. Emilene often stays with us. We do not want her hurt when she is playing near it.'

Spiegel returned. Neumann lifted Emilene off the table and let her run to her grandmother. He stood closely to the three, still pointing his pistol towards them.

'And you were not expecting Guyot to call this morning?'

'No.'

Spiegel was looking out of the window. 'From the boathouse there is a good view of the river and across to its other side. You are aware the factory over there is now the property of the Third Reich?'

'Well yes. But it is of no concern to us' answered Corot wiping some blood from his face.

'That is good. I am pleased to hear it' said Neumann. 'This morning it was attacked by saboteurs. We intend to find those responsible. You must know how we regard people who dare to damage property of the Third Reich or those giving them any assistance. So Guyot was in your boathouse this morning.' He levelled his gun once more at the little girl.

Corot was pleading. 'Yes. But only for a few minutes. I swear to you Monsieur. If this Guyot is one of the people you are looking for. We had no idea. Please Monsieur.'

'Very well.' Neumann stroked Emilene's face again and took her hand. 'However, now I think it best if we take Emilene with us…'.

Her grandparents tried to struggle. Spiegel hit them both.

'…It will only be for a few hours. If you are telling the truth she will be returned to you later today.' Neumann ruffled the little girl's hair. 'You see, we have found that even little angels like this - when they get older - they learn to attack us. We just like them to see what happens to people when they attack us - should they get any similar notions of sabotage when they grow up.' Emilene's grandparents pleaded and struggled. It was of no avail. The two men simply knocked them away. 'Your grand-daughter will be returned to you later.'

The two men strode out of the house carrying a screaming and kicking Emilene with them, leaving her grandparents hysterical and distraught. On their way out both men took great pleasure in breaking and smashing some of the couple's belongings.

38

After changing into the Priest's garments, Mike came from around the screen, making last minute adjustments as he did so. He was embarrassed by what he might look like, his embarrassment increasing when the young woman giggled as he emerged. Cecily Rabelais, apart from being younger than Mike had imagined, was also very attractive. She really looked too young to be helping an Evasion Line.

Feeling rather foolish and, in the best French he could manage, he said 'I think I've put this on incorrectly.'

'Non. Non. It is not too bad. I will just alter these' she replied in broken English. She proceeded to move the garment's belt, tighten the Rosary and adjust the headgear.

Up close to him, as she busied herself making the necessary adjustments, Mike realised how deliciously attractive she was. The Dentist, Doctor Girault, entered the room. Mike heard the front door at the end of the hallway close.

'That was my last patient of the day' declared the Dentist. With amusement he took in the sight in the corner of the room, a young woman with her hands around the waist of a man in Priest's clothing. 'How is it going?' Cecily giggled again. She and Girault exchanged a few words in French which Mike couldn't understand. The Dentist continued.

'Well. Our English friend here could fool me into thinking he is a real Priest!'

Mike was a bit more reassured by the Dentist's opinion, though still did not relish the prospect of merging into the streets of Charleville without speaking much French and, accompanied by a companion who did not speak much English. Somewhere deep within him the thought occurred that, perhaps after all, it would be safer for everyone - himself included - if he had been captured by the Germans after baling out. There was a real possibility now, should he be caught by the Germans, of being shot as being perceived by them as a spy.

Mike's anxiety must have been obvious as Girault started to outline very clearly the plan for getting him away from this "safe house".

'You are Brother Maurice from Lille, recovering here in Charleville after a serious illness. You have been recovering in the Church Retreat to the north of the town. The story is that Cecily is one of the volunteers helping out at the Retreat and she has brought you into Charleville to visit the Dentist. The Germans know I do all the dentistry work for the Priests at Eglise de Saint Remi and those working or staying at the Retreat.' Girault paused as he heard his secretary enter the adjoining room. 'Cecily will take you to the place where the bus stops. The bus will take you both all the way to the Retreat - it stops just metres from its entrance.' Girault turned and selected a walking stick from the umbrella stand and handed it to Mike. 'Use this but Cecily will hold your arm all the way. In the few minutes before you leave, I recommend you practice using it. Remember, you have been seriously ill.'

'But what do I do if we are stopped?' Asked Mike anxiously.

'Leave all the explaining to Cecily and, when you get on

the bus, do not get into conversation with anyone. It will be hard not to, the people of Charleville are naturally friendly and, what with you dressed as a Priest as well. But it is vital you do not talk.' He glanced at his watch. 'Luckily, work had already started on your false papers. I bullied my contact into finishing them quickly. Cecily will give these to you presently. Now, it is important you get on your way. I will just check the street to see if there are any Germans about.' Girault disappeared out of the door, leaving Mike to practice with the walking stick. Within a short while he was back. 'It would be best if you walk to Avenue Pasteur and get to the bus that way. The Boche seem to be all around the station. I wish you both well.' He spoke directly to Mike. 'Monsieur, I cannot say how long you will have to stay at the Retreat but do not worry, word will be brought to you as soon as possible. Now quickly. Off you go.'

Mike just managed to thank the Dentist for all he had done before being ushered out. Once away from the doorstep he felt a mixture of emotions but, above all, very lonely and immensely vulnerable. Cecily took his arm and led him to the left.

Walking with a stick made it slow going. The Germans were cordoning off streets and as they passed a café, Cecily heard a group of people saying the start of the curfew was being brought forward. Fortunately, by threading through a confusing series of right and left turnings and passageways, she managed to navigate a route avoiding many of the roadblocks. Eventually, they reached a point where the bus stopped. There were already a huge number of people waiting.

Cecily cursed. 'These crowds. It might not be possible to get on the bus. We may have to walk.'

'How far to the Retreat?'

'About four kilometres.'

Mike grew more anxious. It wasn't the distance which worried him but the number of troops on the streets were increasing by the minute. A bus drew up beside the waiting queue, people surged aboard and it was filling up rapidly. Mike resigned himself to having to walk and so increasing their chances of being stopped by the Germans. Now the bus was full. There was a young woman with a child immediately in front of them and she turned and spoke. Mike couldn't understand what she said but she stood aside for Cecily and he to board the bus. They were the last to do so. The bus driver was shouting impatiently. With a jerk the bus moved off and Mike asked quietly why the young woman with the child had let them board the bus before them.

Cecily whispered back 'Because you are dressed as a Priest.'

Mike marvelled at the due reverence shown to the clergy of France. As if to underline this, a man sitting nearby offered him his seat. Cecily nodded inconspicuously Mike should accept his offer. As the bus wove its way through the streets Mike took in the sights around him, noting the neat, classical nature of Charleville and its architecture. He remembered some of the buildings, squares, avenues and boulevards Georges and Angeline at the farm had told him and Colin about. After a while the density of buildings seemed to lessen, giving way to occasional clusters of buildings and increasing areas of green space, now and again dotted with buildings built in more of the style of Chateaux.

The bus was nearly empty when Cecily rose from her seat and prompted Mike by nudging his thigh with her knee. She assisted him to his feet whilst quickly casting her eyes around the remaining passengers. None seemed to take an undue interest in them as she helped him on to the pathway, beside which ran a high grey wall. The bus had rounded a bend and disappeared from view by the time they reached a big wooden door inset in the wall. Cecily pulled a long metal handle to the side of the door. Somewhere from over the wall a bell clanged loudly. There was a scrunching of feet on gravel. In the middle of the door a small, square hatch suddenly opened. In the hatch appeared the face of a hooded man who studied their faces for a second or two.

'Ah just a moment.' The face disappeared and there was the sound of a large bolt being drawn back. The door opened to reveal a Monk. A round, smiling countenance greeted them and he ushered Cecily and Mike in. 'We have been told to expect you.'

Waiting for the Monk to slam shut and bolt the heavy door, Mike looked around and saw they were in a pleasant courtyard. A large, ornamental fountain played soothingly ahead of them, in the shadow of which lay a big old brown dog of uncertain breeding. Without troubling to overly stir itself, the animal simply raised its big hairy head as a token of greeting. A few hens picked and scratched amongst the gravel between pots of herbs and ornamental plants. A large tree nodded at the side of a porched doorway opposite. The whole ambience of the place was of calm and serenity.

With a few kindly words, the Monk greeted Cecily and, in very good English, spoke to Mike. 'You will be safe with us. I am sure you would appreciate some refreshment?'

The Monk invited them to cross the courtyard towards the doorway.

Mike's transfer from the Dentist to the Retreat had been arranged as a result of James's "Confession". Then, also, James and the Priest had arranged for Colin to be moved from the brothel on Rue Couvelet and this plan had required more complicated arranging and had begun about the time Mike and Cecily first boarded the bus. During the "Confession" the Priest had told James he had administered the Last Rites the previous afternoon to an elderly man living in a flat next to the brothel in Rue Couvelet. Undertakers had collected his body in the evening, long before the explosion at the factory. James and the Priest, therefore, were reasonably certain that an ordinary elderly man's death, the time of his death and, the subsequent removal of his body by an Undertaker yesterday, would not have caused any interest for the Germans to make a note of. It was an extreme piece of good fortune that had come James's way and he seized on it. The pair thought up an idea whereby another Undertaker would collect "a body" from the dead man's flat today. This "body" would be the hidden British airman - Colin Graham.

The Priest explained to James it would be perfectly normal for him to visit a bereaved family to offer comfort and discuss funeral arrangements. He would be able to keep those bereaved occupied in the flat upstairs as the second hearse arrived and took a coffin into the hallway of the flats. The Madam of the brothel would be informed of what was happening and all Colin would need to do is to slip next door from the brothel and into the coffin. James and the Priest just hoped that even the Germans would not check in a coffin containing someone's body. The Priest assured James that the Undertaker, Monsieur Bercy, could be thoroughly trusted and, after arriving at Bercy's premises, Colin would be hidden there until after nightfall then comparatively easily transferred the short distance to the Church where he would be hidden in a very secret hiding place within its walls.

With the Boche stepping up their search in and around Charleville James was fast running out of options. He had decided the risks were worth taking and had contacted people he trusted to become impromptu employees of

Monsieur Bercy. To use the Undertaker's usual part-time employees could invite disaster.

Just before the planned departure of his younger brother Colin from the brothel, James looked at his watch yet again. At this stage, he had no way of knowing how long Colin would have to remain hidden in the Church, nor how long Colin's Wireless Operator would have to be hidden at the Retreat just outside town. Continuing to walk down the road he couldn't describe his feelings. His younger brother only two streets away, and he could not make contact with him in any way whatsoever - to see how Colin was, to ensure he was properly prepared for his long, arduous and risky journey back to England. Rue Couvelet - just two streets away. The temptation was too strong for James. He just about had time to make a short diversion on his way. There was a little café opposite the entrance to Rue Couvelet and he could, at least, sit in the café and watch the coffin departing. The bravado in James surfaced. At least from the café he would be positioned to do something should something go wrong for any reason. He crossed Rue de l'Arquebuse and turned into Rue de l'Eparyne.

39

James watched Bercy's hearse turn out of Rue Couvelet. Was hugely relieved that this part of the plan at least had passed off uneventfully and Colin was safely on the next leg home to England. True, it was only one tiny part of a journey which James knew, full well, could take weeks or even months to complete and would be fraught with problems and dangers not only for Colin but, also, for the many necessary helpers along the way. He was also relieved that from now on, his younger brother's fate was in the hands of others and the responsibility for the rest of his homeward passage was not his. It was not that James did not love or care for Colin - of course he did - but, he had enough on his mind in his role with the SOE at the moment and trying to avoid his own capture. James left the café. Now he would have time for a couple of hour's rest before preparing to transmit his message to England. Lack of proper sleep for a few days, together with the exertions the previous night in the factory, were catching up with him and he was feeling very tired. His bad leg was also hurting like hell.

As James rounded the corner just before Fouquet's house, he noticed a man standing a few metres up the road. Instinct told him the man was not local. The window of the room the Doctor used for his consultations was open. This room had two windows but, the particular one open now was only used as a warning that something was not as it should be. It was a signal Fouquet and James had devised to alert each other and other Resistance members there was an unwelcome visitor in the house. James was certain the man standing on the pavement was Gestapo. Since James had executed Isobel, the odious but brilliant Neumann had returned a couple of times to the house and had really been turning the screw on both of them. James had known all along, since Isobel's death, Neumann had been waiting for just the right opportunity to arrest both of them. Today could be that day. Neumann was, in all probability right now, in the house. For all James knew one of the factory sabotage team may have been captured by the Gestapo and, under interrogation, talked - told them about his involvement and mentioned others including Dr Fouquet. The best thing he could do now was to get out of Charleville into the countryside for a while. Whilst hiding up somewhere in a "safe house", he could use a courier to obtain information whether anyone had been arrested and to make contact with Fouquet. James ducked back into the side street and thought quickly.

James knew Neumann well enough to know he wouldn't be as foolish as to have his car parked out the front and that it would be tucked away in the service road behind the house. Neumann would probably have his side-kick, Spiegel, with him in the house waiting for his return; another of his thugs waiting at the back of the house. Unlike many Gestapo officers, Neumann's style was not to arrive at a suspect's house with a truck load of troops. He much preferred for himself and his coterie to exact physical and psychological brutality on suspects themselves when arriving.

The side street where James hid was really no more than a passage leading to the rear service road. He knew he had to get as far away as he could and quickly. Over the wall of a house, on the other side of the passageway, he saw a female's full-length coat and shawl hanging on a line. All was quiet, no sign of anybody about. Entering through the house's side gate he grabbed the coat and shawl, returned to the passage and put the coat on over his clothes. The large shawl, he draped over his head and adjusted it to partially conceal his face. James knew Fouquet was careful and, if he had the chance, would have led Neumann into his consulting room at the front of the house. Hopefully this would be the case today and James felt confident he would be able to go round the back of the house unnoticed by those inside. He rolled his trouser legs up so the calves of his permanently-shaved legs were concealed by the hem of the coat and took off his shoes, concealing them inside the top of his trousers. He scraped the ground with the palms of his hands, smearing the dust and grime on his face. The stiletto dagger he always carried he put in the pocket of the coat - his hand around its handle. He affected a bad stoop and started walking towards the junction of the passageway and the service road. During his training in Scotland James had spent some time hardening the soles of his feet. Even so, the cobbles of the passageway were painful to walk on but added a touch of authenticity to his guise as a crippled old woman.

On reaching the corner, he saw two cars parked behind Fouquet's house. The driver of the second car - James recognised as Neumann's driver - sat reading a newspaper. There was no sign of the other car's driver. James hobbled towards the cars. As he got to the rear of the second car he began mumbling incoherently in French and held out his left hand. He stopped just beside the car's open window and turned to its driver begging. He leaned in further, the driver cursed in German and waved him away. James reached into the coat pocket then plunged the dagger into the German's jugular, the cigarette between his lips dropped still smoking onto his chest. There was a strange gurgling sound as he died.

Looking up and down the road, James saw all was quiet with no one around. No buildings overlooked from the far side and the walls and fences, where the cars were parked, obscured from above all but the cars' roofs. Quickly, he hauled the man's body out of the driver's seat and dumped it in the roadway beside the wall. He wiped the dead man's blood off the inside of the car door with the shawl and placed the coat over its blood-stained seat. After rolling down his trouser legs and putting his shoes back on, James pulled the dead man's hat down over his own forehead. He started the car and sped off down the road.

Inside the house, Spiegel pinned Fouquet to the back of a chair as Neumann delivered yet another vicious blow with his fist to the bleeding face of the Doctor.

'You scum, all you need to tell me is when your friend Guyot will be returning' snarled Neumann as he delivered yet another blow. Again Fouquet replied he didn't know. Neumann spoke again, a chilling menace in his tone. 'If you choose not to co-operate with us now, I am sure you will be persuaded to when we get you to our headquarters. I can assure you that you will find the methods we use there are not pleasant.' Fouquet was by now almost unconscious. Neumann threw a glass of water over his face. 'I do not understand you French. Why do you persist with your defiance? We will try another method.' He spoke to Spiegel. 'That poker in the stove should be nice and hot now. Bring it to me?' He turned to the other Gestapo man standing over by the window. 'Haller. Go and see if Trautmann has seen anything out the back?' Neumann perched himself on the corner of the desk, looking directly at the Doctor.

'Fouquet why do you bother to shield this man? Especially as I have proof Guyot or, whatever he calls himself, killed your wife.'

'You are lying. That is ridiculous. Why should he?'

'Guyot is an English secret agent. We know he suspected your wife was passing information to us about the Resistance. That one of his reasons for coming to Charleville was to kill her.'

'Isobel! Passing information to you! I do not believe you.'

'We do know he killed your wife.'

Spiegel came to Fouquet's side. In his hand he held a poker which glowed red hot. With his other hand he ripped open Fouquet's shirt. Neumann grinned horribly.

'Before we take you to our headquarters, my friend Spiegel would just like to give you a little sample of what to expect when we get there.'

Spiegel was about to put the poker to Fouquet's chest when Haller ran in shouting.

'Trautmann is dead! Your car has gone!'

Neumann screamed angrily. 'Guyot!' In his rage, he swept the desk lamp smashing to the floor. He snatched up the telephone receiver.

This distraction was enough for Fouquet. Through a fug of semi-consciousness he reached into his pocket. Weeks ago, he had bullied James into giving him one of his Cyanide pills. When he begun helping the Resistance, he had vowed if ever he were caught by the Gestapo, rather than suffer the torture, he would kill himself. Also, since his beloved Isobel had been killed, life had been so desolate and lonely for him. The idea of her helping the Gestapo, the thought of her deceiving him for so long, was too much to endure. He also couldn't believe his lodger, after becoming such a good friend, would have killed her. Fouquet took the

Cyanide pill and swallowed it before Spiegel could stop him. Dr Fouquet died never knowing whether what Neumann had told him was true.

James sped through the streets toward Rue d'Etion. He was banking on the fact driving a Gestapo staff car, with its siren sounding, he would avoid being stopped at a roadside checkpoint. His gamble was paying off and was waved through at two checkpoints, one at the end of Rue du Palais, the other on Avenue Gustave Gailly. He hoped his luck would continue.

Rue d'Etion was a pleasant tree-lined road and reasonably quiet. He knew he was now taking a tremendous risk by stopping. However, he had no option. Before he went out into the country to lie low for a few days and to plan carefully what he would do, he had to get a message to London. Not only to report on the result of the attack on the factory but, also, to report there was a real possibility his cover may have been blown.

Checking there was no one about he turned into the gateway of the school opposite. It was a school jointly funded by a charity run by wealthy benefactors and the Church. Its aim to care for and teach children either orphaned, disabled or from families who for one reason or another were unable to support them. The school had been established in the 1920's when a large chateau and its extensive grounds had become available and donated to the community. It had a long driveway and after a few metres the car could not be observed from the road. The main building came into view. From atop a slight hill, James could see a group of children playing on a large lawn with what looked like two adults - teachers perhaps - supervising. On his left, the drive opened out to an area where stood two old buildings, probably once inhabited by workers at the chateau but, now James believed, from what he had heard, used as storage areas for tools and equipment and for workshops for the maintenance of the school and its grounds. James stopped the car and got out, crossed to the other side of the drive. From his viewpoint, between two trees and with the cover of the bushes, he was able to see most of the school area and its main entrance. The last thing he wanted was to arrive at the school to find they had Germans as visitors. He scanned the entrance approach and could see three sides of the main building and the grounds immediately surrounding it. There was no sign of what could be military vehicles, Gestapo staff cars or of anyone in a military uniform. He would have to chance it. Crossing back to where the car was parked, he investigated the first old building. Peering inside the windows it was apparent it had indeed once been a house but, obvious now, it had been uninhabited for years. Deposited throughout the ground floor area were work benches, lathes and a whole host of building and maintenance supplies. The adjoining old building was more like a barn, its entrance - sited on the elevation at right-angles to the car - a pair of big wooden doors big enough for a farm vehicle to enter. The doors were pushed closed but unlocked, a large padlock with the key still inside it, hung on the latch. Examining the padlock, James could tell it hadn't been locked for weeks. There was no sound from inside and he pulled open the doors. Inside, were parked a variety of carts. In one corner an unlit blacksmith's furnace with appropriate tools and, along the back wall were stored agricultural and horticultural implements. Importantly though, there was space to park the car. It would be better to conceal the car here, whilst he went to see the person he was seeking.

After locking the padlock, he walked off down the driveway. It was a pleasant evening and he enjoyed the few minutes walk to the school entrance. It was a welcome opportunity to enjoy the sounds and smells of nature, whilst collecting his thoughts and planning the next few days.

The children he had seen playing were just beginning to file in noisily through a side door as he walked the last few metres up the gravelled approach to the impressive front doorway. On seeing him, a middle-aged woman gathered protectively around her the last few children filing through the side door.

'Who are you? What do you want?' She asked defensively.

'I am sorry to startle you Madame. I have to see Mademoiselle Vernet urgently. I hope she is here today.'

'And you are?' She asked suspiciously.

'Andre Marceau.' He used the name Veronique could identify him by. 'I am her cousin and I have some news about her brother. He is seriously ill. I am sorry to trouble you but, things now - communication by telephone or post - are so difficult.'

'Pardon me Monsieur. I apologise.' She instructed the remaining children to go and wash their hands and walked over to him. 'I had no idea. It is just that the Germans were here earlier asking questions. They frightened the children. We have only just managed to settle and calm them. Some of the soldiers were all right, offered the children sweets. The others - well...' she gestured angrily '...I will fetch Veronique for you. I think she is in the music room.' She beckoned James to follow her, inviting him to take a seat in the hallway.

As he watched the woman scurry up the large staircase he had mixed feelings. On one hand he was relieved, if the Germans had recently been here the chances were they might not be around the area when it was time to continue his journey. On the other hand, if they had been at the school, would they have questioned Veronique, could they have been suspicious about what she was doing in this part of France?

Veronique - her code name - had recently been dropped by parachute into France. The recruitment and training of SOE agents and wireless operators had really been accelerated now and, the arrival of a replacement wireless operator in the area had been long awaited. It was a general rule within SOE and preferable for an agent in the field to have as little personal contact with the wireless operator in their area as possible. And, certainly, they should have no knowledge of each other's real identity. All James knew of Veronique was she was French-born, in Bethune, and had lived in England since 1938. He had been immensely relieved when she had at last arrived. Transmitting messages and waiting for incoming ones took up so much time, meant he had to arrange all his other activities accordingly - not always easy or ideal.

He heard footsteps hurrying down the staircase. As the young woman rounded the landing and came down the last few stairs, James stood up, greeting her with a smile. She was in her early twenties, of a chubby physique and had a pleasant, smiling face.

'Andre! It is so nice to see you.'

They embraced and kissed as cousins would. The charade was for the benefit of anyone who may have been in an adjoining room or would happen to see them.

'I apologise for troubling you at your work but I have had some news of your brother.'

'Thank you for coming Andre. I have been so worried about him. It is no problem you're coming here. Besides, apart from supervising the children as they prepare for bed, I have finished my work for the day. Shall we go outside? It is such a nice evening.'

Once outside they selected a bench overlooking an ornamental pond and well out of earshot of anyone.

'I understand the Germans were here earlier. What did they want?' He asked anxiously.

'I did not actually see them. But they were here for a while searching, saying they were looking for someone. They warned Madame Dupont - the Principal - of the penalties for sheltering a spy or a member of the Resistance.'

'They were undoubtedly looking for me. I daresay they could well be back, may well be more thorough and brutal next time.' He told Veronique what he wanted her to transmit later about the results of the attack on the factory and the fate of the train-load of supplies and components. 'When I returned to where I have been staying the Gestapo were there. In recent days they have been drawing the net in on my landlord and I. It is becoming increasingly dangerous for me and the other Group members in Charleville at the moment. I have decided to hide up for a while. I also want you to tell London about this and ask them for instructions as to what they want me to do. Could you send an appropriate message Veronique?'

'Of course.'

He had no idea of where she transmitted from. He did not have to or want to know.

'I am heading out into the countryside, to a safe contact whom I can trust. It is a few kilometres from here but I should be able to arrange for a courier to act as a go-between for messages between you and I. Will it be alright for the messages to be exchanged here when required?'

'Yes. I am in the habit of taking a walk in the grounds in the early evenings. People here are used to me doing that no matter what the weather. Though it will probably not be possible for me to meet a courier personally. If these messages were suitably hidden somewhere?'

James thought for a moment. 'Yes. But it would have to be a very good hiding place and, the message to include a person's name only known to us to verify it is genuine.'

It was her turn to pause for a moment. 'How about "Charles Rocroi"? Charles from Charleville, Rocroi after the town. The Gestapo could never come up with anything like that.'

He was impressed with her ingenuity. 'Yes. Excellent. Where do you suggest as a suitable hiding place?'

'Just off the drive there are some old buildings.'

'Yes I noticed them on my way in. I stole a car from the Gestapo and parked it in the barn and locked the doors. They were left unlocked.'

She gestured in despair. 'Georges! Our maintenance man! We keep telling him that he must always lock them. Oh never mind, he will be away now until tomorrow. When you leave, I will walk up the drive with you - it will look natural to those here for me to do that. When we get there I am sure we will find a hiding place. Apart from Georges, no one ever goes into the barn.'

'Fine. Now Veronique, could you try and do something for me if you can? I need to know the fate of Dr Fouquet, the man I lodged with. Also, any news you can pick up about whether any other members of the Group have been arrested? When I get to my safe house, I will also try to get information on Fouquet and any others.'

'I will do my best. For my work here, there are times when I have to go in to town.'

'Well I think that is all for now. We will walk back to the barn. Now, give me a hug and a friendly kiss?'

Veronique responded and together they walked towards the drive.

Behind the barn was an old well. Examining it carefully,

James found one of the inner bricks loose and removed it by scraping out the loose mortar.

'There we are, plenty of space behind it to leave a piece of paper. This will do fine.' He replaced the brick. 'Remember that Veronique. Third brick from the well handle, second course down.' He looked around them. 'This maintenance man. Is he likely to be working here frequently?'

'It depends. However, he has always gone by three in the afternoon.'

'Right. All messages to be left or picked up after three-thirty.' He started to unlock the barn doors.

Veronique pointed over his shoulder. 'Through the gap in the hedge there, there is an old path which leads eventually to the banks of the Meuse by a disused Church. It is unmistakable. The route is cross-country and will be safer for your courier than perhaps coming along the main roads.'

'Good. I will tell whoever it will be.' He returned the padlock key to her. Instinctively, he touched her arm. 'You take care Veronique.'

'You too.'

James started up the car and reversed out of the barn. Veronique watched him accelerate up the drive - the car's siren wailing.

It was getting dark as James neared Arreux. He knew by now every unit of the army and Gestapo would be on the lookout for Neumann's car. It was too chancy for him to push his luck any further and had to find a place to hide or dispose of the car. From one of his journeys with Fouquet, he remembered him talking of a long-disused and now flooded quarry somewhere near Arreux. James wished he could remember exactly where. Just up the road he could see what looked like a faded white board. "Entry forbidden" the board warned and, underneath, the wording continued: "Danger - deep quarry".

He turned off the road, followed a very rough, gravel track for about a third of a mile around a bend. The car's hooded headlights shone on the surface of an expanse of water merely metres in front of him. James braked violently and killed the car lights in one movement. Stepping round to the front of the vehicle he had no idea of how deep the water might be but, judging by the sheer sides of the water's rocky banks on either side of him, he guessed it was more than deep enough to conceal the car. The car had stopped on a slope of shale, just before an old wooden fence which ran around the edge of the quarry. He examined the fence. It was rickety, appeared not to have been maintained for years and would certainly not resist the impact of a car. After opening all the windows, he released the hand brake and pushed the car and watched as it gained momentum towards the fence. There was a loud crack of splintering wood and the car disappeared over the edge. He rushed to the edge just in time to see the car bounce noisily off an outcrop of rock and plunge into the water, roof first. It began to sink, leaving a froth of bubbles as it did so. James began walking back down the track, on his way picking up a fallen branch of a tree. Meticulously, he brushed the ground with the branch for the whole distance to remove traces of the car's tyre tracks, hoping any searching German wouldn't persist in checking for more than a few metres for any signs of a vehicle entering the gravel track. Meiller-Fontaine, where he was heading, lay roughly a few kilometres away to the north-east. James set off down the road.

A little later, from across a hedge, he heard someone calling in a pet dog or cat. He stopped. Through a gap in the hedge and, by the light of faint moonlight, made out the dark outline of a small dwelling in the trees. James wasn't relishing the walk to the safe house in Meiller-Fontaine and toyed with the idea of creeping up to the house to see whether there may be a cycle he could get his hands on to hasten his journey. Caution however prevailed. Should the Boche call at the house in their quest for him, the resident may report their cycle had gone missing, so leading the Germans to focus their search in this area.. He walked on remembering Neumann's car had nearly a full tank of fuel. He tried to reassure himself that, because it did have nearly a full tank, it might be enough to convince the Germans to search further away.

Using his tiny compass and navigating himself *via* a mix of minor roads, woodland tracks and fields, James at last drew close to the boundary of the farm he would be welcomed and sheltered for however long was necessary. The farm's owners who would give him a haven were two widowed sisters in their early fifties and their niece. Between the three of them they worked their small farm, supplementing their meagre income from spinning and weaving and selling the products in Charleville and other surrounding towns and villages.

It was now late and there was no obvious sign of life at the farm. The three women were almost certainly in bed asleep. For now he would sleep in the barn and make known his presence at first light. Then, he would explain to them the plan arranged with Veronique for leaving and collecting messages at the school.

40

Colin looked at the young woman sitting opposite him engrossed in her book. Throughout the train journey from Rethel not a word or acknowledgement had passed between them. But that would have been dangerous, for she was his appointed guide. In fact, the only words exchanged between them had been on the pathway to Rethel station. It had been a pre-arranged, "stage managed" bumping into each other, just enough to allow her the opportunity of giving him his instructions for the rail trip. She had also told him whereabouts to sit in the carriage, boarding herself at the very last moment.

Much of the train was crowded but their particular carriage less so. Colin looked around yet again. There were various passengers obviously on business or matters of commerce, a few just travelling to or fro between their homes or visiting friends and relatives, two nuns and, disconcertingly, two German soldiers at the far end who spent a good deal of time sleeping or, as Colin suspected, making crude comments about young female passengers.

He though back over his journey so far. His guide to Villers-Semeuse had been a local man obtaining his income by working his way around the area surrounding Charleville, sharpening knives and agricultural hand tools, using his especially adapted cycle for the grinding. Colin had been dressed as his helper, instructed to act as if he was profoundly deaf. Together, Colin on foot - his guide with his cycle - had walked to Villers-Semeuse across country, using fields and tracks. Colin had spent one night there, sleeping in a near derelict out-building of a house, the house owner supplying plentiful but very basic meals and various drinks. At first light, he had been met at the house by a youth with a spare cycle. With the youth cycling several metres in front of him, they made their way across fields, hugging the cover of hedgerows and woodland, to a little hamlet. Colin discovered later this was roughly halfway between Villers-Semeuse and Donchery. There, he was told by the youth to leave his cycle in a barn and hide there for a few hours until someone came for him. On no account was he to emerge from the barn. Colin had been told he would probably have a few hours to wait but, by afternoon, no one had arrived. Despite hearing a woman's voice about the farmyard and children playing around, no one came near the barn. He had been getting increasingly concerned, hungry and thirsty. Of more concern though, for much of the morning, he had heard persistent gunfire in the distance which hadn't ceased by about mid-day. Suddenly, Colin had heard the barn doors open. Peeping down from where he was hiding he saw a woman in the doorway. She was calling quietly and had a tray of food and drink. Apologising for not coming to see him earlier, she explained she had two young children and didn't want to chance them accidentally telling anyone about his presence on the farm. In the early evening her husband came to see him, explaining there had been some hitch in the arrangements for Colin's next move and it could be at least another two days before the move took place. However, his two children would be visiting relatives for the next couple of days, so Colin would be able to leave the barn during daylight if he wanted and hide in the nearby woods, returning to the house after dark for washing and food. Although anxious for the safety of his wife and family whilst Colin stayed on the farm, the couple had made him welcome and were generous in the refreshments provided.

It had been early on the third day when a man in his sixties turned up at the farm for him. Colin had accompanied this man for what he estimated to be about four miles until they came to a cluster of houses gathered around a small square and a church. At the back of a workshop, a horse waited patiently within the shafts of a cart laden with besoms, fencing hurdles and basket ware. Colin's guide introduced him to a man who invited him to join him on the seat of the cart.

The journey by cart had seemed endless but, thankfully, uneventful and it was early evening by the time they stopped alongside a barge moored at a small quay in Donchery. Colin had been quickly ushered aboard and hidden as the merchandise from the cart was loaded.

This journey had also taken ages, the barge crewed by two brothers in their fifties - Louis and Pasquale - continuing the family tradition of conveying cargoes of all descriptions up and down the Ardennnes Canal, the Meuse and Aisne. Colin had enjoyed the days spent with the brothers as the vessel passed along the waterways meandering through the countryside. It had been strangely relaxing. During the trip they had told him all about the traditions and regulations of the work -far more historic and complex than he would have imagined. The two brothers knew the route like the back of their hands, were aware of where the Germans were likely to be found. Consequently, Colin was able to stay on deck for some of the journey enjoying the fresh air and, the information they gave him on the different places and sights they passed.

On a quiet stretch of the Aisne, near Pargny-Resson,

Louis and Pasquale had dropped Colin off on the bank, where he was met by a young woman. Again, cutting through fields and along tracks, she had led him to a house to the south of Rethel where he had stayed for two days.

Whilst in Rethel, Colin had been delighted to be re-united, *albeit* briefly during the evening, with Michael Richards. Mike had been brought by another route to Rethel and had arrived at another safe house on the other side of town two days previously. He was due to be moved on the following day. Their respective hosts turned out to be keen card players and a game of cards, accompanied by a quantity of wine, had been enjoyed. Mike was collected for the next part of his journey early *via* a route kept secret from Colin. After Mike had left, Colin wondered if the two of them might meet up somewhere else along their different routes back to England. During their brief meeting both men had reflected on the fate of their fellow crew members, wondered if there had been any further news of the survivors. There had been none. When the time arrived for Colin to be moved on, he had been given some more French Francs and, the details of his rendezvous with his guide just outside Rethel station.

Although now, as the train slowed just before Reims, Colin's abiding memory had been the shock of seeing wanted posters at Rethel station. Each poster bore a photograph of a man he had recognised instantly - a photograph captioned with an unfamiliar name. The photograph was of his older brother James. Seeing the first poster had stopped Colin in his tracks at, probably, the worst point to show hesitancy, before a ticket barrier guarded by Gendarmes and Germans. It had taken a sharp word in his ear and an inconspicuous nudge by his young female guide for him to hurry on towards the platform. He had been totally shaken by seeing the photograph. Not only by seeing the image but, also, the incomprehension of what and why his brother was doing in occupied France.

Colin waited for his guide to leave the carriage before getting to his feet. A partially crippled, elderly woman got to the door before him and begun to struggle out of the door. Impatiently but concealing the fact, Colin motioned he would assist her down onto the platform. To his horror the two German soldiers were next to follow them out of the carriage but they pushed past intolerantly. Anxious, not to let his guide out of his sight and, after extricating his arm from the old woman's arm and her bags, he hurried as fast as he dared after her. His guide was on the tall side and he glimpsed her camel-coloured coated figure pause just before the barrier making out she was studying the timetable pasted on the wall. Surreptitiously she glanced back towards him and passed through the barrier a few steps in front of him. After an agonisingly-long look at his forged papers, the two Gendarmes at the barrier waved him through. Once outside the station the young woman crossed the road. Straightaway, the differences between Reims and Charleville were obvious to Colin. Reims had all the bustle and rush of a city, whereas life in Charleville had gone about things far more quietly and slowly. It was still a grey, murky day, the rain continuing to fall steadily as he followed his guide, ensuring he kept a distance behind her. During her brief conversation with him outside Rethel station, she had told him when they reached Reims she would lead him to a baker's shop just off a large square.

Despite the weather there were a lot of people about and, at times, Colin was having to step round groups of people queuing at various shops. There were a couple of times when he temporarily lost sight of his guide as she took a turning either to the right or left. At last he saw her go in the side entrance of a bakers on the corner of an alley leading off the square. As instructed, he waited a few minutes before joining a queue of people waiting outside the shop's main entrance.

'Good afternoon Monsieur' called out a rotund woman from over the counter as he entered the shop. 'If you do not mind waiting a moment. We will be closing shortly, then my husband will be able to talk to you.'

As the last customers were served with what little bread remained, Colin looked at some old sepia photographs hanging in frames on the wall. These, together with some written notes hanging below - a few words of which he could understand - led him to believe the family had been bakers for generations. Next to the photos was a cabinet, in which were arranged some bakery trophies.

After ushering out the last of her customers and closing the shop, the rotund woman came to his side. 'Apologies for keeping you Monsieur. Times are so difficult now and we are out of routine. We have to bake and serve whenever we can, whenever we have enough to bake with. We are doing the best we can but times are very difficult for everyone.'

'I understand Madame.'

'How was your journey? We have been expecting you but, nowadays, there is no way of knowing if trains will be delayed or running at all.' Colin had no time to answer her question before she continued. 'Come through to the back. My husband, Gerard, will speak to you.' She showed him through a door before returning to the shop to commence tidying and cleaning.

Colin was in a large room. It was where all the baking took place, the warmth was incredible and a delicious aroma of baking teased his nostrils. There were four big ovens and, in the centre of the room, a large work surface covered with a clutter of baking tins and utensils. Around the walls of the room were storage shelves and hooks on which hung a variety of implements. A man stood in the open doorway directly opposite him holding a glass of liquid.

Seeing Colin, the man came straight towards him and greeted him warmly. 'Greetings Monsieur' and, referring to the glass in his hand. 'Relaxing after finishing the baking. Would you like one - or a coffee perhaps?'

'A coffee would be nice please. Thank you.'

A young woman, Colin's guide, entered from a door to his left.

'Monsieur let me introduce you to our youngest daughter, Colette.' She smiled beautifully at Colin and shook his hand. It was a strange experience for him, not really acknowledging each other since Rethel and, now, to be greeted so warmly by her. 'Colette, our good friend here would like a coffee. Could you please?'

'Of course. It is only ersatz though I am afraid.' She checked whether the water was near boiling and started to clear, tidy and clean the bakery.

The baker motioned Colin to sit with him over in a corner of the room. 'Well, welcome to Reims. You will be staying with us for a while. Initially anyway.' He pointed to a building across the yard from where they were sitting. 'In our storeroom there. It has all been prepared for you and we have made it as comfortable as possible. Hopefully, in a day or two, we will be able to arrange somewhere a little better for you. It all depends on what orders and deliveries I can arrange. Before the war, I had my regular baking and delivery schedules - regular orders to fulfil.' He gestured in despair. 'But now, all routines have gone. I have to bake whenever I can get supplies. So much of what I produce I have to set aside for the damned Boche anyway.'

The baker's wife entered from the shop and flopped into a chair. 'It has been so busy today. I am getting to hate these baking days. Honestly, some of the customers can be so rude and greedy. Do they not realise we are trying to do our best to be fair to everyone.'

The baker got up and put a consoling arm around his wife. 'Poor Edith. I know it is hard. You have the worst of it out there. The people do not mean it. They are just anxious - desperate to feed their families.'

Colette handed mugs of coffee to Colin and her mother. The three remained in the bakery talking for some minutes before Colette showed Colin into what was to be his hiding place.

The store room was of a rectangular shape, at the end of which were stacked to a height of about five feet, sacks of flour. With his help, Colette lifted down three sacks from the top. Colin saw the sacks had been arranged to form a wall leaving a cavity behind of about seven foot square with a small hole in the outside wall for ventilation.

'There is a blanket, a pillow and a candle in the cavity' she explained. Indicating the three sacks they had just lifted down, she added 'If you put these sacks back on the top there, you can use them to block up the gap each time you return. As our shop is not opening every day at the moment and, there is usually just me and my parents here, hopefully you will be able to spend some of the time during the day in the bakery - we are not overlooked. However, if anyone calls on us unexpectedly or, the Boche are around, you must come in here and hide straight-away. Understand?'

'Of course.'

'Then you must wait until one of us tells you it is safe to come out. Now, as it is important you are able to hide yourself quickly, I suggest you spend a little time practising with the sacks. If you will excuse me, I must get back to help my parents finish clearing up in the bakery and to prepare a meal for the evening. I will see you presently.'

41

The system James had devised with Veronique for exchanging messages had worked well. Joan, the niece at the farm near Meillier-Fontaine, had acted as his courier, for over two weeks managing to avoid any brushes with Germans patrolling or at their road-checks. Eventually, Veronique had established that, in the aftermath of the Resistance attack on the factory, none of the Group had been caught and, as far as she could ascertain, none had been injured. But, she had heard the Gestapo had launched a manhunt for Pierre Papon of the factory's transport office who had gone missing after the attack. James had felt a great sense of pleasure and relief on hearing the news about the members of the Group who had been otherwise involved with the sabotage but, had been very saddened to learn of Dr Fouquet's demise. Brave to the end, Fouquet had done so much in assisting the Resistance - assisting him since his arrival in Charleville. Despite losing the wife he worshipped, Fouquet had continued unwaveringly in his help and support for the Resistance. Since the night he had killed Isobel, two things had constantly haunted James. Firstly, how blissfully unaware the Doctor had been of his wife's activities on behalf of the Gestapo - James had never revealed to him what he had discovered about her. Secondly, how Fouquet had always regarded him as a good friend - a friend whom, whilst accepting his hospitality, enjoying his friendship, had terminated his wife's life.

The inactivity, whilst hiding out at the farm, had been driving James to distraction, causing him much frustration and irritation. The first few days had been beneficial in that it had afforded him the time to sleep, rest and regain some strength. He had begun to channel his restored energy and strength into various manual jobs around the farm. This was both therapeutic to him and, he felt in some way repaid the three women there for the risks and hospitality undertaken on his behalf.

He put down the axe and sat on the stump of the old tree he had just felled. He watched Joan walk back towards the house. She had just brought him a welcome, refreshing drink of home-made fruit juice. Whilst sitting there, he reflected on his time in France and what he had achieved. In some ways he believed his mission incomplete. On the other hand, he had been instrumental in dealing a massive blow to the German lines of command in Beauvais; led an operation which helped destroy and severely disrupt the German war machine's efforts for weeks. Perhaps, more importantly, he had also tracked-down and eliminated an important German agent, helped establish and been responsible for the training of a brand new Resistance Group which, hopefully, would continue to grow and cause increasing chaos and disruption for the Germans. However, in reality, he knew it was now the right time for him to leave France - for the time being at least. To stay longer could undermine all achieved so far, could certainly endanger others' lives and their future works of sabotage against the Germans. At last, at the end of a fortnight, the message he had been expecting had arrived. Subject to the weather being right, a flight had been laid on for his return to England. SOE flights were regulated by the cycle of the moon and, to the nights immediately before and after a full moon, when visibility was good enough for the pilots assigned for clandestine operations to find their way. Even then there was always a risk of some other factor preventing a pick-up. James had just over a week to get to the south of Paris, where a local Resistance Group had been mobilised to select and lay out a landing zone. A fresh set of papers had been prepared for him and, in the guise of a criminal, he would be escorted to Troyes by a Gendarme friendly to the Resistance. From Troyes, with a different ID, he would travel by himself by train to the southern suburbs of Paris, staying in a hotel until being collected from there to be taken to a village near Melun for the pick-up.

A week later, near Melun, on the night scheduled for his flight, forecasted squally showers contrived to prevent a pick-up. To James, at the time of the pick-up, the weather conditions had seemed favourable. However James understood how cautious the Met people advising the SOE had to be and, back in England, they had to go by whatever their charts and evidence of weather conditions told them. Angrily, he threw another bit of dried mud to the far end of the barn in which he waited. In a makeshift pen a young, sickly calf noisily disturbed the straw as it got up and went to suckle from its mother. The cow mooed quietly, sniffed and licked its offspring's back. James smiled, wondering again just when he would get out of the barn. Suddenly, he heard footsteps crunching on the ground outside and gripped his knife.

A figure appeared in the entrance. 'Quickly Monsieur. Come with me.'

James recognised the man who had met him at the hotel in Paris. He got to his feet and followed the man out across the yard and into a field. The man ahead was very tall and had a huge stride. Eventually James caught up with him.

'Sorry to hurry you Monsieur' said the man as James drew alongside him. 'We do not have much time.' He anticipated James's question about the weather not being favourable. 'In England, the plans have changed. Word has only just reached us that a plane is coming for you. We have a distance to go before we reach the landing zone.'

They crossed a series of fields, a ditch and a couple of small lanes. James had completely lost his bearings. On their left was a little chapel-like building where a track joined the one they were on. Three figures appeared on this track also hurrying. One of them a female, the second a child clutching her hand.

'Why did we not get to hear sooner?' Demanded the third figure, a man, angrily.

The two groups of people merged on the one track. James now saw the child was a boy of about seven.

'We will sort it out when we get back' replied the man accompanying James. 'We do not have far to go now.'

After a short while the two Frenchmen led their charges off the track and through a narrow belt of trees to a large field. In the middle of the field James saw a group of figures scurrying around busily, realising they were completing the layout of the Landing Zone. He, the woman and child were led to the point where they would board the aeroplane. James instinctively called for silence from everyone. Was it his imagination? No, definitely he could hear a sound in the distance. The sound grew clearer. It was the unmistakable sound of an aero engine - now everyone heard it. The man in charge of the group ordered the flares to be lit. Over the trees at the far end of the field, suddenly they saw the aircraft making its approach and, with his lamp, the man in charge flashed the previously agreed Morse letter. The

Lysander swooped over them - so low its draft parted the waiting people's hair. It climbed again, banked and turned back in the direction from which it had come. For a horrible moment James feared the pilot - after taking a look at the landing area - was unhappy about something. He glanced around the field, saw no obvious problems to prevent a landing. The field had not been recently ploughed, there were no wireless masts or telephone wires, no trees or other obstruction too close. He felt a huge sense of relief when the Lysander levelled out and turned once more over the trees and prepared to land.

During their rush to the landing field, one of the Frenchmen had explained they were not expecting any in-bound passengers off the Lysander but, there would be a couple of boxes of some small arms, forged documents and currency. The Lysander turned and stopped by the first flare in the direction of take-off. Members of the reception party eagerly unloaded the boxes as James, the woman and her child settled themselves in the plane. Within a minute, the door of the aircraft was shut and its pilot released the brakes to start his take-off. The aircraft began its take-off run, the surface of the field causing a slightly bumpy ride. Quickly gathering speed, its engine now roaring, James felt the Lysander lift off the ground. The pilot climbed very steeply and, almost on a wing-tip, banked and turned. Alarmed and frightened by the manoeuvre, the little boy began to cry. Visibility from their position in the aircraft was limited but, as it banked, James could just make out members of the Resistance extinguishing the last of the landing flares. After the short time spent with the Group that had seen him off he was of the opinion they were well-organised and disciplined. He was confident their good organisation and discipline would, within a few minutes, enable them to disperse and disappear in the darkness of the countryside without trace. He made a mental note to make known his favourable opinion to the powers that be when he got back to England. The aircraft had now levelled out and he settled himself in the seat.

James knew the pilots of the "Special Duties" Squadrons navigated their flights in a series of legs, each of about an hour. At the end of each leg, they would get a fix as to where they were. After about 50 minutes, James realised they were changing course. Miles away - off to the north, the night sky was illuminated by beams of light and occasional explosions. An allied air-raid somewhere was being viciously defended. He believed it best to distract his fellow passengers from seeing what was going on. Tentatively, he engaged the woman in conversation. Her son had fallen asleep in her arms.

Smiling, he said 'A certain little person is very tired. What is his name?'

'Jean-Claude. He is rather frightened. It is the first time he has ever flown. Also the first time for me. I am also a little frightened.'

It was strictly against all SOE rules for him to say anything about his background or the reason he was travelling. He knew she would also have been told to say nothing of why she was on the flight. However, James saw no reason why they shouldn't engage in small talk and generalities, as long as they both avoided specifics, didn't give away the true reason for their trip.

'I know. It is also the first time I have flown. I must admit though, I am rather enjoying the experience.'

'I am flying to England to rejoin my husband.' She stopped abruptly, as if she was scared even that was saying too much.

James didn't ask why her husband was in England but wondered if he was a politician, part of DeGaulle's Free

French administration in England. He cooked up a story he was a specialised scientist. 'I have been forced to flee France.'

During the rest of the flight they spoke now and again, both of them deliberately vague. However, he discovered she and her family had lived somewhere near Paris. Using his knowledge of Paris, James and she discussed the various museums and historic buildings there, what life had been like in the City before the Germans took it over. James knew whenever they could the "special duties" pilots chose to fly over points on the Normandy coast. The Lysander banked. He could see they were just crossing the coast.

He turned to the woman. Her son was beginning to stir from his slumber. 'Not too long to go. We are now over the English Channel.'

In all probability they would be landing at Tangmere, invariably now used for SOE clandestine flights to France. As the aircraft drew closer to England, his mind went back to almost two years previously - the many times in his Hurricane he had fought over these very waters. His mind was full of memories of his friends and comrades on the Squadron, many of whom had perished around him. Also others, he hoped during later aerial combats - perhaps now with other squadrons - had not too lost their lives. Soon, whenever he could, he must try and contact surviving former Squadron friends and comrades.

Approaching the English coast they were greeted by bad weather. Suddenly, there was a bright coloured flash of light outside the window. Startled and frightened, Jean-Claude started to cry. The pilot had just fired the colour of the day.

'It is all right Jean-Claude' James called reassuringly. 'It is nothing to be frightened of. The man in the front is just telling the people in England we are about to arrive.'

'The bad weather has arrived sooner than expected' the pilot called. 'I'm afraid it is going to get a bit bumpy. Hang on just in case.' He added 'Apparently, this weather system is due to move across the Channel and spread across most of France.'

James was relieved to have been picked up just in time. He may well have been left stranded in France for the best part of another month.

Despite a strong cross-wind, atrocious visibility and driving rain, the pilot made a landing James would have been proud of himself. As the Lysander drew to a halt at an isolated part of Tangmere, James looked out of the window. He could make out two vehicles driving towards them. Within a little while two cars pulled up parallel. Some official in dark clothing, struggling with an umbrella against the elements, ran up and assisted the woman and her son out of the aircraft.

'Welcome to England Madame. If you come with me, we will go in the first car.'

There was no time even for James and the woman to say good-bye. Before he got out he looked through into the cockpit, saw the pilot like himself - in RAF life - was a Squadron Leader. Through the front screen he saw the first car already speeding off towards - what he remembered as - being the main entrance to the airfield. James couldn't resist congratulating the pilot on the difficult landing.

'Thank you. All part of the service' replied the pilot jovially. Adding 'We sent another Lysander last night. I hope he makes it back too.'

As James stepped down from the plane a man in civilian clothes was waiting. James introduced himself using his code name in the approved fashion.

'Welcome back to England' greeted the man. As the car moved off, the man introduced himself in code as James's escorting officer. 'There's been a change of plan I'm afraid. We were due to drive straight back to London tonight. There's been some hitch or other and we'll be driving up there tomorrow morning now.'

James thought his escorting officer's phraseology strange, considering it was 02.30 hours. He presumed he meant later that morning.

The man sitting beside him continued 'It will mean staying in our cottage here I'm afraid.'

'Never mind. I'm so whacked, I'd rather have a sleep here than dropping off in the car *en route.*'

After a few minutes their car stopped by the cottage just outside Tangmere's perimeter. As they entered, a corporal - the same one as when James flew out to France and acted as an orderly - greeted them smiling.

'I expect you could do with a nice hot drink before you turn in sir?'

'Yes. Thank you. That would be very welcome.'

'We can even offer a rarity nowadays' the orderly added cheerfully. 'How does a steaming mug of cocoa sound?'

'That sounds marvellous. Thank you.'

'You go through sir. I'll bring it in shortly.'

The escorting officer showed James into what was termed as the Op.'s Room. Nothing much seemed to have changed from when he was last there. It still had the cosy, lived-in appearance. The armchairs still looked as comfortable as they did and this was confirmed when he flopped down in the one nearest to him. The escorting officer offered him a cigarette from a box on the table which he declined. There was a knock on the door and the orderly entered with two mugs of steaming liquid. James took a sip. It was delicious - like nectar to him. The last time he had tasted cocoa was whilst at Fighter Dispersals waiting for a scramble.

'Thank you Banks' said the escorting officer. 'That will be all for the night.'

'Right you are sir.' He paused. 'But there's another flight due in?'

'Don't worry. I will see to them.'

The orderly spoke to James. 'Your bedroom sir, is the one immediately at the top of the stairs. It's all nice and warm and ready for you.'

After Banks left the room the two men talked for a while. James was finding it hard to like the other man. There was some questioning, vague as to details and specifics but, nevertheless, enough to make James believe his de-briefing had already commenced. He was very tired, was growing impatient. He finished his drink quickly, made his excuses for ending their conversation and dragged his weary limbs up the stairs. His escort had announced their departure from the cottage as 07.45 - time enough for him to grab a few hours of lovely sleep.

Once in the bedroom, James was too tired to undress properly. He simply took off his jacket, tie and shoes and slumped on the bed. As he drifted into sleep his thoughts were a few miles away, still in Sussex but at his own home with his wife June.

42

During the summer of 1942, after nearly three years of war, the situation was grim for Britain and her allies. The ceaseless tide of war ever-encroaching: Japan's rampant progress in the Far East; the British army in full retreat in North Africa; the German army advancing on Stalingrad and the Volga; U-boats had near-severed Britain's supply lines of food and other commodities. There was a flicker of hope when the United States entered the war but, all in all, good news was hard to come by. Up and down Britain an atmosphere of despair and desolation pervaded like a putrefying smell.

Three days after James landed at Tangmere, Margaret Wilding travelled by train to Cornwall. She and Robert met at a hotel and they had driven to St. Ives. It was a lovely warm day with a clear blue sky and only a few wispy white clouds here and there. They were on the headland above St. Ives - she laying with her head in his lap. He ran his fingers lightly, soothingly through her hair. Gulls wheeled noisily out to sea, their distant cry the only sound to disturb the sublime quiet.

'Oh Robert! Isn't this just heaven. Just the sound of the birds and the breaking of the waves.'

'It's certainly heaven my love being here with you. Just

the two of us.' They kissed. 'Do you know how many weeks it's been since we were last together? Over six.'

'And you have just 48 hours leave?'

'Forty-eight hours! And that a struggle to get.' He paused. 'When we spoke the other evening, we suggested two dates for the wedding.'

Slowly she sat up. There was a hesitancy that worried him. They embraced and kissed again.

'Since we spoke about it Robert I've thought of very little else.' She paused a long while.

'And?' He asked but not impatiently.

'The thing is. Do you not think it best to wait for a while.' Seeing his expression she hastened to reassure him. 'Please Robert. Believe me. I want to get married - since you asked me - there's nothing I've wanted more. It's just that, well, could we perhaps wait a while, until things are more settled?'

Again, without impatience 'Until the war is over you mean?'

'No Robert. Of course not. That could be years away. Heaven knows, you will probably have a better idea than I when that is likely to be. No, it's just - well, I've already talked to Stephen and June about it…'.

'…And?'

'They're both very happy for me - for us. They really are. It's just that I have not heard anything from Richard for ages. I would just like to know his feelings.' She paused. 'I just hope and pray he's safe and well.'

'I'm sure he is Margaret. Mail between POW's and home can only be described as patchy at best.'

'It is so unfair to keep you waiting like this Robert, I realise that. But please, you do understand?'

He embraced and kissed her tenderly. 'Margaret of course I understand. I realise it's so difficult for you at the moment. Anyway, after all, we've got the whole of our lives in front of us. Don't worry. The right time for the wedding will come.' Margaret thought she detected a faint glimmer of relief on his face. He paused a long while. 'Besides, It will probably be difficult to arrange in the very near future.'

'Robert? What is it?'

'Obviously, I can't say too much. But, yesterday, I was at a big briefing. Figures were released of the amount of shipping lost during the last month. Losses are far worse than envisaged.'

'I see…'.

'…The briefing was not only about the loss of shipping. There's also something big being planned. It looks as if I and many others are going to be up to our eyes with it for the next few months.'

That is all he would say but he was referring to the planned attack on Dieppe. Planning and preparation by Combined Operations staff of the operation was now reaching fruition and he and others would be heavily involved.

Margaret clung to him. 'Does it mean you will have to be going away?'

'I just don't know.'

She began to cry. 'Why is it everyone whose been - is dear to me - are snatched away.' She was silent for a while. 'Will anything ever be the same again?'

They remained in each other's arms for a long while. No words were exchanged, each of them were reflecting on their thoughts, each dreaming and hoping for better and happier times.

Eventually Robert spoke. 'How about a spot of lunch? There was that charming little restaurant where we parked the car? After we can go for a drive to Portreath. I have heard it's lovely there.'

After spending the afternoon at Portreath he drove

Margaret back to her hotel. During the drive she thought back over their day together, realised just how close they had grown. They had spent nights together before but, never before, had she yearned so much to be with him for the whole night - for ever.

She had promised to lend Robert a book she had left in her room at the hotel. As she asked at reception for the key, Robert took a seat over in the window. Her hotel was perfectly good and comfortable, run by two spinster sisters, both very prim and proper. The younger sister was on reception and cast a disapproving eye beyond Margaret at Robert which Margaret noticed. There and then, on impulse, she decided on something. Down the road, at another hotel, she had noticed it had "Double Room Vacancies".

'Could you prepare my bill please?'

'But Dr Wilding you're booked in for dinner tonight?'

'I know. I'm very sorry. Something has cropped up. I have to check out now.'

The woman behind the desk looked disapprovingly at Robert again. 'Oh very well' and rather aggressively. 'You realise you will have to pay for dinner?'

'Yes. I realise that. I am sorry.'

After packing, Margaret returned to reception. Robert was still sitting where he had been but now engrossed in a newspaper. After paying her bill she crossed to the side of his chair. He saw she had her case.

'What are you doing with your case? I thought you were here for another night?'

'I was but I noticed there's a hotel down the road with double rooms available. Shall we go there for the night?'

Robert hesitated then took her in his arms. 'Oh Margaret! Yes.' He paused. 'Are you sure?'

'My darling. I have never been so sure of anything in my life.' They kissed passionately.

The woman at reception cleared her throat loudly and called to Margaret. 'I forgot. A telegram arrived for you.' Margaret turned towards her. 'I'm sorry. It only arrived a few minutes ago.'

Margaret read the telegram and returned to Robert.

'What is it Margaret? What's happened?'

'It's from Mrs Fuller. Apparently James has been trying to contact me. He is back. He is trying to get in touch with June. She must be away somewhere with the ATS.'

****

June's secondment to the Sussex Constabulary had ended a month ago. In many ways she had been sorry to leave, especially so as she had enjoyed so much working with the Inspector.

Before June had taken the post with the Constabulary, she had been on the vehicle maintenance training course - mandatory for those ATS volunteers destined to be drivers. It had been different from anything she had done before and she had enjoyed it. She also appreciated the few pennies daily increase to her pay which passing a trade test qualified her for. She was also proud she had recently been promoted, also providing an increase to her pay and daily allowances.

With all this behind her now, June had been given a role of driving officers of the Chiefs of Staff Committee, delivering their messages and documents and generally ensuring their day went as smoothly and efficiently as possible. Much of her work was for an Air Vice-Marshall, a reasonably friendly sort of man with a dry sense of humour but, of the old school and whom June imagined had been one of the many high-ranking servicemen - when plans for the ATS had been initially conceived - not to take the idea of women in uniform very seriously.

As her mother was arriving in Cornwall, June was

driving the Vice-Marshall towards Portsmouth. He was to spend two days on the Isle of Wight observing how the training and exercises by thousands of troops were progressing in the preparations for Dieppe. The RAF were scheduled to provide air support. June had been briefed to drive him around during his time on the Island and, when not required for this, she would be free to spend the time as she wished.

Just outside Cosham, the car started to jerk violently and June managed to nurse the Humber onto a wide grass verge. Since her vehicle maintenance course, she had not experienced a car breaking down and would have preferred it not arising as she was driving this particular senior officer to a vital meeting. Trying hard to appear confident, she reached for the driver's handbook, got out of the car to get its basic tool kit. After a while June discovered there was no "spark" reaching the spark plugs and switched her attention to checking the "high" tension and "low" tension sides of the system. The Humber was a 6-cylinder model and the distributor and coil were located on the offside of the engine. June had her head under the bonnet checking things when she heard the Vice-Marshall get out of the car. Within a moment he was at her side.

'I am getting worried about the time Graham. How long is this going to take?'

'Hopefully not too long now sir.'

'What are you checking here for? I've been driving for years and to me it seems as if the problem is something to do with the carburettor or - almost certainly - the magneto. They are all located over on the other side of the engine. I'm positive it's the magneto that is the problem.'

June replied as politely as she could. 'But there is no spark reaching the plugs sir. I am sure the problem is with these leads.' She paused. 'Besides sir, this model is too recent.

They stopped using magnetos in car ignition systems by the end of the thirties.'

'Really!' The Vice-Marshall looked aghast, not really knowing what to say. 'I see - well I never.' His pride dented, he stepped aside whilst June tightened the low tension lead from the coil to the distributor.

'There we are. The lead had worked loose. Hopefully that has done the trick.' The car's engine fired into life and begun to purr satisfyingly. 'I will just put these tools back and we'll be away sir.'

She closed the bonnet and held open the door for him. Rather humbled he got back into the car. Feeling very triumphant and pleased with herself, she closed the boot.

On the Isle of Wight June was taken aback by the number of military vehicles, either on the move or parked on the roads near the sea front. In the narrow roads, knots of servicemen stood around parked vehicles or stood in groups talking on the pavements outside shops and houses.

She recognised the uniforms they wore as Canadian. After their papers were checked at a barrier the Humber was waved around the corner, past what were once beach-huts, onto a concrete slipway. June observed the concrete was recently-laid and was shocked and bewildered at the scene on the beach before her. Dozens and dozens of stretchers, many of them with soldiers on covered in blankets, were either laying on the sand or being carried to and from assault landing craft. A distance away, other troops were loading a landing craft with equipment. For a moment, still in shock, June was at a loss as to what to do next. The scene before her seemed surreal. The Vice-Marshall offered no comment. Suddenly, came the sound of a shrill whistle. Over to their right an officer, appearing to be some sort of Marshall, waved a flag and shouted something through a megaphone. In an instant, as if by magic, the stretcher bearers immediately stopped what they were doing, the men laying on the stretchers miraculously came back to consciousness and sat up. As soon as June realised it was some sort of training exercise, she fought to restrain a laugh of relief.

'If you drive over there?' A Sergeant, speaking with a Canadian accent, stood by the side of her door pointing to the far left of the beach. 'A soft terrain track has been laid. The car shouldn't have too much trouble getting across there.'

June reversed a bit before steering in the direction indicated. As she did so she was intrigued to see a large group of children gathered around watching the spectacle unfolding before them. For a moment she was puzzled of the security implications of this - if there were any. The Vice-Marshall tut-tutted disapprovingly at the same thing. As June drove along the beach and rounded a little headland another sight unfolded before her. Dozens of troops were disembarking from several landing craft at the beach edge. She parked the car in front of a row of very large tents. As she got out to open the rear door, a middle-aged RAF Officer approached and saluted her passenger.

'Good afternoon sir. There are one or two still to join us. Been delayed by a blocked road near here. A stray Hun bomber paid a visit before the anti-aircraft people got him. If you would like to come this way sir?'

'Shall we say 19.30 hours Graham?'

'Of course sir.'

Before following the other officer the Vice-Marshall paused briefly and, with a gentle smile, said 'And well done Graham for getting that problem with the car sorted out.' He paused again. 'Oh and by the way. You have some oil on the end of your nose.'

Embarrassed, she wiped away the oil but his words of thanks meant an awful lot to her. June went across to a male driver standing by his staff car talking to an ATS driver at his side. It was clear they were flirting.

'Hello. Apparently I'm not needed to later…'.

'…Lucky you love' answered the man in a broad cockney accent. 'We've been told to wait until they've finished.'

June smiled sympathetically. 'I know. Sometimes at these meetings I have had to wait for ages as well. I wonder if you know where I might be able to find accommodation for the night?'

The ATS girl spoke in a "catty" manner. 'Oh of course, your rank get a larger allowance.'

June chose to ignore the remark. The man spoke.

'With this little lot going on, I imagine a room will be hard to come by.' Then, more helpfully. 'After you get off the beach, drive along straight ahead for about a mile. Take the second turning left, then first right. There's a narrow little road. Try up there. You might be lucky.'

June thanked him and got back into the Humber.

She found the road she was looking for. It was more of a passageway than a road and she realised she wouldn't get the car up it, so parked outside a Fish and Chip shop. A notice hanging in the window read: "We apologise to our patrons. Closed until further notice owing to Hitler sinking the fishing boats." June walked up and down the passageway. Every boarding house had the same notice: "No Vacancies". She was getting resigned to having to sleep in the car when out of a front door appeared a woman in a floral apron. In her window was also a notice saying there were no vacancies. Beginning to clean her letterbox, the woman smiled.

'Good afternoon' said June. 'I don't suppose you know where I could find a room for the night?'

The woman looked June up and down suspiciously. 'No I'm afraid I don't.'

'Thank you. Only I have just brought an officer down

here for a meeting. They have their own accommodation arranged. The likes of us though have to fend for ourselves.'

The woman paused, still sizing up June suspiciously. 'Well I suppose I do have a room I could let you have. Mind you it's only a small room, right at the top of the house….'.

'…That would be absolutely fine! I am only here for tonight.'

'I usually save the room for Mr Reynolds - he's a salesman. You know uses the room when he's around these parts. Mind you I haven't heard from him and he usually gives me about a week's notice when he is coming.' She looked at her watch. 'He would have been here by now.'

'Thank you very much.'

The woman looked June up and down again. 'No hanky-panky though. No young men in the room. I don't put up with hanky-panky in this house. Never have done.'

June smiled, holding up her left hand to show her wedding ring. 'Don't worry. I am married. My husband's away. He's in the RAF.

The woman was reassured. 'Oh bless you! Now where is your luggage?'

'A small bag. In the car. It's parked just down there.'

'Well you go and fetch your bag. Come back here and I'll put the kettle on ready and show you your room.'

After having a cup of tea and a chat with Mrs Briggs and installing herself in the room, June went for a walk along the cliffs. She found a modest little restaurant and spent another hour or so enjoying a modest meal before picking up the Vice-Marshall and delivering him to the hotel near the sea-front reserved for senior officers involved in the preparations for Dieppe. When she returned to the house, the kindly Mrs Briggs insisted on making her a hot drink and the two women spent an hour or so chatting.

Since James had been away, June had had many spells of feeling lonely and isolated. This evening, "the time of the month" was also causing her to feel unwell and unusually miserable. She was desperate to speak to her mother.

'Mrs Briggs. Would you mind if I used your telephone?'

'Why of course my dear.'

'Only I see you have a notice that it can only be used with your permission. I will pay for the call….'

'…Oh don't worry my dear. I only put the notice there because some guests I've had have taken liberties with it. You go ahead.'

Hearing Ruth instantly cheered June. However, learning her mother was away immediately dampened her raised spirits. But, when Ruth said James was trying to contact her, she could have jumped with joy. Ruth said she would try and contact James on the telephone number he had left and ask him to contact her in the morning at the guest house.

June re-entered the living room. 'Mrs Briggs my husband is back. I hope you don't mind but he might be able to telephone me here in the morning. Is that all right? I have got to pick up my officer at seven but then I have a few hours to myself. Hopefully, my husband will call at about ten o'clock. Could I stay for the morning? I won't be needing my room.'

'Of course you can. Stay here as long as you like.' She paused. June noticed a tear well in her eyes. 'It's now almost two years since my dear Cyril passed away. I know what it's like to miss someone - not to be able to speak to them.'

'Oh thank you so much Mrs Briggs. You're very kind.'

'Nonsense dear. Would you like another hot drink?'

'No thank you. I am feeling rather tired. Would you mind if I went to bed?'

43

After driving the Air Vice-Marshall back to London, June had been kept busy for some days driving him between a whole series of meetings in London and various establishments in the Home Counties. James had been staying in a hotel near Bond Street and June had managed to arrange to meet him there. She had travelled by Underground. Despite German air raids diminishing significantly, as the train stopped at the stations, June had been surprised by the amount of people still using them as a shelter for the night. All the more surprising as the welter of Government information on the radio news, in the papers had all urged people to abandon this practice.

As she walked out of the station the weather had deteriorated even further and it was unseasonably cold. The rain which had commenced in the morning, if anything, had become heavier. The weather was the same over the Isle of Wight where she had been a few days previously and, in the face of worsening weather, Canadian troops had been embarking most of the day on the assault convoys in the Solent, ready to carry out the attack on Dieppe. June tilted her umbrella to see where she was. Just up the road, on the right-hand side, she saw the name board of the hotel where James was staying.

About three hours after beginning their meal, James

hailed a taxi for June outside the hotel. As he waved her off he was full of regret. A regret which came from the fact their brief time together in the restaurant had been supervised by two SOE officials, *albeit* from across the other side of the room. When they had arranged their reunion he knew it would have to take place under scrutiny, they would not be allowed any private time together whatsoever - SOE rules dictated it would have to be so. So as not to give any indication as to what he was engaged in, he had been told to wear his RAF uniform. As far as anyone was concerned, including his wife, the cover story of being away on RAF matters had to be maintained at all costs. James so wished they could have been able to have even an hour in private. Perhaps at some other time in the future it would be possible. Although the weather was appalling he was pleased to be outside. He took a couple of steps back and stood under the canopy of the hotel to reflect on the de-briefing of his time in France. The process had been exhausting. SOE had been delighted with all the intelligence and other information he had brought back with him. He had been congratulated and commended for eliminating Isobel Fouquet, helping to re-establish a Resistance Group in Charleville and for the acts of sabotage carried out, especially on the factory. At the end of the de-briefing James had been told he would be going back to France - to an area many miles distant from Charleville - but not for a while. For the time being his proven skills would be utilised in training new SOE recruits, mainly at Beaulieu and, in an advisory role, at the small SOE "factories" now springing up and where a great variety of "dirty tricks" gadgets to assist sabotage were being invented and assembled.

James re-entered the hallway, taking comfort from the fact he had been able to tell June, for one or two months anyway, there would be more opportunities for them to see each other. The two SOE officials returned to his side.

During her short taxi ride, June was full of thoughts and concern for her husband. In many ways he was the same gentle and kind man she had married. In other ways he had changed. Sometimes during the evening he had appeared tense and twitchy, as though permanently on his guard and watchful. There had been, occasionally, a haunted - even a hunted look in his eyes, now and again even a frightening coldness about his views on the war. He also appeared to have lost some weight, his uniform had looked slightly too large for him. June was really afraid he was unwell, although he had denied it strenuously. Perhaps it was all her imagination and he was just simply exhausted.

****

After one of his baking sessions the baker had managed to transport Colin, in the horse-drawn van used for deliveries, to his next place of hiding, Reims Cathedral.

The time Colin spent staying with the Priests, in a part of the Archbishop's Palace, had been very relaxing and he had taken the opportunity of learning about the history of the Cathedral since its building beginning in 1211. The Priests had been hospitable and welcomed him as one of their own. One of them, in particular, Dominic, had become a firm friend. Dominic spoke good English and, back in the thirties, had spent several years living and working in England. One day after early morning prayers, he persuaded Colin, provided they were careful and sensible, to accompany him on a walk around Reims to see its architecture and monuments mostly grouped around the Basilique St-Remi.

Looking back at the west façade of the Cathedral, Colin observed 'What a magnificent building.'

'Yes indeed. The west façade is decorated with over 2,300 statues. Above the Great Rose Window, 56 stone effigies form what we call the Gallery of the Kings. At sunset, the light and reflections of that window are fantastic.'

Dominic mentioned the damage sustained by the building during the First World War, still awaiting full restoration. As they walked through the streets toward the Roman Augustan arch at Porte Mars, Colin noticed other areas of more recent damage, obviously sustained during various allied attacks. He was surprised at the small number of German troops and vehicles around. On the illicit radios of some of his previous hosts he had heard much of the German Army, especially its elite units, were now either on the Eastern Front confronting the Soviet Red Army or, on the move there. He presumed that now, with the conquered territories long-subdued, Reims was now only garrisoned by second-line troops - the German Army's priority in the west now one of occupation and defence.

Now and again, on seeing two men in Priest's clothing approach, shabby and broken-spirited individuals - many of them children - begged forlornly for food, something to drink, clothing or money. It was pitiful, saddening to witness. Dominic had brought food from the Refectory and some money with him and endeavoured to distribute what he had fairly to those appearing most in need. Then, as the two men rounded another corner, there would be yet more hapless people equally deserving. It was just impossible to help everyone with what Dominic had with him. Eventually, he ran out of everything he could give.

'Every day some of us leave the Cathedral with a supply of food and things for them' he explained. 'We try and walk by different routes each day so we may help as many as we can but, as you can see, the situation is fast becoming hopeless.' He paused. 'Come my friend? I can see you are getting distressed at what you see.' He turned back in the direction of the Cathedral. 'It's time we should be getting back anyway.'

Colin said sadly 'To see all the suffering and desperation is really awful.'

'Indeed it is. The Germans take much of the available food for themselves, leave very little for the citizens. Many of the husbands or fathers - even the wives and mothers - have been taken away to work in the German factories. Others have been taken prisoner or have become so ill and under-nourished themselves they are no longer able to provide for their families.'

There now seemed an increase in activity of German troops. More road blocks were being set up. Some unmarked cars, Colin presumed Gestapo staff cars - their sirens wailing - tore past them. Jeeps and trucks full of troops began moving around the streets. Colin was relieved to see they were now very near to the Cathedral and relative safety. Thinking about it, he realised it was perhaps foolhardy of Dominic to have invited him to venture out, foolhardy for him to have agreed to go. However, he had been glad to get out and about, more informed for witnessing for himself the suffering of the ordinary French people. If and when he eventually got back to England, flying bombers again, he believed the experience of what he had seen would add to his personal purpose and meaning of defeating the Nazis.

When back within the Cathedral complex, a message from the Cardinal was awaiting Colin. Quickly he made his way to the book-lined corridor, off which was situated the Cardinal's private apartments.

After a few brief pleasantries the Cardinal announced 'Within half-an-hour you are to leave us.'

'To leave here?'

'I apologise for the short notice. The Baker's daughter

left word a short while ago. It seems something urgent has arisen and it is very important you leave quickly. I am afraid I do not know the reason why. She also said you are to remain in those vestments.'

Colin was anxious. 'I wonder what has happened.'

The Cardinal lifted his hand. He paused. 'I am sorry to seem so unhelpful. Here we are always pleased to help the Resistance, to offer a haven for people whenever we can. However, we never ask questions of why they need our help or how they work. We believe it safer and for the best for everyone in Reims if we remain ignorant of these matters.' He got up to bid farewell to Colin. 'I believe you have struck up rather a friendship with Abb$_e$' Dominic?'

'Yes I have. Though everyone here has been kind. I probably get on with him well because we have something in common. As you know he spent some time in England.'

'Abb$_e$ Dominic is a favourite with everyone here in Reims. I am sorry to have to be losing him soon…'.

'…Losing him?'

'Yes. A post suiting his enormous talents has arisen. In Paris.' He moved to Colin's side of the desk. 'However, it really is time you were on your way. It's because of your friendship with him I have agreed with the Resistance that he will escort you on the next part of your journey. He will be waiting for you by now in the corridor.'

Colin shook the Cardinal's hand. As he did so it occurred to him perhaps it would have been more appropriate if he had bowed. 'Thank you for everything you have all done for me.'

'God be with you my son. May he watch over you and keep you safe.' He turned back to his desk. 'Here are a few Francs and a little food to sustain you. Take care now.'

It was early evening when Dominic and Colin reached Troyes. To Colin's immense relief they arrived with about

427

an hour before the curfew began. The old gas-fuelled bus had not been the most speedy or efficient vehicle he had travelled on, there had been occasions when he doubted whether they would even arrive in Troyes before the end of the day. His fellow passengers were mainly devout folk making some form of pilgrimage to one of the many shrines or Gothic churches for which Troyes was noted. During the journey Dominic had mentioned that all Colette - the baker's daughter - had said to the Cardinal about Colin's transfer was a trip had been arranged by some friends of hers. He had also told Colin he was to make for a café located on the square where the bus stopped. That there were two cafes on the square and the one he must go to was named Café Madeleine and he was to ask for Florence.

The two men said their farewells by the bus. It had been arranged that Dominic would remain with the pilgrims whilst Colin made contact at the café. As Colin walked across the cobbled street, he was struck by the delightful tranquillity of the place. Many of the surviving buildings around the square were attractive and half-timbered. Outside one or two of them, elderly women sat knitting whilst they chatted. Over in one corner of the square a group of children played and skipped joyously; in other places, on walls and benches, sat little groups of old men smoking and putting the worlds to rights. On his right, in front of a grocer's shop, an old hand-drawn cart now planted with shrubs and plants had been sited at an artistic angle. Situated behind an ornate stone Well he saw the gaily-painted Café Madeleine, its walls draped with an impressive climbing vine of some sort with, arranged outside it, a number of tables and chairs. Colin was distracted by the sound of pigeons scattering at his feet. As he rounded the Well he hesitated as a Gendarme came out of the café's doorway. He had been told in his evasion and escape lectures and, by his hosts and escorts in France, that some Gendarmes were not always favourably inclined to escapees and evaders. To his relief, this particular officer of the law did not appear overly interested in a man he believed to be a Priest. Colin wondered if he had been dressed as an ordinary man whether the Gendarme noticing a stranger in the square would have been just as disinterested.

The café was cosily furnished, a rich and pleasant aroma of herbs hung in the air. At one table a distinguished-looking old gentleman, dressed in a smart suit and waistcoat, sat drinking a Vermouth of some sort and reading a magazine. On seeing Colin enter, he bowed his head respectfully. At another table, a young man sat with a young well-dressed woman. The pair of them were too engrossed with each other to notice anything going on around them. A young waitress busied herself clearing a table. He stopped himself, just in time, from asking her for Florence, realising it might be prudent instead to ask the man behind the counter who appeared to be the proprietor. The said man, on seeing him approach, straightened up from working on a ledger on the counter.

'Good evening Abb$_e$. How may I help?'

'Is Florence here today? She has a package for the orphanage for me' replied Colin, carefully remembering the exact words he had been told to introduce himself by.

The man looked around furtively, briefly studying the other patrons. 'Why of course. My wife was telling me all about it. If you would like to take a seat, the waitress will bring you a coffee while I go and find her.'

Colin chose a table near the counter and the waitress set a coffee before him. The distinguished old gentleman paid his bill and left. As Colin drank the young couple were still engrossed with each other - the woman giggled as if the man had whispered something saucy or suggestive in her ear. Through the window, he watched as two soldiers on foot patrol approached the café. Colin became anxious - an anxiety short-lived as they were distracted by a couple of youngsters directing cat-calls at them. The soldiers chased the two youngsters now quickly disappearing up one of the narrow passages leading off the square. Colin was beginning to feel ill-at-ease and self-conscious just sitting there. He got up and picked a newspaper from the nearby rack. Returning to his seat he started reading, despite his limited French preventing him from understanding much of what its pages contained. The proprietor returned and turned the sign on the glass door to state the café was now closed. He and the waitress set about tidying the café, preparing it for the next day. At last, the young couple took the hint, paid their bill and left arm in arm - the woman giggling again as her companion whispered intimately in her ear. The proprietor had just begun to sweep when a woman of about the same age entered from behind the counter and came straight to Colin's side.

The woman called across to the waitress 'Maxine you can go now. Benoit and I can finish off.' The waitress thanked her and scurried out the door from whence the woman had entered. After ensuring the waitress had gone, the woman returned to Colin's side. 'Welcome to Troyes. We have been expecting you.'

'Florence?'

'That is how I am known.' Her husband joined them. She eyed Colin up and down. 'Yes, I think the clothes we have got will just about fit. Presently Benoit will fetch them for you.'

Her husband spoke. 'Forgive me Monsieur. Would you mind emptying out your satchel on the table? We need to check you have nothing which would be out of place here in Troyes.' Colin did so. 'I am sorry to have to ask but we are having to be especially careful nowadays. It is surprising how the smallest thing can give one away.' He checked the contents of the satchel carefully. 'You have nothing else on you?' He indicated to Florence he found nothing untoward and passed the satchel back to Colin.

Florence said 'Now if you go with my husband, he will show you where you can change. We have just enough time for you to have something to eat before the curfew. He will then take you to a "safe house".'

After some soup and bread, Colin followed Benoit out of a side entrance. After checking there was nobody about, Benoit said 'It is only a short walk. You will only be staying for a night. At nine tomorrow morning, one of our friends will call for you. He will be wearing a brown tie and introduce himself as Hugo. You will reply by saying: "I have everything ready". Is that understood?'

'Yes.'

After a few minutes they turned into a narrow street - Rue Larivey - which climbed steeply.

'These half-timbered buildings are beautiful' Colin remarked.

'Indeed they are. This street is typical of many in Troyes. Before the war many of these premises were busy manufacturing and selling their knitwear or sausages - "andouillettes" as we call them.' He shook his head sadly. 'Now, most of them have been forced to close, the owners mainly forced to work for the Boche in their factories.'

The street continued to wind upwards. About halfway up on the left-hand side they came to a shabby front door. After looking carefully around, Benoit knocked. He shook his head in frustration.

'The woman living here is very old. She walks with a stick. Oh come on!'

After what seemed ages, they heard a large bolt being drawn back. The door creaked open slowly. In the doorway was a very old lady, well in her eighties. She stood almost bent double and leant heavily on a walking stick. She wore a large shawl over her shoulders and blinked at the two men through tiny round spectacles on the end of her nose.

'Good evening Madame' said Benoit. 'I have a package for your safe keeping.'

'Forgive me Monsieur's' she replied. 'I had fallen asleep.'

'No matter' answered Benoit kindly.

She stood aside beckoning them in. 'Please come in?'

Benoit ushered Colin in. 'Thank you. But I must be getting back before the curfew.' As Colin passed him into the hallway he patted Colin on the back. 'Someone will be here for you at nine. You remember what I told you?' He shook Colin's hand warmly. 'I wish you all the best my friend.'

Before Colin could reply, Benoit had turned back into the street and was hurrying away down the hill.

The hallway was in desperate need of decoration, the linoleum on the floor broken, torn and faded in many places. Numerous potted plants in their stands stood all along the hallway - everyone of them in need of water and re-potting. A strong smell of cats pervaded everywhere.

44

As the last of the group left the room James put away his notes. He had been speaking in one of the classrooms at Beaulieu Manor. For over two weeks now he had been working back here as one of the instructors training SOE hopefuls. His students had either just completed training at Wanborough Manor, used by SOE's French Section, or in Scotland. Some of them had trained at both establishments. There were nine students, five women, four men. He had been appraising them of the risks posed by collaborators and not to believe all French police were sympathetic to or, willing to help an agent in the field. A part of his instruction had been about basic do's and don'ts whilst in France. For example: French etiquette whilst dining in a restaurant and not asking for *café noir,* which would immediately arouse the suspicions of a collaborationist waitress or café owner. Currently in France there was no other way to have coffee. He watched the trainees pass the window, hoping he had imparted his knowledge and experience in a way enabling them to assimilate everything thoroughly without boring them. They had all seemed interested and keen enough, asked numerous, intelligent questions, especially during the part of his talk devoted to getting through German and French check-points and coping whilst undergoing questioning. He considered his initial impressions of the nine. He reckoned five of them would make the grade appropriate for a successful agent by the time they finished the complete course. Out of the remaining four, one - a middle-aged man - was borderline; another - a woman in her twenties - could be suitable for a British-based intelligence officer.

James closed his briefcase. Tonight he was due to meet the other instructors and the Commandant for one of their regular get-togethers to discuss the progress of the current intake of students. It was a lovely summer's day , too good to be cooped up in a stuffy room for most of the time. He had just about an hour before writing up his notes for the evening's meeting and he needed to clear his head. He left by the main door and almost immediately felt the relief of getting out into the fresh air.

When originally agreeing to become an agent he had done so with huge misgivings and trepidation. Now, having experience of working in the field in occupied territory and since being back in England in his present role, he was surprised at how much he missed the action and surges of adrenaline of working behind enemy lines. He had to admit he was feeling a certain frustration at living a more routine existence. Balanced in his mind though - as he passed through the line of trees by the main house - were the positives of being back in England. Firstly, of course, there was not the ever-present danger facing him every minute of every day in occupied France. Secondly, and more importantly, he was now allowed limited contact with June *albeit* only by censored letter or *via* a secure telephone line from Beaulieu and, just recently, to see her in private at SOE-dictated venues under more low-key surveillance. On these occasions though he had to be dressed in RAF uniform and, of course, with a suitable cover story for their being able to meet. However, getting an opportunity to see her was difficult enough in itself, what with his schedule of training SOE students and, with the commitments June had in her present role. Letters between them arrived by a circuitous route *via* fictitious accommodation addresses. In her last letter she had said it was near impossible for her to say what part of the country she would find herself from one day to the next. Neither of them could know the reason for June driving all over the country was that the ill-fated "Operation Rutter" on Dieppe had just been reinstated as "Operation Jubilee" to now commence in August. James really hoped that some day very soon there would be a time when they could at last see each other in private.

James continued to walk through the woods and grounds of the old abbey towards the river. The dappled shade afforded by the mature trees was pleasant and refreshing, the shafts of sunlight penetrating their canopy made delightful and intricate patterns on the ground. Although the many-coloured blooms of the Rhododendrons and Azaleas under the trees and lining the paths had now withered, their rich green foliage still glistened. Coming out of the wood he emerged on a wide edge of the riverbank, at a part a particular favourite of his, where he had previously enjoyed watching busy Kingfishers. He sat on the ground. James knew that between training sessions and lectures some of the students and instructors walked, took physical exercise here - he had been with them sometimes. He hoped none would just now. He just wanted to enjoy the peace, be alone to think and reflect. Out in the middle of the river there was a splash, a silvery flash as some fish jumped out of the water to snap up some unwary hovering insect. Closer to shore, a pair of Mallards marshalled their accompanying brood along - their wash creating a v-shape in the sparkling river; in a clump of water reeds and grasses an unseen Moorhen loudly scolded her mate or offspring. His eyelids became heavy. He laid back on the ground.

James had no idea how long he had dozed but the sun had moved more to the west. Sleepily he glanced at his watch - he had been there for nearly an hour. He still had his report to write. There was a sound behind him. Although still drowsy, his survival instinct kicked in immediately. Almost in one movement he sprung to his feet grabbing for his knife - the one he had used in France and shown his students during his talk. In an instant the knife was poised to be plunged. He stopped just in time before plunging it into the chest of Beaulieu's Commandant.

'Christ! Sorry.'

The Commandant relaxed, immediately recovering his composure. 'It's all right James. My fault. By now I should have known better that to startle you.' He gave a little laugh. 'Anyhow, it shows your training up in Scotland and here was effective.' He paused. 'I was told you had been seen heading in this direction. Mind if I join you?'

'As I say I'm sorry about that.' The Commandant was looking at the knife gripped in James's hand. James put the weapon away.

'Shall we sit down? It's a lovely spot here isn't it?'

'It certainly is.'

'The whole place James is perfect for our work. Secret, extensive and only approachable and accessible to those in the know.' He paused to watch two swans land on the water. 'Before we both have to prepare for tonight's meeting I wanted to have a quick word with you.'

'About the lectures I've been giving?'

'No. Everything seems to be working well with those.' He paused. 'When you rejoined us here, you will remember my saying how important it is to constantly update our knowledge as to what's happening over the Channel, to keep our agents as safe and secure as possible, to ensure the work they do is effective and produces good results.'

James remembered the conversation clearly. 'And how important it is to silence once and for all our critics amongst the SIS and others.'

'Precisely. And to do this, how imperative it is for our new agents and other SOE operatives to learn from people like you on their return to the UK.' Before continuing he took his pipe from his pocket, filled and lit it. 'I will have to make a few changes to our training syllabus to allow you the time but, I would like to bring forward your visits to our "Dirty Tricks" experimental establishments. They're all working like Beavers at the moment. Churning out ideas and prototypes. Many ideas are terrific, others ingenuous but, impractical for use in the field. We need someone with experience of working in occupied territory, to help those working on the experiments to channel their thinking a bit. Help them with advice and tips as to what little gadgets would be best suited and appropriate for sabotage and disruption activities and could be used by the local Resistance groups. Churchill is putting pressure on for us to step up our efforts in causing the Germans problems. At the moment he's a friend and firm supporter of our work. We want to keep him that way. Especially as the likes of SIS are finally being persuaded to relinquish their monopoly on things like clandestine forgery and the supply of radios to agents.' He drew heavily on his pipe and exhaled, sending a cloud of smoke into the early evening air. He looked at his watch. 'I will get weaving straightaway on re-arranging your schedule of talks and instruction. I thought if we plan for something like three days each fortnight for you to go and visit the experimental stations.' He got to his feet. 'Well I must be off. One or two things to attend to. I'll see you at dinner James.'

437

'I must get back as well. I have some notes to finalise.'

They started walking back towards the house. On their way they spoke about the increasing shortages affecting the country. The Wolf Packs of German U-boats were really strengthening their grip, their strangulation of Britain's lifelines was near complete.

When James got back to his room there was a letter waiting. He recognised the handwriting immediately as June's.

...At last, for a few days my driving skills are not required. Something big is about to happen and my Air Vice-Marshall will be totally ensconced in a big house somewhere in the countryside. I have taken the opportunity of a few day's leave to spend a few precious days at our home. The only thing missing here of course is you my darling by my side. I can't wait for the day when we can be together here again by ourselves. I'm feeling desperately tired with all the driving and dashing about here, there and everywhere - it seems all over the country. I just cherish the chance to rest and enjoy the surroundings of our own home and garden, to treasure what we were beginning to create here before we were sent off on our different directions. I do so miss you being here. In some ways I feel a bit guilty as I haven't even told mummy I am back in Sussex for a few days - I just want to enjoy our home but, I will perhaps try and contact her tomorrow so we can catch up on things. I have still not heard anything from either Richard or Stephen. It seems ages since I did. I just hope they are both safe and well. I'm sure mummy would have tried to contact me if she had heard anything.

At the moment I'm looking out the window at our garden, the bit we managed to clear and dig over before your posting. The shrubs we transplanted from Oakfields, when the large bed there was changed for growing vegetables, seem to have taken and are beginning to grow well.

From the date of this letter, I will be home for six or seven days - depending on when you receive it. I pray that perhaps we can be with each other very soon, even if it is only for an hour or so. Wherever you are, I hope you receive this letter in time to telephone me before my leave ends. After my leave, goodness knows where I will have to go and whenever we may be able to see each other again.

Take care of yourself my darling wherever you are. I just yearn to speak to you or see you soon. I take that picture by our bedside into bed with me every night.

God bless.

With all my love and with all my heart darling.

Yours forever.
June

45

June had waved James off from their home just after dawn. They had spent two wonderful days together and, apart from a couple of walks in the surrounding countryside, had spent the time completely by themselves enjoying, treasuring each other's company.

James did not know the Barnet area very well and the lack of road signing hadn't helped. However, from the Commandant's directions, he knew he was almost at his destination. Within minutes he arrived at the entrance of a building which looked, previously, to have been a hotel or pub.

The person in charge of what was now a small factory was a former Captain in the Royal Engineers. Whilst proudly showing James round, the man explained many of the people working there were previously plasterers, worked as architectural experts or for Prop's Departments in the film industry etc. They were working at benches on a whole variety of objects resembling lumps of coal and root vegetables. After, in the factory's office, James was closely examining an object in his hand, a two-piece gelatine mould of a turnip in a plaster case. Explosive material was enclosed in its two halves which were cleated together. The joint and the whole thing was camouflaged expertly and no one would notice it was not the real thing.

'First class workmanship' complimented James. 'Certainly good enough for transporting explosives or fooling a German sentry.'

'Yes we're particularly proud of these. We are trying to perfect the same technique for things such as lumps of coal.'

'And these techniques could be easily adapted for bigger objects?'

'With the experts I've got here, the skies the limit really old boy. You name it, just give us a few days to play around - experiment with whatever you want. Have you anything specific in mind?'

'One of the biggest problems is moving transmitters around. If only we could come up with something appearing to be objects commonplace on the streets. For example, lumps of wood. With all the shortages of fuel for heating and cooking, the French spend much of the day collecting wood. I would often see locals out in the country cutting down trees, filling their carts and barrows with logs and branches. Containers fashioned appropriately would go unnoticed amongst a cartload or stack of wood.'

'I'm sure we could come up with something. Though, as you know, some types of trees are particular to one part of the country. Matching texture and colour would be important, we would need to know in what part of the country the dummy wood is required.'

'There are some contacts of mine able to help with that. I'll be in touch with you. Perhaps you could get working on some prototypes? Chunks of masonry or stonework could be another way of concealing weapons or radio equipment.'

'Slate, granite, marble, ordinary brickwork. Tell us what you want and we'll come up with something.' Suddenly, there was an explosion. James ducked. The Captain was laughing. 'Sorry old boy, I should have warned you. Come with me?' He led James to a window at the back of the building which looked down into an area of waste ground with a high wall around it. Some men in overalls were examining the wheels of a car. 'Another experiment of ours. Some plaster stones and pebbles have had mini-detonators inserted and, when a vehicle passes over them they explode. As you can see the charge is big enough to destroy a vehicle. We want to increase the charges so they are capable of blowing the tracks off a German armoured car or tank.'

They went down to inspect the vehicle and man-made pebbles. James declared an interest in having something similar prepared for SOE's French Section.

During the next two days, James was due to visit two other establishments. One, where he would be informing the people there of the latest style and manufacturing processes of French clothing. Collars, cuffs and seams of French-made shirts were totally different to British-made ones. The other was an office where items like ration cards, identity cards, work passes and birth certificates were forged.

It was evening of the second day when he came out of the garment workshop in Great Titchfield Street. The thought of driving back to Beaulieu did not appeal and James decided to use the accommodation allowance authorised. Originally, he had thought he would travel back *via* his home but June had said in all probability she would be called to resume her duties with the Air Vice-Marshall and wouldn't be there. He recalled one of his fellow instructors recommending a hotel in Langham Street if ever he was in London.

The streets were busy with workers making their way home. Full air-raid precautions were still very much in force. Doorways were still sand-bagged and, every so often, signs indicated the direction or location of a public shelter. Outside an office building an air-raid warden was berating an expensively-dressed man, presumably the owner of the company occupying the premises, about some black-out infringement. As James passed by he noticed the warden writing on an official-looking form. Opposite, on the roof of a taller building, James saw the tin-hatted heads of people manning an anti-aircraft gun, its barrels pointed defiantly skyward. He noticed there were some marked differences about the people since he had last been in London. Firstly, many of them no longer appeared to be worrying about carrying gas masks. Secondly, the majority wore clothing clearly of the "Utility" variety. Very few of them wore apparel which could be described as fashionable. Thirdly and, it occurred to him, perhaps more seriously, the majority of people looked pre-occupied - almost haunted - as if there was no resilience or joy left within them, just a grim acceptance of attrition or inevitable defeat. The atmosphere of depression on the streets was almost tangible. James recalled, when he had last been in London, how tangible had been an atmosphere of a certain cheerfulness - a dogged defiance amongst the population to survive whatever Hitler chose to throw at them. He was surprised how many service personnel were on the streets or in the shops. However, many of these were not wearing uniforms of the British services but, of the United States, Canada, Australia, New Zealand, the Free French, Poland and Czechoslovakia. The majority though were American.

The hotel room was comfortable, the whole hotel well-appointed. After washing, making some notes on his meetings and attempting to telephone home and receiving no reply, he looked at the hotel's dinner menu. He decided his allowance would not cover the cost and would dine at a place down the road. It was just getting dusk when he headed towards it.

The meal in the restaurant, although not cheap, was more reasonably-priced than the hotel. Considering the rationing of food affecting the nation he felt a little guilty about the menu choice available. In stark contrast to the depressed atmosphere he had perceived on the streets earlier, the restaurant was lively and vibrant and he was enjoying the ambience, glad he had chosen to spend his evening here rather than in the hotel which was rather starchy and conservative. James was sitting by himself towards the back of the restaurant. Amongst the civilian patrons were also quite a number of service personnel, either sitting in groups or, in pairs with their dates for the evening. As the orchestra resumed playing, many now took to the dance floor for a waltz. Congregated in other parts of the room, groups of men dressed in American uniforms talked and laughed loudly. During the last few weeks especially, the Americans had been arriving in England *en masse*. Already some RAF airfields had been handed over to the US Air Force and others were under construction.

'Hey Buddy. Would you mind if we join you?'

James turned to see three young men standing beside him. 'No. Of course not. Theses seats are spare.'

'Gee thanks.' The American settled himself beside James. He extended his hand. 'Will Franklyn - Junior, is the name.' The other two men took seats at the table.

'Pleased to meet you.'

James introduced himself. He had already observed from the American's insignia he was a Captain.

'Sorry to barge in on you James. Only the place is a little crowded.'

'I don't mind at all. Nice to meet you.'

As the other two introduced themselves James saw they were both Lieutenants.

'Chuck Montini. Nice to see you.'

'Hi James. Dale Kaplinski.'

Chuck caught the attention of a passing waiter. 'Could

we have three beers please?' He turned to James. 'What about you James? Like a beer?'

James hesitated for a moment 'Well yes…'.

Before he could finish his answer, Chuck said '…Make that four beers please?'

'Thank you' said James slightly taken aback by the American's lack of reserve.

'Sorry for barging in on you like this James' said Will. 'You'll have to forgive us. We Yanks aren't so reserved as you Brits.'

'It's all right. Nice to have you all over here.'

'Many of us' said Dale 'Wanted to get over here sooner and see some action. However, damned politicians and others thought otherwise.'

'How long have you three been over here?'

'We arrived in England five days ago' replied Will. 'We're on our way up to Suffolk but thought we'd like to spend a couple of days in London.'

'What part of the US are you from?'

'Chuck and I are from two little places in Massachusetts. Dale comes from New Jersey.'

The waiter returned with their drinks.

'These ones are on me fellas' said Chuck.

James watched bemused as the American took out his wallet, stuffed full of banknotes.

Before sampling his beer Dale said 'I wonder what this one will taste like. I must say James the beers over here take some getting used to. Um! Not bad.'

Will asked 'I see you're a flyer too James. Fighters or Bombers?'

James paused, instinctively on his guard. 'Fighters - or was. Temporarily ground-based, working in an advisory role. All pretty boring and routine. I'm in London for a meeting. Travelling back tomorrow morning. You're all aircrew?'

'Yeah. On B17's. Dale and I are pilots. Chuck a Navigator.'

The four continued to talk and share jokes. James found the three friendly and warm, discovered more about their homes and lives back in the US. More beers were ordered and consumed as they exchanged views on the war and the differences between the two countries. Dale had lost a cousin in the Japanese attack on Pearl Harbour; Will's father was a judge in Springfield, his sister a teacher; Chuck was the eldest of six children, the next eldest - a brother - had just started training for the air force.

'Now especially for our American visitors' announced the orchestra's conductor. 'You are all very welcome in England. And to make you feel at home we'd like to play some of the music of Glenn Miller.'

James recognised the first few bars of "Tuxedo Junction". Dale whistled loudly and turned to his two countrymen. 'Guys - our type of music. Look, just over there. Some chic's sitting by themselves.' He stood up. 'How about asking 'em for a dance?'

Will and Chuck also got up. 'Yeah swell.'

'Let's go and introduce ourselves.' Will paused. 'How about you James? You gonna join us?'

James declined with a smile. 'No you go ahead.'

He watched them stride over to a table where a group of young women were sitting.

James remained at his table whilst the orchestra played two other Glenn Miller tunes. He admired how easily the three Americans got to know their dance partners. By the time a third tune begun it was becoming obvious they would probably remain with the girls and not returning to join him. It was getting late anyway and he finished his beer.

James said 'Goodnight' as he passed the three couples. 'Nice meeting you. I wish you all the best.'

'Yes. You too buddy.'

'See you James.'

'Night James. Nice meeting you.'

Walking back to the hotel James thought of the three men he had met. He hoped the conviction they all shared - the conviction that strategic daylight bombing would be the American's answer to defeat Hitler - would see all three of them safe in the months ahead. He knew only too well the American theory was still to be proved.

46

To Colin it seemed years since he had baled out of the Lancaster and, not for the first time, wondered if he would ever get back to England. He had just spent two days in Marseilles, staying with a Banker and his wife at their flat. He had now been issued with forged papers and permits as a teacher. The young woman travelling with him had papers identifying her as his new wife. As they walked down the platform at Perpignan Station, Colin hoped their forged documents bore the scrutiny of the Gendarmes waiting by the barrier ahead as they had when Gendarmes and Gestapo Officials passed through the train checking on all passengers mid-way through the journey.

In no nonsense fashion the older of the two Gendarmes told Colin and his escort to stand aside. Colin's heart sank as, unpleasantly, the Gendarme demanded a closer look at their documents and ordered them to open their suitcases. Colin's instructions in Marseilles, should they be stopped during their journey, was to let Jacqueline do most of the talking. Luckily, this ruse worked for, as the policeman busied himself sifting through the contents of their cases, he directed most of his comments and questions at her. Only occasionally was Colin called upon to exercise his very limited knowledge of French. He was truly thankful his hosts in Marseilles had been thorough in ensuring their cases were packed with clothing and other items totally suitable for a few day's holiday of a newly-married couple - their cover story. The master stroke being a specially-commissioned wedding photograph and forged receipts for various wedding expenses corresponding with the date of their forged marriage certificate. On seeing these the Gendarme's attitude thawed somewhat - a smile even appearing - as he offered his best wishes on their recent nuptials.

'Perpignan has a strong Catalan identity' said Jacqueline as they approached an attractive square. 'This is the Place de la Loge where, during summertime, the Sardana is danced.'

'Sardana?'

'Yes. It is a major Catalan symbol. A dance accompanied by a woodwind band.' She looked around them. 'Now we must get to the east of the town and the cathedral quarter of St-Jean. The Vichy spies have less chance of spotting us there.'

Eventually they came to a labyrinth of small streets and squares. Fine 14th and 15th century buildings surrounded them. Jacqueline looked around and spotted a street name on a wall.

'Ah there we are.' She led him towards a narrow street leading off the square to their left. A little way up the street Colin saw a taxi parked. As they approached it she suddenly said 'Now take me in your arms and kiss me?' He was taken aback but did as asked. She whispered in his ear. 'Get into the taxi. The driver will take you to the border.'

'But what about you?' He asked. 'How will you get back?'

'Do not worry about me. Just worry about yourself. There is a place arranged for me to stay the night. Tomorrow I will travel back to Marseilles. There will be different Gendarmes at the station. Now quickly. Get into the taxi.'

'What about this case?'

'Leave it with the driver. He knows what to do.'

Colin got into the back of the taxi. It was beginning to move off as he turned to wave farewell. Jacqueline was already disappearing into the maze of streets.

Outside a little village, the driver swung into the entrance of a pathway. In very broken English he told Colin at the end of the pathway there was a cottage where someone would be waiting for him.

The pathway curved round sharply and as Colin rounded the bend a small, run-down looking house was facing him. On its veranda sat a huge, bearded man dressing an animal skin. The man lifted his heavily-jowled face.

Approaching him Colin said 'I have come to collect the two goatskins ordered yesterday.'

On hearing the words he was expecting the man rose to his feet. 'The two Maurice ordered?' It was the question Colin had been told to expect. The man extended a huge hand. The firmness of his handshake nearly crushed Colin's hand. In very good English he said 'I am Manuel. Welcome. Welcome. Please come in?' Placing a massive hand on Colin's shoulder he steered him inside. 'Our friend in Perpignan got you here in good time. He did well, the roads are not good.'

The little house had one room downstairs, a door to a store room led off to the right. In the far corner a rickety staircase climbed to the next floor. Although run-down and shabby the room had a cosy, snug feel about it but, definitely, was the dwelling of a man living alone.

'Coffee or something a little stronger my friend?'

'Coffee please? Thank you?'

Manuel set a large mug before Colin. The liquid,

although rather too strong for his taste, was nevertheless very welcome. After saying he would return shortly and for Colin to make himself comfortable, Manuel went back outside. Colin studied the room around him. On the wall hung various hunting trophies and a photograph of Manuel amongst others during a hunting trip. Although it was summer, opposite him a fire blazed in the hearth under a large black pot. The room was rich with a delicious aroma of sweet-smelling wood smoke and meat being cooked.

'I have someone who would like to meet you' announced Manuel from the doorway in his big, booming voice.

Behind Manuel's bulky frame stood someone Colin recognised immediately. He jumped to his feet with surprise and pleasure.

'Typical. Trust you to be late over the target. I was wondering what had kept you.' It was Michael Richards. He was reminding Colin about a couple of missions when they had arrived late over targets. The two hugged each other warmly. 'I've been holed up here for a couple of days now' he explained as Manuel poured him a coffee. 'By what route did you get here?' Colin told him. 'I came *via* Macon, Lyon and Marseilles' Mike continued.

Manuel sat at the table, allowing his two guests time to catch up with their experiences before arriving at the foot of the Pyrenees. Eventually, he said 'I plan to leave about midnight. It will be safer then and will give us enough time to reach a certain point by dawn. There we will rest and conceal ourselves for most of the day, before setting off again and cross into Spain under cover of darkness.' He got up to peer into the pot over the fire, giving its contents a stir. 'I suggest we eat now. After, there will be a little time for us to talk, maybe have a drink and then we must sleep for a while before setting off.' He returned to the table. 'Now let me see your footwear?' Colin and Mike stuck out their feet. He examined their footwear briefly and shook his head doubtfully. 'As I suspected, not very suitable. However, we have no choice. I will just have to make the walking and climbing as easy as I can for you.'

His two guests exchanged a look of concern. Manuel fetched some large bowls and began ladling out their meal.

The meal, a type of stew, was accompanied by some crudely-made but delicious bread. The stew was tasty, with a distinctive hint of herbs and, as their host explained, made with a mixture of goat, lamb and venison. During the meal the three talked non-stop and wine was drunk in liberal quantities. The meal finished, the talk continued, complemented by glasses of a potent liqueur-like drink. As well as instructing them on what they would be encountering, Manuel regaled Colin and Mike with a host of sometimes hilarious tales of his exploits and adventures when climbing, hunting and tracking, either by himself or with friends.

It was about nine-thirty when Manuel said 'Now my friends it is time for you and I to get some rest.' As they climbed the stairs he told them he would wake them just before midnight.

The room in which they were to grab some sleep was more like a loft. Two mattresses and blankets were laid on the floor.

As Colin settled himself under his blanket he asked 'Have you been given Spanish money Mike?'

'Yes. A little. And a lot of French cigarettes.'

'Me too. The girl escorting me to Perpignan said cigarettes are like gold dust in Spain. They can prove very useful for bribes when we get there. From what Manuel was saying about our crossing over the mountains, it sounds pretty hairy. I just hope we don't get separated from him.'

Colin felt someone shaking him. The effects of the

alcohol the previous evening together with the previous day's exertion had resulted in both he and Mike sleeping very heavily. Through half-open eyes, Colin saw the heavy features of Manuel immediately above his face.

'Wake up. Wake up. We must be leaving.'

There was just time to gulp down a mug of Coffee. Both Colin and Mike had thumping headaches. Manuel had made up food packs for the three of them, sufficient to last them a couple of days. He said that if need be they would have to hunt for something. Manuel took down a rifle from the wall, fetched some ammunition from a cupboard and put it all in a large shoulder bag.

'Which one of you is the best shot?' Mike nominated Colin as he had been his skipper and was the officer. 'I only have one pistol but it might prove useful should we get separated.' He took out a revolver, two rounds of ammunition and handed them to Colin.

It was a cold night but dry and clear. During bombing missions, Colin had never ceased to be amazed at how beautiful stars looked in the night sky and how vast the universe. And, tonight, as they started to walk, the stars and moon looked all the more special. Out in the fresh night air, with the delicious woodland aromas all around them, Colin's headache started to lessen. After about two or three miles of reasonably level walking alongside and through meadow land, brooks and woodland, the terrain started to rise gradually and then more steeply. Now and again and mainly in the distance, the sound of livestock or a farm dog barking drifted across the still night air. Occasionally, came the sound of a wild animal calling to their mate or offspring or challenging a rival straying into its territory. Ahead of them a dark shape jumped down from a wooded bank and dashed into the trees on the other side of the path.

'A wildcat' Manuel informed them. 'There are a few of

them around here.' He spat in anger. 'Sometimes I shoot them. They kill the farmers' sheep and goats.' The ground now started to rise more steeply, became more broken and rugged, the woods on either side more dense and dark. Their progress was inevitably slowing. 'You will both now have to go carefully.'

The trio continued walking for about another hour. The increase in altitude meant a decrease in temperature and a keen wind now blew persistently. Manuel had supplied Colin and Mike with what old jumpers he could spare but, nevertheless, both were by now feeling the cold. They were also tiring. Their guide sensed this and stopped.

'We will rest here for a while. We are making good time.'

Colin couldn't understand quite how Manuel knew they were making good time, considering all around them was still dark, making landscape features difficult to discern. As they sat on a large boulder beside the track, Manuel reached into his bag. He handed them gloves and battered caps. The caps were of a style that Manuel himself wore.

'These should help keep out the cold' said their guide. Then, taking a flask out of his bag, added 'This too will help. It's Brandy.' He laughed handing across the vessel for each of them to drink.

They were almost at the top of the tree line as the first signs of dawn began to stretch its fingers into the darkest hollows and recesses of the woods and mountainside. To their side and above them a waterfall thundered and tipped the waters of a previous heavy storm down its steep and rocky slopes into a gorge. Manuel brought them to a stop facing a cliff face of about 100 feet.

'How do you two feel about climbing?' The two Englishmen glanced in trepidation at each other. 'We do not need to climb here but, it will save another hour's walking.

Hard walking.' Colin and Mike were by now extremely tired and though the thought of a climb of this nature did not really appeal, the option seemed marginally more attractive than walking for another hour. And, if Manuel considered it a hard walk, it must be hard. As if to really convince them of the merits of choosing the climbing option Manuel added 'It is not too difficult a climb and I've brought proper equipment. I have done this many a time I assure you.'

Mike was first to speak. 'On holiday in Wales once, I did do a spot of rock climbing. Mind you, a few years ago now. I'll give it a go.'

Colin was still not very happy about the prospect but agreed to give it a try. 'Fair enough. Okay Manuel, tell us what we have to do.'

'I assure you my friends. Once we get up there it is very little distance to the place we will rest for the day.'

Manuel took the ropes and other equipment they would need from his bag. He explained and demonstrated how the items were to be tied and used and instructed them as to how they would tackle the climb. Just a few minutes later, Colin and Mike watched carefully as their guide began climbing up the cliff.

They established themselves in a cave just a short walk from the top of the cliff. The cave must have recently been inhabited by some animal as there was a liberal quantity of droppings and animal hair inside. A musty, animal smell seemed to pervade every part of it. Both Englishmen felt a huge sense of pride in what they had achieved although it had not proved such a frightening experience as expected. Colin was even moved to remark that whenever the war was over he might consider rock climbing or mountaineering as a hobby. Before having something to eat and settling to rest, Colin went to the mouth of the cave to take in the landscape stretching below and beyond them. Despite thin shreds of early morning mist hanging over the mountain peaks, the valleys and gorges, the view was truly remarkable and he could see for miles and miles. He looked in the direction of what Manuel had told them was Spain and, to his right, Andorra. It promised to be another wonderful day of weather. In the East, a glorious gold-red orb was emerging from behind a high peak, its rays beginning to polish the multi-coloured hues of the tree-clad slopes and valleys and rocks of the gorges. The ribbon of a winding river wound its way through meadows and pastures far below him. Somewhere in the river's valley, the bells of some village church sounded, sending their melodic chimes up towards him. On the side of a nearby peak, Colin saw what looked like a family of mountain goats or sheep gambolling over rocks. Above these but in the greater distance, a large bird stretched its wings and took to the skies.

He went back into the cave. Mike was already asleep.

Quietly, Colin asked Manuel 'Could I borrow your binoculars please?'

'Of course. What is it?'

'I just wanted to look at some wildlife.'

Colin was adjusting the glasses and pointing when Manuel joined him at the mouth of the cave.

'They're mountain goats with their kids' confirmed Manuel. 'And that's an Eagle. It is a privilege to see one.' Suddenly, the Eagle swooped down onto the back of one of the kids as its parents scattered. Leaving the adult goats bleating the Eagle took to the air again, the hapless kid clutched in its talons. 'Sad. But the Eagle has young to feed as well.'

Colin watched as the Eagle with its prize returned to its eerie.

Manuel said 'Now my friend. I must urge you to have

something to eat and then to sleep. Later, we have a long trip ahead of us.'

'It's just that the view is so incredible. And seeing Spain just over there. Well, for the first time, at last I feel I am nearly home.'

'Of course' Manuel replied kindly.

Colin followed the guide back into the cave.

47

Colin and Mike had just finished eating. Manuel came back into the cave carrying his binoculars. He seemed rather agitated.

'We will be leaving in an hour.'

'Before nightfall?' Queried Colin.

'On the other side of the valley there are trucks of border guards. It looks as if they are on a training exercise which could go on all night. We will have to take a longer route around the mountain to avoid them. It will add hours to our journey.'

The three men walked through the night and, as Manuel had said, the trek was harder and steeper than his preferred route. They could only make very occasional stops for rest and to drink from their canteens of water. During one of these stops, Colin checked his "escape kit" compass. The plan was to head for Barcelona where a British Consul-General could be contacted. He was relieved, the compass confirmed they were still aiming in roughly the right direction and hoped they were still on schedule to reach the point of rendezvous arranged for Manuel to hand them over to another guide. Their progress had been hampered as Mike had received a nasty gash - just above his ankle - from a pointed edge of a part-submerged rock when fording a fast-flowing stream.

Manuel had dressed the wound but it continued to give him a lot of pain and discomfort.

Dawn was breaking when at last they began their descent. The final shrouds of darkness were lifting sufficiently now for them to make out below, in a heavily wooded valley, what appeared to be an old turreted castle and, further down the valley, a small group of buildings.

'That village is the last one in the valley before the frontier' announced Manuel with a note of triumph in his voice. 'A kilometre beyond lies Spain.'

'That's fantastic!' Said Mike.

'To be honest' added Colin 'I was just beginning to wonder when we would reach here.'

Their guide sounded a note of caution. 'Beware my friends. We still have a way to go. We must be extra careful now. The numbers of frontier guards has increased recently.'

As Mike shifted his position he cursed.

'What is it Mike?'

'This bloody ankle is giving me some gyp.' As he lifted his trouser leg to look at the bandage he saw the blood stain had increased. 'It's started to bleed again.'

'Let me have a look?' Said Manuel. He bent down and looked at the bandaged injury. For a big man with big hands he dextrously, carefully, removed the old dressing, bathed the injury again with water from his canteen and applied and bound a fresh dressing.

Completing his first-aid handiwork Manuel said 'The village below us is where I hand you over to your next guide. You will be able to rest for a while. The guide's sister is better able than I to deal with this injury. She has some medical training and will attend to it properly.'

The three set off again and, within a while, took to a mountain track in a gorge. They followed this down through trees towards the foothills, all the time drawing closer to the castle and village they had seen earlier. Although the track was still rough, broken and strewn with boulders, the going got easier and the terrain began to level out. They began to glimpse cultivated vineyards stretching before them. Rounding a bend in the track, suddenly a dog barked fiercely. In a gap alongside the rocky bluff above them were three men, armed with guns and dressed in uniforms. The dog strained ferociously on the lead held by one of the men.

'Frontier guards!' Warned Manuel.

The guards levelled their guns at the trio below them. Were shouting, ordering them to stop. Close at hand, on either side of the track, were woods. Manuel spoke quickly, turning first to Mike. 'Do you think, with your ankle, you're able to make a run?'

The frontier guards shouted again. The dog's straining at its leash increased, its handler fought to control it.

'Yes. I'll take my chances. I'm damned if I'm going to get caught now.'

'We will run to the left' said Manuel.

He charged off into the trees with Colin and Mike hard on his heels - Mike's arm around Colin's shoulder to make it easier for him. Rifle shots cracked, a hail of bullets whistled around them. The dog was now off its leash and rushing after them growling. The guards followed still firing their guns.

Manuel threw himself behind a broadly-girthed tree. 'I must stop the dog. It will track us. I'll catch you up.'

Behind them they heard Manuel fire. There was a whine as the dog died. Colin and Mike reached a deeply-sided gully amongst the trees. It was not possible for them to clamber down the slope abreast so Colin went first and turned to assist Mike. He saw Manuel rushing after them.

Other guards must have been converging on them as, suddenly, from somewhere within the belt of trees, more rifle shots sounded. Manuel was thrown sideways - the rifle fell from his hand and he landed heavily on the ground. Colin thought at least three bullets must have thudded into his body. Briefly, Manuel lifted the top half of his torso and gestured towards the two airmen. Another rifle bullet blasted away a big part of his skull.

Colin and Mike reached the bottom of the gully and found themselves facing two mean-looking individuals dressed in shabby green uniforms. One man had a pistol, the other a rifle. Both weapons were firmly pointed at the two airmen and any attempt at escape would be fruitless. Colin and Mike put their hands up in surrender.

Neither of the border guards spoke English. As the guard with the rifle kept it trained on Colin and Mike, the other guard searched them. As he grabbed Manuel's pistol from Colin, the guard hit him viciously in the face. There was a shout behind and a man, whom Colin presumed was the senior officer, appeared with two other men. After what seemed words of rebuke from the officer, the guard who had struck Colin slunk back to join his colleague. The officer too had only very limited English but Colin and Mike managed to ascertain Manuel had been killed. Both received the news with much sadness and regret and no little feeling of guilt he had given his life for them. They explained as best they could what they were doing in Spain but, it was soon becoming clear that no amount of explanation was cutting much ice with the officer or his men. Without any further ado and, with hostility, the guards marched them off under gun point.

At the border guard's local headquarters, about two miles away, hours of interrogation followed before Colin and Mike were transferred to the prison at Figueras.

48

The telephone in the hallway at *Oakfields* rung about midnight. Outbreaks of Diphtheria and TB in the area meant Margaret Wilding had been working double shifts at the hospital for the past two weeks. She had gone to bed at eight-thirty exhausted and had no idea how long the telephone had been ringing before she heard it. As she got out of bed and made her way downstairs, somewhere in the back of her still half-asleep mind, she wondered why a telephone ring always seemed to have a different sound in the still small hours of the morning. The call was from the hospital, requesting her to return there as soon as she could.

'As the result of a big incident' is all the Consultant would - or was prepared - to say.

If the "incident" was something to do with an allied action on the Germans or, as a result of some enemy attack on England, there was nothing unusual in the paucity of the information he had given her. However, something in her colleague's voice told her whatever it was she was being called in for, it must be pretty serious and on a large scale. Still half-asleep, she had a quick wash and threw on the first clothes she came to.

Although it was the nineteenth of August it was a chilly night and Margaret shivered as she walked across the drive to her car. Her car had been playing up during the last few days and she was immensely relieved when it coughed into life. Things began to add up in her mind. Was the event she was being called in to the hospital for, connected in some way to why June unexpectedly had to leave earlier the previous evening as the result of the telephone call she received, asking her to report immediately to collect the Air Vice-Marshall? Yet June had arrived at *Oakfields* yesterday saying she was able to stay for three day's leave whilst he was engaged in some military exercise.

'Many thanks Margaret.' Leonard Miller had only recently joined the hospital as a Consultant and Margaret got on well with him professionally. He was hurrying along the corridor as she entered the hospital by a side door. 'Sorry to drag you in like this. We were desperate to get in as many staff as we could.'

'Why? What's happened Leonard?' She hurried along the corridor beside him. 'The yard is full of ambulances and military vehicles?'

'They have just brought in the first batch. More are due in about half-an-hour.'

'Batch of what?' She was finding it hard to keep pace with him.

'Troop casualties. I couldn't tell you much on the phone. Still can't at the moment - censorship and all that. A big raid took place on Dieppe or somewhere. A failure by all accounts. Bloody carnage by what I've seen so far - judging by the amount of casualties and their injuries. We've had to clear "Harvey" and "Jenner" Wards, so at least we can begin to assess and categorise the injuries. We are due to start on clearing "Pasteur" Ward any minute. "Jenner" is full up already but I've just been called to "Harvey".'

They had reached the entrance to "Jenner" Ward.

'You've made a start in here Leonard?'

'About half of them. The Sister will bring you up to date'

'I'll continue in here then.'

He nodded and carried on in his rush to "Harvey" Ward. On entering the ward Margaret grabbed herself a fresh white coat which fitted her reasonably enough. There was a voice from the sluice room behind her. It was a young nurse she recognised.

'Hello Dr Wilding. It's been bedlam in here for the last hour or so.'

'Whatever's happened?' Margaret collected together her stethoscope and other instruments she would need initially.

'There was a call just over an hour ago. Telling us to expect hundreds of casualties. All other hospitals for miles around were told the same thing. The vast majority of them are Canadians'

'Canadians! Right nurse. Where's Sister?'

'She is at the far end, dealing with a lad whose lost an arm and both legs.'

Margaret rushed up the ward, as she did, hearing cries of pain and agony from some of the occupants of the beds. During her rush she observed all the casualties were so young - nurses were dashing everywhere. She got to the end of the ward as a Registrar and the Sister were stooping over a patient.

'No we've lost him' declared the Registrar sadly, a note of frustration in his voice.

He and the Sister saw Margaret. The Sister gave instructions to an auxiliary nurse to tidy and clean the area of the bed and to draw round the screen. The Registrar was about to speak to Margaret when a nurse called from the bed opposite.

'Doctor please?'

'I'll attend to it Dr Wilding' said the Registrar.

The Sister began to update Margaret. 'As an emergency measure, before the casualties can be transferred to military hospitals, we and other hospitals were asked to begin surgery and treatment. This ward has been designated for primarily serious limb trauma and preparation for surgery; "Harvey" Ward primarily for burns injuries; "Pasteur" for more minor and shrapnel injuries and to prepare for possible surgery. On this ward, for the more serious of the injuries, we've allocated this half of the ward. The other half we've divided into two - for those deemed as not life-threatening and, I'm afraid, those who are deemed without much hope of survival and our role is to keep them comfortable and as free of pain as possible. Where we have been able to ascertain the patients' names and other details we've opened files and identified the beds accordingly. Where this has not been possible, we have opened files using code numbers.'

'Well done Sister. You and your staff have done well. Let's get started then.'

After quickly perusing the pile of notes the Sister had passed to her, Margaret crossed to join the Registrar at the bedside of a young Corporal from Calgary - in his semi-consciousness calling out for someone she presumed, from what he said, was his wife. She knew from what she had seen and heard so far, many hours of work lay before her and all other staff at the hospital.

****

On the night after Margaret had been called back to the hospital, James was sitting in the office of Beaulieu's Commandant. After spending the evening in the bar of the recreation area with other SOE instructors and the latest batch of trainees, the Commandant had invited James to join him for a drink before turning in for the night. In his office, the Commandant always had very nice Malt Whiskies to hand. He had previously told James the whiskies came from a family-run distillery near Arisaig - the site of his initial training.

After pouring from the decanter and handing a whisky to James, the Commandant said 'I will leave you to add your own water.' He paused. 'On the whole, with the exception of Browne, they seem a first-class bunch of recruits.'

'Yes. All very promising.' James let his palate savour the full distinct flavour of the Malt. 'Browne had no idea I was tampering with his drinks. He allowed his tongue to be loosened a little too much again. I understand he also fell into the trap Molly laid for him at the hotel in Lymington. Have you decided what your recommendations will be as to how he's dealt with when he's kicked out of here?'

'No not yet.' The Commandant unlocked a drawer in his desk, took out a file of notes and studied them for a while. 'Some instinct and, from what I've seen from his file, have been giving me grave concerns for a few days now.' Seeing the questioning expression on James's face he continued. 'I have gone as far as to request Baker Street dig around a bit into his past history. I'm thinking of rejecting him for the usual reasons but, recommending him suitable for some dreamt-up job in one of the War Departments - contriving something so SIS get interested in him.'

'SIS! You mean you think he could be...?'

'... It is possible he could be an enemy agent trying to infiltrate. That's the reason I re-structured the course here at short notice. So he didn't get too acquainted with much of the more detailed parts of our training.'

'God! The SIS? That will be tricky?'

'Yes. Especially, given the contempt and mistrust they appear to have for us here in SOE.'

'If Browne does turn out to be what you suspect, there are only two options open to deal with him?'

'Yes. To be locked away somewhere safe or for him to be eliminated altogether.' The Commandant replaced the file and shut the drawer with a bang of finality. 'It sounds as if Operation Jubilee was a darned awful mess.'

'Yes. Terrible. Early reports suggest losses - killed, wounded, captured - could run into hundreds. Canadians, Commandos, Royal Marines, seamen and airmen.'

'If there is any good to come out of it, hopefully, when the time does arrive for a second front, lessons will have been learnt.' He rose from behind his desk. 'Another Scotch James?'

'No thank you. I'd best be turning in.'

James drunk down the last of his Whisky and got to his feet.

The Commandant was turning the large globe of the world standing in the corner of the room. 'I believe you are returning to France again soon James?'

'Yes. Very soon apparently.'

'I was sorry to receive the news. We will miss your expertise here.'

James smiled. 'Who knows. I might find myself back here at some time in the future.'

'I hope so. Goodnight.'

'Goodnight. Thanks for the drink.'

After James left the room the Commandant returned to his desk and took out Browne's file again. A plan as to how to deal with him was beginning to formulate in his mind.

49

Colin and Mike had spent four days at Figueras packed into a tiny stone room with an Australian Navigator and a Belgian Air Gunner. The only exercise allowed, to leave the cell about three times a day for about five minutes at a time. Mike's ankle appeared to have become infected and was giving cause for concern. In the afternoon of the fourth day, all four were taken under guard and packed with many others into a cattle truck destined for the prison at Cervera.

They had understood Cervera was run by Military authorities and assumed the establishment would be reasonably well run, its accommodation and facilities certainly no worse than what they had experienced at Figueras. Any expectations they held in that regard were very quickly dispelled as soon as they entered the gates of Cervera. The buildings were very old and austere, a high stone wall enclosed all the buildings and what passed as a courtyard.

Colin helped Mike down the short flight of stone steps. The guard, angered by their slow descent, pushed them down the last few steps so they tumbled in a heap on the stone floor of a passageway. The passage was unlit and pitch black. On either side of it were entrances to cells - their doors each secured by massive bolts and locks. Colin's shoulder was hurting like hell as he had landed on it heavily when the guard had pushed them and, he winced as the guard pushed him very roughly through an open door into a cell. The heavy door was slammed shut behind them. Forlornly, the two airmen heard the guard slam home the bolts and turn his key in the lock. The cell had a small, barred window partially below the level of the ground of the yard beyond. In the last vestiges of daylight, Colin saw the uneven floor of the cell was covered with a layer of straw bedding. A filthy and stinking old bucket in the corner obviously served as a toilet. A constantly dripping tap on a pipe hung loosely from the wall, the constant dripping of the tap had caused a puddle to form in another corner of the cell floor which slightly sloped away from them.

It had taken the previous night and most of the day to arrive at Cervera and both men were very tired and sat down on the floor leaning their backs against the wall to get what rest they could. After a while, Colin started itching all over.

'Bloody lice and fleas! Must be in the straw. They're all over me.'

'Me too' replied Mike.

With his feet, Colin started to scrape the straw bedding away. He was getting increasingly concerned about Mike. He was looking distinctly unwell and beginning to shiver. Colin believed Mike was starting a fever.

'Mike, as soon as I can, I'm going to try and get someone to take a look at that injury of yours.'

Mike was now very groggy. He did not answer but weakly raised his head and nodded slightly.

About an hour later there was a coarse voice outside the cell door calling something in Spanish. Colin woke from his doze. By the time he got to the door, the voice the other side was calling more aggressively and the door was being kicked. A hatch in the door was opened and a metal plate with bread on it was shoved through.

'My friend needs medical attention urgently' demanded Colin as he took the plate.

This was met with a hail of angry utterances in Spanish. The hatch was slammed shut again.

Although they hadn't eaten since before they left Figueras, Mike declined anything to eat - no matter how hard Colin tried to persuade him otherwise - and complained of feeling sick. Colin ate half of what was on the plate, leaving what remained should Mike change his mind later. The bread was made with maize and was terribly dry. Nevertheless, it helped to relieve his hunger. Colin made Mike as comfortable as he could, ripping the sleeve off his shirt to act as a fresh dressing for the ankle injury which now looked to be ulcerated. Part of Mike's sleeve he also ripped off and placed under the tap. Not wanting to chance whether the water was potable, he simply soaked the linen to moisten his friend's lips and to hold on his fevered face and forehead.

The middle of the next morning, the cell door was suddenly thrown open. Impatiently, one of the guards shouted, gesturing wildly towards them. Angry at their hesitancy, another guard entered the cell and jostled Colin towards the door. Waving aside his protestations and demands for medical attention for Mike, the guard propelled Colin out into the dark passageway, whilst his fellow guard slammed the door shut and locked it. Colin's continued requests to know where he was being taken were ignored and he found himself being coerced up another steep stone staircase. Within a while he was being thrown into what passed as an office.

It was a big room. Some large, tatty maps of Spain hung on the wall beside a large bookcase packed tight with large volumes of tatty old books. On the wall behind a bulky desk hung a large portrait of Franco. To the side of the desk there was a window, at which stood a portly man with his back towards Colin. A man's cries of pain drifted up from below and through the open window. After a few moments the portly man turned around. He was puffing on a large cigar. Colin wondered fleetingly where on earth he could have obtained such a cigar.

'Forgive me. I was watching one of my officers supervising some punishment' said the man in broken English gesturing with his thumb over his shoulder. 'Utrillo is a good soldier. However, sometimes he does seem - how do you say - rather heavy-handed when it comes to applying punishment' he added rather unconcerned. He settled himself in his chair. 'I am Capitan Martorell, senior officer here at Cervera.' He proceeded to look through the disordered piles of paper on his desk. 'I have only just returned after a few days in Tarragona. I was not here when you arrived.' There was an infuriating relaxation about the way the man went about things - the way he spoke. Finally, after finding the papers he was looking for and reading through them slowly he asked 'You are?'

Colin replied giving his name, rank and number.

Martorell laughed loudly. 'That is what they all say. And you expect me to believe you? I'm afraid you will need to do better than that. First of all you can begin by explaining how you came to be discovered in Spain?'

Carefully, without naming Manuel and only by giving the most sketchy description of their journey over the mountains, Colin recounted part of his and Mike's story before they were confronted by the border guards. Martorell listened intently, referring as he did so to the papers in his hand.

'The man with you, the man we shot is well known to us. He is - what you say - a bandit - a criminal. You expect me to believe you and your friend did not know this, you had never met him before?'

For many more minutes, Martorell continued to press Colin on how long he had known Manuel and more details of their story. Despite Colin's repeated accounts of how long they had known Manuel and their arrival on Spanish soil, his interrogator still did not appear to believe him.

Colin was becoming exasperated, gave up trying to explain and ended by saying 'We are British Officers of the RAF.' Again, he only gave his name, rank and number and added 'I demand medical treatment for my subordinate.'

His demand appeared to fall on stony ground. Still without giving anything away as to whether or not he believed Colin's story, Martorell asked 'You will now tell me something of the mission you were engaged upon when you were shot down? Details of your Squadron, your crew, your aircraft? Anything that may convince me of who you are?' Colin hesitated. For the first time Martorell's relaxed demeanour vanished as he angrily thumped the desk with his fist and shouted. 'You will tell me or you and your friend will rot to death in my cells. You have two minutes to tell me. Understand? Otherwise, I will first throw you at the mercy of my officer - Utrillo.'

As if on cue, more cries of agony came from the courtyard below. Thinking of Mike's deteriorating condition, Colin began to give only the sketchiest details in answer to Martorell's further questions. This done, the Spaniard suddenly referred to other papers in his desk drawer. There was silence for a while as he studied these. Thoughtfully, Martorell replaced the papers and closed the drawer. He got to his feet and walked towards Colin who was fearing what was going to happen next.

Now, almost apologetically, Martorell said 'You must appreciate my friend. Here, in this part of Spain, we are troubled a lot by contraband smugglers and criminals. Hundreds of them a year cross into our territory, bring crime and much trouble. Others try to cause unrest. Cervera is run to punish such individuals and refugees who cross into our country illegally. I believe the story of you and your friend.'

At first, Colin didn't believe what he heard. Martorell crossed to the door and shouted something out into the hallway beyond. He returned to Colin's side.

'There is a doctor living near the prison. Your junior officer will receive medical attention.'

Colin got to his feet. 'Thank you. I appreciate it.'

A soldier hurried into the office and saluted the Capitan sloppily.

'Mendoza take our RAF friend here back. Give him and his cell-mate blankets. I make it your responsibility to make them as comfortable as you can.'

As Colin turned to leave, Martorell shook his hand. 'Please understand. Here at Cervera we have procedures to follow. We have to check. I am afraid though you will have to remain here for a while. You and your subordinate will then be transferred to Miranda del Ebro. Miranda is under the jurisdiction of the British Embassy in Madrid. It will be decided there what happens to you and Sergeant Richards.'

Martorell was as good as his word. An aged but kindly doctor attended to Mike's injury twice. Although Colin still had to clean out their cell, they were provided with fresh, clean bedding and blankets. The doctor had instructed Mike to use his injured leg and ankle as little as possible for the next few days and Mike took great, good-natured glee in watching his Captain - his superior officer - busy himself cleaning out the cell, arranging the new bedding and pandering to his requests for assistance in any way. Colin, also good-naturedly, responded by promising to place Mike on a charge for insubordination to a senior officer when they eventually got back to England or, at the very least, paying for every beer for six months. The pair of them were also allowed out into the courtyard for longer periods during the day, to visit what passed for a canteen for what passed as meals - mainly thin soup and bread - which they had to pay for. Each spell of exercise caused great amusement to Mike as he was relishing his superior officer having to assist him with any physical effort needed. During the rest of their confinement, whenever they encountered Martorell, he was always amiable. However, they soon learnt to keep well away from the brutish and inhuman Utrillo.

On their seventh day at Cervera, Mike's injury was noticeably improved. Colin and Mike were just finishing their soup in the canteen when Martorell approached them. 'The time for your transfer has arrived. You are to go with Mendoza immediately.'

Martorell's announcement was succour to them. At last, their repatriation seemed within their grasp. Quickly, they went with Mendoza out into the yard. Gathered around, standing regimented in two groups, each of about fifty, were in-mates of the prison. One group consisted of a rag-bag of what Colin took to be refugees or criminals, both male and female. The other group comprised of other men, women and children and some members of the military, Spanish, Poles, Belgians, Australians, New Zealanders. Watching over each group were Spanish officers and soldiers unfamiliar to Colin and Mike. The officer in command brusquely ordered Colin and Mike to join the group including the military personnel. Martorell came out of a door and handed two lists to the unknown officer who, with another, started to count those in the groups. Eventually, the superior officer shouted a command and his men began to escort the two groups out of the prison gates with their weapons pointed ominously towards their charges.

After about half-an-hour of walking, the escort channelled the two groups towards a station yard. A train awaited and, although its rolling stock looked old and shabby, it seemed to Colin their journey would be in reasonable comfort. However, the two groups were marched straight past the station entrance in the direction of a distant siding.

The euphoria Colin had experienced, when told they were to be transferred, evaporated immediately as he and Mike and the rest of their group were brutally pushed into the first cattle truck. The truck was already bursting at the seams by the time he and Mike were shoved in. The other group had been taken to another truck and both men had witnessed various incidents of brutality and beatings exerted on various individuals.

Inside the truck it was overwhelmingly hot and sweaty, the stench overpowering, making Colin feel sick - others were sick. A few hours later all were roughly off-loaded and ordered to wait between the tracks of a large siding. Escorted by two soldiers, two civilians carrying a large container eventually arrived and each "passenger" was allowed a ladle of foul-tasting water. The other truck was re-loaded and, with a jerk, it was shunted away and Colin wondered what fate awaited its occupants. Over an hour later, another train arrived and they were pushed into a goods van. There followed an enormous delay and, by the time the train got moving, darkness had descended. Colin and Mike positioned themselves so as to be beside a hole in the side of the goods van and took it in turns to gulp in fresh air. The journey seemed endless. Through the night the train made numerous stops and, on at least one occasion, was shunted into sidings.

Morning had broken when the train again came to a stop. Above the loud hissing of the locomotive, the shouting of orders could be heard. Finally, the group were marshalled by soldiers into the large, walled enclosure of Miranda del Ebro. Everywhere Colin looked, were rows of austere and dilapidated long huts. He didn't know it at the time but, Miranda del Ebro was the most notorious concentration camp in Spain and had been formerly used during the Spanish Civil War.

Colin and Mike were marched, along with others, into an area where they were forced to strip. They were promptly de-loused, their hair shaved and ordered to dress again. The pair were then marched into one of the huts and each shown a crude, bare, bunk bed. As the door was locked loudly behind them, any thoughts, hopes and dreams of a return to England and home had completely disappeared.

The other hut inhabitants were a mixture of nationalities. Some from the RAF, others from the Army and Navy. Colin was exhausted and as he clambered up to his bunk, the man beneath him woke up. He was a Lance-Corporal, taken prisoner by the Germans, and had managed to escape. Colin saw his face was covered in bruises and dried blood.

'What happened to you?' Colin asked.

'The result of upsetting one of the guards. If you're not careful, you will find they're all very eager with their beatings.' The Lance-Corporal turned over and went back to sleep.

The place was run very much like a POW camp. Living conditions and accommodation were at best spartan, the food barely adequate and, usually, inedible. As the Lance-Corporal had said the guards did not need much excuse to mete out physical punishment, seemed to delight in finding the smallest excuse to administer it as Colin witnessed on several occasions. Currently, the senior British officer at

Miranda del Ebro was Bill Cooper, a Wing Commander and Spitfire pilot, shot down over France. Colin met him the day after arriving and discovered he was responsible for keeping records of new British arrivals at Miranda and liaising accordingly with the Military Attaché in Madrid. He was also responsible for maintaining discipline amongst the British in-mates and being their sole spokesman when dealing with the Commander of the camp.

In-mates were allowed four periods of exercise daily. One day, after about six weeks at Miranda, during an afternoon exercise period, Colin became aware something was wrong. Knowing Cooper had been ill for a couple of weeks, he was on his way to see how he was. One hut away from where Cooper was billeted he saw two men carrying out a makeshift stretcher bearing a man. Another man followed them.

'What's wrong with the Wing Commander?' Colin asked the third man when he had caught up with them.

'We're sure its Pneumonia. We are taking him to what passes as the medical block.'

'Can I give you a hand?' Colin was jostled away and prevented from following by a zealous guard.

'We'll let you know any news later' called back one of the stretcher party.

It was early evening, as Colin and Mike waited in the queue for their meagre portion of watery soup and a sort of stew, when they learnt Bill Cooper had died an hour previously.

A Squadron Leader took over Cooper's role and remained as Senior British Officer until his release. By this stage, men were being released every few weeks into the supervision of the Military Attaché in Madrid.

Two weeks after the Squadron Leader's departure, Mike was in the hut playing cards with another Flight Sergeant - a mid-upper gunner and newly-arrived at Miranda. During the last few days the weather had deteriorated and, as the door to the hut opened, a fierce gust of wind followed Colin in and blew laid playing cards off the bunk.

'You're looking pleased with yourself' said Mike retrieving the playing cards. 'Like a cat that's got the cream.'

'You and me my old friend are going to be released.'

Mike was so excited, as he jumped up he banged his head on the bunk above. 'Us released!' You're kidding?'

'No I am not. I promise you. I've just been told. The Military Attaché will be arriving to pick us up tomorrow.'

During their internment by the Spanish, Colin had begun a log of the different things he had experienced since being shot down and of the different places he had either hidden or been sheltered. Later, as he laid in his bunk reading through his log, he realised he may not have recorded correctly some of the dates of all the various events and happenings during the last few months - so much seemed to have happened. However, he made no mistake with the date he entered in his log of when he would be leaving Miranda del Ebro for the British Embassy.

50

Colin and Mike's six days in the Embassy had seemed like luxury. They had been able to bath, enjoy real English meals and sleep in comfortable beds. The Attaché had even spent a good half-day showing them around Madrid. They relished the lovely feeling of freedom offered by this trip. On the sixth day, the Attaché provided transport to Gibraltar. As luck would have it a Royal Navy Frigate, damaged whilst carrying out convoy escort duties, was in port undergoing the last stages of repair and testing. Within two days of arriving in Gibraltar, Colin and Mike were aboard and steaming back towards Plymouth.

After rendezvousing with - and, for a couple of days, supplementing a convoy escort - the Frigate reached Plymouth. The two travelled by train to Paddington and then by Underground to Baker Street. Although given decent clothes by Embassy staff, both men felt rather self-conscious with their appearance. Their hair had only just started to grow again after being shaved repeatedly at Miranda del Ebro and neither had been given a hat. As they exited Baker Street Station, Colin looked at the document M19 personnel in Gibraltar had given him. 'The Great Central Hotel is apparently only a few minutes walk this way' he said.

'You lead the way skipper' replied Mike. 'Don't forget,

I'm a country lad from Somerset. I haven't been to London since my parents brought me up here when I was young.'

Commenting on the bomb damage to various buildings in the Marylebone Road and, in some of the streets leading off it, they continued on their way. On the corner of Balcombe Street, two police officers were questioning a spiv beside his van. Colin heard one of the policemen mention "Black Market" goods.

On arrival at the hotel they were told to wait in Reception until called. After what seemed like ages, a soldier appeared at the bottom of the staircase. 'Pilot Officer Graham?' He called. 'If you would like to come this way please sir?'

After briefly enquiring as to Colin's health and ascertaining whether they had found the hotel without difficulty, the soldier led Colin up two flights of stairs and along a long corridor. Both on the stairs and along the corridor, Colin admired the plush carpeting, the luxurious wallpaper and extravagant-looking chandeliers. Because they were still *in situ,* not taken away for concealment in case of invasion, Colin guessed the large paintings in their ornate frames on the walls must have been first-class reproductions and not originals.

The room allocated for Colin's technical interrogation had formerly been a large double bedroom but was now stripped of all such trappings. Trestle tables now dominated the floor area and on these were arranged groups of wire filing baskets and telephones and, large maps and charts of occupied Europe lay open. Chairs were either side of the tables. At the far end of the room, beside one of the tables, stood a tall gaunt-looking man dressed in army uniform and a shorter man in a grey suit.

'Pilot Officer Graham?' Called the army officer. His voice echoed around the bare walls. 'Come and join us up here please? I understand Flight Sergeant Richards is waiting downstairs?'

'Yes he is.'

As Colin crossed to him, he saw the Officer was a Captain. As the three men sat down opposite each other the Captain introduced himself, stating he was from the Intelligence Corps. He introduced the other man simply as "December" from M19.

'Before we start?' Asked Colin. 'I don't suppose you have any news about any other survivors of my crew?'

The Captain briefly referred to some notes on his desk. 'No. Not that I am aware of. I'm sorry.'

There was hardly a pause before the two men, mainly though the Captain, proceeded to fire all sorts of questions at Colin: about the mission he and his crew were on when Lancaster "F" for Freddie was shot down; what he knew about the fate of the rest of his crew; the baling out of him and his crew and whether appropriate, necessary complete destruction of the Lancaster by the survivors of the crew at the crash site took place; the measures Colin took to evade capture; the names of places he hid or was hidden. The interrogation continued in this manner for what seemed like ages. As Colin told what he knew of the places he hid or was given shelter, the Captain made notes on the papers in front of him or on one of the maps. The man from M19 made his own notes.

The man from M19 asked him for names of the members of the escape organisation or any member of the Resistance that had assisted him.

'I was told never to reveal their names' replied Colin. 'In any case, those people I encountered always used code names.'

Colin's answer did not appear to impress his questioner and he countered in a spiky manner 'We probably know

481

them anyway Pilot Officer Graham. We just like to confirm some of these details from time to time for our records.'

'I'm afraid I am still not prepared to reveal any names.' The man from M19 stared at him for a moment then, with the merest hint of a thin smile, made a note of something.

There was a long silence as the Captain and the official from M19 made yet more notes and marked some of the maps laid out before them.

At last the Captain asked 'Is there anything further you would like to add for our reports Pilot Officer Graham?'

'I would like to register my strong protest at the way Flight Sergeant Richards and myself were treated by the Spanish officials and military.'

After listening to his complaints, the Captain said 'Yes I must apologise. Our Government departments are endeavouring to negotiate with their Spanish counterparts about improving the treatment shown to allied evaders and escapees. But, for obvious reasons, the situation with Spain is very difficult and progress is slow in this regard I'm afraid.'

The two men asked Colin one or two more general questions about how he had coped during the last few months and his general health, then, suddenly, the Captain said: 'Well that's all for now Pilot Officer Graham. Thank you for your help. The Casualty Branch of the Air Ministry may well be in touch with you, should they want any more information about the loss of your aircraft and other details regarding other crew members.' He referred to a file in front of him and confirmed Colin's parent's address. 'You're now entitled to a period of leave. I presume you will be able to be contacted at this address?'

'Yes.'

'You will obviously need to arrange for a new uniform. The information we have gathered today will be analysed and collated and your Squadron informed. I see you have over half of your Tour of Duty to complete?'

'Yes. I presume I will be able to re-join my Squadron?'

'You will be notified accordingly in due course.'

On hearing the Captain's indefinite answer Colin's heart sunk. He had been really hoping to rejoin his Squadron. Did not relish the thought of having to find his way around a new Squadron. However, there was no point in worrying about that for a while. For the time being he would just set about enjoying some leave.

The Captain got up and smiled briefly but kindly. 'And if any news arrives about other members of your crew, someone will try to let you know. That's all I can say I'm afraid.'

The two men thanked him again and wished him good luck.

'How did it go?' Asked Mike as Colin rejoined him in Reception.

'Oh not too bad.'

The soldier standing beside Mike coughed politely. 'I'm sorry sir. But I can't allow you to say too much to each other before you have both finished talking to them upstairs.'

When Mike was called a few minutes later, Colin said 'I will wait for you. Perhaps we'll go for a beer or something. Good luck.'

Colin picked up a newspaper from a nearby table. Sadly, the front page was dominated by news of increasing shortages of food and supplies and Government proposals to revise some of the rationing arrangements.

Mike's interrogation took about the same time as Colin's and, after going for a beer or two then arranging for new uniforms, the two headed back towards Paddington Station. Mike destined for Somerset, Colin for Ealing.

51

Despite the darkened streets, the walk to his parent's house didn't take too long. Colin had telephoned his mother after arriving at Plymouth to tell her he was safe and well and, ascertained she would be at home during the next few days. However, at the time, he hadn't been sure how long the interrogation process in London would take and thought it would be nice to turn up at home and surprise her. Colin knocked on the door twice but there was no reply and he was beginning to regret not telling his mother when he would be arriving. He was about to call next door to see if her neighbours knew where she was when the front door opened.

'Hello mum.'

'Colin!' This is wonderful!' They kissed and embraced, she was crying with happiness and relief her son was safe at last. Still holding Colin she closed the door. 'Why ever didn't you let me know when you would be arriving?'

With their arms still around each other they walked into the sitting room.

'It would have been difficult. Besides I thought I would surprise you. But when you didn't answer the door…'.

'…I was in the back garden.'

'In the dark?'

'Doing my best to secure the housing for the chickens

and ducks. The door broke off its hinges in the high winds this afternoon.' They hugged again. 'Thank goodness you're safe. It's so wonderful to see you after all these months. If you only knew what its been like. Not hearing anything since your Station Commander telephoned and said that he believed you were safe and in hiding somewhere in France. It's been terrible for your dad and I - just waiting for some news about you.'

'I'm so sorry mum you and dad have had all that worry. I have got so much to tell you both.'

'Come and sit down.' She was still holding his hands. 'Unfortunately, he is still away working. He will be so upset about missing you. Especially as he's due back in a couple of days.'

'Then I will see him. If it's all right with you I will still be here. It's normal practice - after making it back home - to be given a few day's leave. Will it be all right if I stay here?'

She squealed with delight and hugged him again. 'Will it be all right if you stay here? Of course it will. That will be wonderful. Oh I'm so happy to have you back safe. Would you like a cup of tea - or something stronger? I think there are one or two beers in the cupboard.'

'A cup of tea would be lovely please mum.'

'Of course - that is - if I've enough left. I am afraid, what with all the rationing and shortages, things are not easy at the moment. I'm doing my best to eke out everything I can.' He followed his mother out into the kitchen. She turned to him. 'Oh Colin are you sure you're all right. You seem to have lost so much weight. And your hair? What's happened? Let me get you something to eat?'

As she made the tea and started preparing a meal from the bits and pieces she had in the larder, Colin started to recount some of the things he had experienced in the last few months.

'That was lovely mum' he said as he finished eating a while later.

'It was the best I could do I'm afraid.'

Colin looked down at himself. 'I must do something about these clothes. They the only things I've got with me. Hopefully, there are still some clothes left upstairs I will be able to get into.'

His mother smiled. 'Well if not, we will go into Ealing tomorrow. There's some clothing coupons we've saved up and might be able to use. If I speak to that nice man your father knows in the tailors he might be able to wangle something.'

Colin smiled. 'Have you spoken to James or June recently mum?'

'At the end of August your father and I had a weekend in Bournemouth with them. James wasn't able to tell us much as to what he's been doing, just mentioned something vaguely about a training job he's involved with. June is still in the ATS - doing a driving job. She was also up in London a few weeks back and telephoned me. We met and had lunch together, looking around the shops in the West End - not that there's much to look at in the windows. She said James had been posted away again somewhere but couldn't, or wouldn't, say whereabouts. She was upset she had not had a letter or telephone call from him.' Colin noticed tears in the corner of her eyes. 'That is what I find so depressing, distressing about the war - much more than all the shortages and everything. Things are so shrouded in secrecy. So many people don't know what their loved ones are doing, where they are, whether they're safe.'

'Before supper you were saying Aunt Lucy wasn't well.'

'Yes. She has been having spells of illness. As you know that is very unlike her. She is worrying about it - she's even been to the doctor. Even more unusual for her. Apparently, the doctor says she is just overdoing things on the farm. She is also getting frustrated and angry. The Agricultural Executive Committee keep changing their minds as to what crops she grows and what the farm produces. It is probably just as well that the number of Land Army girls working there has increased. In her last letter Lucy said she's also got women from the Timber Corps working on the farm.' She piled their dinner plates and crockery. 'I have some dried fruit. Would you like some Colin?'

'No thanks mum. I'm fine.'

'You remember two of those evacuees staying with Lucy? John and Sandra?'

'Yes of course. In fact, Sandra and I have been writing to each other. At least we were until I was shot down. Now I am back I was going to write to her. I also remember what a tyke John was and the problems he caused Aunt Lucy for a while.'

'Lucy was saying she wouldn't know what to do without John on the farm now. He's been indispensable.'

'Oh I am pleased. When Sandra and I were last in touch she seemed to have settled in well with her aunt in Somerset, after the aunt was forced to move from her home in East Anglia.'

'Yes. Sandra is still visiting the farm everyday. Helping Lucy with various things and so on.'

As much as Colin was enjoying talking to his mother, he was beginning to feel very tired and could feel his eyes getting heavy.

'Mum would you mind if I went up to bed? The last few days - last few weeks have been so tiring.'

'Of course - yes you must be exhausted. I should have realised. Sorry. You go on up. You will find your room just as you left it. And sleep in as long as you like in the morning.'

He kissed her goodnight and she hugged him tightly. 'Oh Colin it's so wonderful to have you home again safe.'

When he entered the bedroom it was just as his mother had said. Everything was as it had been during his last leave. Before getting into bed he looked at the photograph on the chest-of-drawers. It was of him and his brother and their parents whilst on holiday on the farm in Somerset five years ago. So much had happened during those last five years - what would the next five years hold in store for them all. Within seconds he was sleeping soundly.

52

It was a lovely late October's day, mild for the time of year. Mellow sunshine enhanced the rich golden-brown of the leaves still remaining on the Horse Chestnut trees on the attractive village green opposite Dr Melville's surgery. June lingered awhile to enjoy the beautiful day and serenity of the scene and, to fully absorb the wonderful news the Doctor had given her. Excitedly, she made her way towards a bench overlooking the pond. Noisily, A Swan saw off two Mallards straying too close. The news June had received had not come as a total surprise just confirmed her instinct, explained how she had felt during the last few weeks and why she had missed her last two periods. Her and James's baby would arrive in early to mid-May.

June remained on the bench for ages. Happy emotions, excitement and anticipation washed over her in warm waves. A young mother pushed her pram on the far side of the green. With a new intensity of interest, June watched the young woman continue on her way. Would James's and her baby be a boy or girl, what would they Christen the baby, the delight when her mother and James's parents heard the news? The only melancholy tarnishing this wondrous moment for her was her inability to tell James and, not knowing when she would be hearing from him or seeing him again. He had simply told her he would be away for some weeks and, if possible, he would try and contact her sometime. Like the time before, when he had been away for months, his explanation had all seemed so vague.

There was no way James could tell her what he would be doing. In fact, he was in France again. He had been briefed by SOE to organise and co-ordinate Resistance activity and sabotage to the German telephone communications and administration centre for the important port and dockyards of Brest.

****

Apart from a new hangar breaking the skyline, some new blocks of Nissan huts and new anti-aircraft emplacements, RAF Church Stephen had not changed much in the intervening months. To Colin, in many ways, it was like returning home. He had been relieved when he learnt he was to be posted back there to complete his tour of duty. Group Captain Burton was also still the Station Commander.

Sitting with Burton in his office, and the familiarity of the room made it seem all the more so to Colin that he had never been away.

'Sixteen missions to complete your Tour' observed Burton putting a file to one side.

'That's correct sir. I am looking forward to getting into the sky again.'

The Group Captain smiled. 'As I said it's nice to have you back with us Graham. But first things first. You will have to undergo some re-familiarisation sorties.'

'Of course. I realise that sir.'

'You will also have to pick a new crew. And, with the number of casualties now piling up, many of those aircrew available will be fairly green. You will see a lot of new faces around here, I am afraid a lot of our more experienced chaps are no longer with us.'

There was a brief silence before Colin said 'I suppose there has been no more news of the other survivors of my crew - those that managed to bale out?'

'No I'm afraid not. The last reports we had said they're all safe but prisoners-of-war.'

Colin paused. 'I believe Flight Sergeant Richards has been posted back here. Would it be possible to have him again as my Wireless Operator sir?'

'I see no reason why you can't link up with Sergeant Richards again' replied Burton.

'Thank you very much sir.'

'There are a few other changes I must tell you about. Your former Squadron Commander - Wing Commander Roberson, as you knew - was shot down. He's been replaced by Wing Commander Gregg - another Canadian. You will also have another Flight Commander, Squadron Leader Yates. Squadron Leader Barber has been promoted and is now with No. 1 Bomber Group. I am sure you'll get on well with them. Both are very experienced. Wing Commander Gregg said he will call in to introduce himself to you. Tonight's briefing finished some time ago. He should be here shortly.' There was a knock on the door and a WAAF entered. She handed a file to Burton. 'Missions are somewhat different now as well. The Pathfinder Force is now properly up and running and expanding. Life is becoming easier for us, our bombing missions are now far more effective.' He was about to explain further when there was another knock on the door. 'Come in?'

A powerfully-built man with a thick mop of black hair and heavy moustache entered. Burton introduced Wing Commander Tony Gregg. As Colin greeted his new Squadron Commander he noticed his DSO, DFC and AFC.

'Pleased to welcome you back Pilot Officer Graham - Colin.' Gregg's handshake was very firm and friendly.

His countenance and whole demeanour was also warm and friendly.

'Tony' said Burton 'I was just beginning to explain how we're working with the Pathfinder Force. I will let you explain.'

'Basically, important targets, all major raids are now marked by Pathfinders - back-up squadrons from 5 Group. They identify the targets by dropping coloured Target Indicators - T.I.'s. If necessary, these are replaced during a heavy raid. The colours of these T.I.'s are always being changed to confuse the Huns. We are now also commonly using Master Bombers to direct our attacking aircraft and to advise if there are any T.I.'s to be disregarded.' He paused for a moment. 'That's basically it but, don't worry too much about it at the moment. Training on the finer details, technicalities of the method will be given to you during your re-familiarisation training.'

'I see' said Colin, almost understanding how it all now worked.

Group Captain Burton smiled. 'Tony, Colin's very anxious to get in a Lanc. Again.'

Gregg grinned. 'Don't worry Colin. As soon as I get an experienced chap like you back in my Squadron the better. Tonight, I suggest you look up some of your old Squadron chums. There are still some you will know who are not flying tonight. Go for a pint or two and relax. Tomorrow you can start picking your new crew.'

Burton interjected 'Colin wonders if it would be possible to have Flight Sergeant Richards as his Wireless Operator. I am sure something could be arranged?'

'Flight Sergeant Richards?' Queried Gregg.

'He made it back to England with Colin.'

'Oh of course. I'm going to meet him later anyway' said Gregg nodding his head in agreement. 'Unfortunately though, apart from one or two experienced aircrew - survivors from bale-outs and crash landings - you may find it hard picking anyone with much experience.'

'Yes. So Group Captain Burton was saying. Though I'm sure I will find some I think have got what it takes.'

'Good man' said Gregg slapping Colin on the shoulder. 'And again, welcome back to the Squadron.' He paused. 'I'm on Op.'s tonight but, how about I look you up about mid-day tomorrow, have another chat before you pick your crew? Now if you will excuse me, there's something post-briefing I need to discuss with the Group Captain.' He laughed. 'I take it you've been allocated accommodation and, you can remember how to find the accommodation block and Mess?'

'Yes thank you sir. All taken care of.'

'Good. I'll see you tomorrow about mid-day then.'

As Colin was about to leave, Burton wished him luck.

Colin made his way out of the building. From the direction of the hangars, way across the airfield, he heard the distinctive sound of Lancaster engines being run up and tested by their ground crews. He stood for a while letting the refreshingly familiar noise of the engines sink into his senses. Beginning to walk towards the accommodation area, he mulled over his first impressions of his new Squadron Commander, what he and Burton had told him. From the decorations on Gregg's tunic, Colin had realised he was very experienced and more than capable. The two of them had hit it off immediately, he knew he would enjoy being back in the Squadron. Two Aircraftsmen saluted as they passed him. Two things though unsettled him: apart from being teamed up with Mike again, Colin wasn't looking forward to picking a new crew, getting to know and work with them - it would be like starting all over again, a whole new bond of trust would have to be built; secondly, it was apparent experienced and seasoned aircrew were thin on the ground. He suddenly felt nervous and unsure. Was it the situation making him nervous or - far worse a prospect - after being shot down and all the experiences which followed, had he lost his nerve? He felt a strange choking sensation.

Back in his room, Colin read the letter awaiting him. It was from the Casualty Branch of the Air Ministry. After reading it thoroughly for a second time, he began to write.

Sir,

With reference to your letter as above, I hope to be able to supply you with information which may be of assistance.

I have now placed the matter with my Base Intelligence Officer, with a view to obtaining target and topographical maps of the area. On receipt of this information, plus the heading of attack and return, I am sure I will be able, fairly accurately, to place the location my aircraft crashed.

Your reference to Resistance reports of what may have been my aircraft and the burial of three bodies at Bouillon, which appears to be near that part of our flight path when I gave the order to bale out, might, I regret to say, indicate the fate of those of my crew who died. Regarding one of the crew being "slim and over six feet tall" and another "very short" it would seem these persons to be Sgt. Geoff Toppin, Flight Engineer and Sgt. Dennis Wilson, Rear Gunner, respectively. The rest of the crew were of average build. As I reported in my earlier statements, F/Sgt. Michael Richards and myself discovered the body of Sgt. Danny Cuthbert, Mid-Upper Gunner, during our retreat from the crash site. As I have said previously, at no time did I see any other crew member actually bale out.

On my return to England I received initial interrogation in Plymouth by F/Lt. Phillips on 23rd October and full technical interrogation at the Great Central Hotel on 26th October. It was during my initial interrogation at Plymouth I learnt Pilot

Officer Ben Cansdale, Navigator, had been taken as a P.O.W. I am concerned to learn you have not received the statement of the latter interrogation but, if you wish, I will be pleased to write another full statement covering the loss of my aircraft and crew members and, if desired, will include the time I spent in France and my route back over the Pyrenees.

Pending the further information from my Base Intelligence Officer, I give below a brief description of the destruction of my aircraft:

On the night of 5/6ᵗʰ June 1942, shortly after delivering our attack on a large "Manufacturing Site" in Koblenz, we were hit by flak and anti-aircraft fire. After making appropriate evasive manoeuvres and assessing the damage sustained, we set course for home. We had sustained minor damage to the fuselage in the area around the WOP's position, flak or shell damage to Mid-Upper turret fairing and turret mounting ring, shell damage to starboard rudder. Over Wittlich we successfully repelled two attacks by a night fighter. Unfortunately, I am unable to tell you whether my Gunners damaged or destroyed the night fighter. West of Bouillon we were again attacked by a night fighter and my aircraft sustained heavy damage to the port side of the fuselage, control cables, port inner and outer engines and port wing. I gave orders to abandon the aircraft and heard <u>everyone</u> acknowledge that order. My Bomb Aimer, Engineer and Navigator made their way to the forward escape hatch. Shortly after, the entire cockpit area was torn apart from the fuselage and I found myself falling towards the ground.

The majority of the aircraft wreckage was about a mile from where I landed. After concealing my parachute, I returned to look for any crew members and to ensure there was nothing which could assist the Germans on discovering the crash site. As I approached the wreckage, the fire was intense and there were still explosions. After checking as best I could for survivors or casualties, I sought a suitable place to hide for the remainder of the night. It was not until early the following morning that I was rejoined by F/Sgt. Richards.

Colin was about to write another paragraph when there was a knock on the door. It was an Orderly.

'Sorry to disturb you sir but I thought you might be pleased to receive some news.'

'What's that Johnson?'

'I believe a F/Sgt. Harvey was a previous member of your crew?'

Colin jumped to his feet. 'Yes that's right.'

'The Group Captain thought you'd be pleased to know, news has just come in he's arrived back in England.'

'Oh that's great. Do you know how he is?' Thought's rushed into Colin's head. Perhaps another former member of his crew might be able to rejoin him.

'Flight Sergeant Harvey managed it back to the UK *via* an evasion line - much as I believe you did sir?'

'Wonderful.'

'Unfortunately though sir, somewhere along the way, he has been injured. It's not yet known whether he'll be passed fit for flying again. That's all we know at the moment I'm afraid. But the CO thought you would like to know.'

'Yes. Thank you for telling me Johnson.'

The Orderly went out. Although disappointed to hear of Doug Harvey's injury, Colin was thrilled he was safely back and knew he would be able to find out more news in the days ahead.

****

'Don't bother to get up Mrs Hughes. I can find my own way out. You just rest.'

Dr Corbett left Lucy sitting in her favourite armchair in the living room at about the same time Colin had walked out of the Group Captain Burton's office.

Lucy had always hated being ill. In fact, it was a rarity for her to be so. But, for the past few weeks she had not felt well - periods of nausea and vomiting, lacking in appetite and energy tired and listless and generally lethargic. She couldn't understand just why she felt like she did and today was the worst she had been. Sandra, on one of her regular visits to the farm, had been so concerned she insisted in calling Dr Corbett. He too was again perplexed by Lucy's symptoms.

As the Doctor emerged from the living room, John and Sandra were talking in the kitchen opposite.

'How is Mrs Hughes?' They asked in unison.

'She says she is feeling a little better than earlier today but still complaining of feeling so tired. I will call back in two day's time. In the meantime. I have written a prescription. Will someone be able to get to the Chemist?'

Sandra took it from him. 'I've got to go into town shortly.'

'Well as I say I will call back in two day's time. Now I want Mrs Hughes to have as much rest as possible. It's also important you get her to eat or drink something. Not too much, just something light.'

Sandra walked him to the front door. 'Thank you very much for coming Doctor. I was getting so worried.'

Lucy called from the living room. 'Is that you John?'

'Yes Mrs Hughes.'

'I'm anxious to hear what the man from the Agricultural Committee had to say.'

Mindful of what the Doctor had said about Lucy getting as much rest as possible, John had a reluctance to tell her but, nevertheless, he was eager to see how she was.

'How are you feeling Mrs Hughes?'

'Better than I did but getting fed up with everyone

fussing so. Now John tell me what the man from the Ministry had to say?'

'But the Doctor said….'.

'…Fiddlesticks! I'm all right. Now what did he say?'

'He gave me a form you have to fill in. It's in the kitchen.' Sandra came in and John continued. 'He said they want us to grow an additional fifty acres of root crops for next year. And an extra thirty of wheat.'

'Fifty acres of root crops?' Lucy thought for a moment. 'Topland and Long Field will need to be prepared then.'

'Me and the Land Girls will make a start tomorrow.'

'Are all the potatoes harvested now?'

'We're just about finishing off. By the end of the day it'll all be done. Oh and another fifteen tons of timber was taken away this morning.'

'Good. Were there any cheques from the Ministry today? I'm fed up with keep having to ask them for payment.'

'Yes the man gave me one which covers the previous three months.'

'I've got to go into town with the prescription the Doctor left. If I'm in time for the bank, I'll pay it in for you.' As Sandra spoke she plumped up Lucy's cushion. 'Now I must get you something to eat Mrs Hughes. The Doctor said to try something light. What do you fancy?'

'A nice piece of toast please Sandra. And perhaps I had better have a drink?'

Sandra picked up the empty jug from the table beside Lucy. 'I'll go and do that for you. Then I must get into town. I hope the bus is running to time today.'

'There were other things the man wanted to know Mrs Hughes' said John.

'I'm feeling a little tired. Tell me later John.' As Sandra

and John turned to leave, she called after them 'And thank you both for all you're doing for me.'

Back in the kitchen Sandra turned to John. 'Oh before I forget John. Mrs Appleford called in about the sale she's organising to raise funds for the soldiers' Christmas parcels. She asked if you could take the paintings you're donating to the shop before the end of the week?'

'Yes I will do. I've got to finish framing one. Perhaps I might have time this evening when we've finished harvesting the potatoes.'

As she toasted the bread she had cut, Sandra hesitated. She was reluctant to ask. 'John I found some papers and forms laying on the floor in the hall?' He looked puzzled. 'I couldn't help but notice - I'm sorry - your name was on them. Forms for enlisting in the army?'

He was embarrassed, paused before answering. 'I was in town the other day and picked them up from the recruiting office. They must have fallen out of my pocket.'

'But why John? You're now officially classed as in a Reserved Occupation. I thought you were happy living here - working for Mrs Hughes?'

'I have been - I am - it's just that...'.

'...What is it then?'

He hesitated. 'Oh I just feel I need to. So many of the young blokes around here are being signed up.'

Sandra had got to know John very well since both arriving in Somerset over two years ago now. Could read him like a book and wasn't convinced by his explanation. 'Come on John. What is it? You can tell me.'

John shifted on his feet awkwardly, uneasily. 'There's a group of blokes in the town. Whenever I go into town, they're always hanging around - waiting to go off into the forces. They keep on at me, having a go about me having come down from London, saying I'm skiving down here avoiding being called up and all that.'

From the time in 1940 when Sandra, John and all the other Evacuees had arrived in the country, to greater or lesser degree, they had all experienced resentment from some of the local people. Now and again, even over two year's later, she still experienced occasional hostile and unfriendly reactions from some of the locals. She also knew John, perhaps more so as a male, had been the victim of incidents of ill-feeling, bullying and being ganged-up on.

'Oh John don't let them get you down, just ignore them. You must realise the work you do on the farm is every bit as important as being in the army, just like the "Bevan Boys" in the mines.'

'I suppose so.' He paused. 'But it's not easy Sandra. Every time I go into town. Then I get to thinking - something about joining the army - I just don't know.'

'But you're so good on the farm. Mrs Hughes often says she doesn't know what she would do without you. And especially now, what with Mrs Hughes not being too well. She needs your help now more than ever.'

They were interrupted by Kitty, one of the Land Army girls, rushing in.

'John, something's gone wrong with the plough. Betty and I have tried fixing it, we've tried everything. And Mrs Hughes wanted that field finished today. Can you come please?'

'Okay Kitty. I'm coming.' Kitty was a nervous, mouse-like girl. She ran out of the kitchen as quickly as she had ran in. John smiled. 'Thanks Sandra. I'll think things over. I promise.'

As Sandra finished putting the plate of toast and the jug of drink on the tray, she watched him hurry confidently across the yard. She was worried. She knew Lucy would be devastated if John left the farm. After seeing the Doctor off she had cut some stems of a late-flowering Chrysanthemum. She put these in a little vase and put this on the tray and took the tray into Lucy.

53

It was the middle of November. Colin and Steve Yates, his Flight Commander, were walking back from the Briefing for that night's raid. The frost had not receded until mid-morning and both men wore their greatcoats as comfort from the raw cold East Anglian air - always worsened by the vast open spaces of an airfield. Because of bad weather over most of Europe, for the first time in days, Op.'s were on for the night. In the Briefing Room there had been an atmosphere of initial excitement, always more tangible when aircrews had been kicking their heels for a few days. Equally tangible, as the Briefing progressed, had been the increasing tension and anxiety amongst the aircrews as details of the designated target emerged.

'Congratulations on your Military Cross Colin' said Yates.

'Thank you sir. I must admit it took me a bit by surprise when I heard about it.'

'You richly deserved it. What you and F/Sgt Richards accomplished by getting back was remarkable.' They stood aside as two large lorries carrying aircraft spares passed them. 'Tonight then, it's the oil refineries at Gelsenkirchen. You've been there before though haven't you?'

'Yes. A few days before I got shot down.'

'You will notice a bit of a difference since then. As they

said in the Briefing, "Jerry" has recently stiffened up air defences around the whole area.' They reached the junction of two roadways. 'I'm going this way to the sick bay to see how Flight Lieutenant Dobson's doing. I'll see you later.'

Continuing to the accommodation block, Colin thought back over his last few weeks back on the Squadron. Since the familiarisation period with his new crew, he had completed three operational sorties. Two other missions had been aborted. One to Saarbrucken to attack a Panzer and artillery training complex and the mission had been called off a third of the way there, because of rapidly deteriorating weather near the target area. The second, when they were halfway across the North Sea *en route* to Bremerhaven and, his aircraft's starboard outer engine failed and the port inner became "iffy", despite the efforts of his Engineer to rectify the problem. Like all other pilots and aircrew, he hated it when a mission was either called off at the last minute or aborted after take-off. There was nothing worse - after all the pre-mission speculation, the Briefing, the apprehension, the anxiety, the preparation, the talk during the pre-flight supper.

Colin was pleased with his new crew. Very satisfied with the way they were all blending into a cohesive and efficient team. The tried and trusted Michael Richards - Wireless Operator; Pilot Officer Clive Whittle - Navigator, fresh from a heavy bomber conversion unit; Pilot Officer Craig Houston - Bomb Aimer, a New Zealander, on his second tour of duty; F/Sgt Steve "Stuffy" Stafford - Flight Engineer, an Australian from Melbourne; F/Sgt John Kieran - Mid-Upper Gunner, a Liverpudlian, and five trips with another crew until their Lancaster crash-landed on the Fens whilst returning from a sortie, leaving him one of only three uninjured survivors; F/Sgt Andrew "Lively" Livesay - Rear

Gunner, a Scot from Perthshire. Knowing them all now, Colin was reassured for tonight's trip to Gelsenkirchen.

Take-off was 23.00 hours. At 21.55, Colin and his crew left the bus parked alongside Lancaster "S" for Sugar. Since his return, it was the third time he had flown this particular aircraft - it was to be its 30th sortie. He was pleased to be assigned "S" for Sugar - so dependable and responsive. However the thing he had always disliked, ever since qualifying as "Operational", was being taken to the aircraft sometimes as much as 1 hour before taxiing. He would have always preferred to be transported to the aircraft with the bare minimum of time before taxi as there would be less time for the nerves to build up.

Colin and his crew hauled themselves aboard and started their checks. The engines were run up and shut down.

'Can we get off for a while skipper?' Asked Craig.

Craig, like Colin and the rest of the crew, also hated the waiting around for the instruction to taxi. Preferring to stand outside on the "Pan" chatting, smoking or, if necessary, to use the latrines by the dispersal pans before take-off.

'Yes we've got bags of time yet. Mind you its cold out there, I don't want all you lot going down with double pneumonia before we get back.'

Around a quarter of an hour passed and, to their relief, no indication came from the control tower to tell them, after all the waiting, the Operation had been cancelled.

Colin called 'Okay chaps let's go.'

All aboard again, the ladder was stowed and the doors locked. Colin signalled the ground crew to stand clear and the engines were started. The Lancaster began to throb, exhaust smoke and gases drifted through the open cockpit window. "S" for Sugar strained to be unleashed and Colin signalled "chocks away". Brakes released, the aircraft began its long taxi to join others proceeding along the taxi-way in their curious "crab-like" motion. Aircraft converged on the end of No. 1 runway from both sides - Colin's Squadron from one side, another Squadron from the other. At last it was "S" for Sugar's turn for take off. The green light from the control van shone and Colin turned the Lancaster onto the runway. Brakes applied, up to zero boost with the engines, a second green light, brakes off and the Lancaster was moving. As always, the Group Captain and other personnel were positioned by the control van and along the runway to wave them off. As the Lancaster rolled past, Colin's feelings were lifted by their presence. He lifted "S" for Sugar into the night sky. As they gained height Colin knew - providing he and his crew survived the mission - they would not be returning for between five and six hours.

The crossing of the North Sea was largely uneventful. About 50 miles from the Dutch coast Colin called the gunners 'We'll be crossing the coast soon. Keep a sharp lookout for night fighters.' Then, to the others 'Everyone else, be prepared for coastal defences.'

A short while later they were crossing the coast above Katwijk. Almost immediately searchlight beams scoured the sky, closely followed by streams of bursting tracer shells and clouds of flak, mercifully, all of it some distance away. Colin was thankful they were in the first wave, before the German gunners had proper track and height of the bomber stream. Suddenly, miles over in the distance to port, there was a huge explosion in the sky some thousand or so feet below them. The German gunners had scored a direct hit on a Lancaster. Quickly, Colin re-checked their bearings. He thought of the poor souls in the stricken bomber - probably a new, sprog crew - probably on an incorrect heading and height. He called up his Navigator.

'Clive. About fifteen miles over to port. A Lancaster

hit. Get a rough fix for the Intelligence people when we get back?'

'Righto skipper.'

They were now leaving the coastal defences behind, continuing across the flat lands of Holland in a series of doglegs. They steered north of Utrecht to avoid heavy air defences, down to the east of Zeist and way to the west of Arnhem, then east of Nijmegan and then over the Dutch/German border and turning southwards. Way over to his left Colin could make out a gleaming, winding ribbon of water.

Clive confirmed: 'The Rhine should be over to port skipper.'

Quickly Colin calculated the flying time to commencement of their bombing run. As if anticipating his calculations Steve, the Flight Engineer, confirmed the fuel levels.

'Night fighter! Fighter, starboard quarter! Prepare to corkscrew starboard' shouted Andrew over the intercom from the rear turret. He gripped the trigger of the four Brownings. 'Can you see him John?'

'No. Not yet' replied the Liverpudlian from the mid-upper turret. 'Yes, yes, I see him now.'

'Stand by to corkscrew' called Colin.

'Corkscrew! Go!' Shouted Andrew.

Colin dropped the Lancaster's nose very sharply. Andrew lost all sight of the night fighter. As they pulled out of the dive, he glimpsed it again. A brief burst of tracer spat fiercely at them.

'I've got him now. I see him' replied John.

Colin was still corkscrewing the aircraft.

'Fire together' called Andrew. 'Ready, Ready, Fire!'

Both gunners squeezed their triggers. Shells from their guns streamed back towards the fighter which coldly, clinically, followed the Lancaster through its evasive manoeuvres. Andrew and John were giving a running commentary. The night fighter was firing short bursts from its cannons but continued to hold off no more than 100 yards away. Then, it closed in for the kill. In the rear turret Andrew waited for death. Colin put the bomber into another violent corkscrew as more shells streamed from the fighter. Together, Andrew and John fired desperately. Suddenly, the fighter's nose dropped and he screamed away vanishing just yards beneath them.

Andrew called 'Can you see him John?'

'No. No, not a sign of him.'

Andrew called Colin. 'He's gone. All clear behind skipper.'

Colin levelled out. The effort of hauling the Lancaster about had made him breathless and sweaty. 'Well done you gunners. Well done everyone. Keep a lookout for others. Everyone okay? We'll be starting our bombing run soon. Any damage to report?'

One by one, his crew members stated they were uninjured, reporting no significant damage sustained. Colin began to climb again. Because of their evasive action, Clive studied his calculations and gave the revised heading. A few minutes later and the Lancaster was approaching the target area. Target indicators could be seen going down straight ahead. Michael switched to the master bomber's W/T frequency. It was confirmed the TI's had been accurately placed. Colin was able to fly straight in on their bombing run at 19,000 feet. The Pathfinders had performed their task efficiently, their flares and markers illuminating the target. Already pools of orange flame glowed, flared and grew. Clouds of light, medium and heavy flak bursts exploded above, below and all around them - the blast draughts buffeted and bumped "S" for Sugar. The sky around the target was angry with bursting tracer shells, many streaking right towards them, the nearer they got to the Lancaster the faster they seemed to be going. "S" for Sugar began to pitch and roll violently, some of this due to exploding shells but much due to the slipstream of Lancasters ahead of them. The bombing run seemed to last an eternity.

Coolly, Craig gave instructions to Colin. 'Right, right - steady - bomb doors open - left, right, right again, now - steady - steady - bombs gone. For God's sake let's get out of here!'

Now un-encumbered by its bomb load, the Lancaster jerked and lifted. There was another minute of fear and anguish as Colin flew straight and level for the obligatory photo to be taken. Suddenly they were in the beam of a searchlight. Despite Colin's desperate efforts at the controls they couldn't escape its brilliance. He and his crew knew they were now the target.

Colin called '3,000 revs, plus 14 boost, maximum speed!'

Shells arched up towards them, the Lancaster pitched wildly as some hit home. Suddenly, at last, they were out of the beam. Colin put the aircraft into a rapid dive - 19,000 feet, 18,000 feet, 17,000 feet, gaining speed, turning and weaving away and heading for home. Night fighters were in evidence in the sky.

'Mike' Colin called up. 'There are fighters around. Help the gunners, keep a lookout from the astrodome for a while?' He called the others 'Everyone all right? Any damage to report?'

There was still some heavy flak but they were gradually leaving it way behind them. Colin climbed rapidly to 23,000 feet. The controller signalled "operations over". Mike switched to the group transmitter frequency before going aft to check the photoflash had cleared the chute. Returning to his position, he prepared for the tiresome business of listening out, the boredom only to be relieved, at the due times of transmissions, by the occasional changing of the colours of the period.

Colin wasn't relishing the prospect of the journey home. He knew the gunners had used a lot of ammunition in repelling the night fighters they had encountered. There was still a long way to get home and, from the pre-flight briefing, knew they could still encounter fighters at various points along the route. Nevertheless, he kept his misgivings to himself and joined in with the others as they enjoyed the usual "immediate post bomb-dropping celebrations". He took a drink from the flask of coffee being passed around. Steve gave another verbal report on the fuel consumption. A Lancaster suddenly appeared at an oblique angle off to port, racing them towards home.

During the briefing, all crews had been told of airfields in England to be used in case of an adverse change in weather, shortage of fuel, aircraft damage or a local emergency at their home base. Colin hoped against hope he and the crew of "S" for Sugar would not need the alternative landing sites tonight. As usual, the return trip was *via* a different route as specified at the briefing. Their route back was over Gelderm, then following the River Maas to Venlo in the Netherlands, steering to the right and over Valkenswarrd, then to Brecht in Belgium slightly south to Terneuzen on the edge of the Westerschelde and crossing the Dutch coast at Breskens. Perhaps, being able to glimpse below him the waters of the rivers Maas and Schelde and, the expanse of the Westerchelde estuary, Colin could identify for himself navigational landmarks on their way back - always good psychologically. He looked down and saw a tiny ribbon of glistening water. They were now following the River Maas. So far so good!

To the south of Brecht, there was a network of important rail links and marshalling yards. The location being very important to the Germans for the movement - between Germany, Holland and Belgium - of troops, equipment and other supplies. As such, as had been emphasised at the briefing, Colin and his crew knew only too well they could expect stiff anti-aircraft defences.

'Andrew, John, everyone' called Colin. 'Keep a sharp lookout. We're approaching the Brecht area.'

Long beams of searchlight pierced the night sky ahead of them, followed by rising streams of streaking, orange anti-aircraft tracer. A mile or so ahead, just over to starboard, a massive orange cloud erupted, fragmenting into a myriad of flaming, falling fragments. As the orange ball disintegrated further, its dying glow illuminated the unmistakable outline of the twin tail fins of a Lancaster. The very rapid demise of the bomber indicated it had received a direct hit. 'Poor sods!' Murmured Colin to himself. 'At least you wouldn't have known anything about it.' Suddenly there were large showers of burning, yellowy, mushrooms of smoke. Thousands of brilliant, flashing lights whirled around and fell.

'Beware everyone. Here comes the flak' warned Colin, using supreme efforts of airmanship to try and avoid the showers of death.

In the front turret, Craig fired his guns at a night fighter which swooped a few yards directly in front of them. Shouting as he did so: 'Night fighter! Night fighter!'

'Gunners! Watch for him coming round the back' screamed Colin.

To port, about 1,500 feet below them, Colin saw a long smear of red. Another Lancaster burst into flames. The orange-red smear, fanned by the airflow, expanded and lengthened all along the aircraft's starboard side. He couldn't identify whether any of its crew were baling out. Briefly he pictured its desperate, frightened crew trying to evacuate from the increasing inferno in the fuselage.

Mercifully, they were now through the worst of the flak and anti-aircraft fire. The strain, sheer concentration of constantly searching the darkness was having its effect on Andrew's eyes. He blinked to clear and refresh them. What was that? For a fleeting moment he caught sight of a bluish-green light. He realised what it was - burning, red hot exhaust gases - a night fighter!

'Fighter! Coming in, port quarter above!' He called. 'Prepare to corkscrew port. Do you see him John?'

'Yes I see him.'

As one, both gunners fired their Brownings at the rapidly closing fighter. It's cannons were already spitting shells. Colin responded immediately. The Lancaster turned and dived steeply, throwing everyone inside off balance. As "S" for Sugar levelled out, both bomber and fighter were exchanging fire furiously. The bomber began to turn and dive again.

'The guns have…'.

The rear turret disintegrated in a living hell of cannon shells, shattered glass and Perspex. The three words Andrew spoke were the last anyone else in the bomber heard from him. More shells riddled the Lancaster's fuselage. Someone heard the Navigator, Clive, scream with pain.

In the mid-upper turret, John watched the fighter circle and come in again. As he watched, his fingers poised to fire, he had a fleeting nightmare of total finality. He let loose with his guns. Perhaps it was the inexperience of the German pilot - sheer good fortune - fate - whatever - but the German somehow got it wrong. The fighter just blew up. Mesmerised, John watched as tiny fragments of fighter bounced off the Lancaster's fuselage all around his turret.

'I've got him! I've got him!' In his relief and excitement he could hardly get the words out.

There was a long pause as the Lancaster pulled out of a steep dive.

The calm, appreciative voice of Colin came over the intercom. 'Well done John. Well done. You're sure he's gone?'

'Positive skipper. Bits of it were dropping all around me.'

Colin, still calm and in control, called 'Okay everyone. We have still a way to go. Keep a close watch?' Near him the Engineer was busily checking his gauges and instruments. Apart from some slightly slower responses from the flight controls, "S" for Sugar seemed, so far, to be flying okay. 'Report all damage and injuries please?' Colin had heard Andrew's curtailed warning and there was still no response from him. The Navigator had responded but, his voice had been barely discernible. He called up Craig in the front turret. 'Craig. Get back and see how Andrew and Clive are?' Shortly, the Bomb Aimer was beside him. 'Take Mike with you. See if there's anything you can do?'

With no information forthcoming from Clive, Colin looked down and around to see if he could discern any visual landmarks by which to get a course bearing. A few miles ahead, just north-east of him he saw an expanse of water which began to widen and bend in the further distance. He believed it was the Westerschelde.

After what seemed like ages, Craig was back beside him. 'Andrew is not too good at all. His turret is a hell of a mess. Honestly, I don't know if he'll make it skipper. We've done what we can for him and made him comfortable on the rest bed. Clive's been hit, his shoulder is shattered. He's just conscious but in agony. Blood all over his desk and charts.'

As if on cue, Clive's voice - very weak and trembly - came

over the intercom. 'Hi skipper. I think I can set a course for our way back. If I get into difficulty, I'll call you.'

'Well done Clive. If you're sure you can manage it. It won't be too long before we are back. Then those lovely nurses will be looking after you. Lucky bugger. Take it easy and thanks again.'

As they crossed the coast they encountered heavy anti-aircraft fire but emerged unscathed.

Over halfway across the North Sea, Steve spoke. 'Skipper, I'm losing oil pressure in the port inner engine.' As he spoke, a small glimmer of flame flickered around the starboard outer engine cowling. The merest hint of panic was in his voice as he added 'I can see flame from the starboard outer.'

'Shit!' Exclaimed Colin. The awful probability of them either ditching or baling out into the freezing waters of the sea loomed large in his mind.

'Shutting down and feathering props now!' Shouted the Engineer.

The options open to him raced through Colin's mind. If he tried to continue they could end up ditching in the sea or crash landing as they reached the coast; if he ordered "bale out", his badly injured Rear Gunner and Navigator would certainly not manage it and he would be signing their death warrant; he had the rest of his crew to consider. Steve's next words were heaven sent.

'The feathering seems to be working. I can't see any more flame.'

Colin adjusted the trim and flying controls accordingly. 'How's the oil pressure on the port inner?'

'Seems to be stabilising - no it's dropping again - no - shit - it's all over the place. Bloody "Jerry" must have shot things up. What are you going to do skipper?'

'Don't take your eyes off those gauges.'

Colin tried to call up his Navigator for their position. He couldn't make out Clive's barely audible reply and called up his Bomb Aimer to go aft again to see if he could glean anything from Clive's charts and instruments. Within a few minutes, Craig was back at Colin's side informing him.

Colin asked his Engineer again about their fuel situation and oil pressure. Considered his answer for a moment and made his decision. 'I'm going to try and put us down at one of the alternative landing fields.'

At their briefing, one of the alternatives given was Manston - a Fighter field. A landing there would be tricky for a Bomber but had been utilised by Bomber Command on several previous occasions. Colin called Mike, now preparing to fire the colours of the day. He stopped what he was doing and signalled Manston. Shortly after, Colin found it hard to contain his relief. He could just make out the English coast ahead.

He called 'English coast ahead. We are nearly back in Blighty.'

Mike switched on the VHF recognition signal.

Colin's euphoria only lasted a little while as Mike called 'Bad news skipper. Manston have just radioed. They can't take us. One of our kites has beaten us to it. It crashed and exploded on landing. Debris and explosions all over the place.'

Throughout the crew a fatalistic depression descended.

'That's buggered that then. We are going to have to make it all the way back. How's the fuel and oil pressure?'

Steve made some quick calculations. 'We'll be flying on the vapour if we're not careful and only two engines working properly.' Colin throttled back as much as he dared. 'Oil pressures are all over the place. But we might just make it.'

Colin recognised the unmistakable outline of the

Thames Estuary slide beneath them. The Lancaster was at 1,500 feet.

By a miracle and a short while after Mike was talking to the Control Tower at Church Stephen. 'Hello "Milkwood". Hello "Milkwood". This is "Dylan" "S" for Sugar calling. Over.'

With a warm, welcoming voice the Controller responded 'Hello "Dylan" "S" for Sugar. This is "Milkwood". Over.'

'Thank you "Milkwood". We have serious casualties on board and damage to engines. Request permission to come straight in. Over.'

'Message understood. Will come back to you.'

Mike's transmitter crackled noisily. The Controller was calling up other incoming aircraft already in the landing circuit.

Whilst Colin and Mike waited for the Control Tower to speak to them again Colin turned to Steve. 'Here's hoping the undercart's still working.'

There was a voice from the tower. 'Hello "Dylan" "S" for Sugar. The circuit has been cleared for you. You are now clear to approach Runway 1. Wind speed: 16mph. Direction: 080°. QFE: 102. Over.'

'Many thanks "Milkwood". Message understood. We will continue our approach.'

The Controller's voice once again: 'Emergency vehicles standing by. Welcome back. Good luck to you all.' There was a brief pause before the Controller added 'We'll have hot drinks and hot toddies waiting for you. Over and out.'

The voice from the tower had been so reassuring. Returning aircrews really appreciated the little postscripts of welcome the people in the tower always added to their messages. Colin selected "undercarriage down" and released the up-locks. He was so relieved as the wheels dropped unquestioningly and the undercarriage locked. "S" for Sugar was now at less than 700 feet. There was now no going back with them so low on fuel and altitude and the undercarriage locked under its own weight. Colin was committed to landing. In the light of the flare path he glimpsed the letters "CS" on the runway beneath them. They were home. All that remained was for him to put the Lancaster safely down.

Passing the Control Tower, as the aircraft slowed on the runway, and silhouetted against the moonlight on the tower roof, Colin saw the control personnel waving to them. The Lancaster slowed to a halt. He saw the emergency vehicles were already in position. They began to race to the aircraft's side. With almost zero fuel left in her tanks and, with substantial damage, Lancaster "S" for Sugar had returned after six hours in the air.

Colin and Steve said together 'Thank you. Thank you "S" for Sugar. How we love you.'

Colin was desperate to get out of his seat. He was anxious to know how his injured crew members were.

54

It was the middle of July 1944 and Margaret Wilding and her daughter June were sitting on the terrace at *Oakfields*. June was doing her best to soothe the crying infant in her arms. Matthew James Peter Graham had been born in May the previous year. June had been so thankful James had returned home just before Matthew was born. However, between then and now, James had been away twice more. On the first occasion for three months working as an instructor back at Beaulieu, then again just after Christmas 1943 - and he was still away. On both occasions his cover story of being in an RAF training role was just the same as previously. During his time at Beaulieu there had been no problem for James in maintaining the secrecy of his work for SOE. Any letters from himself to June and his parents and family had, using the SOE network in England, simply been addressed and posted from different places in the country. For any letters to himself they came *via* the same network and somehow got to him at Beaulieu. The occasional telephone calls from him were made *via* a secure telephone line at Beaulieu. However, when James had been sent away on the second occasion, communication was more difficult. He had been sent by SOE into the Normandy area to co-ordinate and train French Resistance workers in preparation for the D-Day invasion and its immediate aftermath. Telephone calls were out of the question and any letters or telegrams were either written or answered on James's behalf by one of the team of SOE forgers.

Billy, who had been tending the crops in the garden, passed by the terrace with the wheelbarrow. He stopped and came up the steps towards them. Reaching into his pocket and holding open a grubby paper bag he said 'Here Miss June. Would little Matthew like one of these? I got them this morning.'

June laughed kindly as the youth tickled the infant's chest playfully. 'Thank you all the same Billy, but he's a little small for those yet.'

Billy smiled lovingly. 'Sorry Miss June, I just thought.' He picked up a little cuddly toy from the table and gave it to the infant before returning down the steps to his wheelbarrow.

'Bless him poor sole. Billy's a treasure' said Margaret quietly. 'That was his whole sweet ration.' She lifted the still-crying infant into her arms. 'You poor little love. Those little new teeth are troubling you aren't they? Let's see if you'll stop crying for me.'

Ruth Fuller came out of the garden doors carrying a tray with a pot of tea and scones and set them on the table. She crouched down to Matthew. 'Oh the poor little chap. He is unhappy isn't he? If he'll come to his old auntie Ruth, I will see if I can settle him a bit. You have so much to talk about with June Dr Wilding.' In Ruth's arms Matthew stopped crying, for the moment he was fascinated by her shining broach. She started to rock him gently and hummed a lullaby. 'I'll see if I can get him to have a little sleep.'

As Ruth carried Matthew through the garden doors Margaret said 'In his last letter Richard was adamant for us to go ahead with the wedding as soon as we could.'

'I told you he would mummy. Before he left, James said

the same - we were talking one day before he left. I was saying how you really wanted to wait for all the family to be together.' She poured out the tea. 'His feeling was, with the war on and everything so uncertain, you should not wait. One has to take any opportunity you can nowadays. We could always have a big family celebration when the war's finally over.'

'That's exactly what Robert has been saying for ages and ages. It's just me I suppose. I know with the allies now in France - of course there's still a long to go before the war's over - things do seem a bit more certain.'

'Mummy! The wedding's not until November. Things may be even more certain by then. Please God the war in Europe could even be over. At least Stephen, now he's shore-based, may be able to be at the wedding. Who knows, James may be back by then. Most of your family will be around you.'

'Oh I do hope so.' Margaret picked up a list from the table. 'Robert was here yesterday. We've started to draw up a small guest list. It's so difficult now, what with people dotted about all over the place, and the shortages and everything.' She passed the list to June. 'We thought we would invite some of James's family as well.'

'They would love to come.'

'And I spoke to the Vicar the other day. He will be delighted to conduct the service.'

'Oh that's wonderful mummy. You were thinking of having the reception here, have you decided yet?'

'I have been thinking about it a lot' and, after checking Ruth wasn't in earshot. 'The only thing is - by holding it here - well, we want Ruth to be a guest. If it is here, she'll work herself to the bone getting everything prepared. It wouldn't be fair to expect that. And you know what she is like about having people in the kitchen or helping around the house.'

June laughed, remembering an incident a few months back, after Ruth had sprained her ankle or something and her mother had asked a local woman from the town to help out. The fur had really flown between the two women after Ruth had criticised her for not doing something in a certain way.

Margaret continued 'Robert and I popped into the *Crown* yesterday evening. Mr and Mrs Jenkins said they would be pleased to hold the reception in that big room they have at the back. Between themselves and some of the locals they would do their best to put on a good spread for us. They were really kind, saying it would be their way of thanking me for attending to their daughter when she was so seriously ill.'

'Oh yes I remember that occasion now. It would be nice to hold the reception there. It's such an attractive old place.'

There was a sound of a vehicle on the gravel drive at the front of the house.

'How is James's brother? I keep hearing on the news, reading in the paper, about the number of raids the RAF and the US Air Force are carrying out.' She paused. 'And the dreadful news about their casualties.'

'Last week I took Matthew to see James's parents. We stayed overnight. They said Colin's just completed his latest tour of duty. Apparently, he has been promoted again. He was on leave -before taking up a new posting. He had gone down to the farm in Somerset. Mr Graham was saying how his last "tour" had been particularly gruelling and tiring. Colin had just wanted to get right away from everything into the country.'

'I remember James saying how much his family love going down there.'

Ruth appeared through the garden doors. 'I've managed

to get Matthew off to sleep. Bless his little heart. He really is a dear little soul.'

'Oh thank you Ruth. He must be exhausted like me. He's hardly slept the last two nights, I have been up with him most of the time.' June noticed a tear in Ruth's eye. 'What is it Ruth? What's happened?'

'Mr Blake's just delivered the sewing machine he's repaired Dr Wilding.' She wiped a tear away. 'He said the evening paper's full of the tragedy in London yesterday.'

'Why? What has happened?' Asked Margaret.

'A cinema. Received a direct hit. One of those "Doodle" things.'

'A "Doodlebug"! Are there many killed?'

'Dozens and dozens. Could be many more.'

'Oh no! That's terrible! When I was with James's parents, his mother was saying she saw one go over Ealing - close to where they live. They're dreadful things. Make such a horrible noise, then, just before falling, their motor cuts out.'

'All those poor people - their children. When is it all going to end?' Ruth dabbed her eyes again with her handkerchief. The three women couldn't speak for a while. Eventually, Ruth said 'Mr Blake says the sewing machine is now working like new. Thank goodness. I for one, will be glad when all this "Make do and Mend" business is over. Will be glad when we don't have to keep repairing or altering our clothes and things.' She began to gather the tea things together. 'You're staying to dinner Miss June?'

'Well, with Matthew being so tired and fractious, I was going to go home and get him to bed. But, as he's finally gone to sleep I would love to, yes please.'

'It will be wonderful to have you here for a little longer June. I also want to talk to you about what I'm going to wear for the wedding.'

'Dinner is in the oven already' said Ruth. 'A nice Rabbit pie. One of those Rabbits my brother shot early this morning.'

****

During the year Lucy's health had deteriorated. The spells of illness she experienced had been increasing, each time worse than before, each time more prolonged. Her appetite was poor, she had lost weight and kept feeling so tired and lacking in energy, resulting in periods of fierce frustration and irritability. Irritable was something Lucy had never been. Sandra had been a wonderful help to her. In between looking after her own aunt and younger brother, she had spent endless hours at the farmhouse recently generally keeping it clean and tidy, running errands and, if need be, cooking for Lucy. The Doctor had been so concerned, he had referred Lucy to the local hospital. She had then angered Sandra by cancelling two appointments under the excuse of other things cropping up. Eventually, Lucy had gone to the hospital. They had carried out what tests they could - all proving inconclusive, and then referred her to a Specialist at a hospital in London.

As Sandra expected, Lucy had been very sorry and upset when John enlisted in the army towards the end of 1943. Because of Lucy's deteriorating health he had felt very guilty and awkward about making his decision but, much had changed to help John decide to enlist. He had been devastated by his mother's death when an isolated German air-raid obliterated not only the block of flats where she lived but, most of the street as well. It had re-kindled the flame within him to join the army as a way of getting back at Hitler. Lucy could well understand this, she had also been aware of the bullying John had been getting from some of the local lads about to be conscripted. She was also aware of the feeling, growing throughout the country, that time was overdue for Britain and her allies to really hit back against Hitler and his allies and, the consequential need to increase the armed forces. In terms of the working and running of the farm, although very sorry to learn of his decision, the Land Army girls were all very proficient and skilled in the task and fully capable of keeping it going. Especially so, when helped by the occasional advice kindly given by Jack and Dora of the neighbouring farm - should their advice or help be requested.

John had started his basic army training just before the Christmas of 1943. Later, in an infantry regiment, he had been amongst thousands of allied troops to take part in the Normandy landings. He had survived three days before being injured by shrapnel from an exploding German shell. John's injuries included extensive damage to his cheek bone, the loss of the best part of an ear and the sight in one eye. He had been evacuated back to England and to a military hospital.

John's transfer to the hospital coincided with the last days of Colin's leave in Somerset and Lucy's visit to the Specialist in London. Touchingly, because of the loss of his mother, John had nominated Lucy as his next-of-kin. In addition to regarding Sandra as an "adoptive niece", Lucy had come to regard John in much the same way and had been greatly upset to receive the news of his injury.

Sandra was going up to the hospital in London with Lucy. They had decided to set off from Somerset a day earlier so they could visit John as well. Colin said he would go with them and would spend the last days of his leave with his parents.

Many of the raids during Colin's last "tour" had been over Berlin and other German cities and they had been particularly demanding. They had also been expensive in terms of aircrew lives. He had lost many good friends and experienced some very harrowing times. Whilst the break in Somerset, prior to his next posting - a desk job, had allowed him the opportunity to have a good rest and help ease his tension, the memories and experiences of his previous "tours" of duty had drained him. The days of rest and peace in Somerset had still not fully expunged his exhaustion. The movement of the train, as it gathered speed out of the station, had soon rocked Colin sound asleep. Sitting opposite him in the carriage, Sandra could not take her eyes of the sleeping pilot. She was realising what she felt for him now was far more than simply the crush she had formed for him as she first got to know him now roughly four year's ago. She turned her eyes to the window to look at the countryside speeding by, wondering what an interest Colin - a young man from a social class well above hers - could, if ever, have in her.

The military hospital imposed a strict "no more than two visitors at a time" rule so Lucy, Sandra and Colin had to alternate their time around John's bed. As Colin awaited his turn to see John, he thought back to the time on the farm when the Evacuees first arrived. How he had taken an instant dislike to John and his attitude; the times he had taken it upon himself to chastise and bring into line the tough, morose and unreasonable boy from London; how, in more recent years - before he joined the RAF and during brief breaks in his aircrew training and subsequent brief periods of leave on the farm - he had come to like John as a talented, helpful individual and one his aunt had come to trust and rely on.

John was anxious to hear how Lucy was, concerned to learn she was on her way to see a Specialist. Because of his injuries, he found it difficult to talk, to hear and see his visitors. From the depths of his depression, he had been encouraged when the Doctor told him he would eventually be able to speak and eat normally, that sight in one eye was expected to return to near normality and his hearing would not be totally affected. He had talked to his visitors about his journey across the Channel and the actual landing in Normandy. However, regarding the actual fighting and his experiences in the time before he was injured, John found it difficult to express and fell into a shocked silence. After a while he began asking about how things were on the farm and was anxious to know every detail of what was happening in its locality.

Eventually Lucy said 'Well John, visiting time is halfway through and Colin is eager to see you. If we have time after I've finished at the hospital, Sandra and I will come and see you again.' She bent across and kissed him.

'Oh I hope you can.' He reached out and gripped Lucy's arm. 'Mrs Hughes. I'm so sorry.'

'Whatever for?'

'For leaving the farm to join up. Leaving you - with you not being well and everything. I feel I've let you down....'.

'...John don't be so silly.' She squeezed his hand affectionately.

'It's just that I felt...'.

'...I understand. And when you're better, there will always be a job for you on the farm - a home if you want it.' She kissed him again.

'Oh Mrs Hughes! I don't know how to thank you. Please let me know how you got on at the hospital?'

'Of course I will. It's probably nothing serious anyway. And you my lad. You can thank me by getting yourself better.'

Lucy turned away from the bed waving.

Sandra kissed him on the forehead. 'Now you look after

yourself John. And do what the doctors and nurses tell you. We'll come and see you in a day or so.'

'Sandra. Look after Mrs Hughes for me won't you? Keep letting me know how she is?'

There were tears in her eyes. 'Of course John. Now cheerio. See you soon.'

John could just hear Lucy and Sandra's footsteps as they left the ward. He realised then that Lucy, Sandra and the farm represented some of the happiest and most stable times in his whole life. He laid there thinking over the last four years or so.

55

As her appointment was for 9.15, Lucy had previously booked a room in a small, indistinguished hotel near the hospital. After guiding Lucy and Sandra to the hotel Colin made his way back to his parent's home.

In Ealing at about noon the following day, Colin and his mother were sitting in the Graham's garden. He had been digging over a patch of ground after harvesting some potatoes from amongst the whole host of vegetables his parents were now growing.

'I wonder how Lucy is getting on' said his mother. 'I do wish she had agreed to stay here with me.'

'I think she would have had her appointment not been so early. She didn't like the thought of all the crowds on the train at that time of the morning and, whether any problems may have arisen preventing her getting there on time.'

'I'm just anxious to hear what the Specialist has to say. I am really worried about her. When your father and I were in Somerset about a month ago, we were both taken aback at how ill she looked.'

'Yes. I couldn't help but notice how lethargic and lacking in energy she is. Let's hope it's nothing too serious.' He picked up some recent photographs of his nephew from the table. 'It really surprises me how quickly babies change. Matthew seems to have doubled in size since I last saw him.'

His mother laughed. 'Yes, he's looking a real boy now. June brought these photographs with her last week. He is a gorgeous little chap. Some times I can see a lot of June in him, other times he's more like James. But, recently, I think he's got a lot more like James. What do you think Colin?'

'Yes perhaps you're right. How is June?'

'She seems very well. Of course, she wishes James was with her - but then, nowadays, husbands and fathers being away is the norm. She seems to have got very involved with things in her village, keeps herself very busy, what with Matthew and various war effort activities.'

The telephone rung in the hall.

'I'll go. I am expecting a call from one of my friends from my old squadron.'

When he returned, his mother noticed the look of concern on his face. 'What is it Colin?'

'It was Sandra. The Consultant wants to keep Lucy in over night so other tests can be done. I think Sandra's feeling rather lonely up in London by herself. Wonders if I could meet her up there later to give her some company. Sandra's very close to Lucy - she's so worried about her.'

'Yes I know.' She paused. 'Oh damn! Later on I had promised to attend a special meeting called by the local Home Defence Committee. About these Flying Bombs I expect. Otherwise, I could have come with you and gone to visit Lucy if I would be allowed.'

'Never mind mother. Sandra said there's no visiting time at the hospital this evening anyway. I'll go up and get ready. Perhaps I will be able to find out a bit more about Lucy from Sandra.'

Colin met Sandra in the little square near the hospital in the early evening.

'All the Doctor would say is early examination and

tests have revealed some abnormalities with her blood. To confirm what these abnormalities are, he needs to keep her in overnight for more tests and so she can be observed.'

'How did Lucy seem?'

'Very worried of course and also annoyed about all the fuss it is causing. You're sure you didn't mind coming up to London again Colin?'

'Of course not. Anyway mother and I were both anxious to know how Lucy got on. Besides, you sounded very down when we spoke this afternoon.'

'I'm so worried about her.' She paused. 'Also, although I know it must seem strange to you Colin - what with me being born in London and everything - but I felt very lonely here. I don't think I could ever live in London again. And the thought of spending the whole evening by myself terrified me. Thank you for coming.'

Instinctively he put his arm around her shoulder and drew her close to him. She didn't make any attempt to draw back and they walked on, his arm around her shoulder. To Colin it seemed so natural for them to be physically close. They passed a poster advertising a dance band concert in the dance hall nearby.

'Sandra. After having something to eat, how about going to that tonight? This band once played at a dance in the town near my airfield.'

'But Colin! I haven't been to a dance for ages. I can't, I didn't bring a dress that would be suitable.' She sounded very disappointed.

'What about the one I saw you put in your suitcase. That looked pretty.'

'Oh are you sure? Do you think it will be all right.'

'Of course it will be.'

The dance hall was just around the corner and, after

Colin had brought two of the last remaining tickets, they passed a little restaurant.

'This place looks all right Sandra. We'll have something to eat quickly, go back to the hotel for you to change and get ready. There will be plenty of time.'

After queuing for a while, they got a seat towards the back of the large dance hall. There was a broad mix of people in the hall, civilians in pairs or small groups and others in a whole variety of uniforms. Amongst these were a large number of Americans and other nationalities.

'It's a long time since I've seen so many people' said Sandra. 'Colin are you sure my dress looks all right?' She asked anxiously.

'Of course it does. You look very pretty. Now stop worrying.' He squeezed her arm affectionately. 'Those two Americans over there stopped in their tracks when they saw you.'

She was embarrassed. 'Oh Colin don't.'

'Seriously. They did Sandra. Now stop worrying - you look lovely.'

After being introduced by the compere, the band started playing. Almost immediately a number of Americans got up with their partners and started dancing. Soon after many other couples were joining them.

'Come on Sandra. Let's have a dance?' Asked Colin after the band had played a couple of numbers.

She took his hand as they walked towards the dance floor. 'I'm not very good. I haven't danced since John and I went to a dance in the village hall months ago.'

'Don't worry. I'll guide you.' It wasn't long before Sandra's memory of this particular dance was refreshed. 'There. See. I told you you'd soon pick up the steps again' he said as he whirled her around close to some WREN's dancing with a group of American servicemen.

Some while later they returned to their seats laughing happily. Their seats were far enough back from the dance floor to be able to hear each other speak easily. The Band Leader introduced one of the latest melodies.

'The band's fantastic. Did you see some of those Americans dancing - weren't they good? I hope they weren't watching me too closely. I kept making mistakes.'

Colin laughed. 'Not all the time! My toes and ankles are not too bruised.'

Sandra smacked his arm playfully. 'I didn't tread on your toes. Anyway, you're a dark horse. Where did you learn to dance like that?'

He smiled. 'I've just picked it up I suppose. As I said, on my last tour of Op.'s, the airfield was near a town - a busy little place. Between Op.'s a few of us used to go to dances in the town hall. Some of the WAAF's or local girls taught us.'

'Do you keep in touch with any of these girls?' There seemed to be a hint of disappointment in her voice.

'No. None of them were girlfriends as such. We just went around in a big crowd really.' He paused. 'Strange I suppose. But none of my RAF friends or myself really wanted to get involved with any one girl in particular. Probably the uncertainty of our occupation I suppose.'

'Are you happy about your new posting Colin? Where was it you said.'

'In Nottinghamshire. By all accounts, as airfields go, it's meant to be a pretty good airfield to be based. I am sure I will be kept busy there. The squadrons flying from there have really been in the thick of things in recent months. Mind you, it will be very strange getting used to not flying on OP.'s for a bit. And, of course, I'll miss my previous crew and the other friends I've made - there will be a whole lot of new faces. As far as I'm aware there is no one there I know, but who knows.' He took a long sip of his beer.

Sandra reached over and squeezed his arm tenderly. Colin couldn't help but notice the expression in her eyes, the smile, as she looked directly into his eyes. He cupped her hand in his. There was a stirring within him. A deep feeling he had not experienced with any other girl before.

'Oh Colin. I know you will miss all the flying and everything but, personally, I'm relieved you won't be. I've been worrying so much about you - all the danger - you taking off nearly every night.'

The Band had stopped playing. It was announced there would be an interval.

'Quickly, before the crowds get off the dance floor. Would you like another drink Sandra?'

'Yes please. All the dancing has given me a thirst.'

When Colin returned with the drinks he asked 'Earlier Sandra, you said you would never like to live in London again. Did you mean that?'

'Yes I did. Obviously, when I first arrived in Somerset with all the others, it took weeks - months I suppose - to get used to living in the country. Everything was so different. Since then though I grew to love living on the farm, getting to know Mrs Hughes and everything. The space all around and fresh air. Why! Even what Mrs Hughes and all the locals call "town", well its all so quiet and friendly. And now, with my aunt and brother so settled and happy - Robert is so enjoying his school. Even Auntie Enid seems to have got a new lease of life. No, I certainly wouldn't like to live up here anymore. There's no one in London now, no relatives or anything, for me to want to live back here.'

'Lucy has often said how you've got involved with different things going on in the village. Not to speak of the amount of help you give her around the farm and everything.

My family are really grateful for all the help you give her Sandra. We really are.'

She smiled. 'Your aunt has been so good to me. It is the very least I can do. It's my way of somehow paying her back for all that.'

They continued to talk. Their conversation flowed so easily and freely. Most of the time they spoke happily about the times Colin had stayed on the farm during earlier holidays and, later, his periods of leave. The Band returned to the stage, their leader announced a slow waltz tune.

'Colin, let's dance? I love this one.'

As they danced closely together, Colin sensed Sandra had a need to draw even closer to his body. He felt her arms tightening around his back and he drew her close to him. She nestled her head in his chest, the contours of her body pressing against him.

Later, as they left the building and walked arm in arm back to the hotel, she said 'Thank you for a lovely evening Colin. I have so enjoyed it.'

'Me too. It's been wonderful.'

'I'm so worried about your Aunt Lucy Colin. I am dreading what the doctor might have to say tomorrow. It may be hard for you to understand but, since I lost my parents, I've come to think of Lucy as a sort of substitute somehow. I know that might sound dreadful but, in the last few years, as I've been growing up, she was always there to talk to. To help, advise, support me - not only me but for my Aunt Enid and Robert as well. She really has been like a mother to me. I don't know what would have become of me if she hadn't been there.'

She started to cry. Colin held her close to him. 'Oh Sandra! I do understand. It must have been so terrible and frightening for you. You were sent away from your home, with just a little bag of belongings, to whole new and strange surroundings. You lost your father, you were far away from your brother as well. I can't begin to imagine what it must have been like for you.' They had now arrived at the entrance to the hotel. There was an uneasy hesitancy. Colin sensed she wanted to say something. 'What is it Sandra?'

'Colin.' She paused. 'Although I telephoned you because I was so worried about Lucy.' She was finding it very hard finding the right words. 'I also wanted to see you again.' She hesitated again. 'On our journey to London the other day - I was sitting opposite you - I couldn't stop thinking about you. Thinking back over the time, since I've known you, I realised the feelings I have always had for you. I just wanted to see you again.'

They held each other very closely. Colin could feel her body trembling. He kissed her, looked closely into her eyes. She responded fully, their kiss lingered, grew more passionate.

'Oh Colin. I'd better go. It's getting late. They will be locking the hotel soon. Thank you again for such a wonderful evening.'

They still embraced. Colin realised then how much he wanted to see her again, and soon, before he got caught up once more in all the hell and destruction of war.

'I'm not due to report for my new posting for a couple of days. What time did the hospital say Lucy would be able to leave?'

'About 1 o'clock.'

'Say I travel up again with my mother tomorrow morning? We could all meet in that restaurant around the corner from the hospital. Mother is desperate to see Lucy.'

'That would be lovely.'

Colin saw the hotel's night porter peering at them from the doorway. 'Now I had better go Sandra. I'll see you tomorrow.' They kissed again.

He walked off down the street, turning back to wave. Sandra stood on the hotel steps and blew a kiss towards him. He felt happier than he could ever remember.

56

Like other hospitals, the corridors of this one were no different. The main corridor, leading to where Lucy had arranged to meet Sandra seemed endless. The more so, as Lucy's senses were so numbed, shocked, as she struggled to come to terms with what the Consultant had told her. Extensive tests had confirmed his initial, unspoken diagnosis. She had a form of Leukaemia. As she had sat facing the Consultant about an hour ago, there had been something in his expression, something about the careful way he chose his words, which made her fear hearing what he had to say. Although he had been expressly kind and sensitive, there had been a hesitancy in his demeanour. It wasn't until Lucy had really pressed him he revealed the full prognosis of her condition. Hesitantly, he had continued to explain she had perhaps only a short while to live; explained what limited palliative care could be put in place.

At last, Lucy neared the end of the corridor. Silhouetted by the sunshine, she saw Sandra waving as she rushed towards her. With a supreme effort Lucy tried to recover herself, deciding immediately not to reveal, for the time being anyway, the full extent of what she had been told. She resolved instead to hedge around the issue until another time and, meanwhile, to make the most of the time remaining to her.

'Aunt Lucy, how did you get on?' The two hugged each other. 'What did the doctor say?' All Lucy's efforts to act as normal had not fully succeeded as Sandra asked with concern 'What is it? What's wrong? Please tell me?'

'It's nothing Sandra. There's nothing to worry about.' They stepped outside into the sunshine. 'Let's go for something to eat and I will tell you all about it.'

'I have a surprise for you.'

'What's that Sandra?'

'You have come out a little earlier than I thought but, Colin said he'll meet us at a little restaurant just around the corner. And he's bringing his mum with him to see you.'

'That is a wonderful surprise. It will be lovely to see her. We have a lot of catching up to do.'

They started to walk. Although Lucy looked forward so much to seeing her sister-in-law, deep down inside she worried how she could possibly keep her news from her.

For some reason the train had been delayed and it was some fifteen minutes later than expected when Colin and his mother approached the road on which the restaurant was located. It would be some minutes yet before they reached the restaurant itself. There was a weird, unearthly buzzing sound above. Nearer and nearer it came. On the pavement, all passers-by looked skyward. Some people scurried, others stopped in their tracks huddling nervously together not knowing what to do. Colin saw an object approaching, torpedo-like but winged with a spluttering flame behind. It was streaking through the sky at about 3,000 feet. Somewhere nearby an anti-aircraft gun was fired, its shells innocuously, woefully, missing their target by yards. 'A Doodlebug' someone shrieked loudly. Time seemed to freeze for a moment before everyone then scattered in fear for the nearest shelter. Quickly, Colin looked around so he and his mother could follow. There was a shelter in the nearby square but, already, hundreds were thronging and jostling to get in. He realised they stood no chance at all of succeeding. Suddenly the terrifying buzzing stopped. The Flying Bomb's motor had cut out. It dived to ground ahead of them. Instinctively, Colin grabbed his mother and threw her to the ground in an open doorway of a building and threw himself on top of her. There was a tremendous explosion, the ground beneath them shook. There was a "whoosh" and rush of air. Almost immediately, Colin heard a storm of loud clattering as debris and masonry rained down on the pavement behind them. Eventually, he sat up, lifted and held his mother. Together they got to their feet and stood on the threshold of the building - the offices of an insurance company. Everywhere there hung a grey, choking pall of dust and smoke. Thousands of shreds of paper were fluttering down, some landing on the shoulders of his uniform. Up the street, where the bomb had landed, flame and smoke lifted from a vast void once a building. Already, in the distance, the bells of emergency services vehicles could be heard. Apart from these though, all around, a ghastly silence lay.

In the restaurant, Lucy and Sandra had selected a table for four and had not long settled themselves. An elderly woman sat playing a piano in a corner. Because of this music, the lively chatter of fellow diners and the usual hub-hub of such an establishment, no-one heard the Flying Bomb approaching until it was too late. As terrified patrons, including Lucy and Sandra, got to their feet, the bomb was already in its dive of death.

Colin and his mother took in the horror up the road. Now others, slowly at first, began to emerge from cover. Some sort of a warden and a policeman rushed past.

As the warden passed he pleaded desperately and loudly

to anyone nearby. 'Please? Please? We need some help to lift debris. A building's had a direct hit.'

Colin joined others and rushed off after the two officials to see what help he could give.

'Be careful Colin' called his mother after him as she too began to rush to see what she could do.

People were already tearing at the mound of smoking rubble with their bare hands as Colin neared the scene. Flames were also rising from the back of the mound. A cold shiver - a terrible numbness ran through him. "...*er's Rest...*" were the only letters of the only remaining words of the shattered name board laying in front of him. *Rodger's Restaurant* was where he and his mother had arranged to meet Lucy and Sandra. Gently fluttering in the breeze, on a small pillar of blackened masonry, was a portion of woman's dress fabric. It was of the same colour and pattern as the dress Sandra had been wearing the previous evening.

57

SOE's task in occupied Europe was largely complete and Baker Street's mission in France was almost at an end. James had finally returned to England in the early Spring of 1945. He had been re-assigned back to the RAF and was kicking his heels awaiting to hear of his next posting. Colin had completed his tour of duty in the late Autumn of 1944 and, had been posted to a Flying Instructor's job and was currently on 72 hour's leave.

Barber, Barber and Saunders had been Lucy and her late husband's solicitors for years and, for her husband's father before that. Her estate, partly because of the war, partly because of some technicalities encountered, had taken months to finalise. It was to hear the reading of Lucy's Will that James, Colin and their parents had travelled down to Somerset during the afternoon of Monday 7th May 1945 and had decided to combine this formality with a little break in the country. June and little Matthew had journeyed down with them but remained at the farm when they went into town the following day.

A woman, presumably one of the Practice secretaries, showed the family into a large room, the middle of which was dominated by a very large table with ten chairs arranged regimentally around its sides and ends.

'If you would like to make yourselves comfortable Mr Barber, Senior, will be with you shortly.'

Ensuring they were comfortably settled around the table, she apologised again for the delay and scuttled out. As well as the huge antique table and chairs, the room was furnished with other items of similar vintage, notably an immense "dresser-like" cabinet on the far wall stuffed full with leather-bound volumes of books.

After a couple of minutes, Cecil Barber the aged Senior Partner entered. He spent some time settling himself at the head of the table, pedantically arranging some papers and again apologising for the delays in finalising Lucy's estate. For a while he reminisced about the number of years his Practice had looked after Lucy's legal affairs. Eventually, after clearing his throat, he began to recite the contents of the Will.

James and Colin were surprised and shocked by what they heard. Such was their disbelief they didn't fully register what the solicitor continued to say as, in his dull monotone voice, he proceeded to read out the various other details and beneficiaries of their Aunt's Will.

After some clarification of one or two things and codicils, all formalities were completed just before mid-day.

Up a side street, almost opposite the solicitor's office, was a hotel and the family decided they would have lunch there. They were shown to a table by a window overlooking the market.

As each studied the menu, James said 'I still can't believe it. I had no idea Aunt Lucy owned two farms. Neither of you ever said?' He queried of his parents.

'We didn't know ourselves' replied his father. 'All I can remember about the neighbouring one, *Quarry Bank,* was that at one time it belonged to Lucy's husband's family. As far as your mother and I knew it had been sold years ago.

Obviously, the couple there are only tenants of Lucy's and must have been paying rent to her and her late husband for years.'

'But how strange that Lucy never said anything to you about it' said James.

'I know. Although Lucy and I were very close - I loved her enormously - she always was rather a private person. Always did keep things close to her chest. Must have had her reasons for not saying anything about it I suppose.'

The waitress came over and took their order.

Colin shook his head. 'I must admit, after the solicitor mentioned the farms, I was in a bit of a daze, didn't take in what he said.'

'*Quarry Bank* - the slightly larger of the two is left to you James' explained his mother. *Copper Ridge* has been left to you Colin.'

'I just can't believe it. That Lucy should leave the majority of her estate to James and I. I assumed it would all be left to you and father.'

'I am not all that surprised' replied his father. 'Some months back - perhaps a year or so - when I was down there for a few days, Lucy inferred she was anxious the farm remained in the family. She also understood how much you and James both loved the farm. As you know, she never had children of her own and, in a way, always looked upon you two as her adopted sons. Anyway, what would your mother and I do with a farm - at our age. You and James have got the whole of your lives in front of you. Besides, the Will leaves us very well provided for, what with the proceeds of the sale of those two cottages in the village and the small holding that goes with one of them. Again, your mother and I had no idea she and her husband owned those.'

'As I understand it then' said James 'The couple at *Quarry Bank Farm,* Jack and Dora Hobbs, will have to move from there? Or do they stay but, instead of being tenants of Lucy, they become my tenants?'

'For the time being yes. The terms of the Will clarified the point they would be entitled to stay at the farm until the present Tenancy Agreement expires. Mr Barber said that's in two year's time. When that arises, a new Tenancy Agreement has to be agreed between them and you.'

'I see.'

'But as we were leaving his office, Barber called me back and mentioned, off the record, that some weeks before her death Lucy had gone to see him saying Jack and Dora were thinking of retiring before the expiry of the Agreement. Lucy had wanted to clarify where she stood if they did decide to retire but died before the matter was resolved. Therefore, James, you will need to discuss it with a Solicitor and Jack and Dora as soon as you can. So it is possible you could find yourself in full possession of *Quarry Bank* sooner rather than later.' The waitress came over with their drinks and to arrange the cutlery appropriate to the dishes ordered. Well aware in small country towns and villages how gossip such as a farm changing hands travelled around, his father said quickly 'We'll study the documents thoroughly when we get back after lunch.'

After the waitress had turned away, Mrs Graham asked her two sons 'Whatever are you two going to do? With you both in the RAF - the war and everything?'

Colin answered first. 'Just before I travelled down here I was talking with some chaps in the Mess. If what we heard then can be believed, the Russians are already in the suburbs of Berlin, some say already encircling Hitler's Chancellery. There is still some very ferocious fighting, the Russians are still encountering pockets of stiff German resistance. However, I really can't believe it won't be many days now before Germany is completely finished.' He took a long sip of his beer. 'I only have a Short Service Commission anyway. I have no real desire to continue in the Service. I've already been approached to take a Permanent Commission - have been thinking it over carefully. But, to be honest, the thought of peacetime flying doesn't really appeal.' He took another drink of beer. 'It's all I could dream of, to own a farm.'

'And how do you feel James?'

'It's different for me really. I have a Permanent Commission. As far as I was concerned I was - always have been - all set for the RAF to be my long-term career.' He took a drink of his beer, paused a long while as he looked out of the window. His mother discerned an expression of concern on his face. 'It is highly unlikely I'll be involved with anything in the Far East but I'm going to have to discuss it all with June of course and what she would prefer. But now, only days ago, learning we're to have another baby, its put things into a different perspective. To be honest I'm just overwhelmed to have heard the contents of Lucy's Will.'

The family returned to *Copper Ridge* around two o'clock. The Rhododendrons in the small garden at the back of the farmhouse were at their most colourful and best. James saw his wife playing with their son on a rug laid out beneath the large Elm tree.

'Hello my love' said James, kissing June as he sat beside her. 'And what have you been up to little man?' He picked up Matthew and bounced his son on his lap.

'We've been doing nothing much really. Just relaxing, enjoying ourselves. I took Matthew to see the young lambs and we went for a walk around the lanes.' June rested her head on his shoulders and held their son's hand. 'Were things sorted out at the solicitors?'

'I wasn't sure what to expect, having never experienced this sort of thing before. We were in the office longer than

I thought. I'm still a bit shocked and surprised by it all to be honest.'

Matthew wriggled off his father's lap to play with his teddy bear and some wooden toy bricks.

'Why? What did the solicitor have to say?'

James paused before answering. 'How would you feel about living down here in Somerset June?'

'What do you mean?'

'Apparently, unbeknown to any of us, Lucy also owned *Quarry Bank,* the farm down the lane. She's left it to me - to us. And left *Copper Ridge* to Colin.'

June was speechless for a moment. 'But I never imagined…'.

'…No, neither did I or Colin.'

'I don't know what to say. What are you going to do, how do you feel? I mean, with your career in the RAF?'

'No. It's got to be **our** decision June. How would you like to live down here?'

'Would you want to James?'

'I don't know really. I haven't had much chance to think about it. Of course, it would mean me resigning my Commission. I suppose the news hasn't properly sunk in yet. It would mean a whole new life for the three of us.' He looked at his son still playing happily on the rug. 'Soon, the four of us. Also, I don't know much about farming, at least, not as much as Colin does. I suppose, for a while, we could employ a farm manager, until perhaps I've learnt more about it. It would be a real gamble though.'

'We would be further away from my mother. We have another baby on the way as well. That rather worries me. Mummy was such a help and support when Matthew was born. You were away so much.'

'Yes. There's that to consider too - and my parents for that matter. Mind you, with the war looking to be almost over. Transport, the supply of fuel and everything hopefully returning to normal, travelling around should get easier.'

'But James, the war isn't over yet despite those saying it can only be a matter of days before it is. The fighting with the Japanese is still continuing fiercely according to the news. If you do stay in the RAF James and, God forbid, another war starts somewhere else. Well I'll be worrying all over again. I don't know if I could bear that.'

He kissed her gently on the forehead. 'Oh June! Bless your pretty head. After my Hurricane crashed back in 1940, it was made pretty clear to me my flying days were over.'

It was a while before June said anything. 'Today, with Matthew here with me on the farm. Seeing the animals - walking around and enjoying the countryside - it was just beautiful. I know it will be hard work, a life something so different for us - a whole new way of life. I'm sure with some help we can make a success of it.' She paused. 'We can do it together James. It is a wonderful opportunity for all of us. Please, let's take the opportunity. Let's start a new life.'

By one of those miracles which defy explanation, Sandra had survived the Flying Bomb's destruction of the restaurant that had claimed Lucy's life. A fallen steel roof joist had missed her by inches but had prevented tons of falling masonry from crushing her. She had been entombed in a tiny cavity amongst the mound of debris. It had been over five hours before the rescue team managed to extricate her. Her outer clothing had been torn off by the blast, water from a fractured pipe had continuously flowed down upon her chilling her to the marrow. Miraculously, apart from exposure to the cold and wet and severe shock, she had escaped with a fractured shoulder and various nasty cuts and bruises. After three nights in a local London hospital she had returned to Somerset.

After her recovery, Sandra had periodically called into

the farmhouse to keep it clean and tidy, to keep an eye on its condition and maintenance. Although the Land Army girls continued to live in their hostel in the village, they had always been allowed by Lucy to use the facilities of the farmhouse, especially when the weather was not conducive to some particular jobs on the farm. This concession had been allowed to continue by Mr and Mrs Graham as co-Executors of Lucy's estate. During the last day or so, preparing for the impending visit of the Graham family, Sandra had been busying herself giving the house a real Spring Clean and ensuring the house was spick-and-span and ready for them. She was just finishing making up the beds and so on in one of the bedrooms when the Graham family arrived back from the solicitors.

Colin went upstairs to speak to her. She was standing on a chair over by the window as he entered the room. 'You've been busy Sandra.' She stepped down off the chair to greet him and they kissed. 'Mum has put the kettle on. Would you like a cup of tea?' They continued to embrace.

'I'd love one. I'll just finish putting back these curtains. It's surprising how dirty they were. It amazes me how quickly a house gets dirty, even when it has been standing empty for most of the time.'

He kissed her again. 'The house looks beautiful. Just as it always did. We are all so grateful for what you continue to do down here Sandra. Thank you.'

She broke gently away from him. 'I must finish getting these curtains back up and then it's all done. I've never been to a solicitors. I don't know how long these legal things take. I wasn't sure when you all would be back.'

'We were in with Barber - the senior partner - for about an hour I suppose. Then we went for lunch in *The Auctioneer's Arms*. I'll tell you all about it later.' From the window he saw John with one of the Land Army girls trying to coax a cow and her young calf into the barn. 'It is nice to see John again. I only saw him briefly, just before we went into town. He was saying he's been down here for a couple of weeks.'

'Yes. He's staying with Jack at *The Lamb and Flag*. Paying for his keep by helping out in the pub.'

'How does he seem?'

'Depressed and frustrated. It turns out his hearing hasn't returned as much as the doctors thought it would. He is also finding it hard getting used to only having one eye. He's now officially invalided out of the army and hasn't been successful yet in getting a job. He has just been wandering around, not knowing what to do with himself and getting more and more despondent. I suggested he could spend some time on the farm helping out.' She hesitated. 'Oh! I hope your parents won't mind?'

'Of course not Sandra.' A thought had just occurred to him but he kept it to himself. 'It will be good for him to spend some time here until he gets himself sorted out with a job. He has always been good at applying himself to anything.' He smiled. 'When you think what he was like when he first arrived here from London as an Evacuee. It's amazing.'

'Yes I remember. The problems he caused Lucy - us all - at first.' She stepped down from the chair. 'Well that's all done. Do you think the curtains look all right Colin?'

'Yes they do.'

His mother called up the stairs 'The tea is poured out.'

'Coming' Colin called back.

With their arms around each other, Colin and Sandra crossed the room. Downstairs, Mrs Graham was setting cups of tea on the table.

'Hello Sandra' greeted Mr and Mrs Graham. 'How are you?'

'Fine thank you. I made some little cakes for when you arrived. They're in the tin on the kitchen dresser.'

'Oh thank you very much Sandra. That is very kind of you. Now where are James and June?'

'In the garden playing with Matthew' answered her husband. As his wife went out to the kitchen he turned the radio on. He heard the unmistakable voice of Winston Churchill and turned the volume up. He shouted urgently 'Quick! Get James and June in? Anyone else nearby for that matter.'

Colin rushed and shouted out of the window. James and June with Matthew were on their way in anyway, they arrived in the lounge within seconds. Sandra on her way to the kitchen to call out to the yard almost collided with Mrs Graham on her way back into the lounge.

'Whatever is…?' Asked Mrs Graham.

'…Churchill is on the radio' replied her husband and urging her to be quiet.

'…*the act of unconditional surrender of all German land, sea, and air forces in Europe…*' she heard Churchill say. Otherwise there was not a sound in the room. Even Matthew was silent. He was asleep in June's arms.

'…*signed the document on behalf of the Supreme Commander of the Allied Expeditionary Force, and…*'.

Sandra, John and two Land Army girls - Vera and Betty, clattered into the room. More noise was created as John and the two Land Army girls struggled to remove their boots.

'Oh don't worry about those' said Mrs Graham with just a mere hint of impatience. 'Churchill's speaking.'

Everyone sat or stood in little huddles, listening intently with contained excitement to the Prime Minister's words '…*and I therefore beg, Sir, with your permission to move: That this House do now attend to the Church of St. Margaret, Westminster, to give humble and reverent thanks to*

Almighty God for our deliverance from the threat of German domination.'

For a few moments in the lounge of the farmhouse there was a silence of calm. Suddenly, as one, everyone was cheering, laughing, hugging and kissing each other. Matthew was awake, crying. His mother and father were kissing him - everyone was kissing him. It was as though in some way his small being symbolised a whole new beginning of life.

'It's over! It's over!' Everybody was cheering in unison as they danced, leapt and kissed in a jamboree of pleasure, laughter and sheer relief.

Mr Graham clapped his hands to get everyone's attention. 'As the Prime Minister has just said, today and tomorrow are for everyone to celebrate. Therefore, I suggest we have a party here, tomorrow, for everybody on the farm, our neighbours, anyone who wants to come.'

Colin's mother turned to him. 'Your leave pass will have expired!'

He laughed. 'I will contact my new CO. He's an old friend from my first Squadron. He had already said if I needed another day or so to sort things out down here, all I need to do is telephone him.'

Mr Graham turned to Sandra 'Sandra. Jack, the landlord of *The Lamb and Flag* is an old friend of Lucy's isn't he? Would you mind cycling down there to see if he's able to set aside some beer or cider or something for tomorrow? Say, I'm willing to pay extra for it if need be. James, Colin and I will collect it later.'

'I'll go right away Mr Graham. And I'm sure Jack won't want any extra. Mrs Hughes was very good to his family over the years.'

58

For the Victory celebrations at the farm, the Grahams invited Lucy's former friends and neighbours, John, Sandra and her aunt and brother, and the land Army girls working on the farm and their friends working on nearby farms. In total, dozens of people, far too many to be accommodated in the farmhouse. It was decided to hold the event in the main barn as, with the cattle having been turned out in the fields at the beginning of April, it was - save for a couple of calves and three sickly ewes - empty of livestock.

After the initial excitement created by Churchill's broadcast and subsequent joyous evening spent in *The Lamb and Flag,* everyone had turned their attention to transferring the remaining animals to the smaller barn and washing out and tidying the main floor area of the larger barn. This work, continuing during the morning of 9th May, resulted in the barn providing a clean and spacious area for the evening's celebration. A makeshift bar, comprising planking resting on three big barrels, had been set up at one end of the barn; at the other end, a space was provided for an ageing quartet of local musicians to play - one of the instruments being the piano manhandled out of the farmhouse lounge. Along both sides of the cleared space, wooden crates and bales of straw and hay had been arranged to serve as tables. To supplement these "tables", a wide assortment of chairs had been loaned from the farmhouse and various neighbouring homes. Mrs Graham remembered, some years previously, her sister-in-law used to host the Church's Feast Day and, the lengths of bunting and various flags for it were stored in the attic. These had been retrieved and bunting and flags now decorated the walls of the barn. Smaller flags fluttered from the makeshift tables. All in all the barn, with the decoration and preparation completed, took on the appearance of a magical setting for such a happy occasion.

Because the farmers and farm-workers were making the most of the daylight hours available, it was dusk when the majority of the guests finally arrived. The party had been in full swing for almost an hour when Colin spotted Sandra standing out in the yard. She was leaning on the wall looking out over the hills and the valley dropping down to the little river coursing and winding through the fields and woods of *Copper Ridge* land. They had been dancing constantly but had parted for a while as Colin spoke to her aunt. Now, joining Sandra by the wall, he kissed her cheek and slid his arm around her waist.

'I wondered where you had gone. Is everything all right?'

She smiled and kissed him. 'Yes. I just wanted to come out here, absorb the peace of this place. It seems somehow - I don't know - all the more precious and lovely to savour now the war's over.'

The bells of the sixteenth century village church began to peal, their joyous ringing carrying clarion clear in the still night air. A couple of late arrivals, walking across the yard and hearing the sound, cheered out loud and kissed each other.

'Oh Colin it is so lovely to hear those bells after all these years. I do so love it here. From when I arrived here I always have done.'

'I know you have.'

Neither of them said anything for a while. They just stood holding each other, soaking in the quiet, the sounds of the countryside being the only disturbance. The stars in their constellations twinkling in the heavens above seemed extra clear and bright.

Eventually Colin spoke. 'Sandra. I've not yet had the chance to tell you what the solicitor had to say.'

'Of course not. What with everyone being busy getting ready for tonight. Besides, why should you, it's nothing to do with me.'

'Well that's just it Sandra, it could be. You see…'.

She could sense his embarrassment. '…Whatever is it Colin?'

'Apparently, Lucy has left the farm to me. If I want it to be, it can be my home…'.

'…My goodness - but…'.

'…Also, unbeknown to any of us, *Quarry Bank Farm* was also owned by Lucy. She has left that to James.'

'Gosh! But I had no idea.'

'As I say, none of us did. Sandra.' He paused. 'Knowing how much you love the farm - the whole area for that matter, makes what I'm going to say much easier.'

'How do you mean?'

'Would you like to make this farm your home as well?' She was completely nonplussed. He paused. 'Sandra will you marry me?'

'But Colin…'.

'…When Lucy was killed in London, when that restaurant was bombed. I feared you had also been killed. It was just dreadful. I also realised something, I realised how much you meant to me. How much I loved you.'

She stared unbelieving into his eyes. 'Oh Colin! I have

always dreamt.' She hesitated. There were tears in her eyes. 'But I'm from such a different background - you're...'.

He placed his index finger gently to her lips and, said tenderly 'Shush! Will you marry me Sandra?'

'Oh Colin! But I - yes. Yes.'

They embraced, kissed long and tenderly.

'As far as I know, apart from your brother Robert of course, your Auntie Enid is your only relative. I asked her permission. Earlier, when I went to speak to her.'

They kissed again.

'Colin I'm so happy. I love you so much, I think I always have.'

'I believe the band will be having a break soon. We'll tell my family then. Perhaps my father will announce our engagement.' He paused. 'That is if you don't mind Sandra - you know - with everyone in the barn?' He kissed her again. 'Unfortunately though I haven't yet had a chance to buy an engagement ring. And, I want to get you a ring you would like.'

'Could we announce it tonight Colin? It would be wonderful. Tonight being such a happy occasion for everyone anyway.' She laughed. 'I don't mind about a ring. I would be happy enough Colin with one of those curtain rings I was using yesterday. I love you so much.'

They laughed together. 'As soon as I get back to the airfield tomorrow I will arrange for you to travel up one day. There's a jeweller in the town nearby. He's bound to have something you will like.' He started to lead her back towards the barn. 'Well come on then let's go and tell everybody.'

Suddenly she hesitated. There was a note of doubt in her voice. 'Are you sure your parents will be all right about it? I mean, do they like me? Would they want me as their daughter-in-law?'

'Oh you silly little thing.' He kissed her hair and held

her face in his hands. 'Of course they do. They think the world of you, and of course they would.'

'Are you sure?'

'Of course. They will be delighted.'

James came out of the barn. He walked towards them. 'So there the pair of you are. I have been hunting all over the place for you.'

Quickly, Colin whispered to Sandra 'Perhaps we'll tell James now, before we go back in.'

James stood between them, placing his hands on their shoulders. He was very merry. 'I wanted to tell you both. June and I have made a decision. I've decided to resign my Commission. We both want to move down here.' He slapped his hands heartily on his younger brother's shoulder. 'So, not only am I your brother old chap. I am also going to be your next door neighbour - that is if you decide to move down here as well. How do you feel about that?'

Sandra said 'That would be wonderful. We're so pleased.'

She realised she had said "we're" and, embarrassed, she looked at Colin.

'Sandra and I have got some news as well.'

'And what's that Colin?'

'Sandra and I are getting engaged.'

James hugged them both warmly and gave Sandra a big kiss. 'Marvellous. I'm so pleased for you both. June will be as well. Congratulations. Well done. I must go and tell her.' He hugged them both again.

Colin held on to his brother's arm. 'Hang on a bit James. We haven't told mum and dad yet. We were just on our way in to tell them.'

'Oh okay then. I'm so pleased for you both.' He smiled broadly again. 'So Sandra, I can now call you sister-in-law.'

'Yes.' She laughed, kissed and hugged him. 'Yes, I suppose you can.'

Colin asked 'So when did you and June finally decide to live down here James?'

'We have been speaking about nothing else ever since yesterday afternoon. And, tonight, in the barn, what with all the people and celebrations and things. Well, now the war in Europe is over, somehow everything seems different. I mean one thinks in a different way. It would make a totally new start for us and Matthew and, of course, when the new baby arrives. We just made up our minds to give it a go.' He hesitated. 'Mind you, how I will manage on the farm I don't know. Especially, when it's got to be our livelihood. Like you Colin, I've spent a lot of time down here over the years but I don't know half of what you do about it. It's bound to be hard for all of us at first I suppose but, we have both got a lot of friends down here. I am sure with their help and advice we'll learn eventually. I'm sure we will make a go of it in the end.'

There was a movement over on the other side of the yard in the shadow of the barn. It was John and one of the Land Army girls - the one he had always seemed to have a soft spot for. They appeared to be taking the opportunity to get better acquainted.

'We will both certainly need to hire some staff though' said James. 'I have got an idea Colin. How about asking John to start with?'

'He would be someone we could rely on. Since I've known him he's proved he can turn his hand to most things. I would think he's certainly able enough to give him a try. I must admit, I've been worrying - wondering how he, like a lot of those now injured, will get on finding work back in civvies. I reckon he would make a damned good farm foreman working for one or other of us - perhaps both for a while.'

'I agree.'

In the barn the music and dancing had ceased for an interlude. Everyone was taking the opportunity to top up their drinks, help themselves to the buffet contributed to by each household present. On hearing of Colin and Sandra's engagement his parents were delighted and both welcomed Sandra warmly into the family. Like Lucy, ever since they first got to know her, they had always had a soft spot for her. Their fondness for her, as she had grown into womanhood, had increased. Especially, after seeing how happy she and Colin were in each other's company during his periods of leave over the last few years and occasional "Squadron stand-down" times.

Amidst the happy circle of his family, Colin's father noticed the band were about to resume playing. He wanted to use this opportunity to tell those gathered in the barn the news about *Copper Ridge* and *Quarry Bank* farms. Taking Enid with him he headed towards where the band was re-assembling.

'Before the band starts again, I would just like to say how nice it is to see so many of our friends here tonight for this wonderful and long-awaited celebration of Victory. But, as we enjoy ourselves, we must not forget those who still have loved ones a long way from home or, unfortunately, still fighting the Japanese in the far east. Let's all hope and pray the war there will soon be over as well. Before our celebrations continue, I think it appropriate to take some time to quietly reflect and remember all those who have lost their lives during the last five ghastly years of war.' After a period of utter silence, he continued. 'I would now like everyone to join me in raising their glasses - Victory.' A loud, cheering response resounded around the barn.

When this had subsided, he continued. 'Now, just before our celebrations commence again, there are couple of other things I and my family would like to say. Firstly, we are delighted to say that Colin and Sandra have just announced their engagement and I hope you will join my family and Sandra's in congratulating them and wishing them all the best for the future.' He was prevented from continuing for a while by loud cheers of congratulations. 'There is something else I would like to say to you all, and this involves Jack and Dora sitting over there. Jack and Dora were telling me earlier this evening they have decided to retire at the end of the summer and will be moving from *Quarry Bank.*'

This statement was greeted with a mixture of shock, surprise, much head-turning and congratulations and good-hearted banter.

Jack, laughing, responded by calling back 'Don't worry my dears, you won't be getting rid of Dora and I that easily. Like a lot of you here tonight the pair of us are not getting any younger. And we've decided that in the years still remaining to us we're going to take things a little quieter, and we will be moving to one of those nice little cottages in Meadowcroft in the centre of the village.' Adding, good heartedly 'Now if you'll all settle down, Mr Graham has something else he wants to tell you.'

'Thank you Jack and we all wish you and Dora all the best for a long, happy and well-deserved retirement.' He beckoned his wife, James, Colin, June and Sandra to join him. 'Although our family in many ways are outsiders hereabouts, over the years - because of my sister Lucy and her late husband - my family have come to know you all as our friends. We hope you have all felt the same about us. We know that Lucy's death upset many of you here tonight and, naturally, you're all anxious - concerned to know what is going to happen to this farm. We hope you will be pleased to hear that *Copper Ridge* has been left by Lucy to Colin for his home. Also, we are pleased to tell you, James and June will be the new owners of *Quarry Bank* farm and they will move in when Jack and Dora move later this year.'

Before he could finish, James and Colin were surrounded by well wishers extending a warm welcome to the community. Many of the well-wishers also pledging any help and assistance needed, either with moving in or helping out with advice or labour on the farms until the two brothers gained sufficient experience.

After a while people began dancing and celebrating again, the celebrations, laughter and noise growing more good-heartedly boisterous as more alcohol was consumed. It was getting quite late by the time people began to drift off on their way home. James, June, Colin and Sandra were standing together. Matthew was beginning to get fractious in June's arms.

'I must get Matthew to bed James.'

James embraced and kissed his wife and son. 'Of course my love. Do you want a hand?'

'No I can manage. Stay and enjoy the rest of the evening James. You deserve it.' She patted her tummy. 'And with this little being in here, I've been standing for too long anyway.'

As June began to move away, James held her arm. 'And you are happy June - really?' She smiled and looked at him. 'I mean with the thought of moving down here and the farm and everything?'

She kissed and hugged him and looked around the barn. There were still quite a few people remaining in the barn and still celebrating happily. 'Oh yes James. Happier than I think I can remember.'

John came over to them. 'While you all together, I just wanted to wish you all well. I'm thrilled for you. And, again, congratulations to Colin and Sandra on your engagement.' He shook James and Colin's hands firmly and kissed June and Sandra.

'Thank you John. We appreciate that.'

June took her leave. James watched his wife as she did so. He glanced at Colin and turned to John. 'Colin and I have something we want to ask you John. There is an old cottage on *Quarry Bank's* land. With a fair amount of renovation, we are sure it can be made habitable. When that work is done, how would you like to move in there? Colin and I will need to recruit some people to help on the farms and we'll need some sort of foreman. Would you like that job? We'll negotiate a reasonable rate of rent for the cottage with you.'

For a moment John was speechless. 'You mean you're offering me the job?'

'Of course' replied Colin. 'If you'll take it. It would be a start for you.' He paused. 'We don't want you to feel compelled to take it - and we will understand if, in the future, you decide you want to get another job elsewhere.'

'I - I just don't know what to say - how to thank you both. And the cottage as well. I don't know how I can thank you all. It's more than I could ever hope for. It will be a whole new life for me.'

'It's going to be a whole new life for everyone' said James.

Lightning Source UK Ltd.
Milton Keynes UK
UKOW022253281111

182850UK00001B/2/P